# KATE MOSSE

## The Ghost Ship

MANTLE

First published 2023 by Mantle
an imprint of Pan Macmillan
The Smithson, 6 Briset Street, London EC1M 5NR
*EU representative:* Macmillan Publishers Ireland Ltd, 1st Floor,
The Liffey Trust Centre, 117–126 Sheriff Street Upper,
Dublin 1, D01 YC43
Associated companies throughout the world
www.panmacmillan.com

ISBN 978-1-5098-0691-1 HB
ISBN 978-1-5098-0692-8 TPB

1 3 5 7 9 8 6 4 2

A CIP catalogue record for this book is available from the British Library.

Maps by ML Design Ltd

Typeset by Palimpsest Book Production Limited, Falkirk, Stirlingshire
Printed and bound by CPI Group (UK) Ltd, Croydon, CR0 4YY

MIX
Paper | Supporting
responsible forestry
FSC® C116313

Visit **www.panmacmillan.com** to read more about all our books
and to buy them. You will also find features, author interviews and
news of any author events, and you can sign up for e-newsletters
so that you're always first to hear about our new releases.

*For my beloved Greg &*

*Martha & Felix, as always*

*And for wonderful Finn and Ollie*

'They that go down to the sea in ships, that do business in great waters; These see the works of the Lord, and his wonders in the deep.

For He commandeth, and raiseth the stormy wind, which lifteth up the waves thereof.'

Psalm 107: 23–27 (KJV)

# CONTENTS

## PROLOGUE

LAS PALMAS DE GRAN CANARIA

*October 1621*

*1*

## PART ONE

PARIS, LA ROCHELLE & CARCASSONNE

*May–July 1610*

*5*

## PART TWO

LA ROCHELLE

*October 1620*

*101*

## PART THREE

AMSTERDAM

*November 1620–March 1621*

*165*

# Author's Note

*The Ghost Ship* is the third in a series of novels inspired by the Huguenot diaspora, which travels from France in the sixteenth century to the Cape of Good Hope in the nineteenth century by way of Amsterdam and the Canary Islands.

The sequence of religious civil wars between Catholics and Huguenots in France – which began on 1 March 1562 and ended after several million had been murdered or displaced – was brought to an end by the signing of the Edict of Nantes on 13 April 1598 by the previously Protestant King, Henri IV or Henri of Navarre. Henri achieved great things during his reign and his assassination on 14 May 1610 was a catastrophe for France and the Huguenots. Henri's oldest legitimate son, eight-year-old Louis XIII, ascended the throne and a rolling back of Huguenot rights began immediately. La Rochelle, then the third biggest city in France, became a symbol of resistance against the Catholic crown.

When Louis XIII died in May 1643, his son Louis XIV continued the persecution. He revoked the Edict of Nantes at Fontainebleau on 22 October 1685, precipitating the forced exodus of those few Huguenots still remaining in France. The first Huguenot refugees began to arrive in the Cape of Good Hope in South Africa as early as 1671. The governor, Simon van der Stel, set aside land for Huguenot settlement in the valley of Drakenstein (present-day Paarl) and Oliphants Hoek in which to settle. Renamed *le coin Français*, the 'French corner', it later became known by its Dutch name, Franschhoek.

There are many excellent histories of the Huguenots and the influence of this small community is extraordinary, a diaspora that took them, as skilled immigrants, all over the world. The word 'refugee' comes from *réfugié*, a French word first used to describe the Huguenots. Every country which accepted the refugees – including the Dutch Republic, England and South Africa – was enriched by their presence.

The United East India Company – the VOC *(Verenigde Oostindische Compagnie)* – was established in March 1602 by the States General of the Netherlands, seven years before the Dutch Republic was formally recognised by Spain in 1609, if for a limited period, granting it a twenty-one-year monopoly to carry out trade activities in the Far East. I have allowed myself a great deal of licence by allowing the Van Raay fleet to be independent within the VOC. I've also taken huge liberties with the command structure and the piratical activities of the *Old Moon* for the purposes of the narrative: for example, there would certainly have been three lieutenants/watchmen beneath the captain, rather than just two. It is not likely that a 'ghost ship' such as I have imagined could have existed – least of all commanded by a woman – but, in the tradition of most pirate stories, romance and swagger is what drives the narrative. The *Old Moon* is based on two Dutch ships of the period – Henry Hudson's *Halve Maen* (*Half Moon*) and William Barentsz's *Witte Swaen* (*White Swan*). The *spiegelretourschip* the *Berg China* – referred to in Dutch records simply as the *China* – arrived in Table Bay from Rotterdam in 1688.

Finally, the love story at the heart of the novel is inspired in part by two real eighteenth-century female pirates, the legendary Anne Bonny and Mary Read; as well as earlier pirate commanders such as the fourteenth-century 'Lioness of Brittany', Jeanne de

Clisson, and the sixteenth-century Moroccan pirate queen, Sayyida al Hurra. These extraordinary warrior women – and others – appear in my book *Warrior Queens & Quiet Revolutionaries: How Women (Also) Built the World*.

All the characters in *The Ghost Ship*, unless otherwise specified, are imagined, though inspired by people who might have lived: ordinary women and men, struggling to love and survive against a backdrop of religious war and displacement.

Then, as now.

Kate Mosse
Chichester
November 2022

# Principal Characters

IN PARIS & CARCASSONNE

Louise Reydon-Joubert
Marguerite (Minou) Reydon-Joubert, her
    grandmother
Piet Reydon, her grandfather
Jean-Jacques Reydon-Joubert, her uncle

IN LA ROCHELLE

Gilles Barenton
Achilles Barenton, Gilles' uncle
Marie Roux, Gilles' mother
Hans Janssen, former captain of the *Old Moon*

IN AMSTERDAM

Alis Joubert, Louise's great-aunt
Cornelia van Raay, owner of the shipping line &
    Alis's companion
Bernarda Gerritsen, Louise's aunt
Frans Gerritsen, her husband

## IN THE ATLANTIC OCEAN

Hendrik Joost, captain of the *Old Moon*
Jan Roord, first lieutenant
Joris Bleeker, second lieutenant
Dirk Jansz, boatswain
Pieter, a cabin boy
Albert, a cook
Lange, a Dutch mariner
Jorgen, a Dutch mariner
The De Groot brothers, both Dutch mariners
Marco Rossi, an Italian tailor
Tom Smith, an English lieutenant
Ali Al-Bayt, a Morisco mariner
Pierre Rémy, a French gunner
Sanchez, a Canarian mariner

## IN LAS PALMAS DE GRAN CANARIA

Willem de Klerk, captain of the *North Star*
Phillipe Vidal, Lord Evreux
Andries Joost, the father of captain Hendrik Joost
Filipe Arauz, chief prosecutor of Gran Canaria

## IN CAPE TOWN

Florence Amiel *née* Reydon-Joubert, Louise's cousin
Suzanne Joubert, Florence's granddaughter

## HISTORICAL FIGURES

Henri IV, King of France & Navarre (1553–1610)
François Ravaillac (1578–1610), assassin

# PROLOGUE

Today I am sentenced to swing. Before the sun rises, I will be taken from here to a place of execution and there, hanged by the neck until I am dead.

*My pretty white neck.*

Friends, I am innocent of the charge set against me. My other crimes, I do not deny. My actions were measured, they were just. I can still feel the slip of blood between my fingers, still smell the fear. Later, the hate down below deck and the stench of men confined at sea for month upon month. Their disbelief, too, that a woman could be so cruel. So, yes, I confess I have killed, but only ever in self-defence or to protect those I love. Never for gain. Never without due cause.

Those were the words I spoke at my trial, but the men of the Spanish court did not listen. The judges – hypocrites all – gasping for details. They could not believe a woman capable of such devilry, yet they pronounced me guilty all the same.

Outside my window, the sky is growing white, giving shape back to the scaffold and to my cell: the rough bunk affixed to the floor; a blanket lousy with fleas; my trencher and tankard; a night pot. I have scratched my initials upon the bricks so future prisoners will know that, for nigh-on six weeks in the year of Our Lord 1621, a woman was here confined: LRJ, captain and commander, innocent of the crime for which she was condemned.

I can hear the bells of the cathedral of Santa Ana marking the start of another day. At the port, the fishermen will be mending their nets, their wives gutting the morning's catch and their children curing seaweed with smoke on the sand. In the harbour, the wind will be whispering in the shrouds and snapping at the rigging of the tall ships as they prepare to journey south to the Cape of Good Hope where two oceans meet.

How I miss the lilt and sway of the waves beneath my feet, the buck and the tilt. The solitude of the night-watch and the black sky scattered silver with stars. The endless, treacherous, beautiful shifting water.

*Such freedom, such liberty.*

In the Casas Consistoriales, the Town Hall, scribes will be preparing their paper and ink. The priest will be sharpening his prayers and preparing to hear my confession, expecting repentance and a desire for absolution. I shall not give him that satisfaction.

Friends, it was my grandmother who taught me the importance of telling one's own story, of not allowing the words of others to stand for us. Lies that snare and trap. So, in these last moments, I have a final question to put before you, a question I find I still cannot answer for myself.

*Is a murderer born, or is she made?*

The Bible says that God put his mark on Cain and condemned him to be a restless wanderer. Do I have such a mark? Is there such a thing as bad blood?

Some are born to evil. That is what the prosecutor said as he pronounced sentence. And how could I – the daughter of a murderer, the granddaughter of a murderer – refute that? Were the seeds already sown in my childhood spent among the wooden masts of the *fluyts* and flat-bottomed barges of Amsterdam? In that boarding house in Kalverstraat when I became what I am? In La Rochelle sailing with the *Old Moon* into harbour on that late October tide one year ago? Or the instant I realised I was in love, and so had everything to lose?

Even at this eleventh hour, I still believe my lover will save me. After everything we have seen, all we have been to one another, I have faith.

The sky is now the palest of blues. I believed myself composed, but I see how my hand is shaking as I write these final words. I have paid the guard well to smuggle away these papers, and I have to pray that he will be honest.

It is quiet in the gaol. I'm told it is always so on a day of execution. Can you hear it, the silence? No banging on the bars, no shouting or pleas for clemency, tobacco or water, no imagined malady come on during the hours of darkness. Even the rats are still. There is only the clink of keys and boots as the gaoler makes his way, flanked by four soldiers, for they think I am wild.

Outside the prison walls, it is different. I can hear the growing roar and clamour of the populace gathering at the gate. Armed with their needlework and their lace, flasks full of Canarian wine and parasols to shelter them from the rising sun. Until today, this has been the hottest autumn on record.

*It is nearly time.*

I have rejected the hood. I want to see the *burguesía* and the common people alike, all who have come on this dull morning in October to witness the execution of the hellion, the notorious she-captain of the seas. I will give them a spectacle, make no mistake. They will get their entertainment, even though they have dressed me in women's weeds and I can barely breathe. I petitioned to be allowed my own clothes, but they forced on me this last indignation of petticoats and stays. I came into this world as a woman, and I am condemned to leave it as one.

I have heard the guards say that it will be the largest crowd ever for a hanging and that, I admit, also pleases me. They have seen corsairs swing before, at this meeting point of the Atlantic Ocean and the Barbary Coast where piracy is a fact of life, but it is only right that I should be such a draw. I am, indeed, notorious, feared over sea and land. I am the one they did not believe could exist.

I am the commander of the *Ghost Ship*.

# PART ONE

*Eleven Years Earlier*
PARIS, LA ROCHELLE & CARCASSONNE
*May–July 1610*

# CHAPTER ONE

PARIS
*Wednesday, 12 May 1610*

In the gardens of the Palais des Tuileries, a butterfly fluttered in the warm spring air. Soaring, turning, dipping, it flew over the formal lawns and beds of red and yellow tulips, past the elms and the holm oaks, before coming to rest in a haze of lavender.

In the pink of the early morning, the formal box hedges lining the alleyways were already alive with sparrows. A blackbird grumbled at her mate. The first swifts gliding home from wintering on the Barbary Coast, a drift of silky wings skimming the still waters of the ornamental lake. Silk worms, the most recent arrivals in this green oasis at the western edge of the city, were spinning their silent story in the white mulberry trees.

Behind the high stone walls, beyond the tranquillity of the gardens, Paris was stirring. The bells of the city marked the passage from night to day. Hawkers dragged their carts towards Les Halles, wheels rattling over the cobbled streets. Merchants of cloth and preserves, pewter and gloves prepared for another day's business. In boarding houses and attics, the doxies and cutpurses muttered and cussed, waiting for the night to come around again. Kitchen maids held out jugs for deliveries of milk and scrawny boys were sent to buy fresh fish from the Quai de Bourbon. From north to south, within the old medieval footprint of the capital city, everywhere was life.

The coronation was only a day away. Pennants flew blue,

red and gold, geraniums blazed in window boxes. Royalists pinned flags to their balconies and boasted of how they had been invited to be in the congregation at the Basilica of Saint Denis tomorrow. After ten years of marriage to the King of France, Marie de' Medici was finally to be crowned queen in the presence of her husband and the eight-year-old Dauphin. Though the Italian queen was not popular, in taverns, landlords were offering drinks named in her honour – the 'Marie Punch', the 'Medici Malmsey' and the *grosse banquière*. All along the rue Saint-Honoré, the boulangeries were filled with Florentine biscotti and brioches, *pâte feuilletée* filled with cream and plaits of bread in the shape of a crown.

And in her family's temporary lodgings in Place Dauphine, at the western end of the Île de la Cité, slept one who had not been invited. Louise Reydon-Joubert was dreaming of Amsterdam: the twenty-fourth day of April in the year 1596. Of deep waters and wide blue skies that promised adventure, of the glory of ocean-going ships.

*Night after night, the same dream.*

She was ten years old, tall for her age, and remembering being taken out into the IJ for the first time to inspect the ships anchored in the harbour. Smart in her white bonnet and apron, blue dress and clogs.

In her troubled sleep, Louise shifts. Her long brown hair tangles around her throat like a noose. The dream is disconcerting. It is painful to remember how innocent she was, how proud. Holding her grandfather's hand as they walked over the canals of Amsterdam, knowing her beloved mother would be home the next day.

A red-letter day, marked on the calendar.

Louise dreams of being handed down from the quayside into the barge on Damrak, like a sack of flour, then feels the dip and pull of the oars and the slap of canal water on the bow as they make their way past the wharfs at the backs of houses on Warmoesstraat. Under the bridges, past the spire of the Oude Kerk, then disembarking. Walking along a wooden pontoon, the struts cracking and lurching beneath her feet. Clambering into the ship's *boot*, a large rowing boat which would take them out to where the *Old Moon* was anchored in the deep, shifting water of the harbour. She sees a forest of wood, masts and sails – the most glorious sight – and the noise is overwhelming, terrifying. Shouting, gusts of wind, the scrape of metal. The whistle blowing instructions.

The images swirl and merge. Looking up in wonder at the sails and masts, the lattice of rigging. Looking down at the sea, choppier now, white waves breaking as the oars carve a path through the water making diamonds of green. Remembering her grandfather wiping the salt spray from her face with his handkerchief.

Then, they are alongside, beneath the smooth hull of the *Old Moon*. The *fluyt* is bobbing in the swell. Iron nails bleeding red into the timber of the gunwales. Louise sees the polish and shine of a ship almost ready to sail, the chaos of merchants and goods, sailors and civilians. Animals, for trade or food, are being winched up onto the deck.

Strong arms grasp her around her waist, pass her up from hand to hand on the rope ladder, until she, too, is standing on the deck. Her clogs are unsuitable, but Louise quickly finds her balance. She is a natural, they say. Touching the rigging, the polished taffrail, the comforting thickness of the rope. Her grandfather lifts her up to ring the ship's bell and she runs the length of the deck, stern to bow, without slipping.

Louise claps with delight as the sailors clamber barefoot up ropes and balance on the cross beams, like the pet monkeys in the bar on Zeedijk; the galley in the fo'c'sle with its belch of smoke and soot, the rattle of the metal cauldron hanging in its brick prison; the beak at the bow and the grille through which the sailors do their private business. Though she is only ten, she understands that every man has his task. A ship is a floating republic, with its own laws, its own customs, its own rules.

Louise loses her heart that day, swept away by the promise of adventure, of freedom. Everyone is charmed by a girl who loves the sea as much as any boy. All the grizzled seamen, who spend their lives away from the civilising company of women and children, clap their hands. Her cheeks are flushed, her hair has come loose, she is happy.

Then, as always, the dream darkens. Always the same shift from exhilaration to despair. The sailors laughing when she says that, one day, she will be the captain of a ship. Not understanding why everyone is laughing, she feels humiliated. Her grandfather bends down to explain that girls cannot go to sea, though there is much they can do on dry land.

And that is how it begins to end.

Louise runs from him and trips, overbalances. She is falling, spinning down into the sea. Not the familiar glinting surface of Damrak, but the deep waters of the IJ reaching up to claim her. So cold. She tries to swim, but her arms will not move, her legs will not move. Her skirt and petticoats are sodden, dragging her under. Louise sees her wooden clogs come loose and float away from her. She will not need them now.

There is no sound save the beating of her own heart as she is embraced by the silken water, held by the choking weed, sinking down to where the fish dart, quicksilver fast, in the depths.

How much simpler everything might have been if she had drowned that day.

\* \* \*

'No!' Louise shouted, throwing herself bolt upright.

It took a moment for the room to come back into focus. Pale blue curtains rather than wooden shutters. The sounds of workmen arguing in French in the square below, not the cheerful chatter of Dutch bargemen. Louise is not in her chamber in Zeedijk, but in an elegant house in Place Dauphine. No longer a ten-year-old girl learning the limits of her world for the first time, but a woman of almost twenty-five.

Louise Reydon-Joubert let her head fall back against the bedstead and caught her breath. This was Paris not Amsterdam. Yet even here, it seemed, she could not escape the past.

# CHAPTER TWO

One floor below, Louise's grandmother, Minou, lay in her bed staring up at the wooden ceiling of her chamber and thought how, of all places, she most hated Paris.

This was the first time she had returned to the capital city since the terrible night of the August massacre that followed the royal wedding of Henri de Navarre to Marguerite de Valois thirty-eight years ago. Minou wished they had not come though, in truth, there had been little choice. If Louise was to claim her inheritance, she had to be present in person tomorrow to sign the documents, and neither Minou nor her husband, Piet, could have let her come to Paris alone.

She was determined to banish the memories of the past, so they had intended to stay until December. It was a chance for them to see their son, Jean-Jacques, who was in the employ of the Duc de Sully, the King's closest adviser and friend. It would also give her the chance to get to know her Parisian grandchildren, Jean-Jacques' four-year-old daughter Florence and his new baby son. Now, Minou wasn't sure.

Feeling every one of her sixty-eight years, she raised herself on one elbow, and gazed at Piet sleeping beside her. His beloved features, grown white with age, were as familiar to her as her own. Against all odds, they had been by one another's side for nearly fifty years. Together they had faced grief and despair, they had lost their way and been reconciled once more. Blessed with three children and three grandchildren, they had suffered, but kept going. Companions-in-arms, they had stood firm against the vicissitudes of life, the evils of war and the deaths of those they loved. They were old, but they had somehow kept living when those around them stumbled and fell. They had survived.

They would not survive this.

Minou let her eyes briefly close. She could put it off no longer. She had to tell him. She ran the back of her hand down the length of her husband's arm, hoping to wake him gently. He was still a strong man, though the flesh hung more loosely on his bones. In her memory, she could still see the stranger who had first stood before her outside her father's house in Carcassonne and called her his 'lady of the mists'. She had given Piet her heart that night and, though it had been torn and stitched by time, still it beat only for him.

'*Mon coeur*,' she whispered.

Piet grunted in his sleep, but did not stir.

The early morning sun was filtering through the shutters, casting ribbons of light on the wooden floor. Minou thought of other wakeful mornings when they had lain in one another's arms: in their first home in Puivert, destroyed during the fourth war; of their sanctuary on Zeedijk in Amsterdam, where they'd fled after the massacre that had taken her brother and their eldest daughter, Marta, from them, as well as a thousand other Huguenot souls; of all the places where they had been honoured guests, or homeless refugees, as their fortunes rose and fell, and rose again. She did not want to break the spell. Once she did, nothing would be the same.

'My love, I would speak with you,' she said, gathering her courage. She kissed his cheek and breathed in the familiar scent of sandalwood. So vivid, so strong, even after all these years. His eyes opened, for an instant not sure where he was. 'Piet.'

He turned a morning smile towards her. 'You sound very sombre.'

'It is a matter of some importance.'

He laughed. 'There is no need to frown, madomaisèla. There is nothing you could say that I would not be glad to hear.'

'Madomaisèla, ha! You are in need of a pair of spectacles.'

'I do not need an eye glass to know you are beautiful.'

Minou rested her hand against his cheek. 'You are a flatterer, my lord.'

'Speak, for the sooner you do, the sooner we might take breakfast.' He grinned, the lines on his weathered face creasing his pale Northern skin. 'I find I have an appetite this morning.' Seeing her hesitate, he reassured her. 'You can tell me anything, Minou, you know you can.'

'Of course.' She pushed her long hair, the colour of snow now, back from her face. 'It is this. I want to go home.'

Piet sat up and leant back against the bedstead. 'Well, I confess that was not what I was expecting. This does not seem to me so very serious. I admit the timing will need to be the subject of some discussion, given Jean-Jacques is so well-established here. And there is Louise to consider. Once the papers have been signed, I assume she intends to stay on with us in Paris, but I might be wrong. And, of course, Bernarda and Frans are not expecting us back in Amsterdam until the eve of Sint Nicolaas.'

She put her hand on his arm to stem the tide of words. 'No, not Amsterdam.'

Piet frowned. 'Then where?'

For the first time, Minou smiled. 'To Carcassonne. The time has come to go home.'

# CHAPTER THREE

Louise tiptoed past her grandparents' closed door, down the wide staircase and out into the early morning. Her blood was restless, as it always was when she was plagued with bad dreams, and the only way to calm herself was to walk. Walk, and not think. Walk, and not speak.

For a moment, she stood in the centre of Place Dauphine and looked back at the building that, for three weeks, had been their home. Named for Henri IV's eldest son and heir, it was the second of the King's newly designed open spaces for the citizens of Paris and was not yet completed. The sound of hammering and construction had filled every waking hour since they'd arrived in April, save for the Sabbath. It was enough to drive anyone out of their mind.

Of course, Louise knew it wasn't the noise in Place Dauphine that unsettled her. Her mind was too full. This was her first visit to Paris. It was here, in the year 1572, that her mother, Marta, had gone missing as a child. Louise's fingers went to her pocket, where her mother's locket lay wrapped in a scrap of cotton. A talisman, or a good luck charm, she was never without it.

*Try not to think.*

Louise walked through the square and leant on a stone parapet, looking down over the river Seine. Even before she had been old enough to be told the story of how her mother had been lost two days before the massacre – and not reunited with her family for twelve years – Louise had sensed that Marta did not fit within the Reydon-Joubert household in Amsterdam.

It was those missing years, as the adopted daughter of a mercenary and soldier, that had shaped her, not the fortune of her birth.

Throughout Louise's childhood, her mother would often vanish from Amsterdam for months on end and no one would tell her where Marta had gone, or if she was coming back. When she did reappear at the busy house on Zeedijk, she brought Louise lavish presents and told tantalising stories of the places she had seen. Marta was charming to her little daughter, pleasant enough to her brother Jean-Jacques, and civil to her younger sister Bernarda, but with little more warmth than she would offer a passing acquaintance. Only Louise's grandmother, Minou, had ever commanded Marta's unquestioning affection.

But, from time to time, on long, hot summer evenings – when Marta had taken a little wine and was in a mood to reminisce – she would gather Louise to her on the bench in the orchard of the house on the corner, and tell her stories. They always started the same way: 'Once upon a time, there was a little girl, a quick-witted and courageous girl . . .'

She remembered her mother as a glamorous and elegant woman, who had made no attempt to hide her disdain for Dutch society. Louise had her mother's colouring – and the distinctive mismatched eyes of the Reydon-Joubert women, one blue and one brown – but she was broad for a woman and with strong features, at odds with Parisian ideas of female beauty. She had seen her father only once, but knew that she resembled him in build and height. She hated that.

Then two days after that morning in April when Louise had fallen from the *Old Moon* and nearly drowned, her mother was dead and there were no more stories.

*No sense looking back.*

As the bells of the Sainte-Chapelle rang the half-hour, Louise pulled her thoughts back to the soft Parisian morning. Her homesick heart was craving familiar sights and smells – the sound of gulls trailing the fishing boats, the slick movements of the stevedores, the swagger of sailors.

She decided to go down to the port. She had noticed one small ship flying the colours of the Dutch East India Company, the VOC, waiting to depart on the morning's tide. Just the sight of it would help her feel less out of sorts.

Louise picked up her step. Even before she had set foot on the *Old Moon*, all she had ever wanted was to go to sea. She had made herself a nuisance, forever begging her great-aunt Alis and her companion, Cornelia van Raay, to take her with them to see the tall ships come in. The pennants and the flags, the tiny boats bobbing around the bigger ships like flies around a docile mare. Though she was bored by her lessons, she had no trouble memorising the names of different kinds of rigging and sails, nor how to trace a voyage on the lacquered globe that sat on the table in the entrance hall of the Van Raay house in Warmoesstraat. Louise smiled. Her fingers were always getting trapped in the wooden struts as she spun the world round and round, entranced by the sea monsters and shipwrecks and the *terra incognita*.

The Van Raay fleet was one of the smallest operating under the auspices of the Dutch East India Company in Amsterdam, and the only one owned and run entirely by a woman. Louise helped Cornelia, but hated being restricted because of her sex. She tracked cargo, noted the running repairs, paid the captains and crew. It was important work, but it was not enough. To be on dry land, dreaming of adventures happening elsewhere, was not enough.

*Tomorrow, all this might change.*

Louise stepped down off the Pont au Change. After the quiet

of the Île de la Cité, it was busier and noisier on the right bank. Carts and carriages jostled to pass, people bellowed, the smell of horse dung mixed with fried meats from the vendors who set up their stalls in the Place de Grève on days when there was to be an execution.

There was a permanent gibbet set in front of the Hôtel de Ville. Louise saw a crowd had gathered and her heart sank. She thought public hangings barbaric, and would have avoided the square if she could, but there was no other way down to the port.

Already soldiers were patrolling the square, pikes in hand, looking for signs of trouble. Children were running around, women pushing with sharp elbows and the stiff corners of their willow *paniers*, everyone trying to reach the palings first. Louise had little choice but to follow the crowd.

'Excuse me,' she said, trying to squeeze through. *'S'il vous plaît.'*

Lifting the hem of her cloak clear of the muck, Louise made her way as best she could. Then, the crowd roared as the cart bringing the prisoners from the Bastille rumbled into the square, and she realised she was trapped.

Close by, a tall man stood shivering despite the warmth of the morning, his red hair marking him out. He nursed a soiled hessian bag to his chest like a baby.

The voices in his head were loud today, telling him what he had to do. He was a fool, an outsider, someone of no account. They hissed at him, telling him the Huguenot malignancy was still spreading, infecting Paris and every one of the great cities of France. The nation would never become great again until every last heretic had been extirpated. It was his purpose. It was God's purpose through him. The voices told him so.

Those around him gave him a wide berth, he saw that, but he did not care. Was it not always so when a prophet walked among the common people? They would have cause to praise him soon enough. They would fall on their knees to give thanks that the humble saviour of France had graced them with his presence. He was an instrument of God. He would rid France of the cancer of heresy and be blessed for it. Then they would have to believe him.

He kept marching on the spot, his filthy feet uncertain on the cobbled ground. The noises in his head were growing louder. Buzzing, whispering, jeering, mocking.

'You are nothing, François Ravaillac, nothing at all.'

He clutched the bag closer to him. The tip of its hidden blade pierced the hessian weave, leaving spots of blood on his shirt.

'What is wrong with him?'

Louise looked down at the little boy who had appeared beside her.

'Are you lost?'

The child pointed. 'Look. He's bleeding.'

She turned to see a ragged man, tall and unkempt, with russet hair, standing in the shadow of the town hall clutching a bag to his chest. He was clearly afflicted with some malady of mind or spirit. His eyes darted to and fro, as if he feared he was being spied upon, and he seemed to be talking to himself. Then, as if feeling her watching him, he turned and stared directly at her with dark, burning, hate-filled eyes.

'Come away,' she said quickly, taking the boy by the hand. 'Where is your mother?'

'I came with my father.'

'All right, your father. Where did you last see him?'

The child shrugged, his bravado deserting him. 'I don't know,' he said in a small voice.

In the centre of the square, another roar went up. Above the heads of the crowd, Louise could see four prisoners being hauled up on to the gibbet. One was barely more than a boy himself.

*Who would let a child so young wander off on their own?*

'What's your name?' she asked.

'Jacques. I'm four.'

'Well, I would have thought you at least six,' Louise said brightly, trying to divert his attention from what was going on behind them. 'My uncle's name is Jacques, too. Well, Jean-Jacques. He has a little girl, Florence, about the same age as you and a son, also, but he's only a baby. Do you live nearby?'

His bottom lip began to quiver. 'I don't know.'

'Now, there's no need for tears. We'll find your father.'

In truth, Louise didn't know where to start – there were so many people, all pressing forward. Such ugly expressions on their faces. This was not justice, but sport.

A woman in a filthy shawl pushed her arm. 'You're blocking my view.'

'Do you know this boy's father?'

'Get out of my way.'

Another roar as the cart was rolled away and the four men dropped, legs twitching and spasming in the air. Three of them were lucky enough to die quickly, with a clean snap of the neck, but the last, a thin streak of a boy, was too light. His face turned blue as he slowly choked, bare feet twisting in the warm morning air. Louise wanted to look away, but the horror of it held her. No dignity.

*No one should die alone.*

'Excuse me,' she tried again, pushing her way through the crowd, 'does anyone know this boy? He's called Jacques.'

No one was listening. Then, suddenly, she felt Jacques' hand slip from hers and he ran towards a bearded man in a red cape.

'This lady found me,' he said, then staggered back as his father cuffed him around the head.

'I told you not to go running off.'

'Monsieur!' Louise said sharply. 'He was frightened. This is hardly a place for a child to be.'

He glowered at her. 'The boy's got to learn.' He shoved his son forward. 'Say thank you to the lady.'

'*Merci*,' Jacques whispered, trying not to cry.

'This is no place for a child,' Louise repeated, but father and son were already walking away.

For a moment, she stood quite still, infused with a deep sense of sadness, sadness for all the boys like Jacques, for the child-thief on the gibbet, for her ten-year-old self. She knew how easily a child's heart could be wounded.

The bells of Paris started to ring the hour. Louise shook her head, gathered herself. Her uncle was coming to visit this afternoon, so she had a couple of hours yet. She would put the execution from her mind and carry on to the port as she had intended.

Though the Seine was nothing compared to the grandeur of the IJ in Amsterdam, the familiar sights and sounds were soothing. Louise stepped onto the foreshore of the Port de Grève and walked down towards the lapping water, enjoying the squelch of mud beneath her shoes. Boats, barges, ships, scavengers, mudlarks, birds, the river was bustling. Everything that kept Paris going came into this square of riverbank between the floating jetties and bridges: wheat, flour, oats, barley, wine, white-wash and charcoal, all unloaded from a flotilla of tiny craft. She eavesdropped on men bartering and bargaining, in French rather than Dutch, but the hand signals were the same.

And the VOC ship, with its red, white and blue flags, was still there, ready to sail.

'Monsieur,' she said, as the sturdy *boot* taking cargo to the Amsterdam ship pulled up to the wharf. 'Where are you headed? How big is your crew?'

# CHAPTER FOUR

## La Rochelle

Under the same sun, some eighty leagues from Paris on the Atlantic Coast, a ten-year-old girl darted, unseen, through another crowd.

La Rochelle – the richest city on the western seaboard and the most important of the *places de sûreté* for Huguenots within France – had grown rich on salt and wine, and trade in fur and spices with the Americas and the East Indies. A jewel within France's crown, defended by fortifications, castles and towers, a multitude of cannon facing out to sea, it protected itself and its wealth fiercely. The King had been a friend to La Rochelle, providing funds to reclaim the south-eastern marshlands and transforming the city into a star-shaped stronghold of impregnable bastions, pinned by the Tour de Sermaise to the north, and the Tour d'Aix to the south. To the west, lay the sea.

This morning the port, a natural harbour, was busy. It always was. Several trading ships were moored just beyond the sea walls, and a steady convoy of smaller boats were sailing out between the two mighty towers that stood sentinel at its narrow opening, closed each night by raising the mighty underwater chain to the surface of the water.

Beyond the channel, the Atlantic Ocean.

For the girl, none of this was unfamiliar. She relished the familiar bustle of the port in the middle of the day: nets drying in the sunshine, the rumble of carts, stevedores unloading their cargo, the bob and dip of oars, the slap of rigging in the wind. Sailors with skin the colour of charcoal or scorched red by the sun, mingled with blond mariners from the Baltic. Women with baskets of mussels on their hips, the sleek black shells catching the light. Well-dressed merchants and their wives thronged the quays, making the wharves fertile ground for pickpockets and mountebanks. Behind it all could be heard the sounds of hammering and sawing from the shipbuilders. Sounds the girl had heard many thousands of times.

Yet today was different.

Everything she had known was about to change. Tomorrow, they would lay her brother in the ground. Then the day after, she would cease to exist. The ten years she had lived on this earth would vanish, as if they had never been.

A cacophony of bells from the churches that occupied every corner of Protestant La Rochelle began to ring, each slightly out of time. The girl realised with a start she had been gone too long. She had slipped out at dawn and now it was ten o'clock.

Her heart started to race.

'Watch where you're going, boy.'

For a moment, she didn't grasp he was talking to her. A red-faced man, none too steady on his feet, breath thick with brandy.

'*Pardon*, monsieur,' she murmured, stepping out of his way.

The girl pushed her hand through her shorn hair, unused to feeling air on the back of her neck. The jerkin and the uncomfortable breeches irritated her skin, the material so much coarser than her petticoat. The shoes were too big, clumsy on her narrow feet and tied on with string. Everything felt wrong. But she had caught sight of her reflection in the water and knew she passed well enough.

'Pick a card, any card . . .'

She stopped, her attention caught by the odd sing-song voice. She did not want another beating, but the thought of returning to the sordid lodgings in the rue du Port, where her beloved twin lay cold in his box, felt like a weight pressing down on her chest. Might she risk another few minutes?

'Pick a card,' the man repeated in his lilting accent. 'How about you, monsieur?'

A knot of some dozen people was clustered around a *bateleur*, a street entertainer, unusual in the bourgeois Protestant city whose Huguenot soul did not encourage augury or cartomancy or Papish superstition. Unnoticed, the girl slipped through the forest of coats and boots, right to the front of the crowd.

'I don't believe any of this,' sneered a man in a long green velvet coat.

The girl stared at the magician. Dark skinned, exotic in a flounced coat and a blue neckerchief, he had set up a folding table draped in a black cloth with a painted sign: SORTILÈGE. She had never seen anyone like him before. In his hands, he held a stack of rectangular cards, each decorated with bold printed images. The girl had heard of Tarot cards – red, blue and yellow, like the colours of his coat – but had never seen any before. She edged closer and up onto a doorstep to get a better view.

Urged on by his companions, and the promise of a quart of ale if he took the wager, the man in the green coat swaggered up to the table.

'Come on, then, prove me wrong.'

The *bateleur* gave a half-bow. 'You would know what your future holds, is that so?'

One of his companions elbowed him in the back. 'Ask if that shrew of a wife of yours is tupping your neighbour!'

The man spun round, ready to curse, but the *bateleur* merely smiled.

'*Mesdames et messieurs*, perhaps this other gentleman here is asking because that is what he most fears for himself, no?' A rumble of appreciation went through the crowd as the *bateleur* continued. 'You should know that these cards represent our journey through life, the challenges that cannot be changed or fought against. It is, too, man's journey from ignorance to enlightenment. Each of these cards, *mesdames et messieurs*, exists in balance with another. Two sides of the same coin, if you will.'

Entranced by his voice, the girl watched as the cartomancer cast his eye around the circle, drawing each person in. They were conspirators now, a ramshackle congregation. Then, he gave another smile and spoke to his customer, almost in a whisper.

'So, signore, will you try?'

Bucked by the appreciation of his friends, and the attention of the crowd, the man dug a coin out of his pocket.

'Why not?'

'A man of discernment, I could see it at once.' The *bateleur* held out the pack of cards and suddenly, the girl thought, the air seemed to sharpen. 'Shuffle them, cut them, change the order. There is no trick, no sleight of hand. The cards will fall as they fall.'

The customer made heavy weather of the task, dropping several cards on the dark cloth, before handing back the deck.

'*Grazie, signore.*' The magician gave another half-bow. 'Now, place the deck on the table and cut it in three, using your left hand. Very good. Now put the deck back together, the middle section first, then the top, and then the bottom.' While the customer was following his instructions, the magician was looking once more from face to face. 'Remember, mesdames, messieurs, a reading is merely a guide to what might happen, not what will happen. Our fate is in God's hands. He, alone, decides.' A murmur of approval went around the Huguenot crowd. One or two of them muttered 'Amen'. 'Now, signore, pick a card, any card, and lay it down just so.'

The girl held her breath, spellbound as the customer drew a card and laid it down on the cloth. She stood up on tiptoe on her step so she could see the image on the chosen card: a man with a bag on a stick, a little dog snapping at his heels.

'*Le Mat*,' said the cartomancer, 'or, in my language, *il Matto*. The Fool. It is the only unnumbered card and represents someone who stands outside of the ordinary world, invisible and not subject to the rules that others are bound by. Sometimes, a scapegoat or a beggar, his presence in a reading might suggest innocence or unpredictability.'

One of the man's friends slapped him on the back. 'Never a truer word spoken.'

'Draw again, signore.'

The crowd edged closer. The girl had learnt never to draw attention to herself but, she too, leant in to see the next card being placed upside down on the black cloth.

'This card, numbered eight, is Justice,' the magician said. 'It represents one of the four cardinal virtues, alongside temperance, prudence and fortitude. Unlike the other three virtues, Justice is always feminine. You see she holds in her hands the scales of logic and the sword of justice. But . . .' He shook his head. 'As you see, *mesdames et messieurs*, the card is reversed.'

The girl didn't mean to speak, but the words came anyway. 'What does it mean if it is reversed?'

She felt the magician turn his black eyes upon her. She shrank back.

'The Justice card reversed suggests the querent – that's to say this gentleman here – knows that he has done, or is intending to do, something that is morally wrong. It might not be much. Don't we all commit sins for which we must ask forgiveness? But it might also be a greater crime against the laws of man, or against the laws of God Himself.' He frowned, though there was compassion in his gaze. 'But you, little gentleman, I think you know this.'

She couldn't bear it any longer. She had never had anything beautiful, never had anything of her own to treasure or cherish. But as the morning sun glinted on the beautiful card, and with the sound of the sea and the gulls in the harbour beyond, she knew that whatever happened in the days ahead, she never wanted to forget this moment.

The girl jumped down from the step. Her thin hand shot out and grabbed the card. Blocking her ears to the shout of the crowd at her heels, she ran.

# CHAPTER FIVE

## Paris

Minou and Piet were sitting in the salon in Place Dauphine, hand in hand.

'Say something,' she said. Minou liked the room, but it was a place with no history, no echoes of past words, no memories of children's laughter or hearts broken. 'What are you thinking, my love?'

Her husband's face was lined with grief, as if he had aged a decade in the space of this one morning.

'I knew there was something wrong. You have been distracted, unlike your usual self. I should have realised.'

'How could you have known?'

Piet turned to face her. 'And you are certain there is nothing to be done?'

Minou shook her head. 'I consulted a physician in Amsterdam in the spring – Alis accompanied me – then another when we arrived in Paris. The good news is that the canker has not grown. We could have years.' She tried to smile. 'I have accepted it, *mon coeur.*'

'Why did you not tell me?' he cried, his voice stiff with grief. 'You should have told me sooner.'

'I know.'

'Then why didn't you? I am your husband. I am not so feeble that you have to protect me.'

Minou ran the back of her hand down his cheek. 'I suppose

because I did not want to have to witness this very look upon your face.'

He raised her hand to his lips. '*Touché*. And this is why you wish to return to Carcassonne. To die.' His voice faltered. 'Minou . . .'

Her eyes brimmed with tears. 'God willing, we will have years,' she repeated, though she knew this was untrue. Already she felt less substantial, as if her feet no longer left an imprint on the earth. 'Come, my love, you should eat. You must keep your strength up.'

On the table sat a trencher of bread and cheese, as well as Piet's favourite Dutch beer transported in casks from Amsterdam in the spring. Minou filled his glass and placed food on his plate, though she took nothing for herself. Most things made her feel sick these days.

'Louise is much on my mind,' she said.

Piet nodded. 'You fear her reaction when you tell her?'

'In part.' This, too, was a conversation she had put off. 'But I worry in any case. She is not content, Piet. She has great strength of character – and works hard for Cornelia – yet there is a wildness in her that I fear will lead her into trouble.'

'Louise is not like her mother,' Piet said quietly.

'It's not that.'

'Then, what? You think she should marry? Alis never married.'

'She has Cornelia.'

'There was no shortage of suitors in Amsterdam.'

Minou laughed. 'Merchants, Dutch advocates, men of business, none to her taste. Besides, there is no need. When Louise signs the papers tomorrow, she will have control of her father's estate and fortune. She can support herself.' She sighed. 'I don't know what she wants.'

'Of all things, Minou, she craves your love.'

'She has my love.'

He put his hand across hers. 'When will you tell her?'

'After tomorrow,' she said, and tried once more. 'Piet, I need you to accept there is a . . . a sense of injustice in her that, if not tamed, will—'

'Will what?'

She threw her hands in the air. 'Oh, I don't know. She feels everything so deeply. Maybe it is our fault. We kept her too close. She never played with other children, she—'

'Minou, stop. You have been as good as a mother to her, better. Louise was surrounded by children in the almshouse. It is her character to hold herself apart. No one could have loved her more.'

'Perhaps too much.' Minou hesitated. 'And, *mon coeur*, we should tell her the truth about her parents' deaths. We owe it to her.'

'No,' he said fiercely. 'We agreed. Nothing has changed.'

*Everything has changed*, she wanted to cry. But she looked at his dear old face, and she held her tongue.

'You want Louise to be happy,' Piet said, putting down his cup, 'as do I. But you of all people, Minou, know that we cannot save our children – or grandchildren – however much we want to spare them the vicissitudes of life. They have to find their own path.'

Minou sighed. 'I know that.'

Piet took a sip of beer. 'I am in my twilight years, but I am in good health. And you, Minou, you say it could be years.'

She tried to smile. 'Louise will be wealthy. What if we are not here to guide her?'

'Alis and Cornelia will provide guidance,' Piet said reasonably. 'Jean-Jacques, too. For all his disapproval of her boldness, he is fond of his niece.'

'That is true.'

'Well, then,' he replied, as if she had conceded the point. 'Could it not be that your illness is making you see problems where none exist?'

'Perhaps,' she said sadly, having failed to make him understand. Indeed, she barely knew what she felt herself, only that she was always on her guard. In Amsterdam, Louise was kept busy at the harbour. Here, she had too much time on her hands. But maybe Piet was right, perhaps it was the sickness that was making her anxious.

Piet took another swallow of beer and leant back in his chair. A drowsy silence fell over the chamber, the sense of being in between times. His eyes fluttered, then closed.

The maid appeared in the doorway, wisps of pale hair escaping from beneath her cap, and bobbed a curtsey. Minou sighed. The girl always looked sloppy.

'What is it?'

'Mademoiselle Louise has returned, my lady.'

'Ah, thank you. Tell her we are in here, if she would care to join us.'

'Also, if it pleases you, Monsieur Jean-Jacques has arrived.'

Instantly, Minou's fatigue lifted. It was a rare pleasure to receive a visit from her son, even though he lived no more than a few streets away.

'Show him in,' she said, then leant across and put her hand on Piet's knee to wake him.

# CHAPTER SIX

When Louise entered the salon at two o'clock, she found her uncle already there. Forty years of age, and tall, he looked distinguished in his black doublet with grey slashing, white ruff and breeches, polished boots. Her grandmother always said Jean-Jacques strongly resembled Piet in his youth – sturdy, with freckled northern skin, russet beard.

'Here she is,' he said, getting to his feet. 'The birthday girl.'

'Not until tomorrow,' Louise said, offering her cheek to be kissed.

Jean-Jacques was secretary to the Duc of Sully, superintendent of finances and one of the most powerful men in the realm after the King himself. It was Sully who had been able to secure the Reydon-Joubert family such propitious lodgings in Paris overlooking the Pont Neuf.

Louise knew her grandmother hated Paris for what it had cost her family, but even Minou had been obliged to concede that the King's determination to fashion his capital into a city fit for the seventeenth century had borne fruit. And though it was said Henri ran his court as something between a bawdy house and a barracks, his subjects loved him. Louise deplored her uncle's old-fashioned views – he was married to someone who talked only of her children and had no interest in the politics of the day – but she enjoyed their conversations and was pleased to see him.

'I have come bearing gifts,' Jean-Jacques said, reaching to the wooden chest in the centre of the room and picking up a blue velvet bag. 'Here.'

'May I open it today?'

'If you do not think it will bring bad luck.'

'I am not so superstitious!' she said, throwing herself into an armchair and placing the bag in her lap.

'*Ma foi*, wherever have you been?' Minou exclaimed, looking at Louise's feet.

Louise glanced down, then grinned. The hem of her skirts was caked with pale brown mud and her green shoes were black at the tips. 'The Port de Grève. There was a voc ship sailing today. And I saw a double-ended skiff with a single mast.'

Jean-Jacques raised his eyebrows. 'And this is fascinating because . . .'

'Oh, Uncle!'

Piet laughed. 'Come, open your gift. Show us what's inside.'

'Let me guess,' she teased. 'Might it be an emerald necklace, my birthstone for the month of May?'

'I hardly think my stipend would stretch to that, even for my favourite niece.'

'Your only niece.' She smiled. 'Though you spoil me.'

Louise pulled at the drawstring, stretched the neck and pulled out a package. She placed it on her lap, opened the cloth and gasped. It was a beautiful dagger with a single emerald, her birthstone, set in a silver hilt.

'I could stretch to a solitary gem,' Jean-Jacques said gruffly.

'Uncle, it is magnificent. I cannot imagine a more perfect gift. Ideal for cutting rope.'

'I had more in mind letters and ribbons.'

Louise laughed. 'Have you ever seen me wear a ribbon?'

'There is time. After tomorrow, you will be able to buy as many ribbons as the Queen herself.'

\*　\*　\*

They drank beer and ate sweet seed cake, and caught up with family news before moving to the subject of the coronation.

Although Louise was inclined to debate every point, Minou enjoyed listening to their chatter. It was a rare indulgence for them all to be together these days. Not all, she corrected herself, with the usual guilt for forgetting the daughter she had never quite been able to love – Bernarda had never set foot in France, and claimed she never wanted to.

'Except surely,' Louise was saying, 'all the good the King has done will be for nothing if he goes to war against Germany?'

'His legacy is secure,' Jean-Jacques replied. 'The evidence is all around you.'

Piet nodded. 'Ours not to reason why. If I have learnt anything about politics it is that everything – and nothing – can be made to make sense.'

'All part of God's plan,' Louise said wryly. 'Well, we can only pray that He is listening.'

'Niece, you go too far!'

Louise grinned. 'I'm sorry, Uncle.'

'How goes the King?' Minou asked.

Jean-Jacques turned a sober eye on her. 'His Majesty is no longer in the best of health – gout and inflammation of the stomach, catarrh.'

'I would hazard he is weary of kingship,' Piet said, shifting in his chair and waving away Minou's attempts to help him. 'He is more himself in the field with his men than confined within the walls of the Louvre Palace. Am I close to the mark?'

'There is something in what you say, sire.'

'You cannot surely be suggesting that he might provoke a war merely to fill his over-long hours?' Louise protested.

'The King is of the genuine belief that he alone, of all the rulers of Europe, can bring together a Christian alliance.'

'His "Grand Design",' said Piet.

'Just so. My lord Sully and the King have spent many hours in debate on the matter. His Majesty would, above all, curb the influence of Spain. If he could break the alliance between Philip and the Holy Roman Empire—'

Louise raised her eyebrows. 'And should we consider this a noble intention?'

'What can I tell you?' Jean-Jacques let his hands drop. 'The King has had his fill of Paris. He says he does not feel safe here, and that he is plagued by melancholy and bad dreams. This last week has been difficult. My lord Sully is himself unwell, and that has left the King without a politic ear.'

'But—'

Minou put her hand on her granddaughter's arm. 'Louise, enough. Jean-Jacques is here for a respite from politics.'

She had the grace to blush. 'I'm sorry, Uncle. If I have offended you, forgive me.'

'Not at all.'

Piet leant forward and tapped his son's knee. 'But are the rumours true, or is it another attempt by the Leaguers, or Spanish sympathisers, to provoke unrest?'

'There are some forty thousand royal troops mustering in Champagne near the frontier with the Holy Roman Empire. The King's intention is to ride out to join his troops on Wednesday next.'

'War is a young man's game,' said Louise idly, strolling to gaze out of the window.

'Do you mind!' Piet peered at her over the top of his spectacles. 'His Majesty has not yet accomplished sixty summers. A mere sapling!'

Minou patted his hand. 'It is true you have amassed the wisdom of nearly a *vingtaine* more, *mon coeur*.'

Louise turned to the room. 'Common gossip has it, that nothing gives him pleasure since the failure of his latest fancy last winter.'

'Niece!'

'Oh, Uncle, I am not a child! It is common knowledge the King has no restraint in matters of the heart. It is rumoured he threatened to have the poor girl kidnapped, then that he would go to war against her husband – his own nephew – if he did not hand her over. Is that true?'

Jean-Jacques shifted in his seat. 'This is not a suitable topic.'

'But is it true?'

'All right, I confess it is,' he admitted. 'And he might well have pressed ahead with his plans had it not been for the wise counsel of my lord Sully. The matter was resolved with the greatest difficulty.'

Louise started to pace. 'My sympathies are much with the Queen. The King is faithless and allows her to be humiliated.'

'His Majesty believes the Queen never accommodates herself to his humour, nor allows him to approach her with tenderness.'

'You are saying it is her fault, not his?'

'Niece, you are putting words into my mouth,' Jean-Jacques replied evenly. 'In any case, now his blood has cooled for his nephew's wife, of late they have been gentler in one another's company.'

'Hence the coronation?' asked Minou.

'In part, though it is as much a matter of state. His Majesty deems it advisable to have the Queen confirmed as regent should anything befall him when he is on campaign. The King has, much to the surprise of my lord Sully, superintended many of the preparations for the coronation himself. He appears to be enjoying himself.'

'I regret that we will not be there, but my health prohibits it,' Piet said, then smiled at Louise. 'Besides, we have important plans of our own tomorrow.'

'His Majesty understands. It is a pity. Very few of the leading Huguenot noble families will be in attendance, though all were invited.'

'Most are not prepared to risk setting foot in the capital again,' Minou put in. 'And can you blame them.'

Louise's eyes twinkled with mischief. 'Perhaps I should go in your stead, *Gran'père*.'

'Without an escort, that would hardly be appropriate,' Jean-Jacques protested.

'Uncle, you really do have a most antiquated view of what is permissable for women to do or not to do.'

'Louise—' warned Minou.

'Why do we not go together, *Gran'mère*? This is 1610, the world is changing. It is not like in your day, when ladies never left the house without a male guardian. Don't you want to be there to see history made?'

Minou gave her granddaughter an indulgent smile. 'You seem to be of the impression that I have seen nothing in my long, long life. Done nothing. We were not so timid as you seem to think.'

Louise grinned. 'Aren't you just a little bit curious to see what will happen when the former Queen, and all the King's mistresses, and all the King's children come face to face? Those born on the wrong side of the blanket all seated beside the Dauphin? Don't you want to see the look of horror in the Spanish ambassador's eyes? So offended, but having to hold his tongue?'

'It is not a laughing matter,' Jean-Jacques said sternly, and was bewildered when everyone burst into laughter.

'She is teasing you,' Minou said, patting her son's hand.

'I have seen enough pomp and ceremony in my time,' Piet said, 'and our business is more important than a mere coronation, is it not, Louise?'

'It is.' She planted a kiss on her grandfather's head, then headed for the door. 'Uncle, it has been a pleasure. *Gran'mère*, *Gran'père*, if you will excuse me.'

Minou nodded. 'Where are you going?'

Louise looked down at her stockings, stiff with dried mud from the river bank. 'To change my shoes.'

'After all this is over, you should come and visit the children. Little Florence misses you,' Jean-Jacques said. 'She has something of you about her. And my wife would be glad to see you.'

Louise pulled a face. 'I doubt that, though you are kind to say so. And I will. After my birthday. Everything will be different after that.'

# CHAPTER SEVEN

For a moment after Louise had gone, everything was quiet, as if the air itself was settling in her wake.

'She is as spirited as ever,' Jean-Jacques said. 'She would give any one of His Majesty's advisers a run for his money, though I am not certain such strong opinions would find favour at court.'

Minou looked affectionately at her dependable, honourable son. 'Paris is more conservative than Amsterdam. Louise finds the lack of intelligent conversation frustrating. At home, she has Alis and Cornelia. Here, she has too much time on her hands.'

'Will she return to Amsterdam as soon as the papers are signed, or remain here with you and Father for the duration of your stay?'

Minou paused, wondering if this might be the time to tell Jean-Jacques of her plan to return to Carcassonne and the reason for it. But she held her tongue. It would be unfair. He had so much responsibility with tomorrow's coronation and the King's imminent military ambitions. What mother would burden her child with more?

'It has yet to be decided,' she said lightly. 'Louise will be free to make her own decisions. It is up to her.'

'You are not in her confidence?'

Minou gave a gentle smile. 'Louise always keeps her own counsel, you know that.'

Jean-Jacques turned to Piet, now dozing in his chair, and dropped his voice. 'How is he?'

'Paris tires him, but he is as well as can be expected for a man of his age. You should not worry.'

'He seems, I don't know . . . His hand shakes.'

'It is a mild palsy, nothing more.'

'And it seems as if it pains him to walk.'

'We have lived to make old bones, your father and I. If he is a little slower, then what of it? His mind is as sharp as ever it was. We manage well enough.'

'It is just that he seems—'

Minou patted his arm. 'It is hard for any son to see his father age, but he has more strength of purpose than most men of half his years. It is only because you have not seen him for a while that you notice the change.'

Jean-Jacques flushed. 'I would come more often, but my time is not my own.'

'Oh, Jean-Jacques, I am not chiding you. He is so proud of you, so proud. We both are.'

He looked suddenly awkward. 'In point of fact, I would talk to you about Louise. Is everything arranged for tomorrow?'

Minou narrowed her eyes. 'It is. Why?'

Jean-Jacques pulled at a thread on his sleeve. 'Father has not said anything—'

'About what?'

He cleared his throat. 'There is a rumour.'

Minou felt her contentment melt away. 'What manner of rumour?'

'That there might be a counter claim on her father's estate. Possibly a legitimate heir, so I've heard.'

She turned cold. 'After all this time, how can there be? We would have heard something before now.'

Jean-Jacques shrugged. 'I cannot tell you if it is true – I am doing my best to find out – only that there is talk of a boy in

Chartres. One of His Majesty's advisers, who was lately travelling in the region, brought the rumour back to Paris with him.'

'What did he say?'

'Only what I have told you. That there is said to be a boy carrying the Evreux name living in Chartres, rumoured to be the son of Louis Vidal.' He glanced again at his father. 'I had hoped to speak to him about it, but since Louise was here and now he is—'

'Piet has heard nothing, he would have told me else,' she said quickly though, even as she said the words, she wondered.

'It is probably nothing. But if there was any kind of scandal that might be—'

'Louise would never want to cause any embarrassment to you or to Lord Sully,' Minou assured him.

'I was thinking of my niece, not myself.' He hesitated again. 'Louise is not going on her own to the lawyer?'

'Of course not. Piet will accompany her. If there is any difficulty – and I am sure there will not be – he will tell you. And, as Louise is fond of reminding us, she is not a child.'

Jean-Jacques leant forward and kissed her cheek. 'I will leave it in your hands. I travel with the duke to Saint-Denis tonight, to be on hand for the King, and will return to Paris with him after the coronation. The Queen is to make her official entry into Paris on Sunday morning. Then, if my duties allow, I will visit Monday next and tell you all about it.'

Minou nodded. 'And if you hear anything about the other matter?'

'That too, of course.' He took up his hat. 'Likewise, if anything untoward happens with the lawyer, you will send a message to me?'

'Of course. God speed, my love.'

She listened to Jean-Jacques' footsteps going down the stairs, heard the front door open and close, before finally allowing herself to sink back in her chair. Everything ached, her bones, her limbs, now her head. The whole day had been exhausting: talking to Piet, hiding her discomfort from her granddaughter and her son, and now this.

Minou rubbed her temples. Despite the manner of his death, Louise's father's will had not been contested. Piet had seen to that. Louis Vidal, Lord Evreux, had been a wealthy man, with significant estates in Chartres, and his illegitimate daughter was his sole heir. But what if Louis had married and had a legitimate child with a better claim?

Louise's inheritance had been a fixed point in her life for fifteen years. That promise of independence had allowed her to live as she did. No need to marry, able to help Cornelia without thought to the longer term. What would it mean if that certainty was snatched away?

Two things had shaped Louise's life. The first – her accident falling from the *Old Moon* – might not have been so significant had her mother not been lost two days later. Overnight, Louise had changed from a light-hearted, open child into a fierce and withdrawn girl, secretive and angry at the world. Had they over-protected her? Piet thought not, but Minou wasn't sure. As a woman, Louise was self-possessed and affectionate to her immediate family, but kept most other people at an arm's length.

She pressed her fingers harder to her temples, trying to keep the incipient headache at bay. She did not want to believe Piet could have heard the rumour from Chartres and not told her, but he often spared her what he thought would be distressing news. As she did him. She prayed it was nothing.

And Minou knew she had to tell Louise about her illness, and the truth about the day her parents had died. How long could she keep putting it off?

# CHAPTER EIGHT

Louise stood at the window of her chamber in Place Dauphine watching the light fade from the sky. She pulled at a thread on her bodice. Why couldn't she settle? An apothecary in Amsterdam had given her powders to help her sleep, but Louise had never taken them. Perhaps, tonight, she would.

*Tomorrow is my birthday.*

The thirteenth of May. Except this year, her life would change. She would be wealthy. That she would receive her inheritance at the age of twenty-five had been a fixed point in her life. No one knew why her father had set it so late, only that those were the terms of his will. Many times, Louise had tried to ask her grandmother and grandfather about him, but they claimed they knew nothing. Maybe, tomorrow, she would find out more.

Her day-to-day existence was confined and dull, but settled. After tomorrow, she would be free to go anywhere. She would no longer be obliged to remain in the house on Zeedijk where she had grown up. Louise loved her grandparents, Alis and Cornelia, too, but her aunt Bernarda was trying. A woman who made a show of piety and Christian duty, but was always looking to criticise and apportion blame. Perhaps she might buy a little modern canal house or somewhere near Begijnhof? Except Louise cared little for the idea of her own home.

*There is only one thing I want.*

She started to pace, thinking about the conversation she wanted to have with Cornelia. The *Old Moon* was the only thing that meant anything to her. Would Cornelia agree? Might she allow her to sail with the ship? Sailors were superstitious about having a woman on board, they thought it would bring bad luck. But if Cornelia agreed, and gave her permission, no captain could object. For a moment, Louise allowed her dreams to soar. She imagined herself not just sailing on the *Old Moon* but owning it, even commanding the ship on the high seas.

She smiled. One step at a time. All it took was courage.

# CHAPTER NINE

## La Rochelle

Many hundreds of miles away, the light was also fading over La Rochelle. The sea was still, shifting green and blue, as the last few small boats came back into the harbour.

The girl stood on the ramparts beside the Tour de la Chaîne and watched the sun sink below the horizon. The backs of her legs were smarting from that morning's beating, but it could have been so much worse. Her mother had not found the tarot card, hidden in her shoe.

Seeking comfort in familiar things, the girl had come to watch the nightly closing of the harbour. And here it was, a sound just beneath the water. The judder of metal and the grind of the winch as it slowly began to turn, like the growling of a giant monster waking from a winter's sleep. The jolt of iron against brick as the mighty chain was dragged up and across the narrow gap of water between the two towers. It was a tradition many centuries old, both to prevent ships weighing anchor under cover of darkness and to keep privateers out. The girl had never seen a corsair ship, but she had heard sailors in the taverns talk of the pirates' cruelty and wildness. How they showed no mercy and lived by their own laws, their own loyalties.

On the other side of the harbour mouth, preparations were underway for the celebration to be held in the Tour Saint-Nicholas to give thanks for the safe return of the son of one of La Rochelle's richest shipowners. In the softly fading light, beyond the shipyard, the girl could see lanterns set along the path to the entrance, the flames licking up the sides of the tower. She wondered how it would feel to be so loved that a feast was held in your honour. How it would feel to not live every moment of your life in fear.

The gulls wheeled and dived above the fishing fleets at rest. Sailors singing in the taverns, a fiddle and whistle playing old shanties of the sea beneath the *grosse horloge*, the grand clock tower, that marked the boundary of the port and the town, the usual carousing heard on a fine evening in early summer. The spot where the cartomancer had dealt his cards was deserted now. The Devil's Picture Book, that's what the preachers called the Tarot. Despite everything, the girl smiled at the thought of her treasure.

Then, she shivered.

Tomorrow morning, she would have to watch as they laid her beloved brother in the ground. Then, at eleven o'clock on Friday, her mother would receive her estranged brother, Monsieur Barenton, and the deception would begin. The girl tried not to think of what would happen if she failed to convince her uncle that she was the heir he had come to meet. Her fingers slipped to the bruises on her arm, evidence of another beating two weeks ago, her skin still yellow and green. She vowed to do better. What choice was there?

The broad beam of light from the Tour de la Lanterne began to shine out across the Atlantic Ocean. The girl knew that prisoners were held in the dungeons of the tower, men from England, or Holland, and Catholic France, common criminals and seafaring men with the misfortune to stray into enemy waters. Did they lie awake dreaming of home? Were they missed by their families or were they, like she, grateful to be freed from the circumstances into which they had been born? The girl had heard it said that they scratched their initials on the wall and tallied each sunrise to keep count of their days of imprisonment.

The bells began to ring for seven o'clock.

She heard soldiers swapping tales as they handed over to the night watch. Someone laughed: shifting, ordinary, night-time sounds. Outside the Tour Saint-Nicholas, the carriages were starting to arrive. The band struck up, recorder and viol, the notes thin in the soft evening air. A steady drum beat to see the honoured guests into the banqueting chamber.

Clutching her cap in her hand, the girl jumped down from the sea wall and made her way back towards the town, avoiding the rectangles of light spilling from the taverns and boarding houses that ringed the port. No one saw her, she was a ghost child. Her muscles began to burn as she walked faster, then broke into a run. She could not be late back for a second time today.

One day to go, then there would be no going back.

# CHAPTER TEN

## Barbary Coast

On the Atlantic Ocean, more than a thousand miles from La Rochelle as the crow flies, mariner Hans Janssen sat cross-legged atop the high platform of the main mast of the *White Dove* listening for the eight bells to signal the end of his watch.

The *White Dove* was the flagship of Cornelia van Raay's fleet operating out of Amsterdam. There was always a moment, when a ship sailed out of Mediterranean waters into the more oppressive climate off the North African coast, where the wind might drop. But this voyage, luck was on their side. A brisk north-easterly was driving them forward at a fair pace. The generous square sails were full, the rigging was singing. Janssen thought they might even arrive in Las Palmas de Gran Canaria ahead of time.

He smiled, thinking of the pink cheeks and unmarked skin of his girl in La Rochelle. Janssen was not a sentimental man, and he had not thought he was the marrying kind, but Marie had captured his heart. She was plump and pretty as a picture and he was minded, when they got back to harbour in the autumn, to ask her to be his wife. They would have two sons and two daughters. The boys would go to sea, the girls could stay home and keep his Marie company while their menfolk were away.

Content with his vision of the future, Janssen cleaned his nails with the tip of his knife. He noticed that one of the ropes on the yardarm on the leeward side, outside the lift of the spar, was worn and needed replacing. He considered doing something about it, then decided to leave it to the next man on duty. A miserable dog from Haarlem, Wouter was lazy and always shirked his duties. It would do him good to pull his weight for once in his miserable, pox-ridden life.

The wind dropped and, for perhaps half an hour, his mind wandered. Then in the fading light, out of the corner of his eye, Janssen saw movement. Some distance behind them to starboard. He swivelled round on the platform, squinted, then raised his spyglass.

'By all that's Holy,' he muttered.

No doubt about it, they had company. He couldn't make out the colours they were flying, but he could see it was a double-masted vessel. He adjusted the setting. Now he could make out the long, slender hull and low freeboard. A galley driven by oars and manpower was less reliant than they were on the wind. There looked to be two lateen sails and a beak at the bow. Perhaps as many as twenty oars. The question was, was it friend or foe?

He lay flat on his stomach and shouted down to the deck below.

'*Schip aan stuurboord.* Ship a'starboard.'

An answering whistle told him the message had been received. Cursing the ill fortune that might prolong his watch – the roll of the ship was considerably worse this high up – he continued to keep the vessel in his sights. He started to make out the sound of the dip of wooden blades in the water. Yes, at least two dozen oars.

The galley seemed to be gaining on them. It was common knowledge that galleys were the favoured ships of the Barbary corsairs from the port of Salé, but they rarely sailed alone. They hunted in packs. Though Janssen was apprehensive, he was not unduly concerned. A single galley was more likely to be an ally than an enemy ship.

Moments later, his confidence was rewarded. Flying from the top mast, he spied the distinctive red, white and blue of the newly established Dutch Republic. He shouted down again.

'She's flying our colours!'

Janssen exhaled. No disaster today, not on his watch. Like every Dutchman, he'd heard the stories of Jan Janszoon, a privateer from Haarlem, who had overstepped his letters of mark and taken to attacking Dutch ships. He snorted. Nothing good came out of Haarlem. Wasn't the filthy dog, Wouter, evidence of that?

The galley was getting closer. Janssen adjusted his spyglass again. Eighteen oars, in fact, with five poor devils on each bench. He couldn't see the commanding officer, though he could see sailors scuttling around on the deck. He wondered what they wanted. Perhaps the captain was running low on provisions, or had suffered a fire down below.

The captain of the *White Dove* ordered their sails to be trimmed, to allow the galley to come alongside more easily.

Janssen sat back, resigned to being stuck up on the platform for a while longer, as the galley gained on them. He heard his captain hail the ship, and the response from his opposite number. From his station in the sky, he saw the rope ladder being thrown down and a pale-skinned man being welcomed on board the *White Dove*. He spat, hearing the harsh accent of the north-east of the country. Haarlemers all sounded as if they had something stuck in their throats.

For the rest of his life, Janssen wouldn't be able to remember quite what happened next. But suddenly there was a violent shout, like a command, from the bowels of the galley. Grappling irons were thrown and the oarsmen on their portside pulled on the ropes to bring the two vessels against one another. In an instant, the *White Dove* seemed to be swarming with corsairs. Men with cutlasses and fierce eyes, some pale skinned, some dark, shouting in a language Janssen didn't understand. Then a Dutch voice.

'*Leg je wapens neer.* Lay down your arms, and you will be spared.'

Wouter was the first man down. He threw himself at one of the attackers, but before he could land a blow, his neck was sliced open with a scimitar. His compatriot from Haarlem jabbed forward with his knife. For his pains, his forearm was slashed to the bone.

The crew of the *White Dove* fought bravely, but were no match for the superior numbers and skill of the corsairs. It seemed like hours to Janssen, lying flat on his belly on the platform, before the captain of the *White Dove* ordered their flag to be lowered indicating their surrender. Peering through a crack in the boards, Janssen watched undetected as his colleagues were bound and tied by rope around each of the masts. Scarcely able to breathe, he saw the Dutch colours replaced by a Morisco flag, green with three crescent moons, hoisted in its place on the mast of the galley.

Then, as if Nature herself was against them, the wind picked up and Cornelia van Raay's flagship continued on its journey. Not to Las Palmas and a Christian welcome, but to Salé where the slave markets awaited. From his eyrie in the sky, Janssen thought of Marie waiting for him in La Rochelle and, finally, the tears began to fall on the rough boards of his secret hide-away high above the deck.

# CHAPTER ELEVEN

'*Gran'père*, the carriage is ready.'

Now the moment had come, Louise was suddenly nervous. This morning, for her birthday, her grandparents had made a great fuss of her, serving warm white rolls and honey for breakfast. They had wished her happiness, but Louise thought there was an odd tension between them.

'Is everything all right, *Gran'mère*?' she asked again.

Minou started. 'Of course.'

'It is just you seem distracted.'

'I am a little fatigued, that's all. You look a picture, *ma belle*.'

Louise gave a half-bow, her green gown pooling on the polished tiles of the hall. The yellow flashing in her sleeves caught the light.

Her grandfather nodded. 'You do, indeed.' Although Piet wore the sober black attire worn by most of the older Huguenots, and Minou herself dressed in the more modest Dutch style, Louise knew he secretly loved the colour and flamboyance of Parisian fashions. 'Your grand-aunt Salvadora would have approved.'

'I remember you speaking of her,' Louise said.

'I forget you never met her. She lived in Toulouse, but always followed the fashions of the Parisian court.'

Minou smiled. 'She was a wonderful lady. Set in her ways, firm in her opinions, but we owed her so much.'

'What happened to her?'

'She died ten years ago, having seen ninety summers. Surely, you remember that?'

Louise shook her head. Again, was it her imagination, or did everything sound false this morning, as if her grandparents were both playing a part?

'Are you all set, *mon coeur*?'

Piet nodded. 'We are.'

Minou took Louise's hand. 'You are a most worthy representatives of the Reydon-Joubert family. You take great care of your grandfather, young lady, do you hear? And never forget, this is the very least you deserve. This is your rightful inheritance.'

She watched as Minou placed her hand on Piet's cheek. 'You take my love with you.'

'My lady of the mists,' he whispered.

Louise looked away, feeling unaccountably sad.

'*Bonne chance*,' she heard Minou whisper.

'Will we need luck?' Louise asked, feeling even more the weight of words unsaid.

## SAINT DENIS

Some three leagues north of Paris, the coronation was about to begin.

The throng was ten people deep in front of the Basilica Saint-Denis, waiting for a glimpse of the royal party. The spectators were held back by armed guards, but the atmosphere was festive. In the narrow alleyways behind the church and the abbey, the cutpurses and hawkers were working the crowd but, for the most part, all eyes were on the spectacle of the royal court.

The Swiss Guard, dressed for the occasion in velvet vests of the Queen's own colours – tawny, blue, crimson and white – led the procession towards the west door. They were followed by some two hundred nobles of the leading Catholic families of France, many wearing habiliments of tawny-coloured satin, braided with gold, others pourpoints of white satin and tawny breeches. Next, came the lords of the bedchamber, chamberlains, and other great officers of the royal household, followed by the Knights of the Holy Ghost wearing the collar of their Order. A body of trumpeters dressed in blue velvet walked after them, then the heralds in full armour, and the Ushers of the Chamber with their maces.

Everything was opulent, speaking both of ages-old tradition and modern power. If the King had wanted a clearer demonstration of how, under his reign, France had transformed herself from a bankrupt and war-torn country to one of the richest thrones in Europe, he could not have found a clearer way.

No one noticed the red-haired man, clutching a hessian bag to him like a shield. He kept his head down, trying to lose himself in the stream of Parisians wanting to pay their respects to the heretic king.

François Ravaillac looked from right to left, to right again. Was anyone watching? He remembered the woman with the mismatched eyes on the Place de Grève, observing him. Looking at him.

As if she knew.


## LA ROCHELLE

In La Rochelle, it was an ordinary Thursday morning, people going about their business. Although the King had showered money on the Huguenot capital, and given the city unprecedented independence, the pomp of the Catholic court in Saint-Denis meant nothing to them.

In a corner of the Protestant cemetery, a fleshy woman of middle years, in a soiled plain bonnet and collar, stood holding a child tightly by the hand. The girl kept her head bowed, aware of the sharp pinch of her mother's fingers on her hand. She bit her lip, trying not to cry, looking down at the open grave as the tiny wooden coffin was lowered into the damp earth, where the worms and spiders dwelt. She prayed silently for her beloved brother's soul, hoping he had been taken to a place kinder and safer than this one.

At the head of the grave, the pastor continued to mumble the words of the burial. The girl did not think his heart was in it; it was as if it meant nothing to him to be burying one so young. She would have liked to see her brother sent to his eternal rest by a man of greater faith.

'In the name of the Father, the Son and the Holy Spirit. Amen.'

The pastor made the sign of the cross, lingered a moment, then walked away.

The girl felt a shove in her back. Obediently, as if her hand belonged to someone else, she dropped her posy of flowers. Watching a flash of colour spiralling down through the warm air and landing with a soft thud on the coffin lid, taking her heart with it.

'God speed,' she whispered, wishing for a moment that she was to be laid in the grave with her brother.

Then, it was over. The same spiteful fingers on her wrist, and she was being walked from the graveyard. Her mother said nothing, but the girl could read her humour, and judged she was not angry. She swallowed a sigh of relief. Yes, she must have played her part well. No one had challenged her, or thought she was anything other than she pretended to be.

But the girl was under no illusion. The true test would come tomorrow morning when her uncle arrived, and her future became her present. And all the time, the same five words echoed in her head, repeating over and over like the chorus to a cheap song.

'Pick a card, any card.'

# CHAPTER TWELVE

## Paris

Louise sat straight-backed in the carriage as they crossed the Pont Neuf.

'There is no need to be anxious,' Piet said.

'I'm not,' she replied. 'Are you sure *Gran'mère* is quite all right? She did not seem herself this morning. Nor do you.'

Her grandfather took her hand and squeezed it. 'Let us take one thing at a time. This is a momentous day, Louise.'

'I know.' She paused, then added: 'Will I learn anything?'

'What do you mean?'

'About my father. About why he left his estate to me, though not until I turned twenty-five? I know so little. Perhaps someone from Chartres might be present?'

'It is possible,' Piet replied, in a tone that made it clear he was not going to speculate.

'Because it would be—'

'Louise,' he said sharply, 'we will find out soon enough.'

Bemused, she looked away.

*Why is he more nervous than I am?*

The carriage rattled on through crowded streets towards the rue de Rivoli. Some minutes later, they arrived at the lawyer's office and a clerk showed them upstairs to a chamber on the second floor. Inside, a lawyer dressed in black with a white collar, his nose dripping with a spring cold, nodded in greeting.

'Monsieur Reydon-Joubert, Mademoiselle Reydon-Joubert, you are welcome. Please, take a seat.'

'Are we expecting anyone else?' Louise asked.

Both her grandfather and the lawyer looked at her.

'Er, no.' The lawyer sniffed. 'The matter is straightforward. Your grandfather had sight of the will some years ago when –' he cleared his throat – 'the situation arose.'

'When my parents were murdered,' Louise said bluntly.

The lawyer sniffed again, and addressed himself to Piet: 'And you, monsieur, you took guardianship of your granddaughter—'

She interrupted again. 'I already lived with my grandparents.'

'Louise,' Piet murmured, 'let him finish.'

'I would have thought it mattered to be accurate under the law.'

'Indeed. Quite, quite . . .' This time, the lawyer did look at her. 'Shall I continue, Mademoiselle Reydon-Joubert?'

Satisfied she had made him acknowledge her presence in the room, Louise nodded. 'Please.'

The lawyer dabbed his nose with his handkerchief. 'As I said, the matter is straightforward. On attaining the age of twenty-five on the thirteenth day of May in the year of Our Lord 1610 – that is to say, today – Mademoiselle Reydon-Joubert comes into the sum of fifty thousand crowns.'

Louise caught her breath. This was much more than she had been expecting. '*Gran'père*, did you know it would be so much?'

Piet swallowed hard. 'I had no idea. It is a great deal of money.' He frowned. 'And you said the sum was to be paid in crowns? The will stipulates crowns, rather than *livres tournois*?'

The lawyer nodded. 'It suggests Lord Evreux – that's to say, your late father, mademoiselle – saw how the currency was being devalued and thought to protect his income by converting it.'

'What of the estate itself?'

The lawyer raised his eyebrows. 'Forgive me, I thought you knew. There is nothing else. Lord Evreux sold his father's estate outside Chartres shortly before his death.'

'All of it? The house and land?' Piet asked sharply.

'So far as I know, yes. No parcel was retained.'

'Do you know why? Or to whom he sold?'

'*Gran'père*, does it matter?'

The lawyer cleared his throat. 'I never met Lord Evreux and everything was handled by his own advisers in Chartres. As I said, the matter is straightforward. Mademoiselle Reydon-Joubert is simply here to sign the documents pertaining to her fortune. Once this has happened, and the papers have been duly witnessed, then we can discuss how she might—'

'And there are no conditions?' Louise interrupted again. 'I receive the money outright, is that correct?'

'Well, er, that is so.' The lawyer sniffed. 'But I would hope that you would see fit to take our advice as to how best to protect your assets. You will be a very wealthy woman, which might attract the attention of unscrupulous men. Scoundrels. It would be wise to retain expert counsel.'

Louise smiled coldly. 'I have my family to advise me.' She pointed to the desk. 'Are these the papers?'

'They are.'

She stood. 'If you might summon a suitable witness, monsieur, then we can conclude our business.'

Her grandfather put his hand on her arm. 'A moment, *ma belle. Monsieur le Notaire*, you are certain that there is nothing more to be done. No proof of identity, nothing? Absolutely certain.'

The lawyer shook his head. 'All that was taken care of by you in Amsterdam, Monsieur Reydon-Joubert.'

'And nothing has changed since then?'

Louise looked at him, wondering at her grandfather's questions. The lawyer clearly felt the same.

'Should it have done?' he asked with a touch of impatience.

Piet raised his hand. 'It is merely that it has been fifteen years. A great deal has changed in France, new laws governing property and inheritance. There is no one else who needs to countersign?'

'The will is valid, monsieur,' the lawyer replied firmly. 'Everything is as it should be.' He turned the paper towards Louise and passed her a quill. 'Mademoiselle, if you will.'

Within a half-hour, Louise and Piet were back on the rue de Rivoli. All arrangements had been made for the transfer of funds to a bank in Amsterdam, the paperwork signed and sealed. There was nothing outstanding.

Louise thought she would feel something. She didn't. She turned her hands over in the sun, holding her gloves in her hand, as if looking for a sign, for stigmata. She was disappointed to feel exactly as she had when she had woken up this morning.

*Nothing has changed.*

But her grandfather seemed to have undergone a transformation. No longer taciturn or anxious, he was in the best of spirits. And soon, his enthusiasm ignited hers. Her fingers went to her mother's locket and, for a moment at least, she felt a sense of excitement, of one chapter ending and a new one beginning.

'What say you we walk back to Place Dauphine,' Piet said. 'I could manage, if you can adapt your pace to mine. I will be slow, I warn you.'

'Are you sure you can manage?'

He beamed. 'I feel equal to anything. You have your inheritance, it is your birthday, the sun is shining. I would be honoured to walk with my beautiful granddaughter through this wonderful city.' He held out his arm. 'Shall we?'

Louise smiled. 'It would be my honour, *Gran'père*.'

# CHAPTER THIRTEEN

PARIS
*Friday, 14 May*

The day after the coronation, the hedgerows in the gardens of the Palais des Tuileries were again alive with the shimmering of sparrows. Their cheerful song soared over the formal lawns and the beds of red and yellow tulips. In the white mulberry trees, the blackbird still called for her mate. Another glide of swifts, home from the Barbary Coast, skimmed the still waters of the lake.

And in Place Dauphine, Louise sat turning her mother's locket over in her hand after another sleepless night. An oval of silver, containing a single lock of brown hair, it was her most treasured, most secret, possession. No one knew she had taken it.

Louise's sense of well-being had not lasted beyond the evening of her birthday. She had prepared the sleeping powder in a glass of water but, in the end, could not make herself drink it. In consequence, she had sat awake most of the night, thinking about the boarding house in Kalverstraat where her mother had been found. Her memories were incomplete, faint images that came in and out of focus. But she remembered the floor drenched in blood and her despair at having arrived too late. A child's red handprint on a whitewashed wall, that was her true inheritance.

*Always too late.*

She had not been in time to save her mother. She would never forgive herself for that.

Louise dressed quickly and again left the house before anyone else was stirring. She'd heard her grandparents whispering behind their closed door late last evening and the relief in her grandmother's voice. It was as if some burden had been lifted from their shoulders. All the same, Louise knew something was wrong. Several times last evening, as they enjoyed a traditional Dutch meal of pancakes and smoked pork for her birthday, she had felt her grandmother's eyes on her. But every time she had thought she was about to say something, Minou had pulled back. It was very strange.

Louise lifted the handle of the kitchen door and slipped out into the morning sunshine. Her red-letter day had come and gone. The papers were signed, she was wealthy now and, yet, she felt exactly the same. Restless, unsettled.

Guilty.

In the corridors of the Louvre Palace, courtiers shuffled from room to room, their eyes averted, hoping not to attract the displeasure of the King. Although the coronation had gone precisely according to his wishes – and the French court had shown itself the envy of Europe – Henri was out of sorts.

The King had returned from Saint-Denis to Paris the previous evening. Today, he intended to settle his private affairs. Tomorrow, he would undertake a progress around Paris. The state arrival of the Queen was scheduled to take place on Sunday, the official coronation banquet would take place on Tuesday next, then he would ride out on Wednesday to join his troops in the field. But, for all this to proceed, he needed his right-hand man and the Duc de Sully was indisposed. So unwell, indeed, that he had taken to his bed in the Arsenal. It had fallen to his secretary to bring the bad news.

Jean-Jacques bowed once more. 'It is my lord Sully's greatest regret that he is unable to attend Your Majesty in person. Not for anything would he offend you, sire, but his physicians have confined him to bed. He would not imperil the health of Your Majesty by bringing any sort of pestilence or malady into your presence.'

He waited in respectful silence, knowing his wisest course of action was now to hold his tongue. Attired all in black, Henri impatiently strode up and down, the heavy buckles on his shoes tapping on the floor, the jewelled cross of Saint-Esprit hanging from his neck by a broad ribbon. His hair was almost white above his starched ruff. But for a man of fifty-and-seven, who had enjoyed no more than a few hours' sleep, he still cut an imposing figure.

'If the mountain will not come to Muhammad, then Muhammad must go to the mountain. Isn't that what they say?'

Jean-Jacques frowned. 'My lord?'

'It is a phrase I have heard from the Moroccan ambassador,' Henri said, waving his hand. 'Never mind.'

'Is there a message I might convey to my lord? Or papers I might carry to him for his attention?'

'Tell him . . .' Henri stopped, then sighed. 'Tell him, I do not feel safe in Paris.'

'Were the duke here,' Jean-Jacques ventured, 'I feel certain he would note that you will be in the company of the royal army within the week, and away from Paris.'

Henri threw himself into his chair. 'My nights are plagued with bad dreams, Joubert, yet by day . . .' He let his hands drop. 'I find the hours drag upon me.'

Jean-Jacques glanced to the Swiss guards standing at the door to the chamber, the courtiers in their yellow silk set around the room, and willed the King's aide to return. It was not his place to receive such confidences.

'I am sure my lord Sully will be recovered tomorrow,' he started to say, but Henri smacked his fist onto the embroidered arm of his chair.

'That is not good enough!'

'Sire, I only meant—'

Henri jabbed a finger at him. 'I know what you meant, but this is what is going to happen. You will return with haste to your master and inform him that His Majesty the King will call upon him within the hour. He may remain in his bed – I will not be offended – but I would he should hold himself in readiness for my visit.'

Jean-Jacques bowed. 'Very good, sire, I will inform him. He will be honoured to receive you.'

There was a brief pause then, to his surprise, the King roared with laughter. 'Honoured! Do you know how many of the fairer sex I have honoured in such a manner, Joubert? *Le Vert-Galant*, they call me, did you know that?'

Jean-Jacques flushed, horrified either that he should have to answer and offend, or else risk rousing the King's temper again by holding his tongue.

'I shall deliver your message, sire,' he murmured, starting to withdraw.

Henri clapped his hands, and a courtier came running. 'Inform the master of the guard that I would have the wagon made ready. I will go to the Arsenal to "honour" my lord Sully as I might any fancy of the bedchamber!'

Jean-Jacques turned and fled the hall, with the King's ribald laughter echoing in his ears.

François Ravaillac watched the King's carriage leave the Louvre Palace and could not believe that God had so favoured him. Though it was common knowledge that the King was intending to make a progress through Paris on Saturday, he had not thought anything due to happen today.

And yet . . .

For the time being, the voices in Ravaillac's head were quiet and he was grateful for it. Clutching his bag, he fell into step alongside the royal wagon, rattling over the cobbles of the rue Saint-Honoré, a lumbering wooden affair, suspended by leather straps on huge wooden wheels and drawn by eight horses. The velvet curtains were pinned back and, although there were courtiers sitting with the King and eight footmen walking before and behind, there was no sign of the customary contingent of Swiss guards that usually accompanied the heretic.

For a moment, Ravaillac wondered if he was mistaken. Might it be some other member of the royal family in the carriage? But then the King turned his head and Ravaillac recognised the distinctive plume of Navarre in his black, wide-brimmed hat, and knew he had his target in his sights. Henri was wearing his breastplate over his black doublet, but it was unfastened.

'*Deus vult*,' Ravaillac muttered under his breath, picking up his pace.

The wagon jerked to a stop. There was a jam of carriages at the corner of the rue de la Ferronerie. A man with an ox-drawn cart was trying to turn and had become stuck, blocking the road in both directions. A crowd formed, calling out the King's name. Ravaillac slipped closer, edging his way to the front. The courtiers were shouting at people to move, but there were too many horses, too many gawkers. The royal carriage remained at a standstill.

Louise heard the commotion as she turned into rue de la Ferronerie. She was on the point of turning back, when she saw a man with red hair jump up onto a small pillar at the side of the road, muttering and twitching. She recognised him.

*The tortured soul from Place de Grève.*

He was clutching that same hessian sack as he had on the day of the executions, as if it held all his worldly goods.

Then, everything seemed to happen at once.

The man pulled something from the sack and ran full tilt at the wagon. One of the King's courtiers turned, a frown creasing his soft features, then his eyes widened and he spread his arms wide. Behind him, Louise now saw the occupant of the carriage was Henri himself. She opened her mouth to shout, but no sound came as the man with red hair launched himself at the King. Louise saw the glint of a knife in his hand.

'God wills it!' he shouted.

Beside her, a woman screamed.

Louise saw the King throw up his arm to ward off the blow, but it left his flank unprotected. The assailant plunged the knife into Henri's ribs, then struck a second time. She watched in horror as soldiers dragged the man away, stamping on his hand until he let go of the knife. A shot was fired and, suddenly, the street was filled with yelling, shouting, weeping. People were running in every direction, trying to force their way through the barricade of pikes and soldiers trying to seal the road. Others were trying to get to the King.

The man with red hair lay quite still, face down on the filthy street, making no attempt to flee. For a moment, their eyes met, and Louise knew that he remembered her too.

# CHAPTER FOURTEEN

An hour later, in Place Dauphine, Louise was clutching her hands tightly together to stop them from shaking. Her breath was ragged in her chest. She had run all the way home.

'You must be mistaken?' her grandfather repeated.

'I know what I saw.'

'He must only have been injured,' he insisted. 'They would have rung an alarum else.'

Piet broke off as the carillon of the Sainte-Chapelle began to sound, followed almost instantly by Notre-Dame and all the churches on both sides of the river, until the air was filled with the clamour of bells.

'There,' Louise said, her face ashen. 'The King is dead!'

'We must leave,' Minou said suddenly. Her voice was level, but Louise could see the alarm in her eyes. 'While we still can.'

'*Gran'mère?*'

Her grandfather also looked bewildered. 'Minou?'

'We cannot risk staying, *mon coeur*, we cannot.'

'This is not history repeating itself,' Piet said. 'It cannot be.'

Louise looked at them, distressed to realise how instantly their thoughts had flown back to the night of the Paris massacre. Thirty-eight years ago, yet the trauma was still there only just beneath the surface. For all their comfort and security, her grandparents were still refugees, always ready to flee at a moment's notice.

'This is not the same,' she said, forcing a confidence into her

69

voice she did not feel. 'He was a mad man, a lost soul. I'd seen him before. There was no one else.'

'We do not know who he is,' Minou said. 'You say he acted alone, but what if he is funded by someone powerful, or was encouraged to act on behalf of one faction or another?'

Piet was shaking his head. 'The Duc de Sully will move to proclaim the Queen as regent. Her ascendancy, at least, cannot be challenged after the coronation.'

'But will the Queen be accepted by the council, by the court?' Minou pressed. 'You often tell me Paris is alive with spies and plotters. And there will be some who question the timing of this murder, coming so soon after the coronation. Some might even think the Queen was responsible.'

'There is little honour in Paris,' Piet agreed.

'People hear what they want to hear, see what they want to see, in order to shore up their own power, their position,' Minou continued urgently, fear fuelling her words. 'Even if there is no evidence the Queen is involved in any conspiracy, that will not stop the rumours. The Spanish faction and the surviving members of the Catholic League – they all would benefit from a weak crown. The Dauphin is only a child.'

Louise reached for her grandmother's hand. 'It will be all right.'

'So many years of war, then so few of peace,' Piet said. 'Is it possible that France can be so quickly thrown into turmoil once more?'

'We don't belong here, Piet,' Minou said. 'I cannot be trapped here, you know that. I cannot.'

Louise saw his shoulders sag, and her heart tightened another notch.

'It will be all right,' she said again, though her words held no conviction. She went to the window. Outside, the city was bathed in warm, gentle sunshine. Only the relentless tolling of the bells betrayed that this day was any different from the one before, or the one before that. 'What can I do?'

Her grandmother turned gratefully to her. 'Gather your belongings, inform the groom we will be leaving without delay.'

Minou moved to the desk, pulled out a sheet of paper, dipped her quill in the ink, and scribbled a few words. 'Have the boy deliver this to Jean-Jacques – he will be at the duke's residence at the Arsenal.' She sealed the letter, then held it out. 'Here.'

'Should we not wait to see what happens?' Piet asked, his voice robbed of its strength.

'If we wait, it might be too late. The city guard will not hesitate to seal the city. The people loved their king. They will mourn him, then look for someone to blame. Without him, who will we be?'

'Though if it is nothing to do with us—' Piet began to say.

Minou interrupted. 'In the years of his reign, there have been, what, some nineteen attempts on his life? Only close confidantes, like Jean-Jacques, know that there have been so many. Some were the work of malcontents, funded by Spain or by disaffected Leaguers. Others, I regret to say, were financed by Protestant extremists.' She caught her breath. 'I pray Jean-Jacques is safe.'

'He will be,' Louise said, trying to reassure her. 'The duke will make sure of it.'

'These immediate hours are the most dangerous, Piet. Rumour and allegation will spread like wildfire, you know what Paris is like. There are foreign dignitaries here, too, representatives of the Pope, all of them still within the city walls. It's a tinder box. They always want someone to blame, and we are the most obvious target. Although we are not the only Huguenot family in the capital, our name is known.'

Louise looked at her grandparents, wishing more than anything she could spare them more pain. It was only because of her they were here in Paris at all. She knew how much it had cost her grandmother to come back. She watched as her grandfather reached out his hand. Minou put her arms around him and Louise heard her murmur in the old language.

'*Si es atal es atal*,' she said. 'What will be, will be.'

For a moment, they clung together, like two swimmers struggling against the tide, then Piet kissed her forehead and stood back.

'You, Minou, have been the greatest blessing of my life,' he said quietly. 'If you think we should go, we will.'

# CHAPTER FIFTEEN

## La Rochelle

In the great Huguenot port city on the Atlantic coast, no one was yet aware of the tragedy unfolding in Paris.

The girl felt her uncle's stick tap the back of her sore legs, and she flinched. She felt like an animal, or a slave in a Morisco market, submitting to questions and examinations.

'You are small for your age, boy.'

'But he is strong,' her mother fawned.

'Can he not speak for himself? Does he not have a tongue in his head?'

The girl felt another swish of the stick.

Her uncle's grey ruff and doublet, fine cape and buckled shoes were out of place in their modest lodgings, in sharp contrast to her mother's threadbare and sweat-stained clothes. She had not realised how wealthy this uncle of hers was – a successful producer and merchant of wine. She had walked past BARENTON ET FILS in the rue du Temple many times and admired the name in gold above the door without knowing they were kin. She wondered what had brought about the estrangement between brother and sister.

'Answer your uncle.'

Feeling the pinch of her mother's fingers on her neck, the girl kept her voice steady. 'I am strong, and can work hard. My eyesight is good.'

Monsieur Barenton huffed, but she didn't think he was

displeased. 'And his sister's malady?' She felt another swish of the stick. 'He doesn't suffer from the same weakness?'

Her mother shook her head. 'From birth, she was the lesser of the two. Always prone to catching cold, afflictions of the stomach.'

The girl marvelled at how easily her mother lied, exchanging their two life stories. She was, in truth, ten minutes the older, born one side of midnight and her brother, Guillaume, the other. He had always been their mother's favourite. The lion's share of household chores – chopping wood, fetching water, delivering the garments her mother sewed for the rich ladies who lived in the rue des Gentilshommes – had always fallen to her. Meanwhile, her brother was kept quietly indoors. All the same, he had always tried to stand between her and their mother's punishments. He could always charm her and, sometimes, deflect her anger. Even when he failed, and she was locked in the cellar with rats running over her bare feet, Guillaume would whisper to her through the grille when their mother fell into an ale-soaked sleep, and help the night to pass.

'Of course, he grieves for the loss of his sister.' Her mother dropped her voice. 'As do I. She was the sweetest soul that ever lived, too good for this world.'

Her uncle huffed again. 'Would you come and work for me, boy? We shall have to do something about your . . . your . . .' He pointed to her drab breeches. 'Not suitable, not suitable at all.'

The girl raised her eyes, wondering how it was he could be so easily gulled. She saw her mother's expression darken, and then the look of slight bemusement on her uncle's face. She did not want to answer, but could not fail to do so.

'Yes, Uncle,' she said, and her mother's fingers tightened on her neck, then released their grip. 'I will do my best.'

'Very well.' Her uncle put the tip of his stick under her chin.
'I will provide a home for you, and for my sister. Family is
family. But if you disappoint me, or shame the Barenton name,
you will be back in this slum before you can count to five.'

'Yes, monsieur. Thank you.'

Her uncle let his stick drop, and tapped it twice on the floor
as if a bargain had been struck.

'Very well, we understand one another.' He took a step back.
'I will send a cart for your belongings this afternoon. Are there
any debts outstanding on these . . . lodgings?'

Her mother clasped her hands. Red hands, like slabs of meat.
'I fear we owe until the end of the month, Brother.' She named
the sum. 'Is it too much?'

His expression did not alter. 'I will settle that with the land-
lord.'

'You are too kind.'

The girl saw the obsequious look on her mother's face. Did
that mean she was pleased? She smiled back, co-conspirators,
then saw the contempt in her mother's eyes. The familiar dread
pressed down on her chest. Had she done something wrong
again? What had she done wrong?

'If you are to work for me, I would know your name,' her
uncle said.

'He goes by—'

'By all that's Holy, let him answer for himself, Sister! A mute
boy is no good to me in the shop.'

This was the moment the girl had been dreading, when she
would step into her brother's shoes and cease to exist. Guillaume
would cease to exist. What she was doing was criminal and, if
caught, she did not think either her age or her sex would protect
her. But fear of her mother outweighed everything and, perhaps,
this new life would be better? Her uncle had a large household

by all accounts, so surely her mother would have to temper her behaviour? That was her only spark of hope.

'My name is Guillaume, monsieur,' she said, but her brother's name sounded disloyal in her mouth and she realised she could not live with it. 'Though, if it pleases you—'

'What is it?'

The girl met her uncle's gaze for the first time. All or nothing. 'If it pleases you, monsieur, I prefer to be known as Gilles.'

The die was cast. She was a he.

# CHAPTER SIXTEEN

## Paris

Louise sat holding her grandmother's hand, looking from right to left as their carriage jolted over the cobbles of the university quarter.

*This is all it takes. A twist of the knife, and the world is ruined.*

In the hours since the assassination of the King, news had spread to every corner of Paris. It seemed to her that, in this neighbourhood on the left bank, the streets were less in the grip of panic, as if it would be vulgar of the philosophers and theologians to give way to such base emotions. All the same, shopkeepers were boarding their windows, and there were no children playing in the streets.

'I can see nothing amiss,' she said again. It had taken little more than an hour to collect the few objects of value they had brought with them from Amsterdam. With their belongings pushed underneath the seat and hidden behind the sweep of their skirts, they had quit the house in Place Dauphine. They kept the curtains on the carriage open, so it would look as if they had nothing to hide. 'There are no soldiers, at least no more than I would expect. What can you see?'

The groom stood up on his platform. 'They have set up a blockade at the gate.'

Louise tried to ignore the hammering in her chest. What if there was already a warrant out for any Huguenots known to be in the city?

'*Gran'mère*, what do you want to do?'

'We press on,' Minou replied.

They came to a halt at the Porte Saint-Jacques. A mass of people was waiting to be allowed to pass. Others, on the far side, were petitioning to be permitted to enter. Was it possible that they did not yet know that the King was dead?

After what seemed an endless wait, they reached the front of the line. The sentry held up his hand.

'State your business.'

'I am taking my grandparents outside of the city for the air,' Louise said, holding her voice steady. 'We are headed for Troyes, to the abbey there.'

'No one is to leave the city.'

'We are not subject to any general order,' she responded, holding up a letter with the crest of the Duc de Sully. It was an old letter from Jean-Jacques that she had refashioned by dripping a thimble of red wax to reseal it. 'This contains express instructions from the duke allowing us passage. My uncle is his secretary and would have the duke's instructions respected.'

Behind her, she heard the sound of horses' hooves. Minou twisted in her seat, then whispered to her: 'The Swiss guard.'

Meanwhile, the crowd was growing, the voices getting louder and more fractious. Louise suspected it was only a matter of time before a general curfew was imposed.

'May we pass?' she said with as much confidence as she could muster. 'Is the Duc de Sully's word not enough?'

The young guard stared at the letter, too intimidated to take it, then at the opulence of the carriage and the two inoffensive elderly people sitting side by side. Louise watched his eyes flicker to the increasingly restive queues on either side. He could smell the trouble brewing. He dithered a moment longer, then waved them through.

'Let them pass.'

Louise found a smile. 'May God bless you.'

The groom cracked his whip and the carriage jerked forward, over the cobbles of the narrow gate. Then they were out, and turning towards the woods of Saint-Michel. At their backs, she heard the sound of the heavy gates slammed shut.

The noise of the city gave way to birdsong and quiet country roads, the dusty and warm air of the world beyond the walls. News of the King's murder had not yet reached the villages outside Paris, though Louise knew it soon would.

She felt exhilarated to have talked her way to freedom, but when she looked at her grandparents, their grey and defeated expressions, her elation faded. Then she remembered the murdered king, his cold and dead eyes, and she shivered.

*Si es atal es atal.*

It was a phrase she had heard a hundred times from her grandmother's lips, but Minou was silent now. Louise leant back and allowed the rhythm of the wheels to soothe her rattling heart.

The hours passed. They travelled through villages and hamlets, peaceful in the sunshine. They saw a country wedding, the bride resplendent in a red gown and headdress trimmed with glass beads, the sound of bagpipes and flute filling the small square. The simple joyous celebration was a reminder of how life could be – how it ought to be – away from the intrigues and politics of Paris.

Louise wasn't sure if Piet was sleeping or simply conserving his strength, but Minou seemed to have disappeared into herself. She felt emotion catch in her throat. For all of her life, her grandmother had been steadfast and strong. She had held her family together, despite everything, through the best of times and the worst of times. Now, she seemed to have suddenly aged in the space of a few hours. Then Louise felt Minou stir beside her and suddenly, quietly, she spoke.

'I am not well, Louise.'

'Of course, this has been too much. You will feel better in the morning.'

'No. I have not been well for some time.'

Louise turned cold. 'What do you mean?' But even as she said the words, she realised that she had known in her heart that something was wrong. Her grandmother's lack of appetite, her pallor, the times when she found even the lightest of walks around the square too taxing. Only she had been too preoccupied to say anything.

*Thinking only of myself.*

A shudder shook her whole body.

'It is serious?' she asked.

'God willing, I will have a few months yet.'

'*Gran'mère* . . .' Louise whispered, in a voice that seemed to come from a long way away. 'Are you in pain?'

'Sometimes.' Minou squeezed her fingers. 'I am sorry. You know I don't want to leave you.'

'It is I who should be sorry,' she cried. 'I should have done something; I should have noticed—'

'Hush now, I did everything to make sure you did not.'

'And *Gran'père*?' she demanded. 'Why has he not—'

'I only told him two days ago. We did not want to spoil your birthday. He holds to the idea that I might recover.'

Louise made no attempt to wipe her tears away. 'What will we do without you?' she murmured.

'You will thrive, Louise, I promise you. You are a fine young woman; you are principled and courageous. There are people who love you.'

'I will be lost.'

'No, you won't. You have already suffered a great loss in your life, *ma belle*, and yet remain steadfast. But you must find something to express your undoubted talents. Promise me you will.' Minou smiled. 'And that you will look after my old man when I'm gone. This will be hard for him.'

Louise felt her heart was breaking. All the colour had gone from the world, all the light.

'I can't bear it,' she sobbed. 'Does Jean-Jacques know?'

Minou shook her head. 'I was waiting to tell him until after the coronation. Alis and Cornelia know. Alis came with me to the first physician in Amsterdam.'

'You have known for that long?'

'Don't be angry they kept it from you, I asked them to.' Minou closed her eyes. 'But I am glad to have told you now.'

Louise could hear the relief in her grandmother's voice, and that she understood. Hadn't she herself kept a secret from everyone she loved for most of her life?

They fell into silence. Louise felt there was much she still wanted to say and yet, at the same time, there was nothing that could be said. The world without her grandmother in it was no world at all.

She took Minou's hand, and held it tight.

They continued on, not stopping until it was dusk and the horses needed to rest. In the distance, Louise could see a cluster of houses and the spire of a church in the fading light.

'Do you not want to know where we are going?' her grandmother asked, as they came into the village.

Louise began to shake her head – this village or that, what did it matter – then she stopped. They had been heading south. No, not due south, but south-west. She caught her breath.

'To Carcassonne,' she replied, and was rewarded with a pale smile.

'Ah, how well you know me, *ma belle*. I will show you everything, all the places I've told you about. You will not believe the beauty of La Cité and the bustle of the Bastide. And, if fortune favours us, we might visit Puivert, where your dear mother spent the first seven years of her life. I have so wanted to show you.'

'That would be wonderful,' Louise said, fighting back fresh tears.

'Yes.' Minou exhaled. 'We are going home.'

# CHAPTER SEVENTEEN

## CARCASSONNE
### *Saturday, 10 July*

Standing on the battlements on an early morning in July, with the Pyrenees shimmering on the far horizon, Louise could scarcely believe they had been in La Cité for three weeks. Though everything was tinged with sadness, she had lost her heart to Carcassonne and felt closer to her grandmother because of it. She slept in the chamber that had once been her great-aunt Alis's, listening out in case her grandmother needed her. Through the open casement, she could hear the sound of the night watch, the ancient tramp of men-at-arms marching down the centuries. A generation ago, a hundred years ago, back to the time of the Cathars and the Saracens. Before them, the soldiers of the Roman garrison who had created the modest hilltop fort of Carcasso.

When her grandmother could spare her, Louise explored every corner of the old town. She followed the tracks down to the river where the angelica and the ragwort grew, and listened to the song of the water carried on the paddles of the old mill in the river Aude. She imagined herself as the warrior queen, Dame Carcas, commanding her troops. And every afternoon, she brought her impressions home to her grandmother and begged for every detail of her childhood growing up in the rue du Trésau in return.

Louise knew she could not settle in Carcassonne. It was too

far from the sea and the Midi heat was fiercer than anything she had known. But here, for the time being at least, the restlessness in her blood was quiet. Here, she was freed from her past.

*No more dreams. No half-memories.*

She took a deep breath, and jumped down from the walls. With the sun rising at her back, Louise made her way through the alleyways of the old city to the little house with roses around the front door.

'*Gran'mère,*' she called, as she stepped inside. 'I'm back.'

# CHAPTER EIGHTEEN

## La Rochelle

What the girl had learnt after two months in her uncle's house-hold was that people saw what they wanted to see.

With her hair shorn like a boy's, dressed like any other above-stairs servant of the house in breeches, jerkin and cap, no one doubted she was who she said she was. A boy called Gilles. She took care never to wash or piss in the company of others, and slept by herself at the top of the house. Her fingernails were black with ingrained coal dust from lugging crates up from the cellar. She copied the coopers who rolled the barrels along cobbled streets, sitting with her legs apart or with one ankle balanced across the other knee. She spat in the street and practised throwing stones at the cats in the courtyard of the house opposite.

Gilles' uncle's own son and wife had died from the flux in the winter of 1604, and he had chosen not to marry again. The household accepted her without question as the destitute nephew of Monsieur Barenton, who was being trained in the wine trade. Sharp-witted, small for his age, but willing to work hard.

As each day passed, the girl grew more into her new skin. And though her mother was always there in the background – and ready with a slap or a spiteful pinch – she was less at her mercy. As a boy, she could run away from a beating. Though her uncle rarely addressed her directly, he let drop enough comments for her to realise that he, too, had lived in fear of his vicious older sister when he was a boy. This shared suffering disposed him to an affection for her. He wanted to do right by his nephew, allowing him the run of his library when business was done, and began instructing him on the making of wine and bookkeeping. Gilles was an eager student, determined to earn his uncle's trust.

Gilles also discovered that things were easier for boys in other ways. She'd heard stories about the depravity of sailors – and, some said, the monks in the Augustin Abbey – but, in the streets of the town or around the port when the ships from Amsterdam or the Americas came in, no one tried to lift her skirts, or take her chin between dirty fingers and tell her to smile. No drunken hands circled her waist and jested about how she would break a man's heart when she was older. As Gilles, once her day's work was done and the shop was closed, she was free to come and go as she pleased. Provided she did her duty, said her prayers and kept out of trouble, her life was better than it had ever been.

Often, she went down to the port hoping to catch a glimpse of the Italian cartomancer. But nobody seemed to remember the man with the brightly-coloured coat. After a while, she stopped asking. It was only the Justice card that proved he had been there at all.

So it went on, day after day, week after week. She pushed from her mind the thought of what would happen if her uncle discovered their deception. Perhaps because of the card hidden beneath her pillow, the girl knew her good fortune would not last. It could not last. Her deceit would eventually catch up with her.

# CHAPTER NINETEEN

## CARCASSONNE

Minou heard her granddaughter call out, and smiled. She loved how Louise crept out into the streets of La Cité every morning, just as she, her sister Alis, and their brother Aimeric had done half a century ago.

It also gave her great pleasure that her granddaughter had so fallen in love with Carcassonne. As they had rounded the final corner on the road three weeks ago, and seen the citadel like a crown of stone on the green hill, Louise had stood up in the carriage and stretched her arms wide at the sight of it, the glory of it. Minou had laughed and taken Piet's hand and, in that moment, her pain had vanished like a summer mist.

No longer.

Lying in her childhood bed, the sheets tangled and stiff with sweat after another wakeful night, Minou could not say she was grateful to see another morning. The canker was like a living thing, bringing constant pain. Both Piet and Louise fussed endlessly. Minou knew how hard it was to watch someone you loved suffer, and wished she could spare them. She did not believe there was glory in death – she had witnessed too much bloodshed, too much cruelty for that – but now she prayed nightly for her failing body to set her free. Though Piet was not ready to accept it, she had already said goodbye to this world. Louise, she thought, understood. The loss she had suffered as a child had shaped her. For good or ill, it had taught her the frailty of life.

Minou tried to find a more comfortable position, comforted by the thought that her mother and father were waiting for her on the other side, her brother, her aunt and her beloved Marta, too. She had not expected Alis or Cornelia to be able to leave Amsterdam, though she would dearly have loved to see her sister and her children one last time. Jean-Jacques was kept in Paris by affairs of state – Sully's steady hand was helping ensure an ordered transition from the rule of Henri IV to his wife and the Dauphin – but she did not fear for him. As for Bernarda, the daughter that Minou, to her shame, had never been able to love, she was with her husband in Amsterdam. They had taken over the running of the almshouse some years previously and Bernarda took her duties too seriously to consider travelling to be at her mother's side.

Minou knew how loss and grief sent people back to familiar traditions, taking refuge in customs and prayers that had sustained those through the ages who were weary and sought rest. There were only two things left undone. One was to help Piet to accept that she wanted to receive the last rites and be buried in the Catholic faith of her parents. She knew her decision would wound him, after how much they had suffered for their Huguenot religion, but her failing heart was more determined than her sense of duty to the Reformed Church. All that mattered now was God's grace. She wished her body to be taken to Puivert and laid to rest in the glade in the woods beside her father. No monuments, no effigies of weeping angels. Just a simple headstone set in the land that she loved.

Her second task was to speak to Louise about the day her parents died. Piet clearly never would, so the duty fell to her.

Death was standing in the shadows, the sand had all but run through the glass. There was no time left.

'I am awake, *ma belle*,' Minou called out. 'Come and sit with me.'

In the lower town, Piet made his way along the rue du Marché, his walking stick marking a counterpoint to his steps on the cobbles. The gout in his leg pained him. His foot had swollen to twice its usual size, but he refused to take the carriage for such a short journey.

Piet hated being in Carcassonne, though he could not have told Minou that. Things seemed much the same, but beneath the surface he could sense the trauma of a town that had been at war with itself for a generation. Worse, on every street corner, he seemed to come face to face with his younger self. An idealistic, headstrong man, so sure in his opinions and his friendships, courageous and yet so naïve. Being here, he was forced to confront all he had failed to do, the many ways in which he had let down his family or his brothers-in-arms, his friends. Now he was just an old man, in the autumn of his life, trying desperately to save his wife.

This morning, he was visiting an apothecary who came highly recommended to seek advice on Minou's condition. He had not told her of the appointment – he did not want to get her hopes up without due cause – but if the physician was in agreement, Piet hoped to persuade her they should quit Carcassonne and travel south to Puivert. The mountain air would do her good.

With his shadow rising to greet him, Piet continued his painful pilgrimage, regretting the passage of time that made even the simplest task a challenge of stamina and will.

\* \* \*

Louise ran upstairs, her face flushed with the early morning. Her smile faded at the sight of her grandmother. Minou's face was grey, furrowed with discomfort. Each day, she seemed a little less substantial.

'Can I fetch you anything?' she asked as brightly as she could. 'Did you sleep?'

'A little.' Minou held out her hand. 'Tell me, where have you been this morning?'

Louise pulled the chair close, and sat, knitting her grandmother's fingers in her own. 'I watched the sun rise over the cathedral Saint-Nazaire. I caught that moment when the tip of the steeple turns golden.'

'And the light catches those grotesque faces of the gargoyles. Wonderful.'

'Yes! Then, I climbed onto the walls – earning quite disapproving looks from the men-at-arms – and looked out over the fields. Yellow broom and silver olive trees, such vivid colours, just like you promised.'

'Everything is brighter here. Purple lavender and pink dogbane—'

'– and grapes on the vine, everything so beautiful. The swallows were swooping through the orchards on the lower slopes.'

'So very beautiful,' Minou murmured.

'You must have missed it so much, *Gran'mère*.'

Minou gave a long sigh. 'I carried it always in my heart, *ma belle*. We had no choice. You, all things being well, can decide where you want to live, and how. War took that from us: Carcassonne, Puivert, Toulouse, Paris, Amsterdam, we had no choice where we lived.'

'But you love Amsterdam.'

Her grandmother smiled. 'I am grateful to Amsterdam for welcoming us in. It is a wonderful city, and the Dutch are the kindest people. I made it our home and I knew our family would be safer there. But love it? No.' She caught her breath. 'What of you, Louise? Amsterdam is your home, but do you love it?'

'The only thing that matters at the moment is what you need.'

'There is no need to rush, but you should decide what you want from life. You are in a fortunate position. Make the most of that.'

'I will.'

'I know you think the world is unjust, but—'

'It is unjust!' Louise cried, then took a deep breath. 'All right, I will tell you. If I could, I would command a ship.'

'I know that.' Minou laughed. 'That has been your wish since you were a child, and you have never wavered in it. Things are changing, Louise, though I fear not so quickly as you would like. But there are many paths open to you. Do not dwell on what is not possible, but rather what you might do in the world.' She paused. 'It would be easier with someone at your side.'

'I don't need anyone.'

'There are different kinds of love,' Minou continued. 'Your grandfather and I have been so lucky. Alis, too. Jean-Jacques, in his way.'

'His wife's a goose.'

'She is a good mother. I would that you had someone to share your life.'

'I don't want to share it.'

'One day, you might.'

'But look at how *Gran'père* is like a ghost in the house at the thought of losing you,' Louise protested. 'The cost is too high.'

'Ah, grief and loss are the price we pay for love.'

'And what of my mother?' she said, then felt instantly

ashamed at the look on her grandmother's face. 'Forgive me, *Gran'mère*, I did not mean to upset you.'

'What your father felt for your mother was not love,' Minou said firmly. 'That was obsession, and ownership, and wickedness and—'

'*Gran'mère*, tell me. I know there is something. You and *Gran'père* have been whispering for weeks now.'

Minou squeezed her hand. 'When I tell you, you must understand that your grandfather thought he was acting in your best interests. And it was not that we did not want to tell you the truth, but rather that there was nothing to be gained by doing so. And the money is rightfully yours. It was the very least you deserved. But I have to tell you that your father—'

'– killed my mother. Yes, I know.' Louise saw shock, then relief in her grandmother's eyes.

'Ah, I always wondered,' Minou murmured.

'Not at the time, of course. But later. It never made sense that someone would have, by chance, found them together in Kalverstraat. I heard *Gran'père* tell the advocate that they were victims of an assassination, though he never suggested why that should be, beyond the fact that my father was wealthy. But why did no one pursue it?'

Minou closed her eyes. 'We think Louis followed Marta to Amsterdam in order to try to take you from her – from us. When she refused to let him have you, he killed her and then turned the knife upon himself.'

*But that doesn't make sense either*, Louise wanted to shout, but she could not. No one had ever known she was there.

'I only wish you had not worried about telling me.'

Minou sighed. 'We thought it would be hard for you to bear.'

*My mother was taken from me, and I was left unable to trust anyone, or love anyone, what could be harder than that?*

'Louise,' Minou sounded determined. 'In Amsterdam, you will find my journals. All bar the one I had with me in Paris, which was forgotten in Place Dauphine when we left so suddenly. I've kept a record, of all of it – our lives, your aunt's and uncle's lives, what we witnessed. There is much there about your mother, a little about your father too, and his father before him. He was once a close friend of your grandfather's, did you know that?'

Louise shook her head. 'You never talked of him.'

She could picture the brown leather notebooks so clearly, the scraps of paper pressed like dried leaves beneath the covers. She thought of all the times she had come into her grand-mother's chamber and seen her sitting at the table at the window in Zeedijk, her long hair – brown then – loose around her shoulders. Louise's fingers went around her mother's locket in her pocket and, for an instant, she imagined unburdening herself of her own secret. But she held her tongue. How could she inflict any more pain on her grandmother now?

'I bequeath them to you, *ma belle*. Read them wisely.'

'What do you mean?'

Minou squeezed her fingers. 'You will understand. It is so easy to forget, to overlook what matters.'

Louise could see her grandmother was tiring, but there were still so many questions she wanted to ask. 'Do you still miss her, *Gran'mère*?'

'Every single day.' Minou closed her eyes. 'I miss Marta every single day, as I know do you. But I will see her soon.'

Louise swallowed hard. 'I don't want to lose you.'

'Nor I you, *ma belle*, but I am ready.' Minou smiled. 'Now we have no more secrets between us, there is one more thing I would have you do for me.'

'I know. Take care of Grandfather. Will he want to return to Amsterdam?'

Minou shook her head, and Louise could see her bones sharp beneath the thin material of her nightgown. 'He refuses to discuss it with me, but I think so. Amsterdam was always more his home than mine. But no, what I was going to say is this. See him settled, but then leave if you want to. Do not sacrifice yourself, Louise. Women always do. I would not have him be lonely, but Alis and Cornelia will care for him. Bernarda, too, in her way.'

Minou reached to her nightstand. 'These are my last letters – one for Bernarda, one for Jean-Jacques, one for Piet, one for you. For after I am gone. I have already written to my beloved Alis.'

'I will see they are delivered.' Louise's eyes were brimming with tears.

'Thank you.' Minou paused. 'And this service, too. It will be hard for your grandfather to accept, but I would like you to fetch a priest.'

'Is that not where *Gran'père* has gone this morning?'

Minou gave a resigned smile. 'I fear he has gone in search of another cure.'

'He should be here with you.'

'Do not judge him harshly, he is doing his best. But, no, not the pastor from the Temple. A priest.'

'A Catholic priest, do you mean?'

'There is little time left, Louise. I would receive the last rites.'

Louise sat back, unable to believe what she was hearing. 'I don't understand. All these years, after everything you have suffered – we have suffered – you would turn back to the Roman Church.'

'I am not sure I understand either,' Minou said quietly, 'but I want to die in the faith of my mother and my father. I want to rest with them.' She paused. 'Will you fetch him? He lives in the square beside Saint-Sernin.'

Louise had ceased to believe in a kind God, or a just God, on the day her mother died. Her family had been driven from their home by religion, had seen their friends and family butchered in the name of religion. France was scarred by the blood of Christian spilt by Christian. But Louise had always thought her grandmother's faith was the bedrock of her life. Now, it seemed, she had not understood at all.

'Are you sure?'

'Ah, yes.' A final squeeze of the hand. 'After Piet, you are the greatest blessing of my life, Louise. Find purpose. Find your place in the world. Make your life count.'

'Can't I send someone else? I don't want to leave you.'

'I know, *ma belle*. But I shall be here when you return.'

Louise bent forward and kissed her grandmother on the forehead. Then, with her hands balled into fists, she left. Every step felt like a traitor's step, taking her away from the one person in the world she loved the most. Down the stairs and out into the bright July sunshine. Her heart was beating at twice its normal rate, she felt as if she could hardly breathe.

She looked with disbelief at the people in the street. How could it be that the world continued the same as ever? Women going about their business as if nothing was happening? Children laughing. Why were the bells not tolling? Why was the rue du Trésau not shrouded in black?

'My grandmother is dying,' she wanted to shout. 'My world is about to end and yet you carry on in the streets as if it was any other ordinary day.'

*Once upon a time, there was a courageous little girl.*

Louise started to run. The sooner she found the priest, the sooner she would be back at her grandmother's side.

*A courageous little girl, whose heart was broken.*

# CHAPTER TWENTY

Minou jolted awake. She had fallen asleep again. For a moment, she panicked. Where was Piet? Where was Louise?

She rang her bell. No one came.

Minou rang again, wondering if the maid had gone to the well. The sound seemed to echo empty through the house.

Steeling herself, she slowly swung her feet down to the floor, feeling the customary tilt and slip of the room, the pain that rattled her bones. No sudden movements. She waited until her breathing had settled, then carefully stood up. Fingers on the bedpost, threading her feet into her slippers, trying not to fall. She could not bear being so helpless.

*'And I saw the dead, small and great, stand before God; and the books were opened: and another book was opened, which is the book of life: and the dead were judged out of those things which were written in the books, according to their works.'*

Minou slowly recited the words so precious to her father, to take her mind away from the pain. The Book of Revelation. It was natural, surely, to think of judgement at this time? She prayed that, for all her sins, she would not be found wanting and she would be granted peace.

She walked slowly across the chamber, holding on to every piece of furniture for support, and out onto the landing. At the top of the stairs, she paused to steady her fading heart, then putting her hand onto the wooden banister, she slipped and fell into nothing.

* * *

Returning with a pail of water, the maid found Minou unconscious at the foot of the narrow flight of stairs. She was still breathing, but there was a gash where she had hit her head on the newel post, and blood pooling where she lay on the flagstones.

Floating gently inside her own mind, everything still and clear, Minou was aware of what was going on around her, though she could no longer speak. She did not fear death. She was fire, she was fire. No longer in pain, no longer tethered to the earth. In the absence of the priest, she murmured her own words of release and transition. Ashes to ashes and dust to dust.

Though no one she loved was at her side, she did not feel alone. She knew her mother and father were waiting, her brother Aimeric and her aunt Salvadora were waiting. Her adored Marta. And she held the faces of her sister and her son in her heart, of her beloved husband and of her wild, beautiful granddaughter, and prayed that they would find the strength to comfort one another.

Then, even those thoughts began to fade. She was mist, she was air, floating free of the world. As the bells of Saint-Nazaire began to strike for midday, Minou Joubert drew her last breath, and her soul took flight.

# CHAPTER TWENTY-ONE

A week later, Louise was standing in the woods of Puivert, the castle estate where her grandparents had begun their married life together. Her face was drawn and pale, but her cheeks were dry. She had cried every tear she had to give in Carcassonne. Now, she felt nothing. Numb and so cold, despite the heat of the day, as if she would never be warm again.

This was the place where her mother, Marta, had been so cherished, where she had played with her little brother, Jean-Jacques. Dappled light in the glade where the family had picnicked in summer, yellow-tipped broom and purple cypress on the ridge, everything was exactly as her grandmother had described it.

'*Gran'père*,' she said, placing her hand upon his arm.

He was like a spectre. He had barely slept, barely eaten, since returning to the rue du Trésau on the morning of Minou's death, believing he had found a remedy to save his wife, and instead had discovered her gone. Louise knew he blamed himself for not being there at the end, and blamed her for leaving Minou alone in her final hour. That Louise was following her grandmother's wishes made no difference. When Piet had arrived to find a Catholic priest waiting in the hallway, he had ordered him out of the house and wept.

Louise bowed her head as the plain wooden casket was

lowered into the ground. Eagles soared above in the hot July air, indifferent to the tragedy being played out below.

'*Gran'père*,' she tried again, offering him a wreath of mountain flowers. He refused to take them, so Louise let them drop herself, a splash of blue and pink falling down onto the lid of the coffin.

She took his arm. He didn't look at her, or say anything, but did allow himself to be guided to the cart that would take them to the village, then to the carriage to return to Carcassonne. Behind them, the labourers began to shovel the earth into the grave.

Louise lingered a moment longer, looking back at the two grey headstones at the heart of the glade. It had been her grandmother's wish to be buried alongside her father, Bernard Joubert, who had died at Puivert nearly forty years previously. Louise had spoken to the mason and had made the arrangements, though she did not feel the words Piet had chosen did justice to the life her grandmother had lived.

MINOU REYDON-JOUBERT
BELOVED WIFE, MOTHER & GRANDMOTHER
31 OCTOBER 1542 – 10 JULY 1610
TAKEN HOME BY THE LORD

'Goodbye, *Gran'mère*,' she murmured to the empty air. 'God speed.'

Her grandfather didn't look at her or say anything as she climbed up beside him.

'Drive on,' she said.

The cart jolted forward. Though she had no idea what would happen next, Louise was certain of three things: first, that she would never return to Puivert; second, that her grandfather would not stay long in a world without his beloved wife; third, that the cost of loving was too high if it left a heart broken beyond repair.

# PART TWO

*Ten Years Later*

La Rochelle

*October 1620*

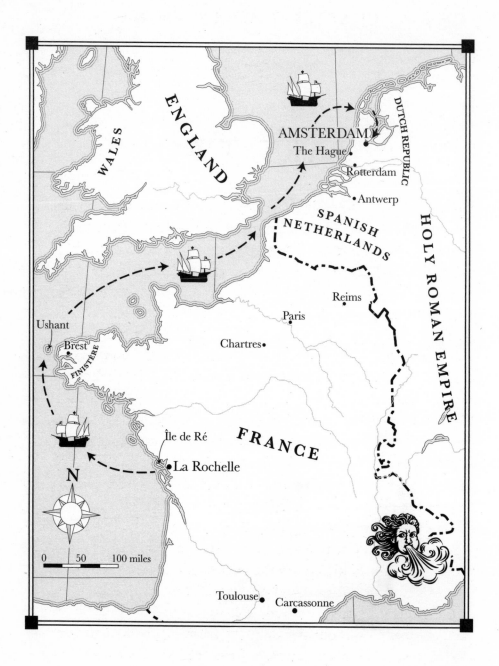

# CHAPTER TWENTY-TWO

## LA ROCHELLE
### *Wednesday, 7 October 1620*

In the port of La Rochelle, a gull wheeled in the damp air. Its wings outstretched, it hovered over the rows of cannon on the ramparts facing out to sea, as if inspecting the fortifications. It swooped between the Tour Saint-Nicolas and the Tour de la Chaîne, the two apostles protecting the entrance to the harbour, then soared up and higher, carried on a gust of wind.

From the stern of the *Old Moon*, Louise Reydon-Joubert tracked the bird's progress until it was a distant white cross against the grey sky. Standing on the quarterdeck in black boots and black gloves, she was the only woman in a world of men. Today, the sea was wild, the colour of turquoise, the waves angry. Louise pulled her cloak tighter around her shoulders as the wind sliced through her like a knife. White foam chopped against the hull as the ship bounced through the water, making her hold tight to the wooden taffrail to keep her balance.

The *Old Moon* was one hundred feet long and quite narrow, designed to carry as much cargo as possible. It had three masts and a large low hold beneath the main single deck, above which the fo'c'sle rose forward and the quarterdeck aft. There was a rope store and general storeroom beside the galley at the bow, and another storeroom aft beside the helmsman's compartment at the stern. The main and fore masts carried two square sails apiece, the third mast, a lateen sail of faded white. The draught, when loaded, was a little over seven foot deep, though today she was carrying no more than ninety casks of Canarian wine back from Las Palmas de Gran Canaria.

Although the *fluyt* was still part of the Van Raay fleet sailing beneath the colours of the Dutch East India Company, the VOC, the ship now belonged to Louise. She had persuaded Cornelia to let her buy the *Old Moon*, when she'd come into her inheritance ten years ago, and had never regretted it.

More than anything, Louise wished to command a ship. Not travelling as a passenger or representative of the company, making short journeys between the ports in which their ships docked, but as a true sailor: swearing an oath upon the Bible, her jewelled dagger with its needle-sharp point at her waist. Dancing to fiddle and pipe on the deck after dark, carousing and gambling, numbing her emotions with the intoxicating mixture of rum, water, sugar and nutmeg the crew called bumboo. She had always wanted to travel to the *terra incognita*, to navigate by the stars and the wind, and see whales – like the monstrous sea pigs and sirens who lured men to their deaths, the wondrous images on the lacquered globe in the hall of Cornelia's house on Warmoesstraat that had delighted her as a child. But it was considered bad luck to have women on board, even in these modern times – and, though Louise travelled with the fleet when she could, she knew some of the sailors resented her presence.

All the same, her wealth and position as a friend of Cornelia van Raay, gave her privileges denied to most women. Two hours ago, she had been rowed out into the Atlantic to greet the *Old Moon*, just so she could sail with her back into port. The sea was choppy, but her stomach was equal to it, and it was worth it. Louise's favourite view of La Rochelle, her home for nigh on a decade, was the one she saw coming back into harbour from the sea.

It wasn't enough, it was never enough, but it was better than nothing.

Around her, all was activity as the captain and crew brought the ship safely home. It was late in the season. Soon, the weather and the seas would be too rough, the crossing too dangerous. Louise glanced aft and saw storm clouds were now bumping along the horizon and threatening rain.

She remained in position while the heaving line was thrown across to the jetty. Men scrambled to catch it, then pulled the attached thick berthing hawser across, winding it round and round the bollard on the quay to secure the ship at the bow. The same process was repeated at the stern, then they were docked. Sailors instantly began to stow the cannon and shut the gun ports, the two wooden shutters snapping closed like gunshot.

The *Old Moon* was a merchant ship, not a warship, so the two cannon on the upper deck provided only very basic protection. On this voyage, Louise knew they had not been needed. She was relieved. Cornelia had lost her flagship ten years before, in a pirate raid off the Barbary Coast, and lived in fear of such a loss happening again. But the *Old Moon* was home in one piece on this blustery late afternoon in October, having sailed into the most powerful, the most successful Huguenot city of France, the gateway to the new world. La Rochelle traded in wine and salt, furs from Saint Lawrence in the Americas and sugar from the Caribbean Sea.

The port was filled with sound. Sailors shouted to one another, the rattle of coin and the banter of coopers with their carts grew as the first of the casks were unloaded from the *fluyt* onto the dock.

*All so familiar.*

Except although the scene at the port seemed unchanged,

Louise knew there was an undercurrent, like the tug of the deepest tides. Behind closed doors merchants and religious leaders alike talked of the ascending power of the King's chief adviser, Cardinal Richelieu, and the changing dynamics at court. The independence of La Rochelle was surely being eroded. Once more Huguenots were being portrayed as the enemy within. As a counter-measure, it was an open secret within the walls of the town that a plan was being put in place for a national assembly of the Reformed Churches to discuss raising an army to protect their interests, if and when the time came. La Rochelle was seen as a state within a state. From the last letter Louise had received from her uncle – now in the employ of the Huguenot leader Henri de Rohan, after the Duc de Sully had retired to his country estates – she knew the threat was serious.

And what of her fellow citizens in her adopted city? Louise was certain every woman, man and child in La Rochelle was aware the clock was ticking, although most buried themselves in their prosperous day-to-day lives. They were bourgeois, comfortable and successful. They did not believe themselves to be the kind of people trampled by history.

Louise knew better. Change was coming, she knew it was coming. She could smell it in the air in the harbour, in the damp copper leaves that carpeted the slopes outside the city walls. She didn't know what, only that something was going to happen.

'Madame Reydon-Joubert? May I help you disembark?'

Louise turned. 'My thanks, Captain Janssen, I appreciate your kindness in allowing me to join you.'

The old sea captain bowed. 'You love this ship.'

'I do.'

She was due to take his report this evening. It was his final voyage for the Van Raay line and Louise was hosting a dinner in his honour. After a lifetime of service, Janssen was retiring to run a tavern in the town. His wife, Marie, was unable to attend this evening – she was expecting their sixth child – but the captain had sought her permission to bring another relative, a cousin, in Madame Janssen's place. Louise already knew there had been no significant incidents on the journey from the Port of Las Palmas in Gran Canaria to La Rochelle – no storms in the Bay of Biscay, no privateers in the Atlantic, no drag from barnacles slowing their progress – so they could celebrate his retirement tonight.

Louise allowed the old sea captain to accompany her to the side of the boat, but refused his hand. She stepped onto the wharf, careful not to slip, with her head held high.

'Until this evening, captain.'

# CHAPTER TWENTY-THREE

Gilles Barenton was watching Madame Joubert, having spotted her distinctive long emerald cloak and hood from afar. He thought she looked like a painted figurehead standing on the deck – imposing, inscrutable, indomitable.

A tall, handsome woman of some thirty-five years, her reputation was for fairness, though she did not suffer fools. He knew she was wealthy in her own right – some said from a husband long-dead, others from her father – and remained unmarried. She lived in one of the finest houses in rue des Gentilshommes, but held herself apart from the leading families of La Rochelle. She was barred from city affairs by virtue of her sex, but she was known as a shrewd negotiator, ready to drive a tough bargain. Some people hated her, looking always for the chance to undermine her authority or sabotage a deal. Gilles was not one of them.

Had he the courage to approach her?

His uncle's vines and shop were doing well, but they were a relatively small producer and Gilles thought they could do better. In a city awash with Cognac and Pineau des Charentes, it was hard to get their wines noticed. Gilles had conceived a plan that Barenton et Fils should become the sole purveyor of wine for the Van Raay fleet. If they had some kind of warrant, then they would have the opportunity to grow. His uncle, reluctant at first, had finally given his assent.

Gilles wondered if he might simply walk up to Madame Reydon-Joubert and present their case. He doubted there would be an opportunity later at dinner. His uncle would think it vulgar to mix business with pleasure.

Over ten years in his uncle's household, he had risen through the ranks, learning each part of the business. He was now the chief bottler in the shop, transferring wine from the casks to the family-crested glass bottles servants brought to be filled. He had delicate penmanship, so he also drew the labels and had designed a crest for their bills of sale – a capital letter B for Barenton, with a vine entwined through it. He was personable, had a steady hand when decanting the wine, and remembered everyone. Tall and broad, Gilles had inherited his mother's shoulders and heavy features, which would have made him a plain woman but gave him a pleasing appearance as a man. The King, Louis XIII, favoured long hair, which suited Gilles and drew attention away from his lack of a beard. Women, in particular, enjoyed being served by him.

He had stayed awake much of the night practising his speech. How he would invite Madame Reydon-Joubert to their oak-framed barn filled with copper tanks and wooden barrels, and allow all the inimitable aromas of fermentation to work their magic while he explained how their Pineau was made. How legend had it that a winemaker in the harvest of 1589 accidentally decanted grape juice into a barrel containing eau-de-vie. Then later, after the mixture had fermented, how the end product was considered pleasing, so the distinctive local drink was born. How their Vieux Pineau was exceptional – cherry red and sweet – fine enough to grace any captain's table.

He had made up his mind. He was going to approach her. Then, everything changed.

'Here you are!'

His stomach plummeted. Gilles had not heard the hated voice for years, but it might just as well have been yesterday. He had allowed himself to hope that she was dead. His heart started to race. He was twenty years old, a man now, not a defenceless girl, but the years of beatings and punishment had scarred him. That he had not seen his mother for eight years meant nothing.

'You,' he said.

She narrowed her eyes. 'Well, here's a fine welcome, I don't think.'

'I am on my uncle's service.'

'You're idling,' she snapped. 'Standing doing nothing, I've been watching you.'

For some time, he had been aware of a thrumming beneath his skin, a dread that his contentment was about to be destroyed. He had tried to blame his unease on the rumblings of war, though the feeling was more visceral and more personal than that. Now, in these split seconds between hearing his mother's hated voice and finding his own, he realised she was the reason for it. He would never be free of her.

'Let me pass.'

'Aren't you pleased to see your own mother?' she said, grasping his elbow and pushing him along with her. 'We are going to have a little conversation, you and I.'

'I have not the time,' he protested, but already she was steering him away from the main thoroughfare and into one of the narrow roads that ran in shadow between the buildings that fanned out from the port. Gilles hated himself for going with her, but he couldn't help it. Back when he was a girl, the threat was always of violence and humiliation. Now it was different. The more his uncle had come to rely on him, the greater the power his mother had to ruin everything. As a child, he had been terrified of her rage. Now she was suddenly back, he was immediately terrified of what havoc she might wreak.

Gilles was under no illusion. His uncle was a decent, but

unyielding man, and he was proud. The death of his own son many years ago had left him without an heir. In the past ten years, Gilles had, if not filled the dead boy's shoes, brought his uncle some comfort that his business would stay in the family. The betrayal Achilles Barenton would feel at learning he had been duped would destroy all that, as well as the quiet affection that had grown up between them.

He stumbled, his shoes slipping on the greasy cobblestones. 'Where are we going?' he asked, hating how small he sounded.

'Keeping walking.'

It was the same cold voice that still haunted his dreams at night. Why was she here? His mother had been banished from the house eight years ago after helping herself one time too often to his uncle's wine stock. She had been given money enough to support herself beyond the city limits of La Rochelle on the understanding that she could never come back. His uncle feared lack of respectability more than anything else.

And now? From his first impression, Gilles could see that she seemed to have risen in the world – lied, or tricked, or gulled another fool. Her clothes spoke of comfort and respectability, wide sleeves, a wired collar, good-quality cotton.

'If you let me go, I will say—'

A slap to the side of his head silenced him. He was taller than her now, stronger than her now, yet her malignant power was undiminished.

'I am on my uncle's service,' he said again.

'And?'

'I would not court his displeasure—'

A second slap. He could feel the burn of her hand on his cheek.

She shoved him back against the wall. 'I know everything about you. Everything you have, you owe to my kindness and goodwill. You will do what I tell you.' She poked her finger at his chest, then laughed. 'Flat as a board, very convincing.'

He flushed. He had been taught to bind and strap effectively by the doxies in the bawdy house on the port to hide every indication of his born sex. They had shown him how to manage his monthly courses, too.

'Never mind your uncle, you should fear displeasing me.'

His mother left the threat hanging. There was no need to say more. She steered him to the left, into the rue du Port, which ran up from the harbour to the town. Only a stone's throw from where they had lived when Gilles was a girl.

'What do you want?' he asked, despising the sound of defeat in his voice. Flat and submissive.

'To introduce you to a friend of mine. That's to say, my husband. There is a service you might do for him.'

Then she leant forward and whispered in his ear.

# CHAPTER TWENTY-FOUR

Gilles' mother hammered with her fist on a low door in the dark alleyway. Finally, it opened. Without a word, she shoved him inside.

The lamps were unlit, though there were slits at the top of the wall, enough for Gilles to see a servant exit through a door at the end of the narrow corridor.

'I cannot do what you are asking of me,' he repeated. 'My uncle has been good to me.'

'Hold your tongue.'

His mother's breath was sour and he tried to step away from her. He thought about how the filth of the alleyway would have splashed his stockings, and how his uncle would be displeased. Achilles Barenton was a fastidious man.

'Why are we here?'

'As I said, for you to meet my husband. Are you so unnatural a child that you care nothing for the fact your mother is provided for? You have shown me no concern or filial feeling.' She cracked a smile. 'If that is, indeed, the right word. Filial!'

She laughed again. Gilles said nothing. The lesson had been well learnt in his childhood. A word out of place always meant a blow.

'Roux will tell you what you are going to do.'

Gilles closed his eyes. He needed to stand up to her. Somehow, he had to find the courage to be loyal to the man who had taken him in and given him a home, a trade.

'I will not do what you ask.'

Gilles heard the crack as the bone in his little finger gave, seconds before pain exploded up his arm. He swallowed a scream.

'I warned you not to provoke me,' she hissed.

'I'm sorry,' he whispered, hating himself for begging.

Ahead of them, he heard the sound of the door opening and a square of light fell into the corridor.

'About time,' his mother muttered, then plumped her voice with charm. 'Monsieur Roux, Husband, here you are.'

In the doorway stood a man like a weasel, eyes too close together, with a thin, pockmarked nose. His straggled hair was unwashed, his red beard and moustache unkempt. His clothes looked too big for him, and somehow too fine. A cotton shirt with lace cuffs, wool stockings rolled above his knee held in place with a ribbon, loose breeches, a once-white neck stock. Over the top, a brown felt coat with brass buttons over a long waistcoat, and a wide-brimmed tricorne hat.

'You found him?'

'As promised. If I might introduce my *son* to you.'

Gilles could not say if she meant him to understand that Roux knew what he was, or if the emphasis was intended as a warning to him alone, but he knew he was limed in any case. If he did not do what they wanted, she would expose him and everything would be lost. But if he agreed to betray his uncle, everything would be lost anyway. There was no way out.

'Does the whelp know what we would have him do?'

'He does,' she said in the same honeyed tone.

The man took a step forward and, without Gilles even seeing him move his hand, he felt the point of a dagger at the base of his throat.

'You understand what will happen if you attempt to warn him?'

Gilles looked into the vicious eyes. What if he could find a way to speak to his uncle, persuade him not to attend the dinner? Then the crisis could be averted. For today, at least.

As if Roux could read his mind, he pressed the tip of the blade harder against his skin until Gilles felt a bead of blood appear.

'Make no mistake, I don't care who or what you are. For your dear mother's sake, I would not harm you, but . . . You understand?'

'Yes,' he managed to say.

'So long as we're clear.' The man slipped his dagger back into its sheath, then turned to his mother. 'What time do the festivities commence?'

'At eight o'clock, in the rue des Gentilshommes. It is all arranged with Janssen, I paid him well enough. The man has five brats to feed, and most of 'em girls.'

There was a pause, then a sly smile cracked Roux's face. He grabbed at Gilles' mother's skirt and pulled a fist of material up above her knees.

'I know just how to fill the time.'

She laughed. 'What about him?'

The man was pawing at her bodice now. Repelled, Gilles turned away.

'Lock him up,' he said, taking a key from his pocket. 'I'll take him with me when I go.'

'No, I will not warn him,' Gilles said desperately. 'I give you my word.'

'Your word!' his mother sneered. 'What makes you think the word of an invert like you is worth a sou?'

She pushed him through a dark doorway and slammed the door. Gilles found himself sprawled on the floor of an empty chamber. Ten years of normal life vanished as if they had never been. From the street outside, he could still hear the cry of the gulls and the laughter of sailors drinking in the tavern on the corner. Now, they were toasting their safe return from the sea. Later, the sounds would turn ugly. Gilles wished he was with them.

He covered his ears so as not to hear the grunts of his mother and Roux making the 'beast with two backs', as Rabelais called it. In his uncle's library, he had read the words in the story of Gargantua, where the giant had tethered his son Pantagruel to his cradle by one of the chains that was drawn across the harbour of La Rochelle each evening.

His uncle had given him everything – a home, food, education, the chance of a better life. How could he betray him? Gilles pulled his knees up, put his head in his hands, and wept.

# CHAPTER TWENTY-FIVE

'Who brought this?' As Louise brandished the letter, shards of red wax fell to the floor.

'Just a boy, madame.'

A solid and pious individual, her steward had come with the house when she had purchased it some ten years ago, and Louise had never seen any reason to replace him. He was wholly without imagination or curiosity. He worked, he went to church, he slept and never touched a drop.

'Well, who gave it to him to be delivered?'

'I regret to say I did not ask.'

'Why ever not?'

'It did not seem necessary. I gave him a sou and sent him on his way.'

Realising the steward was still waiting, she dismissed him. She flung the letter on the table and continued to pace up and down the chamber.

Night had fallen over La Rochelle. Flaming torches were burning outside the grand buildings of the rue des Gentilshommes, sending shadows dancing up and along the elegant stone walls. Despite having visited the Chateau de Puivert only once, Louise had heard enough of her grandmother's stories to want to bring a little of the Pyrenees to La Rochelle. Her house had a turret set above the colonnades facing west and south, giving an impression of a castle from Languedoc. She had no doubt her grandmother would have thought the house too grand, but Louise suspected her mother, Marta, would have appreciated it.

Louise calmed herself and sat down. She stared again at the letter: fine cream paper, the Evreux family crest at the top, red wax where she had cracked the seal. Evreux had been her late father's estate outside Chartres, sold many years ago. Who owned the estate now? How had the letter even found her? La Rochelle was a long way from Chartres.

*Is the claim true?*

She needed time to put her thoughts in order. To try to work out if the letter was genuine and, if it was, what she was going to do about it. But her guests were about to arrive. Louise cared little for the good opinion of others – her wealth shielded her from the need to please or to flatter – but Captain Janssen deserved his farewell feast. He had always welcomed her on the *Old Moon*, although he remained unaware that Louise was the owner of the ship. He was one of the few men in La Rochelle to accept her presence at the harbour, and she was fond of him because of it.

Janssen had worked for Cornelia for many years, having started as a cabin boy, and worked his way up to captain. In 1602, he had helped Cornelia and Alis petition to be part of the newly formed VOC and had remained in their service ever since. He had been on the *White Dove*, Cornelia's flagship, when it was captured by Barbary corsairs in 1610 and was one of only a handful of the crew to escape the slave market of Salé and live to tell the tale, a tale he was fond of recounting. Janssen's loyalty and skill had been crucial in the success of the Van Raay fleet, but the new Governor-General of the VOC had expansionist plans in the East and a year ago had established Batavia as its regional headquarters. Janssen had not liked what he'd heard of the expedition and had decided this sailing season would be his last.

Louise wasn't sentimental. The old captain was perhaps a

little too fond of the bottle and was not always the best judge of men. But she would miss him. It was for that reason that she was prepared to endure an evening of small-talk and tittle-tattle: hypocritical merchants and their painted wives, some twenty local importers and exporters who would petition her for support, eager for gossip about the new trading terms of the voc. Louise could script every conversation.

*But now this.*

She looked again at the letter as if its devastating words might somehow have vanished.

'*Madame, s'il vous plaît?*'

Louise turned to see her housekeeper, a stern woman with a low brow, now standing in the doorway.

'What is it?'

'The first of your guests are here.'

Louise picked up her lace collar and turned it between her fingers. 'I will be down presently.'

The housekeeper glanced at the bed, where Louise's over-gown lay untouched. 'Shall I send your maid up to help you dress, madame?'

'No, I can manage.'

Louise moved to stand at the window. If only she could speak to Alis or Cornelia, to her uncle even. Any one of them might know if the claim in the letter might be true. But they were all several weeks' ride away.

Then, she had an idea. What about her grandmother's journals? The last time she had been in Amsterdam in the dismal months after her grandfather had died – Piet had followed his beloved wife into the ground only a few months after her death – Louise had read them all. But Louise had been grieving for him, as well as for Minou. Maybe she had missed something?

\* \* \*

With Roux's coarse hand on his arm, Gilles stumbled towards the house in the rue des Gentilshommes as if he were a prisoner being taken to the gallows. His mother had bound his finger in a splint to hold it straight, but it was still throbbing cruelly.

For weeks, Gilles had been looking forward to accompanying his uncle to this dinner. He had walked past the house countless times and admired the elegance of the architecture, the unique precision of the turret. Boasting a wide double door at street level, with a brass knocker in the shape of a carrack in sail, narrow timber-framed glass windows on its five floors behind which candles flickered, it was one of the finest in the northern *quartier*. As someone who had been raised in the worst of places, Gilles had looked beyond his miserable existence to the world around him for beauty and found it in the fine houses and churches, the bell towers and convents of La Rochelle. And he had been looking forward to meeting Madame Reydon-Joubert, the one woman in this man's world.

Now, Gilles wished himself anywhere but here. He could hardly breathe. The cotton strapping he wore around his chest had become a band of steel. He felt as if his ribs might, at any moment, splinter and crack. He could imagine the mark of Cain visible on his forehead. No, not Cain, Judas. That was his role. The beloved disciple who betrayed his master.

Gilles was pierced with a despair so sharp that he would have thrown himself from the top of the Tour de la Lanterne without any thought to his immortal soul. Obliterating all guilt, all responsibility. Because even if tonight's deceit passed off without his uncle ever knowing his part in the matter, he knew it would not stop here. Their blackmail would continue.

His hours of imprisonment had done nothing to make his

path clearer. Perhaps if he could find a scrap of paper and write a message to his uncle? But Roux was watching his every move. He couldn't imagine how the man had acquired an invitation in the first place, then he remembered what his mother had said. They had bribed someone – Janssen, he thought was the name?

He would never be free of her.

'I wish you were dead . . .' he said over and over in his head. 'I wish you were dead.'

Louise paused at the top of the stairs, stepping behind a pillar for a moment, so no one could see her.

The hall below was already full, her guests milling about. A long walnut table had been set in the centre of the space. Covered with a white tablecloth, two silver candelabra revealed oysters on a pewter dish, whelk and crab, two large seabass and several lobsters. Sweetbreads and loaves of white bread, and trays of black and green olives, completed the feast. Venetian wine glasses sparkled in the candlelight, to be filled with the local Pineau, though Louise had also instructed the kitchen to ensure there was a supply of rum for Captain Janssen.

*Twenty-one for dinner.*

She spotted a few Medici collars and paned sleeves, but mostly sobriety and Protestant austerity were evident in the women's gowns. Flat white ruffs, damask and velvet the colour of autumn leaves glowed in the flickering light, felt doublets and cotton breeches for Janssen and most of the city's merchants.

Achilles Barenton, one of the city's smaller vineyard owners, who kept a shop in the rue du Temple, looked ill at ease. She wondered if he had supplied the wine for this evening. Close to the door, she glimpsed a delicate-featured young man with long hair and a makeshift bandage on his little finger, looking as if he might bolt at any moment. He was standing close to a thin, wiry man with red hair and beard in badly fitting clothes, chatting with Captain Janssen. Louise assumed he must be Janssen's cousin. She felt an unexpected pang of loss, remembering her grandfather's stories of how his red hair had caused him trouble in his youth. Considered the mark of the Devil by some, as proof that he wasn't truly French by others, he'd had to dampen down the colour with soot.

Then, an image came to her of her father. Black hair with a white streak.

Louise pushed the memory away. She let her eyes continue around the hall until she saw the Huguenot pastor, his leonine head crowned by a mass of white hair beneath his black cap. Long, lace cuffs elegantly hid the stump where his left forefinger should have been. He was an ambitious man.

'*Post tenebras lux*,' she murmured, the Calvinist motto. After darkness, light.

Steeling herself, Louise stepped out of the shadows and descended the stairs. She was wearing a wired collar and low bodice, and a single emerald on a chain. Her birthstone. She had dressed to remind her guests of her status in La Rochelle. Velvet and lace, split sleeves with green ribbons. As her uncle had predicted in Paris the day before her birthday, Louise could now afford all the ribbons she wanted.

One by one, the company fell silent. Her steward was in his place behind her chair, the liveried servants waiting. She said nothing, there was no need, merely took her place at the head of the table. With a simple gesture of her hand, she invited the pastor to lead the prayers. Everyone bowed their heads and murmured the responses.

'Amen,' said Janssen loudly to her right. 'Amen.'

Now, for the first time, Louise spoke. 'Captain Janssen, honoured guests, ladies and gentlemen, you are most welcome. Please, sit.'

# CHAPTER TWENTY-SIX

Gilles pulled out his uncle's chair, then took his own seat.

After expressing his disappointment that Gilles had failed to meet him at the shop as arranged, his uncle had not addressed a word to him. With Roux sticking close to his side, Gilles had had no opportunity to whisper in his uncle's ear, or warn him against the man with whom he was now making small talk about the wine business.

An oyster was placed upon his plate. The smell of the sea, of salt and brine, was overwhelming; the drip of liquid, the clatter of spoons. Gilles felt his stomach lurch and clamped his napkin over his mouth, wincing at the pain from his finger. He raised his eyes and saw Roux was watching, sucking a thumb of crab meat from a claw.

His nausea took over. Unable to hold off any longer, Gilles pushed his chair back and scrabbled up to his feet.

Louise watched the young man with long, Catholic hair stumble from the table. Beside her, Monsieur Barenton half rose.

'Your nephew has a delicate constitution, monsieur.'

'I can only apologise; I can't imagine what has got into the boy. He is not usually so . . .' He tailed off.

Louise noticed that the red-haired man had also risen from the table to follow, and wondered why.

'It is of no matter, though I wish your nephew better.' She glanced to the door. 'That gentleman? He is in your service?'

Barenton frowned. 'Indeed no, madame. I've never seen him before this evening. I believe he is a cousin of Captain Janssen's.'

'Oh? He seems very concerned for your nephew.'

Barenton frowned. 'Well, it seems so. I cannot account for it.'

'Perhaps you should see if he needs assistance. Your nephew, that's to say. Even in La Rochelle, oysters can be treacherous.' She paused. 'What is the boy's name?'

'Gilles, madame. His mother – my sister – well, she was not a suitable guardian. He has lived with me for some ten years and I've never had cause to regret taking him in.'

'You gave him a home and trade, that was most commendable.'

Barenton puffed out his chest. 'He has a hunger for self-improvement, always reading. And a pretty hand. He is responsible for our distinctive crest – you might have seen it?'

Louise inclined her head. 'All the more reason to find out if he needs help.'

Caught between embarrassment and concern, Barenton dropped his napkin on the table and stood up.

'You are most gracious, Madame Reydon-Joubert. Please accept my apologies for this unwarranted disruption.'


Gilles hurtled through the kitchen, sending servants leaping out of his way. He only just made it to the alleyway behind the house before doubling over, the despair of the last few hours burning his throat.

He fell to his knees, coughing and puking, until he felt his innards had been turned inside out. He felt a slick of sweat in the small of his back, damp beneath his strapping. Another dry spasm gripped his stomach. There was almost relief as the retching blotted out the thoughts in his racing mind. When he heard two sets of footsteps, one behind him, and one coming from the street, he could not even summon the strength to lift his head.

'What the Devil is going on?' his mother hissed.

Gilles flinched as Roux prodded him with his boot. 'Ask him.'

His mother grabbed his jacket. 'Well? Did you get the keys?'

Gilles felt another wave of nausea and vomited on her shoes, enjoying the moment of rebellion before Roux kicked him, and he sprawled forwards into the dirt.

'What are we going to do?' she said.

'You take him back to the lodgings,' Roux replied. 'He can try again tomorrow.'

Gilles felt himself being hauled to his feet. He had no strength, his legs were like water, he had no fight. But he was free. He no longer cared what they might do to him. Pain was better than betrayal.

'Nephew, how now?'

'No!'

Gilles didn't know if he spoke the word aloud, but his sense of reprieve vanished at the sound of his uncle's voice. He heard the familiar tap of his stick coming closer. He wanted to shout at him to leave, but the words stuck in his throat. Then, despite the sombre light in the alleyway, Barenton recognised his sister.

'You,' he said in disbelief. 'And you, sir? You were at the dinner. Declare yourself.'

'It's nothing to do with you, old man.'

Barenton took another step closer. 'Tell me the meaning of this? What are you doing to my nephew?'

'Nephew!' his mother shrieked.

It was the final straw. Gilles twisted himself free, and lunged at his mother.

'Stop, stop this instant!'

Gilles heard the confusion in his uncle's voice, but it did not matter. He had the power of ten men. He was sitting astride his mother now, his hands on her throat. He wanted to kill her. He knew he would hang, but it was the only way. Only then would there be peace. He'd been a fool to think otherwise.

Then, he saw the flash of a knife, the metal catching the flicker from the torches at the kitchen door. Roux struck, but he misjudged. The blade missed Gilles and nicked his mother's neck instead. His mother screamed. His uncle was shouting. Roux slashed again. This time his aim was true. A bolt of pain exploded in Gilles' shoulder, but he didn't release his grip on his mother's throat.

'Nephew, do you want to swing? Do not let that woman be the cause of more—'

His uncle's words were silenced, as Roux swung round and sliced across the older man's throat.

'No!' Gilles shouted.

For a moment, Barenton stood still, as if suspended like a marionette. He looked down and seemed to register the red bloom of blood on his doublet. Then, as if in slow motion, he started to sway, and fell.

Gilles leapt up to catch him, the man who had shown him nothing but kindness and respect, trying to stem the blood, while his uncle grew heavy in his arms. Roux dropped the dagger and fled, his feet slipping on the bloodstained cobbles.

'Uncle,' Gilles whispered, 'stay with me. Help will come.' He turned on his mother. 'Fetch help!' he screamed. 'Can't you see he's dying?'

Choking and clutching her hands to her bloodied throat, his mother dragged herself to her feet, and staggered after her husband without a backward glance.

Gilles sat back on his haunches, and cradled his uncle's head in his hands. As the old man's life ebbed away, he murmured the same words over and over again as a light rain began to fall.

'Forgive me, forgive me.'

# CHAPTER TWENTY-SEVEN

The candles had burnt down, pooling wax around the silver base of the candelabra, forming a hard crust like the shell of a crab.

Louise glanced impatiently at the door. When she had given Barenton permission to leave the table, she had not expected him to be gone for so long. His nephew and the man with the red hair had not returned either. Their continued absence was not only discourteous to Captain Janssen, but an insult to her hospitality.

The pastor was still holding court at the far end of the table. Louise could see if she delayed the citations much longer, he would be too intoxicated to speak with any measure of propriety. She thought of how much she disliked the man. Preaching from the pulpit on Sundays about sin and the temptations of the flesh, when, common gossip had it, he spent much of his time in a flophouse down by the port.

She summoned the steward. 'Is there any sign of Monsieur Barenton? It is my impression we should begin the formal part of our proceedings sooner rather than later.'

The steward looked at the pastor. 'That would be advisable, madame.'

Louise turned to Janssen, who had also been drinking heavily. He had delivered his report succinctly and with admirable clarity, but now he was slurring his words. His set-piece narrative of how he had been captured by Barbary corsairs – not to mention a wild and rambling tale about being pursued by a ghost ship crewed by dead men off the coast of Morocco – had become more elaborate with each retelling. Louise had had her fill of the lot of them and wanted nothing more than for them all to be gone, never mind the empty chairs.

She got to her feet and, instantly, the hubbub ceased. Even the pastor stopped talking.

'Ladies and gentlemen, honoured guests, we are gathered here to honour the long service of Captain Hans Janssen to the Van Raay family and the VOC. Many are called to the sea, and it is a perilous and dangerous occupation, but Captain Janssen has shown that, with fortitude and good companionship—'

'Madame—'

The steward had interrupted her. Louise had never known such a thing. He was standing in the doorway and, though his professional demeanour seemed unchanged, his skin was the colour of chalk.

'What is it?'

'If you might come.'

Louise stared at him in astonishment, then back to her guests. 'It seems there is some pressing matter that only my attention can remedy.' A ripple of polite laughter. 'I'm sure it is nothing. Captain, if you might excuse me? Pastor, if I could prevail upon you to begin your address.'

'Of course,' the cleric replied, his face flushed. 'It would be my honour.'

In the alleyway behind the house, Gilles was rocking backwards and forwards, still cradling his uncle's head on his lap. The autumn drizzle had soaked through his jerkin and hose, his hair hung in strands around his face, but he could not stop. His shirt was thick with blood, though he felt nothing more than a dull ache in his shoulder where Roux's knife had gone in.

Around him, a tide of crimson spread on the wet cobblestones as the rain continued silently to fall.

He became aware that he was no longer alone. He looked up to see a woman casting a long shadow from the doorway of the house, a man in black standing beside her. His mind registered that it was Madame Reydon-Joubert herself, and the steward.

'Did you do this, Gilles?' she asked.

The sound of his name shocked him. He had not realised she knew it.

'I loved him,' he said simply.

'Men kill just as often for love as for hate, or greed.'

He raised his head. 'I didn't kill him.'

'Do you give me your word?'

He gave a soft laugh. 'Why would my word be worth anything?'

'Why would it not?'

Their eyes locked and he saw a depth of understanding, compassion even, in her expression. Gilles didn't understand how she could be so calm, or why she would show him any pity.

'Will you come inside?'

He shook his head. 'I cannot leave him, not—'

'I will have him laid out indoors,' Louise said, beckoning her steward. 'Or he can be taken to his own house, if you prefer. Do you?'

For the first time, Gilles realised that Roux and his mother might have gone straight to Barenton et Fils, even without the keys they had tried to make him steal, to take what they wanted by force. A violent shudder convulsed his body.

'No!'

'You are cold,' she said, misunderstanding. 'You have had a dreadful shock.'

Gilles thought she sounded kind. Why would she be kind to him?

He looked down at his uncle's face. All the life had gone. Close at hand, her steward was standing with a sheet over his arms. Behind him, two servants from the kitchen were lurking, their eyes alive with excitement. They darted looks at one another, no doubt already planning how they would sell their story for a quart of ale.

Gilles continued to rock, but more slowly now, like a clock winding down. The haze of rain still hung in the air, silent and silver, painting the world in a watery light. Gently, he laid his uncle's head on the ground. Then, like a parent with a sleeping child, he gently slipped himself out from beneath the body. The wound to Barenton's throat gaped.

One of the kitchen boys muttered an oath.

'Hold your tongue,' the steward snapped.

Gilles looked down to see the whole of his shirt was soaked with his uncle's blood. He staggered to his feet. His right arm was hanging at his side and his legs were shaking, but he forced himself to put one foot in front of the other and walk towards the open kitchen doorway. Behind him, he heard the swish of the cloth as the steward shrouded his uncle's body and murmured instructions.

'Find the boy some clothes,' Madame Reydon-Joubert said.

Gilles barely heard. His mind had gone to another time and place.

'Pick a card, any card . . .'

The same memory. The cartomancer reading fortunes with a deck of Tarot cards. He had stopped that day, seduced by the vivid colours, red and yellow and blue: *le Mat*, the fool, with a little dog snapping at his heels; and the card Gilles had stolen, *la Justice*. He had it still, the only possession he had from his former life. It had been April, perhaps? No, May. Of course, the day before his brother's funeral. Two days before he became a boy.

Gilles reached for the doorframe. Was a person's fate fixed or had he the power to change it? Protestant doctrine was clear. Man would be saved by God's grace alone. Sufficient to stand, yet free to fall. But, on that one day in that long-ago spring, he had been seized with the possibility of something different.

'Is this my fault?' he whispered.

'You did not kill him,' said Madame Reydon-Joubert. 'You gave me your word. Is that true?'

His raised his eyes to hers and was destroyed by the pity in them.

'I did not.'

'Well, then,' she said quietly. 'Come inside.'

Gilles followed her obediently into the house. Had his uncle always been destined to die in an alleyway on a wet night in October, or could another story have been told? Was this his fault? After ten years of deceit, was this God's judgement?

# CHAPTER TWENTY-EIGHT

Barenton's body was carried to a small ante-chamber off the main hall and laid out on a table beneath a clean sheet. Louise looked at the distraught boy as he knelt down beside his uncle, his head bowed.

'He will not let me examine him, madame,' the physician murmured, having been summoned by the steward. 'As well as the wound to his upper arm, he has a broken finger.'

Louise nodded. 'Gilles, how old are you?'

He looked up at her blankly, as if she was speaking in a foreign language, but he answered.

'I have seen twenty summers, madame.'

Louise raised her eyebrows. She had thought him much younger.

'In which case, you are old enough to understand that if the wound is not treated it will become infected. There is nothing you can do for your uncle. Let us help you.'

'No! Nobody can touch me!'

Louise held up her hands. 'No one is going to hurt you.'

The boy kept shaking his head. 'I need nothing.'

Louise looked at the physician, who shrugged.

'Gilles, will you at least take a draught of brandy. It will help with the shock.'

The slightest of nods. She gestured to the steward, who fetched a glass from the hall.

'There,' she said gently, slowly passing it into the boy's hands.

The amber liquid slopped over his fingers, but he sipped a little, cupping the glass in his shaking grasp until Louise was relieved to see a little colour come back into his cheeks. 'And if you will not change your clothes, then at least cover yourself. You will catch a chill.'

Again, he looked up at her, then nodded. The steward passed a blanket to her and she handed it to Gilles, very slowly, as if he was a horse who might bolt at any moment.

'Allow my physician to splint your finger properly,' she said carefully. 'He won't touch you anywhere else.'

'I do not deserve this,' he whispered.

Louise kept her voice level. 'You were attacked, your uncle is dead. You deserve any kindness I might offer.'

She waited until, again, he nodded. The physician opened his bag.

'Lift up your hand, Gilles.'

The boy did what she asked him. Louise watched as the physician strapped his fingers together.

'It's not a bad break,' the doctor said. 'It should heal within a couple of weeks.'

'If you might leave some ointment and a bandage, Monsieur Barenton could tend to the wound on his shoulder himself. Would that be all right, Gilles?'

The physician scowled, as if his skill was being criticised, but he took a wad of dressing, poured alcohol on it, and put it on the table beside a fresh strip of bandage.

'Dress the site twice a day,' he said curtly. 'Any white spirit will do, or brandy, if you have nothing else. It looks like a clean cut. God willing, you will have a full recovery.'

Louise murmured her thanks. 'My steward will see you out. Thank you for coming at this inhospitable hour. You will not find me ungrateful.'

The door closed and now they were alone. There was no fire, and the candles gave scant warmth, so their breath misted in the damp night air.

'What can you tell me, Gilles? Who did this?'

He did not answer.

'My steward tells me the man you came with was called Roux? Is he a friend of yours?'

Gilles shook his head.

'Yet you arrived with him,' Louise pressed. 'He followed you from the table.' She waited.

'He came with Captain Janssen,' Gilles said eventually, so softly that Louise hardly heard. 'Tricked him.'

'Tricked him how?' Louise asked. 'Was someone else there in the alley? With Roux?'

This time, an unmistakable look of fear flashed across his face. Louise didn't know what to make of it. Why would he protect his uncle's murderer?

'This dinner was to honour Captain Janssen. He has sailed for the Van Raay fleet for many years. This was his last voyage on the *Old Moon*.'

She kept talking, hoping somehow that the swell of words would encourage him to let down his guard. She would have to report the murder to the *Prévôt* in the morning – indeed, she should have done so already – but she wanted to have the facts clear beforehand.

Gilles did not respond. She still didn't understand the impulse that was causing her to take such risks, but there was something about this boy. He was nothing to her, yet his predicament had touched her when she had seen him holding his uncle's body in his arms. A blood-stained pietà, not Mary and her dead son, but just as true. Then, another image came to her. She was a child, cradling her mother's head in her lap. Looking up at a man standing over her. Black hair with a white stripe. She shook her head, but nothing else came.

*Half-memories.*

'The other guests have been told there was an accident,' she reassured him, though her voice sounded too loud in the silent room. 'There is no one else here, you need not worry.'

In truth, she knew there was no chance of stemming the gossip. La Rochelle was a city that thrived on the traducing of reputations. Those who disapproved of her influence would use it as a way to undermine her. An unmarried woman who kept her own house, who could say what manner of miscreants and deviants such a person might attract? No smoke without fire, wasn't that what they'd say?

'I will leave you now,' she said. 'If you need anything, my steward will assist you. I have powders that could help you sleep?'

Gilles looked up at her with dull eyes. 'I will never forget your kindness to me, never.'

In Louise's chamber, a fire was burning. It was rarely cold in La Rochelle in October, but damp air was slipping between the cracks in the floorboards. Or maybe the chill was inside her?

It was now nearly midnight. Louise was sitting at the table, the letter from Chartres in front of her, a glass of wine at her elbow. The violent events of the evening had banished it from her mind for a while. She asked herself the same question.

*Is it true?*

She swilled the glass, sending pearls of refracted light scattering across the polished wood, then put it down. She needed to keep a clear head. She walked to the window and looked out, leaving a faint imprint of her hand on the glass. It was still raining, a fine drizzle that had filled the streets with mist.

Crossing the room to put another log on the fire, she was acutely aware of the grieving young man in the unheated chamber below her sitting vigil. Would he stay until dawn? She hoped he would.

Louise continued to pace. Counting her steps, she felt suddenly lonely. A wave of nostalgia rushed through her. A sharp longing to see her great-aunt Alis, and Cornelia, and her uncle, Jean-Jacques, and his daughter, Florence. Even her great-aunt Bernarda, who had never approved of her as a child born the wrong side of the blanket.

Returning to the table, Louise smoothed the letter flat, and wondered. Was there anyone who would know if the claim might be true? And if it was true, then why wait until now? Her father's will had been proved ten years ago and there had been no challenge. Then, a trickle of fear went down her spine. She sat back in her chair, suddenly remembering how nervous her grandfather had been that day. The off questions he had asked the lawyer. Had he known something wasn't right? Louise tried to marshal her thoughts. Even if he had, no legitimate heir had stepped forward to claim the inheritance then. So, why now? She caught her breath as the magnitude of what could happen swept over her.

*I could lose everything. Everything.*

Her independence, this house, her freedom. Above all, the *Old Moon*. Louise picked up her glass and, this time, drained it in a single gulp.

# CHAPTER TWENTY-NINE

Gilles was cold, from guilt or pain, he wasn't sure which. During his vigil, his thoughts had clarified and sharpened. Now, he was resolved. Surely everyone in the house would now be asleep?

Placing his hand lightly on his uncle's chest, in a benediction, Gilles lifted back the sheet. Skin the colour of marble, his lips a streak of pale blue, he looked like a wax effigy. He bent forward and planted a kiss on the chill forehead, then took the keys from his uncle's pocket, before replacing the shroud. He shook the blanket from his own shoulders, folded it and put it on the chair. Every movement was precise, neat, despite his weakened right arm and splinted finger. Madame Reydon-Joubert had been more than kind and he did not want her to think him a thief.

Gilles almost laughed. If his mother spoke out, he would be revealed as worse than a thief.

He crossed the dark hall, and unbolted the front door. He had no certain plan, only that he suspected his mother and Roux might attempt to take the gold from his uncle's strongbox tonight all the same, with or without the keys. Then they would be at the front of the queue as the gates to the city were opened in the morning and gone before anyone could catch them.

'Justice', he whispered.

In the chamber above, holding her hands to the fire, Louise heard the creak of the front door. She rushed to the window in time to see a shadow vanish into the mist and, though she couldn't see clearly, she knew it was the boy. Suddenly, another half-memory came back to her. Herself as a child following her mother through the streets of Amsterdam.

Louise snatched up her cloak, and followed.

It was so long since Gilles had moved like a fox through the streets of La Rochelle at night, but he still remembered every short cut, every abandoned alleyway. His muscles held the memory of his past more than a map ever could. Silently, he traced his way back to the premises in the rue du Temple that had been his home for a decade.

How easily he had slipped back into old habits, the past ten years of respectability gone as if they had never been. How could he have believed that a life built on deceit would last? This was his punishment – he accepted that now – for having believed himself worthy of safety, a home, a future.

At a sudden outburst of sound from a neighbouring tavern, Gilles pressed himself into the shadows. He waited for the drunken mariners to stagger past, holding one another up, before stepping back out.

On through the familiar streets. Though his uncle had led him to believe that he would be provided for, Gilles had no idea what that meant precisely. But he deserved nothing, so what did it matter? His mother's blackmail, and the whispered conversation between her and Roux, suggested that there were papers in the strongbox they wanted, in addition to the bar of gold given as down-payment on a shipment of wine to be sent to Nantes.

Gilles stopped and looked up at the sign above the door – BARENTON ET FILS. The wine shop was in darkness, no tell-tale signs of a lit candle flickering amongst the bottles and casks. Most of his uncle's employees – his book-keeper and men who worked the presses – lived in premises attached to their storage barn on the outskirts of the town, leaving only a small overnight staff here at the house. There was a boy of all trades, Antoine, and a cook-cum-housekeeper who, Gilles knew, had been released for the evening to visit a sick daughter.

He cast his eyes up to the first floor, half expecting to see his uncle silhouetted in the window. Higher still, and he could see his own room at the top. It had been his sanctuary, a place of safety and calm, with a small window looking west to the wide ocean beyond.

His fingers found the purloined keys in his pocket. The front door would have been left unbolted, since his uncle was out at dinner. Antoine slept in the kitchen, so if Roux and his mother had attempted to break in that way, surely, he would have raised the alarm?

Daring to hope that he was mistaken, Gilles put the key in the lock, quietly turned it, and stepped inside.

# CHAPTER THIRTY

Louise watched Gilles disappear inside the vintner's house. She was torn. The boy was nothing to her, yet she cared what happened to him. Why that would be, on a moment's acquaintance, she had no answer.

*He is a man, not a boy.*

She waited, and waited. The town clock struck two. Gilles had been in there for some fifteen minutes. What was he doing? Louise hesitated a moment longer, then approached the tall, narrow building, and pushed at the door. It swung open, releasing the scent of a cold house on a damp night.

It took a moment for her eyes to adjust. A metal sconce with a candle burnt down almost to the wick sent shadows flickering along the wall. To her right, a painted black door stood open. Louise peered into the shop itself, casks and empty bottles waiting to be filled, a row of glass stoppers beside them. A pile of promissory notes and receipts in a wooden tray waiting to be processed.

The air was still, settled. No one had been in here.

She stepped back into the corridor and now noticed drops of blood on the tiled floor, like a string of rubies, leading deeper into the house. Gilles' blood or someone else's? Her fingers stole to the hilt of her knife. Louise continued forward, pushing open a door at the end of the corridor that led to the kitchen.

The smell hit her first. The warm, metallic scent of fresh blood. She stopped on the threshold and cast her eyes around.

An open fire glowed, with a kettle suspended above the embers, blackened with soot and woodfire. Pans hung from a rack above the table, on which stood jars containing flour and barley and honey. It was an ordinary kitchen, apart from the body of a kitchen boy slumped against the wall, his throat cut from ear to ear. Louise exhaled to steady herself. His eyes were wide open, caught in surprise at the moment of his death. Louise dipped her finger in the blood and found it still warm. A swift death. She closed the boy's eyes, then looked around. On the floor were splinters of wood from where the back door had been forced. Gilles would have had no need to break the lock. So, who? Roux? Had he come here?

Louise saw that the drips of blood continued up the stairs. Desperate not to betray her own presence, she took careful steps, her feet at the very edge of each tread, until she reached a generous landing on the first floor. Refracted silver moonlight through the window, smudged in mist, revealed a heavy oak blanket chest, a side table with an unlit silver candelabra, and a crumpled rug, as if someone had caught his boot or slipper on it.

And the same ripe smell. Louise was aware of the thud of her own blood in her veins, the accelerated beat of her heart, as she walked into the chamber. Bookshelves lined the walls. A large desk with inkwell and quill and blotter dripped with spilt ink, a small spring-driven timepiece lay shattered on the floor. Louise recognised the design, from a clockmaker in the rue des Bonnes Dames. She had one herself. It was a precise and ordered room, except someone had wreaked chaos. There were papers all over the floor, books pulled from the shelves and the drawers of the desk had been prised open. Behind the chair, where Barenton would have sat to study his accounts, there was a niche in the wall, empty now. The protective wooden door hung broken on its hinges, like a bone pulled from its socket.

Then, she heard a sound – a soft whimpering – and she rushed forward. Someone was lying on the floor behind the desk, face down. She recognised the clothes, the long hair now matted with blood.

*It is happening again.*

She rolled Gilles onto his back. He was bleeding heavily from his temple and the wound on his shoulder had come open.

'I tried to stop him—' the boy whispered.

'Save your strength. I will fetch help.'

'No!'

His voice was surprisingly loud in the quiet room. Louise felt a sense of *déjà vu*, as if the conversation from earlier was repeating itself.

'You need a physician. Your shoulder, now this.' She touched his forehead, and the boy flinched.

'Nobody can know.'

Louise put her hand on his chest. 'Was Roux here?'

Gilles nodded. 'I found him . . . tried to . . .'

Louise looked at the empty safehold in the wall. 'He took your uncle's strongbox? Do you know what he was looking for?'

The boy was still dazed, his delicate features almost translucent as if there was no blood left in him. She suspected he was intending to lie, then a change came over him, as if he had no more fight left, and he slumped.

'Gold,' he answered. 'Papers too, perhaps.'

Louise let the silence stretch. In this one moment, nothing seemed as important as the unknown boy, this stranger, deciding to put his trust in her. But would he?

'Who are you protecting?' she asked quietly.

Her words seemed to float suspended in the air. Seconds passed, and she realised she was holding her breath.

Then Gilles exhaled. 'My mother . . .'

Louise held out her hand. 'Tell me,' she said.

# CHAPTER THIRTY-ONE

At eight o'clock the following morning, Louise was standing outside the main entrance of the Hôtel de Ville.

*How could anyone treat a child in such a way?*

Louise was certain Gilles hadn't told her everything, but he had told her enough for her to want to see Madame Roux behind bars for the rest of her life. What she didn't understand was why Gilles had begged her not to tell the *Prévôt* that his mother had been with Roux in the alleyway last evening. He was so desperate that, in the end, she had promised. Back in her house at close to dawn, he had accepted the laudanum she offered him and she had left him sleeping.

The main building of the town hall sat magnificent behind the enclosure wall, with towers, battlements and gargoyles built more than a hundred years previously. The belfry tower was housed in a Gothic cartouche, the upper coat of arms representing the arms of the throne with the cordon of the Order of Saint-Michel surrounded by two angels. The entrance gate featured rich flamboyant Gothic pinnacles; carved figures of small animals with human faces, and the arms of La Rochelle, a three-masted ship with a figure climbing the rigging. Everything boasted of prosperity, conspicuous wealth and status, and was a deliberate challenge to the authority of the Crown. Louise thought the posturing ridiculous.

'The *Prévôt* will see you now.'

Louise followed the servant into the interior courtyard, past the Pavillon Nord, and into the Great Gallery, her calm expression masking her racing nerves. The interview would require skill and her nerves were stretched thin by the events of the previous night and her lack of sleep. As she walked through the arcades, she glanced up at the ceiling to see the monograms of Henri IV and Marie de' Medici. Those days were gone.

'Madame Reydon-Joubert,' the servant announced, and Louise stepped inside.

They had been talking for some time.

Louise was struggling to keep her temper in check as they asked her the same questions over and again. Six men were sitting at the bench. She had been positioned on a chair in front of them, as if she was on trial, a latter-day Joan of Arc. All of the men she knew, and some had cause to feel in her debt – including the pastor from the Huguenot Assembly, who looked rather green around the gills. But *Prévôt* Arnaud was known for his Calvinist views of women, and his disapproval seeped from every pore of his body.

'We have heard what you have said, Madame Reydon-Joubert,' he repeated, 'but I confess I still fail to understand why you delayed reporting this regrettable situation until this morning. A prominent citizen was murdered last evening, his servant a few hours later, yet you decide not to inform the authorities until now?'

Louise looked up at him. 'As I said, at first it was out of consideration for my guests.'

'Consideration?'

'I was hosting a dinner for a senior captain of the Van Raay fleet – as your eminent colleague here knows, for he was kind enough to grace my house with his presence.'

The pastor, whose head was clearly swimming, sat up straighter. 'Indeed, indeed . . .'

Louise kept her attention fixed on the judge. 'Moreover, it was extremely distressing.'

Arnaud glanced at the pastor, then to the *intendants* beside them on the bench. 'Madame, to be in possession of so delicate a nature does you credit, of that I have no doubt. But the law is the law. Why did you not send your steward to raise the alarm instantly?'

'I was under the impression – wrongly, as it now seems – that you, and the other esteemed gentlemen, would not wish to be roused from your slumber at so late an hour.' She met his gaze, challenging him to rebuke her. '*Mea culpa.*'

'I am sure you did as you thought best, madame,' the pastor interjected. 'I wish only that you had confided in me. I could have provided succour and advice.'

'I hardly wished to impose upon you further.'

Louise wondered if her flattery was too much, but he took her insincerity as no more than his due.

'Of course, of course. I am yours to command.'

'Where is the body of Monsieur Barenton now?' snapped Arnaud, sensing the interview was slipping away from him.

'He remains in my house.'

The judge shuffled his papers. 'And the servant? Antoine, was that his name?'

'My steward fetched Monsieur Barenton's housekeeper from her daughter's house. She supervised Antoine's body being taken to the mortuary.'

'It should have remained in situ.'

'Since there was no doubt as to the cause of death, there seemed no reason to delay.' Louise stopped, hoping that silence at this point would serve her better than words. Arnaud wanted to chastise her, but he could not quite find the means to do it and she could feel his support on the bench was dwindling.

'And this nephew,' he continued, 'Gilles Barenton. I still remain unclear as to his role in the matter?'

Louise pretended to consider. 'As I said, I am of the strong conviction that the murderer was the man Roux, a person who, it seems, inveigled an invitation to my house with Captain Janssen. He claimed to be a distant cousin.' She waved her hand. 'The good captain is a simple man, an honest man, and is mortified to have been the cause of such disaster. He admits now he had never set eyes on Roux before, though he had no reason to doubt his credentials.'

'So that man was *not* called Roux?' queried one of the *intendants*.

'I have no reason to think he is not named Roux,' she replied slowly, as if talking to an idiot. 'But he is not Captain Janssen's cousin.'

'A warrant has been issued for his arrest. Whoever he is, we will find him,' Arnaud said.

'I have no doubt of it, monsieur.'

He threw her a sharp glance. 'To return to the nephew. His actions still seem highly questionable. I would have him brought before the court.'

'I am afraid that won't be possible.'

Arnaud flushed. 'You forget yourself, Madame Reydon-Joubert. You are not in a position to instruct the court. Where is he?'

Louise held up her hand. 'You misunderstand me. I have no doubt the young man would wish to assist the court in any way that he can. But, as I said, he was injured trying to defend his uncle. Then, subsequently, Roux struck him a blow to his head and rendered him unconscious. My own physician is caring for him, but his fever is high and he has not yet recovered the ability to speak.'

He glared at her. 'Is that so.'

'It might be hours; it might be days. He was devoted to his uncle —' She broke off, as if in the grip of a new thought. 'And it is important to keep the boy safe until the murderer is apprehended.'

The pastor was nodding. 'You think Roux might return?'

'Gilles Barenton is the sole witness to a vile act of murder, and the subject of a cowardly attack by the same hand. His testimony could see Roux hanged, so yes, I think that is to be feared.'

Arnaud flushed again but, before he could say anything further, Louise stood up. Taken by surprise, he dropped his quill, splattering ink across the surface of his document.

'Messieurs, you have my gratitude for the manner in which you have listened to me. I very much regret not coming to you sooner to defer to your wisdom and experience. I can see, now, that it would have been a wiser course of action.'

Dabbing ineffectually at his papers, Arnaud raised his voice. 'I must speak to Barenton's nephew.'

Louise ignored him. 'I am aware how many demands there are on your valuable time, gentlemen. This sordid matter must be so far beneath your attention at this critical time for our city.'

The men shifted on their bench, both gratified that the difficulty of their current situation was understood and perturbed that a woman should be lecturing them on their civic responsibilities.

'I would like to make arrangements for Monsieur Barenton to be buried,' she continued. 'Pastor, might you be able to call upon me at midday?'

He raised a limp hand. 'Dear lady, of course.'

She nodded her thanks. 'I am due to meet with the harbourmaster and Captain Janssen at ten o'clock. I presume you have no objection to that?'

'I suppose not.' Arnaud was still dabbing his kerchief in the puddle of ink. 'You will be at home thereafter, should we need to speak to you further?'

'I am at your service, *Prévôt* Arnaud.'

Louise gave a slight bow, then walked from the chamber, leaving the men with the impression that it was they, not she, who had been called to account. All the same, she had to force herself not to run as she retraced her steps back through the ornate building. Only when she was standing back outside the main gate on the rue des Gentilshommes did Louise pause to catch her breath.

# CHAPTER THIRTY-TWO

'Do you need anything?' asked the steward.

Gilles slowly raised his head.

'A glass of brandy, something to eat?'

Now he understood. 'No, no thank you.'

The steward glanced at the grate. 'I could lay a fire?'

Gilles felt panic rising in him. Nothing made any sense. 'I need nothing.' Deserve nothing, he added in his mind.

He did not understand what was happening. He had not told Madame Reydon-Joubert everything, but his tongue had run away with him: his impoverished childhood, his rough treatment at the hands of his mother, his uncle's quiet affection and kindness. Only one thing had he withheld, the reason his mother still had so firm a hold over him.

But she had seemed to understand the gaps between what he said and what he had not. She had not judged him, nor shown a pity he could not have borne, but rather listened with gentle detachment. Then she had left for the Hotel de Ville before eight o'clock and had not yet returned. He had put his trust in her and hoped he had been right to do so. He wasn't certain, how could he be? All he wanted was to be able to give his uncle the burial he deserved, and he believed she would help him do that.

From the Hôtel de Ville, Louise walked directly to the port, where the harbourmaster was expecting to witness the paperwork releasing Captain Janssen from his service.

In comfortable quarters on the first floor that smelled of leather and polish, the papers were laid out on the desk. Dated the eighth day of October in the year 1620, the document was ready to authorise the relinquishing of Janssen's command of the *Old Moon*.

*Is what I am about to do unwise? Dangerous, even?*

Louise hesitated on the threshold, still not sure if her plan was absurd. It was not in her nature to act hastily, irresponsibly, yet it seemed the only course of action that made sense. During the long night, her thoughts had crystallised. She could kill two birds with one stone. She could help protect the boy from his mother and, at the same time, find out if the letter from Chartres was genuine.

If it was, Louise would be deprived of her fortune. She would be reliant on Alis and Cornelia's support or, worse, her uncle's charity and his idiot of a wife. And how her aunt Bernarda would crow at how far she had fallen, and deem it the wages of sin. No, she had to do everything to protect her position and that began with finding out whether or not there was any substance to the claim that her father had a legitimate child.

Resolved, Louise walked into the room. 'Messieurs, good morning.'

The harbourmaster leapt to his feet. 'Madame Reydon-Joubert, you are most welcome. Please, make yourself comfortable.' He waved to the chair set in front of his desk and summoned the captain forward.

Janssen was looking rather the worse for wear. His gait as he entered the chamber suggested that the combination of last night's Pineau, brandy and, no doubt, rum in a tavern into the small hours, had not entirely left his blood.

'If I can again apologise, Madame Reydon-Joubert. It was a

wager. Roux promised that . . . that's to say . . .' His words petered out.

'You were paid to invite him,' she said, more a statement than a question. 'You admitted as much to me last evening.'

The old seafarer flushed brick red. 'I cannot apologise—'

'You were duped, captain, I am prepared to accept that.'

The old man sighed with relief. 'Too trusting, that's my—'

'The documents are ready to sign,' the harbourmaster interrupted, unsure what was being discussed.

Louise smiled. 'I regret I am going to try your patience a little.'

He leant forward. 'Is there a problem?'

'Not of your making, monsieur. Rather a change of plan, if Captain Janssen will indulge me.'

He blinked at her in confusion. 'Ma'am?'

'We had intended to moor the *Old Moon* here for the winter,' she began. 'Since her cargo was all intended for La Rochelle and cities on the western seaboard, there seemed no need to sail her back to Amsterdam. Any repairs that needed to be done, could be carried out here. She would be ready to re-join the rest of the Van Raay fleet when they sailed via La Rochelle in the spring.'

The harbourmaster nodded. 'That is correct.'

Louise turned to Captain Janssen. 'You intend to retire here in La Rochelle, do you not?'

The old man nodded. 'My wife is French, ma'am, and prefers the milder climate. I had thought to take on the running of a tavern.'

'A wise woman,' she said, drawing back to escape the stench of sour brandy on his breath. 'However, things have changed. Thanks to your report last evening, captain, I know the *Old Moon* is in good condition and could easily put to sea once more.'

'Yes, ma'am. They are careening the hull for barnacles and weed, but she is sound. A few minor running repairs to the rigging and sails are required, nothing more.'

Louise paused. 'This, messieurs, is the difficulty. As of last evening, I find that my presence is urgently required in Amsterdam. It will take some time to find another captain to take on the command. So, while we still have the crew – some of whom, I am certain, will welcome a few more coins in their pockets – I am asking, Captain Janssen, if you might, for appropriate renumeration, be prepared to keep your command for a little longer and sail the ship on back to Amsterdam?'

Janssen's bloodshot eyes bulged. 'I am not certain my wife will—'

Louise fixed him with a look. 'I am sure your wife is a sensible woman, captain. I know you have a growing family to provide for, and after last evening . . .'

Now understanding this was to be his penance for having brought Roux into her house, he simply nodded.

'I am in your debt, captain. I presume, with no cargo and only two passengers, you will not need a full crew?'

'No, ma'am. Provided my two lieutenants will stay on as watchmen.'

'Very well. If you call on me this afternoon – say, at three o'clock – I will provide you with the funds you need to secure your men's continuing service, and also to cover any costs you might incur in the coming days.'

'Very good, ma'am.'

The harbourmaster pulled the candle towards him and held the document to the flame. It burnt up quickly and he got up to drop it in the cold hearth.

'I also appreciate your understanding, monsieur,' Louise added. 'The port will lose the income for the winter mooring, but I would not wish you to be out of pocket. If you might suggest suitable recompense?'

'Most kind, Madame Reydon-Joubert.' He paused. 'Weather permitting, when would you sail?'

'Monday next.' She thought that would be time enough for her to get her affairs in order, to arrange Barenton's funeral and to persuade the boy to come with her. Louise stood up. 'If that is everything?'

'One final thing, madame,' the harbourmaster said, pulling the ledger towards him. 'You said two passengers would be joining the ship. Might I know the name of the person travelling with you?'

'Is that necessary?'

'We are obliged to keep close accounts of anyone who comes in and out of the harbour,' he explained hastily.

Louise hesitated, then nodded. 'Gilles Barenton.'

The harbourmaster looked up. 'The nephew of the wine merchant?'

'The same.'

He dropped his voice. 'There is a rumour that some misfortune has befallen Barenton.'

Louise despised gossip. She hated the way men's eyes lit up when they prepared to revel in someone else's tragedy under the guise of Christian concern. In her experience, they were worse than women. On the other hand, she needed the harbourmaster's continuing cooperation and all of La Rochelle would know of the murders soon enough.

She inclined her head. 'I regret to say that is true. He was killed last evening, shortly after leaving a banquet at my own house held in Captain Janssen's honour.'

'No!' The harbourmaster's eyes bulged. 'Did you know of this, Janssen?'

The old captain nodded. 'And one of Barenton's servants too, I heard.'

'I have this morning put the matter in the hands of *Prévôt* Arnaud. He, no doubt, will bring the perpetrator to justice.'

'Do they know who—'

'Good day, gentlemen.' Louise turned to quit the chamber. As she walked down the stairs, she heard Janssen scrape his chair closer to the desk and begin to tell his side of the sordid tale.

*Worse than women.*

# CHAPTER THIRTY-THREE

*Monday, 12 October*

On a mild and muggy morning five days later, the *Old Moon* was ready to sail. Since dawn, they had been waiting for the tide and the wind, and conditions were now as good as they could be this late in the season. With a light south-sou'westerly, and good visibility, they would tack through the clear stretch of shallow water up to the headland, into the open sea, then sail north.

By invitation, Louise waited in the captain's cabin at the stern of the vessel while preparations were underway. When she heard the instruction to weigh anchor, she came up on deck to properly take her leave of La Rochelle. In the height of the season, there might be as many as four vessels waiting for the tide. This late in the year, they were the only one. She looked and found Gilles beside the main mast, keeping out of the crew's way. She had been astonished to discover – during the conversations where she persuaded him to accompany her to Amsterdam – that, even though he had lived in La Rochelle for his entire life, he had never set foot on a boat, let alone a ship. Everything he knew of the sea was gleaned from the pages of the books in his uncle's library, or listening to the stories of the seafarers on the quay at dusk.

Glancing at him, Louise recognised a mixture of trepidation and anticipation in his expression. He seemed younger than his twenty years. Children in Amsterdam grew up surrounded by water, living beside the narrow canals and playing on the floating pontoons in the harbour. Even before she had been taken out into the IJ to visit the *Old Moon* for the first time, Louise couldn't remember a time when she hadn't felt part of the sea.

*At home.*

She still felt the same fluttering excitement beneath her ribs when she boarded one of Cornelia's ships. Each new voyage brought a moment of possibility, even one such as this from La Rochelle to Amsterdam that she had done as a distinguished passenger several times before. All being well, and with no interference from English privateers or storms, they should be in Amsterdam in eleven or twelve days' time.

'It is impressive, is it not?' she called.

'Yes, madame,' Gilles replied, edging closer to where she stood.

'The *Old Moon* is the first ship I ever set foot on. I was ten years old and was taken by my grandfather to see her anchored in the harbour of Amsterdam.'

Louise was pleased to see interest glint in his eyes.

'The ship is important to you.'

'Yes.' She hesitated. 'In point of fact, I own her. Very few people are aware of that.'

'It is a beautiful ship.'

It was another sign of the boy, she thought, that he made no comment about a woman owning such a vessel.

'She is.' Louise paused, then said: 'The sea can be rough in the Bay of Biscay. If we are unlucky, you must take to your berth until the worst is over. It may take time for you to get your sea legs.'

'Yes, madame,' he said politely, but she saw a little life had returned to his eyes.

Louise left him on deck. Having talked to her freely on the night of the murders, Gilles had barely spoken since. He was courteous and humbly grateful for her assistance, but grief had made him almost mute. She remembered how her grandfather had been the same after her grandmother's death, a ghost in the house. Gilles had retreated to somewhere inside himself, where his uncle was not dead and his mother could not hurt him.

*That, too, I understand.*

Of Roux, there had been no sign, though Arnaud had put out a warrant for his arrest. Louise had asked to be kept informed, without expecting him to respect her wishes. In truth, there was no reason why he should. Even though she had taken the boy under her wing, she was not a family member.

Gilles had agreed to come with her willingly enough. He did not seem to care what happened to him. She explained his presence to Janssen as her secretary and general factotum. He had an excellent hand and was quick-witted. When they arrived in Amsterdam, Louise was minded to see if Cornelia might find a position for him until his uncle's will was found – it had disappeared in the strongbox stolen by Roux. Until it was recovered, it was not clear what would happen to the business, nor to Gilles himself.

Captain Janssen was on the quarterdeck, shouting the final orders before departure, navigating a path through the narrow exit to the inner harbour. One rogue gust of wind and they could be blown off course onto the defensive wall. He gave the order to let go the berthing ropes and the sails. The few women and men watching from the quayside cheered and began to wave. Then, with a gentle lurch, the *Old Moon* began to sail. The Dutch flag fluttered at the stern, the green and gold ensign of the Van Raay fleet at the bow, and Louise's own private colours, a single emerald-green drop on a silver background, below. Snapping like pennants at a joust atop each of the three masts, was the red, white and blue of the VOC flag.

Louise felt her spirits soar.

'Go aft to the stern, starboard side; you will have a better view,' she called to Gilles. The look on his face reminded her that he didn't know what that meant. 'Starboard is the right-hand side, and larboard the left. The stern is the rear. A ship has its own language. It can be confusing at first, but you will learn soon enough.'

As the *Old Moon* slipped easily through the water, driven by the south-westerly wind, Louise pointed out the landmarks: the twin towers, the lighthouse, the Île de Ré. The sea was a deep green, purple in places, crested by white waves. From a distance, La Rochelle was shaped like a star of fortified stone, strong bastions linked by the defensive walls.

Louise wondered when she would return. When she glanced at Gilles, standing as still as a statue by the rail, she wondered if he was thinking the same thing.

The next day, the sun rose in a milky sky, and later set over an endless ocean.

Gilles had never felt such glorious isolation, surrounded on all sides by the dark, shifting ocean. Occasionally, in the far distance, he saw the welcoming beams of a lighthouse keeping a ship away from the rocks. Dusk to dawn, he watched the sky turn from royal blue to misted grey.

In the Bay of Biscay, the sailors told him, storms could whip up out of nowhere, especially when the wind blew from the south-east. There were perilous pockets of shallow water where a ship could run aground. Even seasoned sailors crossed themselves when they saw the clouds chasing in from the Atlantic.

Gilles started to distinguish the crew, one from the other, though he never spoke to them unless invited. It was a world that never slept. He learnt that this was a small crew because they had no cargo, though the ship had been ballasted to make sure it did not roll in rough seas. He was told how no one should approach the captain's cabin without invitation and that the biggest fear, aside from bad weather or a pirate attack, was fire. So, there were no lighted candles below deck without a safety case and no pipes without a cap. He discovered, in calm seas, there was often music and that the cook was a man to keep on the right side of. He learnt that Janssen was considered a good captain, though prone to bemoaning the size of his family when he was in his cups and telling tall tales about previous voyages. He learnt that the log line, stowed on the upper deck close to the cannon at the end of the waist of the ship, was the instrument for measuring their speed: a quadrant weighted at the bottom edge to enable it to float upright in the water, attached to a long rope. He examined the brass disc and marvelled at the wisdom of the ancients that had created such an instrument to calculate latitude so many thousands of years ago. He discovered, too, that it was very unusual for a woman to travel on board a ship such as this – bad luck, some thought it. All the same, they admired Madame Reydon-Joubert. A stomach as strong as any man, they told him. Finally, he realised that sailors were superstitious, each having his own tricks and talismans, prayers to Saint Nicolas or Saint Christophe, always looking out for signs and portents.

Gilles still felt he was in a dream, as if everything happening to him belonged to someone else. He was entranced by the endless motion of men and ship, the way in which every part of the vessel seemed to speak – creaking, lilting, moving, moaning, the rise and fall in the waves, bouncing and crashing against the swell. The ship had come alive. He stood with his knees partly braced, realising that if he embraced the motion of the vessel rather than fighting against it, he could survive on board. He listened to the whistles and tried to understand what each sound meant. He learnt that time was measured differently – eight bells, one for each half-hour of a four-hour watch, struck each time the hourglass was turned – and that there was always someone on watch, someone at the helm, someone trimming the sails. No hand was ever still.

The sea grew rough as they neared the English Channel, zig-zagging their way with the wind from astern. Huge rolling waves from the Atlantic, steep and unforgiving, set the ship bobbing like a cork. Waves broke across the waist of the main deck, making the wooden deck slippery and perilous.

Mostly, they left him alone with a cup of rum to settle his stomach; he took care to visit the front of the ship to do his personal business when no one else was there. And, when the sea was calm again, they allowed him to listen to their stories of shipwrecks and monsters of the deep, of ships deliberately lured too close to the rocks. Each man had a clay pipe of foul tobacco. Gilles tried it once, and coughed his guts out. They told him that tensions could run high on long voyages, when the weather was against you and the captain harsh. But most of the crew were Dutch, this was a home-coming, and there was no appetite for conflict.

The days went by quietly enough.

Somewhere out of sight, they passed the rocky coast of Brittany and Normandy as, blessed with a westerly wind, the *Old Moon* sailed homeward. Under the last queen of England, the sailors told him how these waters were infested with pirates and ships had been forced to route past Ireland and the north coast of Scotland, before sailing the length of the North Sea down towards Holland. These days, the channel was less dangerous.

Two days later, Gilles looked with awe as magnificent white

chalk cliffs appeared off the portside bow while they sailed through the channel's narrowest stretch. As they followed the flat coastline of the Spanish Netherlands, the wind grew stronger again. Violent waves hit the quarterdeck, setting the ship rolling and plunging in the water, and it was all hands on deck to reef the mainsail. Then, the wind dropped as quickly as it had come, and the voyage continued.

Each night, when the sky was covered with silver and white stars, Gilles returned to the hammock allotted to him in the sailor's quarters in the hold. There, lulled by the motion of the waves and comforted by the teeming life around him, he curled into a tiny ball, and slept. He had nothing of his own, except the clothes he stood up in and the Justice card tucked in the lining of his shoe. But for the first time since his uncle had died, he felt he might trust in providence and live.

He was free.

# PART THREE

AMSTERDAM
*November 1620–March 1621*

# CHAPTER THIRTY-FOUR

AMSTERDAM
*Sunday, 8 November 1620*

It was with relief that Louise walked through the heart of Amsterdam towards the house Cornelia and Alis shared. They had been out of town when the *Old Moon* docked – she had not been expected back until the spring. So, despite their mutual antipathy, Louise had been obliged to lodge with her aunt Bernarda and her husband Frans for the past fourteen days in the old family home on Zeedijk.

Bernarda had talked a great deal of her Christian duty and made a fuss, not least about Gilles and his position in her house. Was he a guest, an upper servant, or a poor relation? Respect for status and hierarchy were the rules by which Bernarda lived and ran the almshouse. Minou and Piet had established the *hofje* to care for the scores of displaced children – innocent victims of the wars in France and the Dutch Provinces – who found their way to Amsterdam. Refugees like them. It had been their way of expressing their gratitude to the city that had offered them sanctuary. These days, the children were clothed and fed, they were dutiful and obedient, but it seemed to Louise that there was less laughter in the *hofje* than in the old days.

Since Gilles did not speak Dutch, he was protected from Bernarda's tongue, though not her critical glances. To Louise, every hour dragged, and she felt her grandparents' absence in every room. But finally, a message had been received that morning saying that Cornelia and Alis were home and would be glad to see her this afternoon. Louise was hoping they would invite her to spend the rest of her time in Amsterdam with them.

A great deal had changed since she had last been in the city of her birth. She had spent only a handful of weeks here in the past ten years, choosing to settle instead in La Rochelle where there were no ghosts to haunt her. No troubling half-memories.

Amsterdam had expanded significantly both to the east and the west. Everything was on a grander scale. Three new grand canals to the west of Singel were in various stages of completion with magnificent gabled townhouses. The city's fortifications had been enhanced, the Stadhuis on Plaats renovated, and every church was full on Sunday with Calvinist burghers and their wives dropping heavy coins onto the offertory plate. There always had been a babel of languages and nationalities around the port itself and Louise, though she had not yet visited, had no doubts the rough quarters behind Sint Nicolaas still existed – the far end of Zeedijk was known as the 'rat's nest' for the number of pickpockets, rough taverns and brothels in its teeming streets. But bourgeois Amsterdam had come into her own.

Everywhere there were signs of the influence of the Dutch East India Company, voc, and evidence of the ways in which a modest, if ambitious, port – which had suffered much during the long wars against the Spanish – had transformed itself into a harbour to rival the finest in the world: hops, cheese, fish, beer, wine, cloth, soap, hemp, timber, nails, rope, in this great trading city anything could be bartered and sold. The grain ships of merchants trading with the Baltic and France sat beside the clippers and *fluyts* heading for the Islas Afortunadas, the Indian Ocean and Batavia. It was from the Shreierstoren, the weeper's tower, that Henry Hudson had set sail in the year 1609 to find a faster trading route to the East Indies and, instead, discovered a new world in the Americas.

Louise stopped to watch a knife-grinder working his stone, then continued on into Warmoesstraat itself. The red-brick merchant houses were some five storeys high, most with elegant neck gables and ornate pediments. Steps led up from street level to narrow front doors, with long leaded-glass windows to the side. Above each door, carved decorative tiles of painted plaster and gilt boasted the year of construction. In this city of traders and merchants, success had to be visible. Appearances mattered.

Louise stopped in front of the Van Raay house and glanced up. The tile set between the stone-arched windows showed a richly dressed man, standing in front of a cargo ship bearing the family ensign, grain slipping through his fingers into a basket. She pulled a face. Surely, by now, the tile should have been replaced by an image of a woman commanding a fleet? But, then, that would not have been in character. Cornelia disliked ostentation.

Louise walked up the steps, knocked and was admitted into the hall by a maid with raw, angry skin. She smiled. The old globe was still there, its surface a little more yellow. She ran her fingers over the wooden surround, looking at the *terra incognita* that entranced her as much now as it had when she was a child.

*Everything just as it always was.*

Then, the door of the salon opened and there was her great-aunt Alis throwing wide her arms. In her sixty-sixth year, she was a wiry woman with a mass of curls turned grey by the years held beneath a white bonnet. Her eyes were as bright as ever.

'*Lieveling*, how we've missed you! I am so sorry we were not here when you arrived.'

Louise let herself be buried in a hug. 'And I you.'

Cornelia appeared behind them. A slightly older woman, stout and sturdy, her face was a map of the years she had lived. Her heavy brows were white now, but her glare was still forthright, making it seem as if she was furious even when perfectly sanguine.

'Dear, dear Louise, come and sit by the fire. Has Bernarda been driving you to distraction?'

Louise laughed. 'You cannot imagine.'

In the way of old friends who have been apart for a while, the three women took a little while to settle. Dutch beer and pancakes were brought to the table, soused herring, welcome tastes of Amsterdam after the Pineau and oysters of La Rochelle. Though she was very aware of the letter from Chartres in her pocket, Louise felt the strain of the past few weeks fading away as they caught up on several months' worth of news. Over the summer, Cornelia had lost another ship, the *New Star*, in a storm off the Strait of Gibraltar. That had been a bitter financial blow and there were problems, too, with the levies she was obliged to pay to the VOC. Louise listened, sympathising and worried for Cornelia, whilst being conscious she was putting off sharing her own news. She did, however, tell them about the banquet she had held in La Rochelle for Captain Janssen, and what had followed.

'I can hardly believe it,' Alis said, when Louise had recounted the events of the night. 'That poor young man. And they have not caught this man, Roux?'

'They had not when we sailed.'

'And you have brought the boy with you, you say?' Cornelia asked, peering at her under her white brows. 'That is, how shall I say, surprising?'

Louise felt herself blush. 'His situation is unclear until his uncle's will is found. I couldn't leave him.'

Cornelia fixed her with a look. 'You could have. He is hardly your responsibility.'

'If you knew how his mother treated him. Even now, he goes in fear of her.'

'Bah!' Cornelia puffed out her cheeks. 'You would not have come without a good reason, I know that. But here is my question. Why are you here in Amsterdam?'

Louise held her gaze for a moment, then reached for her purse and handed across the letter. 'Because of this.'

After nearly two weeks at sea, Gilles had found it difficult to get used to being on dry land again. He'd felt a camaraderie with the sailors and crew, had felt accepted and safe. Now he was in yet another unfamiliar situation and, unable to understand the harsh Dutch language, he felt constantly ill at ease.

He suspected Madame Reydon-Joubert felt the same. There was clearly little love lost between her and her aunt – they were made from different clay. Bernarda Gerritsen was austere and judgemental, and seemed to take pleasure in pointing out everyone else's short-comings. Her husband Frans, a heavy bear of a man, was kind though he said little. In the evenings, he brought Gilles a quart of beer and sat with him on the porch smoking his pipe, content in the silence.

But Gilles liked the house itself, liked imagining Madame Reydon-Joubert growing up here. Four storeys high, it sat at the eastern end of Zeedijk, one of the original dykes of medieval Amsterdam that curved along the northern boundary of the city at the harbour. Most of all, he loved the small orchard at the back of the house, where the orphanage children played in the afternoons, and slept in an old converted stable block at night. Though Amsterdam was prosperous now, there were still Huguenot refugees fleeing persecution in France, and plenty of abandoned children with no homes or parents to care for them. Though he could not understand them, nor they him, they sensed he had some fellow feeling with them.

He tried to make himself useful.

'What?' Louise asked, seeing a look pass between Alis and Cornelia. 'I read all my grandmother's journals that summer after she died – after grandfather died. There was nothing in them to suggest my father had married and had another child. Nothing.'

'There wouldn't be.' Cornelia shook her head. 'Minou only heard of the rumour when she was in Paris.'

Louise was taken aback. 'When I went to sign the papers, *Gran'mère* knew?'

Cornelia nodded. 'When Minou was dying, she wrote to us. She said that your uncle had come to her the day before your twenty-fifth birthday, saying there were whisperings of a legitimate heir to the Evreux estate. One of the King's advisers had been in Chartres that spring, and had brought the story back to Paris. Jean-Jacques was intending to investigate, but obviously circumstances changed.'

Louise got to her feet. 'Why didn't she tell me?'

'I imagine because, when you went with your grandfather to the lawyer, there was no suggestion that your inheritance might be challenged. So they felt they could dismiss it as a baseless rumour.'

Louise paused, remembering how suddenly happy her grandfather had been that afternoon when they left the lawyer's office, and how relieved. Then, her grandparents laughing behind their bedroom door that night after her birthday dinner.

'Did you ever ask Jean-Jacques about it?'

'There was never a chance,' Alis replied. 'The murder of the

King kept him in Paris and, as Cornelia said, because the will was proved, I suspect he also felt it was a false alarm.'

'But that being so, why did *Gran'mère* mention it to you at all?'

'Minou was very sick, and that was a burden on her. Since there was nothing proven, she did not want to cause you distress,' Cornelia explained in her measured way. 'Don't be cross.'

'I'm not cross. But you should have told me before now, both of you. Jean-Jacques should have told me.' She brandished the letter. 'And now this.'

She picked up her glass and found it empty.

Louise waited while Cornelia rang the bell and the maid brought a second jug of beer, before continuing. 'In her notebooks, *Gran'mère* wrote that my mother always refused to say who my father was.'

'That is true,' Alis said. 'Then we all travelled to Chartres for the coronation of the old king in February of 1594, and Marta saw him there. It all came out.'

Cornelia nodded. 'Minou realised. Marta's behaviour and expression confirmed it. And your name – Louise, perhaps named for Louis?'

Louise frowned. She had never considered that before. 'Then what?'

'After that, Marta changed,' Alis said. 'She became obsessed with the idea that he – Louis – would find out about you and take you from her.'

'Could he have done that?'

Cornelia gave a dry laugh. 'Of course. As a man, the rights were all on his side. There was a further complication. Louis' father was an old adversary of Piet's. They were distant cousins, and there was a suggestion that some of Vidal's wealth might rightfully belong to your grandfather.'

'Yes. *Gran'mère* wrote about that too.'

Cornelia continued. 'For a while, it was all Minou and Piet talked about. But, in truth, we all thought it would be impossible to prove. It is hard to explain how it was in those times. Any papers that might have proved your grandfather's case would, more likely than not, have been lost in the Huguenot–Catholic wars.'

Louise put the letter carefully back on the table. 'And then?'

'And then,' Alis replied, 'he tracked Marta down.'

She exhaled. 'Do you think he knew about me before seeing us in the cathedral in Chartres? I presume that is where he saw us?'

'Yes. Marta saw him first, then he caught sight of her as the service was finishing.' Alis shrugged. 'But we never knew if he realised who you were.' *And that chance moment led to murder.*

Louise pushed the memory away, with the same nagging sense that there was some crucial part of the story missing.

'This letter,' she said. 'There are two things I do not understand. If there is any truth in the claim, then why wait so long? Even if there were rumours – my uncle heard them some ten years ago – this is a very, very long time after the event. Is it possible no one knew he had married?'

'Of course,' Alis said. 'But *he* would have known.'

'It is easy for the rich and powerful to keep their secrets,' Cornelia added.

'Or,' Alis continued, 'his wife was estranged from him, so he didn't know there was a child. Perhaps that is the reason for the stipulation you would only inherit when you were twenty-five years of age.'

Cornelia considered. 'Giving Louis time to find this possible legitimate descendant? That, too, could be an explanation.'

Louise shook her head. 'Are we truly prepared to countenance that, on *two* occasions, this man – my father – had a child of whom he was unaware? Or that a woman who was legally married to such a wealthy man, whatever the reasons for their estrangement, would not instantly have presented herself when she heard of my father's death?' Then she stopped, suddenly picturing her grandmother on that last morning in Carcassonne. She tried to remember the exact words Minou had used. She held up her finger. '*Gran'mère* left her final journal behind in Paris when we fled after the King's assassination, she told me so. Is it possible that she did write about the rumour of a legitimate heir – she was always honest in her journals – and someone found it?'

Alis nodded. 'And is now trying to make use of the information?'

'The same objection applies,' Cornelia said. 'Why wait so long? They would have used the information long before now. Neither solution explains the long gap in time.' She reached across the table and drew the letter towards her. 'This letter has the Evreux seal, but it is not signed. Louise?'

She realised she hadn't been listening. 'I'm sorry?'

'I said the letter is not signed. 'So, we have no idea if the letter has come from this supposed claimant or from someone else. A servant, or a representative, a lawyer.'

'Or someone hoping to make mischief,' said Alis.

Louise shrugged. 'Could be. The letter simply asks me to acknowledge receipt and agree to meet.'

Cornelia shook her head. 'That you should not do. Not until we know more.'

Silence fell over the chamber. Alis refilled their cups and lit the lamps, the weak November sun having long since faded from the sky.

'I may have a half-brother or a half-sister,' Louise said, then smiled at the shocked expressions on the older women's faces. 'Oh, yes, I have thought of that. And of what it would mean if the claim is true. I could lose all of my inheritance. All I would have left is the little my grandparents left to me.'

'I cannot believe it will come to that,' Alis said.

'It could. If they could prove their case.'

'Your grandmother's journals are here,' Cornelia said. 'Why not go back to them? There might be something you missed, now you are looking for clues.'

Louise thought this could be true. She had read them in the grieving months after her grandmother's death, watching her grandfather slowly slipping away.

*The price of love is too high.*

'They are not still in Zeedijk with Aunt Bernarda?'

Alis and Cornelia exchanged a glance. 'I think Minou felt they might be better in our safe-keeping,' Cornelia explained. 'Alis took possession of them and brought them here.'

'There are so many things of which my niece does not approve,' Alis added. 'What do you think, *lieveling*?'

Louise let her hands fall. 'That the letter is a hoax.'

'For the purpose of?'

'As you said, for cheating me out of what is rightfully mine.'

'But as *you* said, why wait so long?'

Louise put her thoughts in order. 'I think that someone close to the Evreux family – who, for some reason, had been prevented from speaking out – can now do so. I intend to reply and see what comes of it.'

'I do not think that wise,' Cornelia said quickly.

'What else can I do? If I just ignore the letter, it will always be there at the back of my mind.'

Cornelia nodded. 'Very well. I will arrange it.'

'Of course,' Alis added, 'there is another possibility. Perhaps someone else was there when your mother died, someone who overheard something.'

Louise turned cold, her thoughts racing with the idea of a new threat.

*Was it possible that, all those years ago on Kalverstraat, on the day her parents died, someone had seen her?*

# CHAPTER THIRTY-FIVE

'What is the meaning of this?'

Gilles scrambled to his feet. 'Mevrouw Gerritsen, *excusez-moi*.'

Bernarda's French was heavily accented, with sharp Dutch corners, but Gilles could not pretend he did not understand.

He looked at her moon-like face, her pale skin blotched red with rage, then to the Tarot card in her hand. And cursed himself for letting down his guard. He had only sat down for a moment on the terrace in Zeedijk in the pale November sunshine, after playing with the orphanage children. Madame Gerritsen and her husband had gone to church, for the second time that day. He must have fallen asleep. Now, here she was in front of him, holding the Justice card as if it was poison.

'I will not have such blasphemous material in my house. It is an affront to decency.'

'I meant no harm.'

She took a step towards him. 'This is not something that belongs in a Christian household.'

Gilles felt himself shrinking away from her. He had no position here, no place. Without Madame Reydon-Joubert, he was nothing.

'*Vrouwlief*, my dear, is something wrong?'

Frans Gerritsen, a gentle giant of a man who lived in the shadow of his wife's ill-humour, came out into the garden. Gilles didn't understand his words, but the look in his eyes was kind.

'This person,' she spat, switching to Dutch, 'has brought this abomination into our house.'

'Ah.' Frans gently took the Tarot card from his wife's hand. 'I am sure he meant no harm by it,' he said, in careful, simple French as he handed it back to Gilles. 'Keep this for yourself, you understand? Put it away where it is hidden.'

'*Oui, merci, monsieur*,' Gilles said, then attempted again to apologise to Madame Gerritsen. '*Het spijt me.* I am sorry.'

She looked at him with disgust, then walked away.

Frans dropped a friendly hand on his shoulder. 'She is a good woman,' he said sadly, then followed his wife into the house.

Gilles was left in the twilight of the garden, wondering what he should do. He was always in the way. When Madame Reydon-Joubert was there, he could write letters on her behalf, run errands and, though Amsterdam was not a city of wine, there were French traders to whom he had been useful. He had a knowledge that outstripped men twice his age. But when she was not here, Gilles was lost.

He returned the card to his shoe. Gilles wished he had the courage to ask what she intended for him, but he feared her answer. Of course, he was grateful she did not pry. Gilles was content in her service, as he had been content serving his uncle. She had saved him. But he dreamt of being back at sea. The nearly two weeks spent on the *Old Moon* as they had sailed from La Rochelle to Amsterdam he looked back on as the happiest of his life. The ship was a world unto itself, with its own laws, its own time, its own customs. He would not leave Madame Reydon-Joubert, who had shown him such kindness, but more than anything he wanted to accompany her on her next voyage.

'Your behaviour leaves much to be desired, Louise.'

Vexed by her husband taking the Dutch boy's part, Bernarda was looking to quarrel. Her niece had arrived back from

Warmoesstraat and appeared to have walked through the streets without a bonnet on the Sabbath. That gave her the excuse she needed.

'What will people think?' Bernarda needled. 'That you did not accompany me to church is bad enough, but that you show no regard for the customs of this house, that is another matter.'

Louise stared as if her aunt had lost her wits. 'Of course I wore my bonnet in the street. For my part, I resent the assumption that I do not know how to behave. Amsterdam is as much my home city, as it is yours.'

'*Vrouwlief*,' Frans said ineffectually, 'might I talk to you about the accounts?'

'The books will wait,' she snapped. 'You are a guest in this house, Niece. You would do well to remember that.'

'You forget, Aunt, that this is my house too.'

Bernarda gave a thin smile. 'And you forget that *my* mother and father left the house and the *hofje* to me.' She pointed a stubby finger at her niece's chest. 'You are here on sufferance.'

'My dear,' Frans muttered.

Louise laughed, her mismatched eyes shining with fury. 'That is at least something we are in agreement about.' She took a step closer, causing Bernarda to stumble back into the dresser. 'But you do not need to concern yourself further. Since my presence here is such a trial to you, I have pleasure in informing you I will be leaving. I had thought to wait until tomorrow, it being the Sabbath, but I think it best for everyone if I remove myself without delay.'

Frans bustled forward. 'Come, Louise, I am sure my wife did not mean for you to go. Did you, my dear? You are family. You are always welcome here.'

Louise smiled at Frans, whom she had always liked. He had

been one of the first children her grandparents had taken into the orphanage, and had never left.

'*Dank u*, but I will be spending the remainder of my time in Amsterdam with Alis and Cornelia. They extended the invitation this afternoon.'

Bernarda's face reddened. 'And I hope you will be taking that "servant" with you.'

The smile slipped from Louise's lips. She took another step closer and had pleasure in seeing a flash of alarm in her aunt's face.

'And what, pray, might you mean by that?'

Bernarda's eyes glinted with malice. 'It is not appropriate that you should have a male servant, and so young, to wait upon you. People are talking.'

Frans put his hand on Bernarda's arm. 'My dear, I beg you . . .'

She shrugged him away. 'This is not your business.'

'You say people are talking . . .' Louise said in a cold voice. 'And what kind of things are these people saying, *Tante*?'

She pronounced the word in French deliberately to rile her aunt, who had a violent hatred for anything that was not Dutch. She had particular contempt for the French, despite her mixed heritage, whom she considered decadent and immoral.

Fuelled by righteousness, Bernarda squared up to her niece. 'You know very well what I mean. You are an unmarried woman. You conduct yourself imprudently and here you are, in this decent Christian household, with a young man whose status is far from clear. How did he even come to be in your service? There is something strange about him. He creeps about like a cat. And as for the wickedness of bringing such an idolatrous image into a decent home, where innocent and impressionable children live, I can scarcely credit—'

'I have no idea what you are talking about.'

'Your aunt found him with a Tarot card,' Frans explained unhappily.

'He is unnatural,' Bernarda continued, her voice steadily rising. 'What say you to that?'

Louise refused to be provoked. 'What I say to that is that you, dear aunt, clearly have a mind like a sewer.'

Her aunt flew at her. 'How dare you!'

Frans stepped in between them. 'Ladies, please. Please.'

'Get out of my house!' Bernarda shouted, wisps of brown hair coming loose from beneath her white hood.

Louise laughed. 'There is nothing that would please me more. All I will say is that my grandparents would be distressed to see what you have done here. You have turned a place of light and warmth into something miserable. If that is your faith, then you can keep it. Pride is a sin and you, dear aunt, are guilty of it.' She gave a formal bow. 'Frans, thank you for your kindness. Aunt, I will be gone within the hour. Thank you for your Christian charity, but I will not call upon you again. Your reputation will not be further sullied.' She gave a wintry smile. 'I have no doubt that anyone in Amsterdam who has the misfortune to know you, will understand my decision.'

'Get out!' Bernarda shrieked, and Frans put his arms around her to prevent her laying an angry hand upon her niece.

Louise swept into the hall, more shaken by the encounter than she cared to admit. Too many things Bernarda had said gave her pause for thought. She almost collided with Gilles at the foot of the stairs, and felt herself flush.

'There you are,' she said, to hide her embarrassment. 'We are leaving immediately. Please pack my things, and your own.'

'*Oui, madame.*'

Louise watched him climb the stairs, tracking his footsteps across the floorboards above. She heard the sound of the drawers in her chamber opening and shutting. She knew Gilles could not have understood her aunt's accusations, but the tone had been clear. Had Bernarda spoken his name? She didn't think so.

She had grown accustomed to being the subject of gossip and speculation in La Rochelle, and had closed her ears to it. Her wealth protected her and it was not unusual for women in French households to have upper male servants. But Calvinist Amsterdam was different. There were many like her aunt who spent their lives sniffing out sin. Had she been naïve?

Louise took her cloak from the hook beside the door, something she had done a thousand times before, then realised she might never again set foot in her childhood home. Where all, bar one, of her memories of her mother existed: the secret corners where they had sat, the table at which they had eaten, the terrace where Marta told her stories of Paris and stroked her hair.

She heard a creak on the stairs. Gilles was coming down, carrying her wooden travelling chest in his arms. She seemed to see him as if for the first time. He was tall and broad, his face smooth, with bright, intelligent eyes. Her aunt's words were still ringing in her ears. He was the sort of young man who would grace any drawing room. Educated, courteous, knowledgeable. As he drew level, their eyes met and, for an instant, they looked at one another on equal terms. Then Gilles dropped his gaze, the perfect servant once more.

'Forgive me, madame, if I have been the cause of some estrangement.'

*So he did understand.*

'The fault is not yours,' Louise said, her voice sharp with an emotion that confused her. 'Come.'

Frans met them beside the door to the street, his lugubrious face speaking a silent apology. 'Your aunt means well. Give it time for her anger to blow over, she did not mean for you to leave.'

Louise smiled. 'Dear Frans. I will be with Alis and Cornelia if – and I think it unlikely – my aunt wishes to apologise. Thank you for your kindness.'

Louise walked with Gilles in silence through the chill November streets. At this moment, she was very aware of the small distance between them. Along the canals and over the narrow, curved bridges back towards Warmoesstraat. Several times, she was on the point of asking about the Tarot card, but held back. She did not want to pry.

'The card is a memento from my childhood,' he said, as if reading her mind. 'I am sorry to have offended Madame Gerritsen.'

Louise stopped. 'She is easily offended.'

'Card number eight. Justice,' Gilles said quietly. 'It is the only thing I have from the before times.' He paused. 'The picture reminds me of you.'

Louise felt the unspoken words shimmering in the air between them. Out of the blue, the story of how her grandparents had met for the first time came into her mind: February in Carcassonne, in the year 1562, the great ship of the cathedral of Saint-Nazaire rising out of the darkness. A Catholic girl hurrying home, a Huguenot boy fleeing through the foggy night, darting in and out of the alleyways of La Cité. It was why her grandfather had always called Minou his 'lady of the mists'.

Louise looked away, down into the inky waters of the canal. Grief swept through her, for those she had loved and lost. Longing, too, for the possibility of devotion like her grandfather and grandmother had shared. Despite everything they had endured, theirs had been a true love.

Suddenly, standing in the grey November light of the late afternoon, she wanted to ask this boy again what he meant and why a Tarot card was so important to him.

'Gilles, will you tell me—'

He raised his eyes, but she saw only the poised and dutiful secretary. Not a boy who shared his secrets. Disappointment washed through her. Servant and mistress for nigh on a month now, yet still he did not trust her.

# CHAPTER THIRTY-SIX

*Monday, 9 November*

Cornelia was as good as her word. At eleven o'clock the following morning, a messenger arrived at Warmoesstraat intended for Chartres.

'Thank you for arranging this, Cornelia,' Louise said.

'If you are sure this is the right thing?'

She nodded. 'If I do nothing, the uncertainty will stay with me. Every day, I will expect another petition.'

'Better to know,' Alis said.

'Better to know.'

'Though if you chose not to make contact, they would not know where to find you,' Cornelia explained. 'There is no reason anyone might be aware you are in Amsterdam, as the original communication was sent to La Rochelle.'

Louise laughed. 'There is the entire crew, and dear Captain Janssen. He is loyal to you – and to me – but has a loose tongue when he is in his cups, a condition I fancy is habitual with him.'

Cornelia nodded. 'I fear so.'

Louise's face fell. 'If there is a legitimate claim, I will lose all that I have,' she said, repeating the fear that had occupied her nights since the letter arrived. 'A child – a girl – born out of wedlock has few rights.'

Cornelia took her hand. 'It will not come to that,' she said firmly. 'We will not let it.'

Louise nodded, though she knew Cornelia could guarantee

no such thing. Her business was not exactly failing, but it was hard work to keep such a small fleet profitable. The loss of the *New Star* had been a blow, and Cornelia would struggle to support Louise as well as herself and Alis if the worst came to the worst. They all knew that.

*I would have to sell the* Old Moon.

'What do you intend to do this morning?' Alis asked, cutting into her reflections.

Her hand went to the locket. Though she loved her great-aunt and Cornelia, she did not want to tell them where she was going, for fear they would try to dissuade her. Their conversation yesterday afternoon had stirred up all the old emotions – and new fears besides. She could do nothing about the risk to her fortune. Assuming the messenger would arrive in Chartres by the end of the month and allowing for a response to be delivered back to her – if there was a response – Louise was bound to remain in Amsterdam at least until January. But she could put her mind at rest on the other matter.

'I shall continue to reacquaint myself with the city,' she said lightly. 'Much has changed – improved, dare I say – since last I was here.'

'To be fair, a great deal of that progress can be laid at the door of the voc,' Cornelia said. 'Since any resident is empowered to buy and sell shares in the company, there is a common purpose these days. Unlike our European rivals, wealth here is vested in the people not the crown. You should visit their headquarters on Kloveniersburgwal. Most impressive.'

Louise smiled. 'If one investor profits, all profit, that is clever.'

'Something like that. Having said that, the voc monopoly on trade in the Far East soon will come to an end. Then, we will see.'

'Do you think there will be significant changes to your licence? Captain Janssen certainly believes there will be.'

Cornelia snorted. 'Janssen is a fine seafarer, but he is not a diplomat. As I said, we will see. I would be grateful to talk to you about improvements to the fleet. The *Old Moon* is in excellent condition, so I was thinking she should return to the Islas Afortunadas in the spring, if you would be happy with that.'

'That would suit me well.' Louise paused. 'In point of fact, Cornelia, I wondered if I might sail with her.'

'To Las Palmas?'

Louise nodded. 'After all these years, I would see the island for myself. Provided, of course, the new captain will have me on board.'

'The new captain will do as he is told,' Cornelia said firmly. 'He can hardly refuse you passage on your own ship!'

'True, but I would rather he welcomed me willingly than under duress.'

'Then we must choose our man wisely. Now, let us talk about this boy you have rescued.'

'It was hardly that.' Louise flushed, cursing Bernarda for making her self-conscious about the relationship. 'He is very capable of looking after himself.'

Last evening over supper, she had explained the quarrel with her aunt, though she had turned the confrontation into something amusing. As she'd intended, Alis and Cornelia had put her high colour down to temper, not embarrassment.

'You may be right,' Cornelia said mildly. 'You know his value better than I.'

'In point of fact, I was wondering if there was some role Gilles could take within the company? He works hard, he is loyal and discreet, and his knowledge of wine is impressive. He might be put to good use while he is here in Amsterdam. He was taken in to his uncle's business when he was ten years of age, and received an excellent training. He has a steady hand, and can read. Though he has no Dutch, he has advised several French exporters in the city already.'

Aware she was talking too much, she tailed off.

Cornelia raised her eyebrows. 'Actually, I could make use of someone of his knowledge to advise our quartermaster. I do not think we are always striking the best bargains with our suppliers in the Islas Afortunadas. As for the language barrier, there are plenty of people who speak passable French in our offices. I cannot see that as being an insurmountable problem. Send him to see me this afternoon at the harbour. Three o'clock.'

Louise sighed with relief. 'Thank you, Cornelia, you won't regret it.'

At the top of the house in Warmoesstraat, Gilles looked around the attic room that was to be his for the next few weeks, perhaps more. Plain, clean, functional, he thankfully had his own chamber pot beneath his bed. His concern was the distance to the privy and access to any source of water. He had been lucky on the ship, but now he felt the familiar drag in his belly and knew that very soon he was going to have to find a way to keep his bleeding private and find somewhere to rinse his cotton cloths without being seen.

At his uncle's house, it had been just the two of them, plus the servants. Antoine, the boy of all work, and the cook, who rarely strayed from the larder or her kitchen except to visit her sickly daughter. But here he was constantly in the company of women and, though he knew that it was a monthly curse that afflicted young women rather than old – and Madame Reydon-Joubert's great-aunt and her friend were both of later years – they were observant. The kitchen servants were young girls, and already he felt they were looking at him with suspicion. He feared being exposed. If Madame Reydon-Joubert sent him back – or even threw him out on the streets – he did not know what he would do.

Gilles supposed his best course of action was to find a public laundry and manage his business there. In La Rochelle, there were several and both male and female servants made use of them for their masters and mistresses. But in Amsterdam, he did not have the language to ask.

He sat on his narrow wooden chair, then stood up again. He was not certain how he should occupy his time, but sitting in this chamber being idle was doing no good. He could hear his mother's voice in his head, jeering at him. Even now, so many leagues away, her voice still haunted him.

He went down the back stairs to the kitchen, thinking he might be able to make himself useful, in time to see Madame Reydon-Joubert take her cloak from the hook beside the door and open the front door. On an impulse, Gilles hurried out into the street, and followed.

At several times in her life, Louise had been homesick for Amsterdam and thought of it as home. Now she was back, she realised she felt differently. The child she had been, the young woman raised by her grandparents in the almshouse now owned by Bernarda, seemed little to do with her any more. Her brief sojourn in Paris and Carcassonne, her years in La Rochelle – looking out to sea and dreaming of distant lands – had all weakened her ties to the city of her birth. Oddly, the realisation gave her comfort. The idea of a fresh start, of not being defined by her family name or her heritage, appealed to her. She only hoped that there would be a prompt response from Chartres, so she would know once and for all where she stood.

Fleetingly, her thoughts went to Gilles.

*If I lose everything, will he still want to stay with me?*

Louise walked faster. She was resolved to sail to the Canary Islands in the spring, whatever the news from Chartres. Perhaps remain there for a while. In the sodden November air in the city of tears, as her grandmother had always called Amsterdam, the thought of blue skies and white sands gave her something to look forward to.

She walked along Warmoesstraat, through de Wallen and over the wide waters of Rokin into Plaats, where the Stadhuis stood proud in the smudged November sunshine, then left into Kalverstraat.

A long and narrow street, which led at the far end to the religious community of Begijnhof at the border with Singel, Kalverstraat had always been filled with artists' ateliers, print makers and map makers, booksellers and engravers. Though some of the facades were smarter now, with glass in their windows rather than wooden shutters folded down on chains, there was the same smell of peat and herring Louise remembered from her childhood. A street that represented both the best of merchant Amsterdam and the darker, poorer side that lurked beneath its prosperous surface.

Louise picked up her pace, a little nervous now. She paid no heed to the curious glances, or the children peering at her from behind their mothers' skirts, just kept walking until she reached her destination. At ground level was a cloth merchant, just as it had been all those years before. Bolts of material – black, blue, brown, little of colour – stood nose to tail against the panelled wall. Behind the glass, a small woman with swollen knuckles, the tip of her nose pink with the cold, was talking to another woman. A customer, or perhaps a relative? It was still early.

*The same woman as back then?*

Louise looked up at the windows on the first floor. She had not been inside this building for twenty-five years but, somehow, she still felt she could smell the blood and the violence, the rage. In her mind's eye, she could see that red handprint upon the white wall at the top of the stairs, the size of a child's hand.

# CHAPTER THIRTY-SEVEN

A coin changed hands. Within minutes, Louise was standing in the upstairs chamber. There was a smoking oil lamp in a sconce on the wall, otherwise the room was bare.

She had once been told that places where something of great trauma had happened held the memory of it – an echo of pain or loss or agony. But here, she sensed nothing.

Slowly, Louise turned around, fixing every corner of the chamber in her mind. Remembering. Everything seemed smaller, of course. There, between the windows, had been a chest of drawers with two candles burning. And over there, beside the door, a wooden settle with two embroidered cushions.

She crossed the room. Here there had been a screen painted with a version of the ubiquitous Cornelis Anthonisz map of Amsterdam. There was a print hanging above the fireplace of the family salon at Zeedijk, a gift from Cornelia's father to Piet and Minou when they had first settled in Amsterdam. It was why her ten-year-old self had recognised the image.

Slowly, Louise breathed out, relieved. Whatever else, she had answered the question that Alis had put in her mind yesterday afternoon. There was nowhere for anyone to hide. No hidden crevice or alcove, no recess. No one could have seen her, or overheard anything. She could put her mind at rest over that, at least.

But she was also aware she was poring over tiny details to avoid remembering the worst hour of her entire life. She did not want to fill in the missing moments. Trying not to remember her mother's brown hair, loose and matted with blood, her blue dress, the bodice unlaced, her petticoat and skirts pulled up above her knees. One foot bare, her slipper lying discarded. A knife on the floor. Trying not to remember her father, a white strip in his black hair, his doublet undone and his shirt untucked. Standing. Not speaking, not moving, just standing. Then something else. What else? A glimpse of something skittered across the surface of her mind, then was gone.

*So much blood.*

'Madame?'

Louise's hands flew to her chest. Alone with her ghosts, shifting presences so clear she might have reached out and touched them, she wasn't sure the voice was real. Then, the word repeated.

She spun round. 'Gilles!'

Still caught between her present and her past, she closed her eyes and held out her hand. He came towards her across the room. Louise felt him take her fingers in his. Such soft skin, she thought, the hands of a scribe or a scholar, not someone who worked for a living.

Now she allowed her eyes to open and saw his concern for her in his face. Before she had time to check herself, she was leaning forward and kissing him on the cheek. Then, lightly, on the lips. Louise had kissed a man once before, and been vaguely repulsed, though he had been kind enough. Bristles and a hint of Pineau on his breath. This time, it felt different. She did not know how. A sense, perhaps, of a conversation being completed.

'Oh,' she said in a whisper. Then, she stepped away. 'Did you follow me?'

'I saw you leave and I was worried about you – a place like this. Don't be angry.'

'I'm not angry.' Louise looked around the room again. 'This is where my father killed my mother,' she said, amazed that she sounded so calm. 'I was too late to stop him.'

She heard him catch his breath. 'I didn't know, I'm so sorry.'

'I was ten, almost eleven.' A strange laugh bubbled in her throat. 'No one else knows I was here. It seems you are the holder of my secrets, Gilles Barenton.'

He took both of her hands between his. 'It must have been terrible.' He hesitated, then asked: 'Is that why you rescued me?'

'I—' Louise stopped, struck that he used the same word as Cornelia, and didn't know how to answer. 'Is that how you see it?'

'I do.'

The silence between them filled with words unspoken. 'I was too late,' Louise said again. 'She was already dead.'

*Always too late.*

He paused. 'And did you find what you came here for today?'

Louise gave a light laugh. 'There are things I can't quite remember, but it is a beginning.'

For an endless moment, they stood in the empty room, matched for height and build. Louise had no idea what she was feeling, nor what she hoped might happen, only that time did not exist. She was not herself. Perhaps Gilles was not himself. He had not pulled away. They were no longer mistress and servant but something other. She kissed him again, this time lingering longer. She felt his arms go around her waist, pulling her to him. Louise had no idea how long they stood there, only that they fitted perfectly together. This time, it was Gilles who broke the spell.

'Madame, what do you want from me?'

Louise felt the world come crashing back. She was suddenly

cold, and she shivered. What *did* she want? From him, for herself?

'If I have offended you, I am sorry.'

He smiled. 'You haven't.'

She met his gaze. 'I am not myself today.'

'There is nothing to explain.' He paused. 'Aren't you going to ask what I want?'

Louise felt hysteria building in her chest. Nothing of this was appropriate, but yet it was the most natural conversation she had ever had.

'Tell me.'

Gilles held her gaze. 'Simply, to stay with you. And if you leave, for you to take me with you.'

Louise chose to misunderstand. 'I'm not leaving yet. We cannot sail until the spring. Besides, there are things that keep me here.'

'The letter from Chartres, I know.'

Her eyes widened. 'How do you know?'

'I heard Madame Alis and mevrouw Cornelia talking about it. The door was ajar.'

'You should not have listened.'

Another faint smile. 'How can I serve you if I do not know what I should pay attention to?'

'I see.'

For a few moments more, they stood opposite one another.

'We should return to Warmoesstraat,' she said calmly, in a voice that sounded nothing like hers. 'Cornelia would have you join her at the harbour this afternoon. She has a proposition for you.'

Gilles took a step back. 'That would be good. I would like to work while we are here.'

'We?' she said, in a voice that seemed to come from a long way away.

'I told you. I want to stay with you.'

Louise felt untethered, as if she might do anything. For good, or ill. Finally, she allowed herself to answer.

'I want that too,' she said quietly, taking his hand.

# CHAPTER THIRTY-EIGHT

Louise took a last look around the chamber, then they went down the narrow stairs in single file and out into the cold November morning. Though the sky was overcast, threatening rain, she thought everything seemed brighter, shimmering with possibility.

'Actually, before we return to the house,' she said, 'there is someone I would like you to meet.'

A few minutes later, they were standing beside a black door in Sint Luciensteeg, the small alleyway that led to the city's main orphanage. Unlike most of the other commercial premises around Kalverstraat, there was no display outside. No tile on the wall to indicate the owner's trade. It looked like a private house.

Louise knew she was crossing a boundary with every step she took. She had heard of women falling in love with their servants, and had not believed it. Why would any woman debase herself to offer her heart to a man in her service? To any man, indeed.

*This is different.*

Because of the way they had met, she told herself. With all etiquette swept aside by the violence of his uncle's death and her own subsequent actions, their relationship stood outside of the real world. Maybe that was it.

Gilles stood patiently beside her. She liked that about him, his stillness. It was the perfect counterbalance to her restless nature.

Louise lifted the star-shaped metal knocker and let it drop.

A single, heavy thud echoed through the quiet alley. A small grille slid back, and a pair of dark eyes peered out.

'*Ja?*'

'*Voor een tarotlegging,*' Louise said, gesturing to Gilles. '*Voor hem.*' A Tarot reading for my companion.

The old woman glanced at Gilles, then opened the door. A ribbon of light spilled out into the street.

'*Jouw naam?*'

'My name is of no importance.'

Another pause. '*Meekomen,*' the old woman finally said.

She showed them to a parlour on the right-hand side of a long, panelled corridor. The wooden shutters were closed, but two lamps revealed a necklace of stars hanging from the ceiling, spinning silver on gold thread. On the walls, rather than paintings of still lives that graced most drawing rooms in Amsterdam, an astrological chart and signs of the zodiac were displayed. A dark wooden box sat on the single square table, covered with a black cloth, with two ladder-backed chairs set either side. The scent of incense lingered. Louise had been here only once before, seeking answers about her mother's death, but she had never forgotten.

'What is this place?' Gilles asked, his eyes wide with wonder.

Louise smiled. 'Another place where the real world does not exist.'

'*Even geduld,*' the woman said. Wait here.

She shuffled away. Louise heard a door slam and, minutes later, a man walked into the room. He looked different from the last time she had seen him: thinner, but more prosperous. His light brown hair, cropped close to his head, was flecked with grey and he wore a long black robe with a soft white ruff in folds at his neck. He might have been any age between thirty and sixty. Beside her, she felt Gilles fall back.

*Trust me, Gilles. Believe in me.*

'Monsieur, thank you for seeing us without an appointment,' she said in French.

The man opened his hands. 'I am here when needed, madame. You come for yourself?'

'For my companion.'

Gilles glanced at her, and she could see he was wary.

'*Bonjour, monsieur*,' he said, bowing. 'You are welcome. Shall we begin?'

'Begin what, monsieur?'

The cartomancer smiled. 'Your reading. Is that not why you are here?'

Gilles frowned. 'I don't understand.'

Louise touched his arm. 'Since the Tarot card was the cause of the disagreement between you and my aunt Bernarda, I thought, perhaps, that this would be something you would welcome. If I am wrong, we can go.'

'How did you know?'

Louise paused, not sure she could answer. 'Wouldn't you like to hear what the future might hold?' She watched his face, his expression mired in indecision, but also curiosity.

'Would you?' he asked.

She hesitated, then nodded. 'Because it might mean a different story could be told.'

'And you might not have been too late.'

Louise caught her breath at how well he understood. 'Yes. But this is your choice.'

With a final glance to her for reassurance, Gilles went towards the chair. The cartomancer stepped forward.

'Madame, if you might sit over there. The usual rates apply.'

Louise withdrew to a settle beneath the shuttered window as the men sat down on opposite sides of the table. The cartomancer opened the teak box and took from it a deck of cards. Wrapped in black silk, he revealed them, yellow with age and their edges smudged.

The cartomancer invited Gilles to cut the deck and spread the red and white-backed cards, vivid on the silk.

'We will undertake a four-card reading.' He looked across at Louise, then back to his customer. 'I think that will best suit your purpose.'

'Pick a card . . .' Gilles murmured under his breath.

His mouth was dry. The cartomancer was nothing like the person he had seen on the quay at La Rochelle all those years ago. That man had been a performer, a *bateleur*. This man was as austere as a Dominican priest.

His emotions were in turmoil after what had happened with Madame Reydon-Joubert – with Louise, as he might now allow himself to think of her. He wanted to hear his future, but feared it, too. He feared being exposed, or being told something he did not want to hear. But he also felt poised for adventure as if, for the second time in his life, he might let down his guard. Nothing was as it had been. For one brief hour, on this day in November, the usual rules did not apply. Louise had made that happen, and he adored her for it.

'May I draw any card?'

The cartomancer swept his hand over the brightly coloured fan on the table.

'The choice is yours, gentilhomme. There are twenty-two cards here in the major arcana – *arcana* is Latin for secrets – numbered one to twenty-one. *Le Mat*, the Fool, is unnumbered. The other fifty-six cards are the minor arcana and divided into suits – cups, coins, batons, swords. Each suit has an association. Swords, for example, are the suit of air, appropriate for this city where our wealth is built on the power of the wind. They represent fire, the suit of energy and conflict, again significant in a city where the fires of conflict have burnt for so long. Cups are associated with water and emotion, again most fitting in the city of tears. And coins make up the suit of earth. In each, there is a king, a queen, a knight and a page.'

The cartomancer gathered the cards, then handed the deck to Gilles to shuffle. 'A word of warning. The cards are only a guide to what *may* happen, not what will happen.'

Gilles remembered the *bateleur* saying much the same. As he reordered the pack, he felt as if he was floating. 'There,' he said.

'Now, put the cards back together – the middle section first, then the top, then the bottom,' the cartomancer instructed. 'The first card you will draw is called the significator, the card that represents you, the querent, the person you are this day with a question to which you need an answer. The sex on the card is not important. Each card carries with it archetypal feminine or masculine qualities and characteristics. Do you understand?'

'Yes,' Gilles replied softly. Had he not lived the last ten years of his life in-between? He understood better than the cartomancer could possibly know.

'Then, please, draw a card.'

Gilles pulled a card from the end of the deck and laid it face up.

The cartomancer peered. 'The *valet d'épées*. The page of swords, the suit of air, if you remember. A powerful card, though often someone not fully connected to others. Perhaps because of his youth, or perhaps for some other reason. It can represent someone at the beginning of a journey.'

Gilles studied the image of a young man, a sword in his hand. He appeared reflective, not a fighter.

'What does it mean?'

'It is unequivocally a card of strength and goodness,' the cartomancer replied. 'One of the few sword cards to be so. Draw again, and put this next card beside the *valet*. This will describe your circumstances as they are now.'

With nervous fingers, Gilles slid another card from the deck and placed it on the table.

The cartomancer smiled. '*Dix de coupes*, the ten of cups. Ten is the number of completion, marking the end of one cycle of life. But that supposes the beginning of another, does it not? Might you be on a threshold, gentilhomme?'

'I cannot say,' Gilles replied hesitantly, conscious of Louise sitting behind him.

'It suggests change is to come,' the cartomancer said, his ruff bobbing at his neck. 'Whether this might be good, or bad, is up to you.'

'I see,' Gilles said, though he wasn't sure he understood anything.

'Draw again, and place this next card below and to the right of the significator. This will indicate the obstacles in your way, the people or the circumstances that might prevent you from moving on.'

Gilles drew nervously, and heat flooded through him. Card VI, an image of a young man between two women, Cupid above about to fire his arrow.

'*L'Amoureux*, the lover,' the cartomancer intoned, in his same steady voice. 'You will note that the lover wears the same red shoes as *le Mat*, the Fool, suggesting perhaps youth and inexperience. Some of my brethren believe that the two female figures represent the past and the future, the mother and the lover-to-be, but I –' he paused – 'I incline to the reading that each figure represents the possibility of love within ourselves.'

'But it is upside down. Should I turn it around?'

The cartomancer shook his head. 'No. When reversed, it might suggest that there is a foolishness in hoping for love. Or, that there is a distance that cannot be breached between the lover and the object of his affection. A complication that is insurmountable.'

Behind him, Gilles heard Louise catch her breath.

'But you said the cards say what *might* be, not what *will* be.'

'That is correct. The cards give guidance only. Your destiny is in your own hands, and subject to the Lord's will.'

Gilles swallowed a laugh. God had looked away every time his mother hit him. Everything he had, good and ill, came not from Heaven but from people on this earth: his mother, his uncle, now Louise. She had rescued him, saved him, whether she acknowledged that or not.

'The final card will indicate your future, gentilhomme. It will indicate something you are about to discover, a shifting between past and present, drawing everything together. Do you want to know?'

Before Gilles had even turned the card over, he had a sudden premonition of what he was going to see. He laid it carefully in position on the cloth.

'*La Justice*,' he said. This time he could not stop himself from turning round. For a moment, their eyes met, and he was sure Louise was also thinking of how he had compared the image on his own stolen card to her.

'Card VIII. It is a powerful card,' the cartomancer told him. 'It might indicate you will be called upon to right some ancient wrong, or that you are being exhorted to keep a balanced view – that you should take care not to be led astray. It could be that you have suffered a great injustice and the time will come for that to be rectified.' He paused. 'But set with these others,' he indicated the cross of cards on the table, 'I confess it is hard to be sure. There is something hidden within you that refuses to reveal itself to me.'

Gilles was aware of his mistress behind him. He knew she would be sitting with her hands upon her lap. He knew she would be staring straight ahead with her extraordinary mismatched eyes, one blue and one brown. He knew she would not speak until he did.

For a moment longer, he stared at the vivid images and saw his life laid bare. Shimmering with possibility and challenge, and also with the wrongs done to him. They were exhorting him to be powerful and determined. Past and present and future, all there in a single moment revealed by the cards on the table. A mirror to his heart.

Then, the light seemed to fade and he was back in the same room in Amsterdam, a servant living a dishonest life.

Gilles put his hands on the table. 'Monsieur, I am in your debt,' he said quietly. He turned. 'Madame Reydon-Joubert, this is a gift beyond anything I deserve.'

Louise retraced her steps along Kalverstraat. She did not trust herself to speak to Gilles. There was both everything, and nothing, to say: *le valet d'épées*, the ten of cups, air and water, the Lover and Justice, the very card Gilles had brought with him from La Rochelle. What did it all mean? Her thoughts were spiralling round and round in her head, leading her nowhere.

*And yet . . .*

What was Gilles thinking? Had the reading disturbed him? Had the fact that she had put him in such a position distressed him? The impulse that had driven her to kiss him, then to take him to Sint Luciensteeg, had faded, leaving her feeling foolish. Wrong-footed.

Louise did not know what to do. For a few hours today,

everything had felt possible. She had felt lighter, more herself. Had she had ruined everything?

Her thoughts spiralled. The fault was hers. She had taken them out of the real world and now they had to return to a routine of duty and society, not stars and possibility. Though she had always said she cared nothing for her reputation, it was not entirely true. Her wealth protected her, but that might soon be gone. And Gilles had no such defence. Bernarda's words were still sharp under her skin, and didn't she owe it to Alis and Cornelia not to allow any breath of scandal to attach itself to them?

*What had she done?*

They arrived back in Warmoesstraat as the bells of the Nieuwe Kerk began to ring for midday. Louise was astonished to realise so little time had passed. She hesitated on the top step.

'Gilles, what happened between us today, what *I* did today, it was a mistake. I acted wrongly. We should never talk of it.'

She wanted him to argue, to plead his case, but of course he took his lead from her.

'Whatever you wish, madame,' he said, and Louise was filled with a crushing sense of loss.

'We should leave here at half past two in order to be at the harbour at three o'clock.' She paused, then allowed herself to say: 'Thank you for looking after me.'

Finally, he smiled. 'It was my pleasure.'

She went inside, leaving Gilles to walk through the yard to the kitchen. Louise removed her cloak, and spun the globe in the hall, watching the colours shift and turn. Her words had been dishonest. Whatever she had said, they couldn't go back. Though they might never speak of what had transpired between them on this November day, she would not forget.

# CHAPTER THIRTY-NINE

November passed slowly. Louise's emotions gradually settled. What she felt for Gilles was affection, but not love. At least, that is what she told herself.

She managed to find a new equilibrium so that she was comfortable in his company, whilst taking care never to be alone with him. Louise felt, somehow, she had compromised him, taken advantage of her power over him, and resolved that the intimacy in the house in Kalverstraat was never to be repeated. Only when she was alone, lying in her bed at night, did she permit herself to remember the touch of his hand and the card, *l'Amoureux*, he had drawn.

'*A distance that cannot be breached between the lover and the object of his affection.*'

All the same, her spirits lifted whenever she caught sight of him unexpectedly in the house. Each time she did, she smiled, and he smiled, too. Several times, Louise was on the point of asking if he had returned to the cartomancer in the Sint Luciensteeg, but caution stayed her tongue. He had become a valued member of the household. She didn't want to jeopardise that.

Her parents were much in her mind, too. She asked herself the questions she had never thought to ask before. Why had her mother gone to Kalverstraat to meet her father? Another realisation came to her – Marta had put on her best dress, so what did that mean? Did she love Louis? Had she ever loved him? Had she feared him? Why was she there at all?

November faded into December. On the eve of the feast day of Sint Nicolaas, children thronged the streets with their voices and their joy. They placed clogs outside their doors to be filled with gifts and the streets were thick with the aroma of roasting chestnuts and sweet biscuits. Every pew was taken in the Nieuwe Kerk and the congregation had to arrive early at Zuiderkerk to secure a good position.

Sint Nicolaas was followed by the Feast of the Nativity, followed by the tipping of the year, then Twelfth Night on the sixth day of January. Cornelia and Alis called upon Bernarda and Frans with greetings of the season. Louise stayed home in Warmoesstraat.

Still, there was no word from Chartres. Louise spent the mornings in good works, visiting the poor with sisters from Begijnhof, as her grandmother had done before her. The afternoons, she spent with her great-aunt, or with Minou's journals spread out around her. When she had first read the notebooks, grieving for the loss of her grandmother and witness to her grandfather's sad and rapid decline, she had done so to feel close to the people she had loved. Now, ten years later, Louise was searching for clues. She understood how devastating it must have been for her grandparents to discover that the father of their granddaughter was the son of a man who had attempted to destroy their family many times over.

'He had killed before,' she said to Cornelia and Alis, when she joined them for dinner one night. 'He killed his own father. A man who has murdered once, will surely do so again.'

Minou's last journal had been with her in Paris, then left there in the wake of their abrupt departure for Carcassonne. Louise didn't know what had happened to it after that. There were gaps. After Marta's murder, the journal was silent. But there was nothing in their pages to suggest Louis had married and fathered another child. It was not proof, but she was conscious the knot in her chest was loosening a little.

The days passed.

February saw a resumption in local coastal trade as the ice melted and canals started to fill with smaller barges and lighters. Then one late afternoon, when the lights were lit, and snow was in the air, Cornelia took her aside.

'Forgive me for speaking plainly, but you should take care with Gilles. If not on your own account, on his.'

Louise frowned. 'Has something happened? Is his work not satisfactory?'

'His work is excellent. It is not that.' Cornelia put her hand on Louise's arm. 'The boy loves you.'

Shocked, Louise tried to pull away. 'Nonsense!'

'You know it is true. There is a great difference between you – in age, in status, in position – but if you have an affection for him, that need not matter. However, you must be certain of your feelings, *lieveling*. If you want him to sail with you on the *Old Moon*, be careful. He has everything to lose and I would not have the ship set on its heels.'

'Cornelia, I give you my word there is nothing.'

The older woman did not smile. 'You will be confined at sea, Louise, you know how things are. There is more to that young man than meets the eye. Do nothing you will regret, that is all I am counselling.'

Louise was about to argue, then she changed her mind. 'I understand.'

By early March, the first signs of spring were in the air. The bitter damp and cold of the winter were replaced by a mildness that shimmered over the waterways. Green shoots appeared on the trees that lined the new grand canals.

The new season was scheduled to begin in the third week of the month, weather conditions permitting, and the boatyards were busy. Louise's thoughts turned to her voyage to Las Islas Afortunadas. She felt she had survived the winter, that her life had settled again and that she was the mistress of her emotions. She put everything else from her mind and focused on practical things. Though she was still restless, she was hopeful.

Cornelia was known to be a fair employer, and one who paid promptly, so there was no shortage of candidates for the position of captain of the *Old Moon*. On Cornelia's urging, they chose an up-and-coming young man, the son of a powerful family from Leiden who brought investment into the Van Raay fleet.

At the same time, there was much talk about a new trading consortium, the Dutch West India company, the GWC. The chatter in the Stadhuis and the VOC offices was loud and forceful. Not only that, the Twelve Years' Truce signed between the Dutch Republic and Spain to suspend hostilities and protect colonial trade was soon to expire, and VOC and Dutch ships were arming once more.

In common with the other owners, Cornelia was concerned for the security of her fleet and their crews when the truce came to its end, and a succession of meetings was held as the burghers of Amsterdam debated how best to protect their trading routes. Cornelia had no plans to extend her trade beyond the Islas Afortunadas, had no desire to sail to the Caribbean or the new colony at the mouth of the Hudson River, nor to engage with the highly profitable, but abhorrent, trade in human beings. This put her out of step with most other members of the VOC. Louise thought she was right. It was an affront to Christianity that women, men and children should be sold like cargo.

Working with Cornelia gave Louise a pretext to visit the office in the harbour. Gilles was always there. She didn't forget Cornelia's warning, but she was pleased he was so highly thought of. Having been trained in a city of wine makers, here in Amsterdam, where beer not wine was the everyday drink, his expertise was valued. In a matter of months, he had gone from advising only Cornelia's quartermaster to other members of the VOC, too. Though Gilles struggled to learn more than a handful of Dutch words, his character and willingness to learn made him popular. He had become the young man his uncle had trained him to be, and Louise could not help but be proud of him.

Life went on.

# CHAPTER FORTY

*Thursday, 18 March 1621*

'Ah, you're back,' Alis said, waiting in the hall.

Louise removed her gloves and cloak. 'Is something wrong?'

Alis pushed her grey curls back from her face. 'Not so much something, as someone. A person. I put her in the parlour.'

Used to the subtleties of Dutch society, Louise understood the visitor was not someone her great-aunt considered likely to be a friend or an equal.

'She did not give her name?'

'She declined to do so, awaiting your arrival.'

Louise's heart contracted. She had replied to the letter concerning her inheritance in November and had been impatient for a response. But as the winter had passed with no word, she had stopped expecting a reply.

'Has she come from Chartres?'

The older woman shrugged. 'She is French, but she did not say. Only that she would speak with you in private. Would you like me to come with you?'

'No, it's all right. I will see her alone.'

Alis patted her arm. 'I hope it is the news you want, *lieveling*. I will be here if you need me.'

Louise paused to check her reflection in the looking glass. She thought she looked pale, the brown velvet of her bodice stealing the colour from her cheeks. No matter.

As she entered the parlour, her first impression of her visitor was of colour and frills, too much for the modest panelled room. An ample woman with coarse features, wearing a cartwheel ruff and cuffs, wide sleeves showing a yellow gown beneath, and a long waistcoat with a fur trim. She gave the impression she was wearing her entire wardrobe at the same time.

'Good afternoon, Madame . . .?' She left the question hanging.

The woman gave a half-curtsey. 'Madame Roux, if it pleases you.'

Louise was certain she had never set eyes on the woman, but her features were somehow familiar. The name, too.

'Have you come from Chartres, Madame Roux?'

'Chartres?' Confusion flashed across the woman's mottled face. 'No, I come from the same part of the world as you.'

Louise frowned. There were plenty of French Huguenots in the city, mostly in Jordaan, but she had never heard of the Roux family.

'You are from Amsterdam?'

'La Rochelle,' Madame Roux said. 'Your departure was the talk of the town. So late in the year to be sailing.'

Louise felt a trickle of dread run down her spine. Now she remembered the name. 'What might I do for you, Madame Roux?'

'It is rather more a matter of what we might be able to do for one another,' the woman said, with a look that spoke of dishonest bargains struck. 'Here is the situation. I regret to say that I find myself in a position of some financial distress. My husband was a violent man, Madame Reydon-Joubert. He brutalised me.'

'I am sorry to hear that.'

'He's gone now,' she added, 'and good riddance to him. Left me with nothing but debts. Hanged at the last quarter.' She paused. 'Arrested on information received.'

Louise kept her expression neutral. 'As I said, I am sorry. But I fail to see what business this is of mine.'

'No?' The widow grimaced. 'Let me explain myself better. I am fortunate to have a son. He was a good boy, and I always did my best for him, but he turned against me. My own brother took his affection from me.' She fluttered her hands. 'But family is family. I feel sure my boy would wish to support his poor mother, if he knew of the misfortune that had befallen her.'

Louise caught her breath. No doubt, now, that this was Gilles' mother – the woman who had bullied and abused him during the early years of his life. She was also complicit in the death of Achilles Barenton, even if she had not wielded the knife. Louise took a step forward, and was pleased to see alarm spark in the older woman's eyes.

'I know what you are, and what your husband did. If he is hanged, you should have been hanged with him. I should have you arrested.'

'Ah, but you won't.'

Louise stopped, unnerved by the woman's confidence. 'What is it you want?'

'My brother had no wife or child. Wanting only the best for my son, and at great personal cost to myself, I gave him up so he would have a chance in life. The light of my life, he was. But how could I stand in the way of his advancement? My brother promised he would inherit the business and keep it in the family. The shop lies empty because my brother's will cannot be found. I am his closest living relative.' Her eyes glinted. 'I accept my son does not want to see me. If, however, he might be encouraged to hand over the business to me, then I cannot think that I would ever have to call on him again. Once would pay for all.'

Louise struggled to remain civil. 'Are you attempting to blackmail your son, Madame Roux?'

'Just trying to be helpful, Madame Reydon-Joubert.'

Louise's thoughts were spiralling. Gilles was certain his uncle's will had been in the strongbox stolen from Barenton et Fils on the night of the murder. Had it favoured him, it would have provided Gilles with a trade and income for life. He would no longer have to be a servant in someone else's house. She had to assume that Roux, and now this creature, had it.

'You have travelled a long way to have this conversation, Madame Roux,' she said coldly.

The woman smiled unpleasantly. 'In sensitive matters, it is always wiser to discuss matters in person, don't you think?'

'You are intimating you might lay your hands upon this will? How do I know you are telling the truth?'

Her eyes sparked. 'When you return, with my son, to La Rochelle, I will show you. Or, he can write a letter now handing the business over to me, negating the will.'

Louise gave a sharp laugh. 'I am at a loss as to why you think Gilles would hand over control of your brother's estate to you. He has worked for it, earned it. And you, Madame Roux, are an accessory to the act of violence that ended your brother's life.'

'You have no proof of that.'

'It is what Gilles told me.'

The widow narrowed her eyes. 'What makes you so certain that his version of events is the true one? He was there, too. He had everything to gain after all.'

Louise held her gaze. 'He is honest. I trust him.'

The woman let out a shriek of laughter. 'Honest you say!'

*Why is she so sure of her ground?*

'What do you mean by that?'

Madame Roux pulled a kerchief from her cuff and dabbed her face.

'Why don't you ask him? Or perhaps it would be best if I put my proposition to him myself?'

'He is not at home,' Louise said quickly.

'At work, is he?' Madame Roux pulled a face. 'Well, perhaps I should go and find him. Down at the harbour, will he be? Quite a valued member of the Van Raay company, so I have heard.' She placed her hand on her heart. 'I could not be prouder of my boy.'

*Has she been watching us?*

'I strongly advise you to put my proposition to him, Madame Reydon-Joubert,' the widow continued, her voice hardening. 'You will find he will see things my way.'

'I am certain he will not,' Louise said, ringing the bell to bring the interview to an end. 'There is no reason why he should.'

'Let's wait and see. You do not know my child as well as you think.'

'When I have spoken to him, where can I find you?'

'I have lodgings on Rokin. If I do not hear from you by Friday, I will return here to receive his answer. *A bientôt.*'

Louise remained standing in the parlour until she heard the maid close the front door. Then, she sank down on the wooden settle and waited for her heart to stop racing. She had watched Gilles becoming less and less anxious the longer they had been away from La Rochelle. He had come out of his mother's shadow and learnt to forgive himself for his uncle's death.

*Almost forgiven himself.*

Louise knew guilt was a powerful thing. Could she keep the news of his mother's arrival from him? The woman was here and Louise had no doubt she would make good on her threat to seek out Gilles at the harbour and confront him if Louise did not get her an answer. And even if she could persuade

Madame Roux to leave, having got what she wanted, Gilles would always fear she would return.

And why was the woman so confident that Gilles would agree to her terms? Round and round she went, trying to work out if there was some way she could spare him, some way she could keep his mother away, at the same time wondering what hold the woman had over him. But she always arrived back at the same conclusion.

In the hall, the clock began to spin and whirr before striking. She glanced towards it. Gilles would be at the harbour now. Best to do it there, rather than wait until he returned home this evening.

She had to tell him the truth.

# CHAPTER FORTY-ONE

Gilles nodded a welcome to the watchman as he walked along the quay, then into the offices of the Van Raay shipping line. The long corridor was half panelled and oil paintings of each of Cornelia's ships hung on the plain wall above the wood. Tied to two of the frames was a small black ribbon to honour the vessels that had been lost: the *White Dove* to Barbary corsairs in 1610; and the *New Star* sunk the last season in a storm off the Strait of Gibraltar with the loss of all hands.

He could still not believe his good fortune. In five months, he had become a respected and valued member of the company. Gilles had no pretensions, he did not think himself better than the common sailors, and showed no signs of wishing to rise above his station. He knew everyone found his attempts to speak Dutch amusing and, though he never joined his companions to drink in In't Aepjen or visit the doxies in the houses behind the Oude Kerk, they put that down to his youth.

'*Goedemorgen,*' he said, as he walked to his narrow, tall desk in the office. The word sounded heavy in his mouth, but he persisted. He had learnt to say 'mevrouw' rather than 'madame', 'meneer' rather than 'monsieur'. Last evening, he had asked Madame Reydon-Joubert to teach him a new phrase.

'*Het is een mooie dag,*' he attempted. 'It is a nice day.'

'Nice enough, I suppose,' the clerk replied, dabbing his handkerchief to his nose and sniffing.

Gilles took the lid from his inkwell, wiped the nib of his quill with a cloth, then opened the ledger. Mevrouw Van Raay had provided him with new clothes, a plain doublet and white collar, black breeches and stockings, a black felt hat. Apart from his lack of a beard, Gilles looked like any other Dutch secretary who worked in the office, and a sharp contrast to the men who went to sea with calloused hands and weather-beaten faces, their skin the colour of worn leather.

The full crew for the voyage of the *Old Moon* to Gran Canaria had now been engaged. A young captain from Leiden, Hendrik Joost, was taking his first command. Joost was rather too pleased with himself, Gilles thought, and was rude to the staff in the office when no one else was there to witness it. Gilles was not supposed to know, but he was aware Joost's father had made a significant investment in the company. He could only hope the son would prove worthy of Cornelia's trust and be a good and fair captain for the ship.

The first lieutenant, Jan Roord, originally from Antwerp, was of an old Catholic family. He was quiet, with an expression of permanent bewilderment on his face. A second lieutenant, Joris Bleeker, suffered with pock-marked skin from a childhood illness. Gilles particularly liked the boatswain, a short squat man by the name of Dirk Jansz. He had grown up in Zeedijk and his father had served mevrouw Van Raay as a steward. There were six other crew members, including a cook and a cabin boy. With him and Louise, that made twelve in all.

Over the winter, Gilles had studied hard. He had learnt about the vineyards of the Islas Afortunadas, and how the vines were ungrafted and ran in horizontal rows close to the ground. How the soil was contrasting on different islands, some volcanic with beaches of black sand, some soft like the land around La Rochelle. How they produced wine from bananas – a strange pendulous yellow fruit that grew in clumps like fingers in tall trees – as well as from grapes. Most of all, he learnt that, although the islands were under Spanish dominion, the islanders' allegiance was to an older history, not to the conquerors who had raped their lands for the benefit of Madrid and Castille.

His hard work had paid off. A week ago, it had been formally agreed that he would accompany Madame Reydon-Joubert when the *Old Moon* sailed next week from Amsterdam to Gran Canaria, then back via La Rochelle to Amsterdam. It was a voyage the reliable *fluyt* had done many times before.

Gilles now knew the *Old Moon*, like all *fluyts* designed for shallow Dutch waters, was flat-bottomed. She sailed beautifully on a calm sea, but in rough waters she struggled not to be pushed sideways. It meant that the sailing time varied enormously depending on the direction of the wind.

Every man was praying for clement weather, no one more so than Gilles. He wanted nothing more than to acquit himself well and justify Louise's faith in him. And, of course, he was concerned about how he would keep his nature hidden in the confined quarters of the ship. He had learnt how to be private and had to pray that he would be able to manage on board. He could not let fear of what could happen stop him living his life. Had the cartomancer not told him that he was at the beginning of a journey when he drew the *valet d'épées*, the page of swords? Had he also not drawn the *dix de coupes*, the ten of cups, a card marking the end of one cycle of life and the beginning of another?

Card number VI, *l'Amoureux*, he pushed from his mind. The case was hopeless, after all. He did not know if Louise thought of him as he often thought of her, and Gilles accepted that there could be nothing between them, but he loved her with all his heart. It was enough to be at her side and serve her.

In just under a week, they would sail. There was a great deal to do before that. He knew mevrouw Van Raay was concerned with the changes proposed by the voc, and the charges associated with it. Foreign currencies were flooding the market, the costs of timber and taxes were rising, and the company's finances were far from secure.

Gilles' practised eye scanned the first document on the desk, a bill of lading from a wool merchant's cargo out of Rotterdam. He dipped his pen in his inkwell, and began to write.

# CHAPTER FORTY-TWO

Louise looked around the panelled room, noticing the familiar, acrid, scent of wood and tar.

'Gilles, might I speak with you?'

She hadn't meant to startle him, but he dropped his quill.

He leapt up. 'Madame Reydon-Joubert!'

Louise looked at the blot of ink, and remembered how the magistrate had dropped his quill when she had gone to report the murder at the Hôtel de Ville, spoiling his papers.

'Is something wrong?' he asked.

Mindful of the promise she had made to Cornelia, Louise had taken care in the past weeks never to put herself or Gilles in a compromising position. Now, however, she closed the door.

'Madame, has something happened? Is there a reply from Chartres?'

She almost laughed. The threat to her inheritance had been hanging over her for five months, except the longer nothing happened, the less pressing the matter had come to feel. Only the thought of losing the *Old Moon* concerned her.

'No,' she replied. 'No letter yet.'

'Then what?'

'Will you sit down?'

He came out cautiously from behind his desk. 'Is it mevrouw Van Raay? Madame Alis?'

'They are both fine. Please, Gilles. Sit.'

Although she had rehearsed what she was going to say, she

found she didn't know how to begin. She looked at him, waiting patiently for her to speak. He was always so still. She took a deep breath.

'Gilles, a few hours ago, I learnt that Roux – the man who murdered your uncle – was caught and hanged in La Rochelle last quarter.'

He did not move, but Louise noticed his fist clench in his lap. 'I thought you would like to know.'

'Yes, thank you.' He exhaled. 'This is good news, but how have you come by this information? Did *Prévôt* Arnaud write, as promised?'

'He did not trouble to inform me.'

'Then how?'

She looked down at her hands in her lap, dreading the words she had to speak.

'Louise?' he said again, forgetting himself enough to use her given name.

'Gilles, your mother is here. In Amsterdam.'

The colour drained from his face.

'She arrived without an appointment at Warmoesstraat, asking for me. Alis admitted her and I spoke to her.'

'I am sorry,' he murmured.

'Don't be,' she said, wanting desperately to comfort him. 'It is not your fault.'

Gilles clenched his hands. Louise could see his knuckles were white. With fear, or with anger, she wasn't sure.

'What did she want?'

'The woman seems to think that you should hand over control of your uncle's business to her. Her proposition, if one might call it that, is that since your uncle's will is missing, and she is his next of kin, it should come to her anyway.'

'I see.'

'It may be, though, that she has the document and it favours you.'

Louise was watching Gilles for a sign of what he was thinking, but he had withdrawn into himself. A wave of sadness overcame her. A few words were all it had taken to return him to the terrified boy he'd been when they had first met. How had she thought that a mere five months in Amsterdam could mend everything that had gone before?

'Let her have what she wants,' he said in a flat voice.

'Gilles, no! You cannot let her do this,' she said fiercely. 'As an accessory to your uncle's murder, she can have no claim, regardless of what it might say in your uncle's will. We can expose her. I will help you, I—'

'I don't care.'

'Why?' Louise cried. 'You cannot let her win. She has no power over you, not unless you give it to her. You have friends, you have all this,' she swept her hand, taking in the room. 'You have me.'

Something between a cry and a sob slipped from Gilles' lips. 'I don't deserve anything.'

'Hush,' she said, forgetting all her previous resolutions and taking his hand. 'I will send her away. Have her arrested. We will fight for you to have what your uncle intended you to have. Your mother has no case.'

He exhaled. 'Ah, but she does.'

Louise felt a shiver run down her spine. 'What do you mean?'

Gilles looked up at her. 'That day in Sint Luciensteeg?'

Louise didn't understand. 'Yes—'

'The third card, *l'Amoureux*. You remember?'

Her heart began to thud. 'I do.'

'But it was reversed. Which suggested, so the cartomancer said, that there was a distance between the lover and the object of his affection that cannot be breached. A complication that is insurmountable.'

Louise held his gaze. 'He also said the cards prophesied only what *might* be, not what *will* be.'

Gilles sighed. 'I cannot keep lying, not to you.'

'Lying? Gilles, I don't understand.'

Gently, he placed her hand on his chest. 'I was born the same as you,' he said quietly. 'I bleed, like you. I have wanted to tell you, every day since you took me in, but I feared you would send me away.'

The instant he said it, Louise realised she had always known. No, that wasn't true. What she had known was that there was something different about him, something other: his lightness in the world, his unblemished skin; the sense that, when she looked at him, she was looking at herself in a mirror.

*Ten is the number of completion.*

'This is the hold your mother has over you?' she said, in a voice so faint that it seemed to echo from underwater.

Gilles nodded. 'My twin brother died when we were ten. She did not want to lose the chance of my uncle's estate, so—'

'— so, she exchanged him for you,' Louise finished his sentence.

'Yes.'

*Gentleness and strength, the page of swords.*

She thought a moment. 'Did your uncle know?'

He shook his head. 'Except for my mother, no one knows. Perhaps she told Roux.'

'And now me,' she murmured though, as she said it, she wondered if Cornelia had suspected. Several times, she had noticed the older woman looking at Gilles as if trying to understand something.

'And now you,' he echoed. 'So, you see, I can't win against her.' He fell silent, then added: 'If you want me to go, I will.'

Louise felt weightless, as if the world had come untethered and it was up to her to put it back together again. Nothing made sense, and yet everything was somehow as clear as crystal.

'We all have secrets,' she said quietly, putting her arm around his waist and drawing him to her. 'Together, we will work out what to do for the best.'

# CHAPTER FORTY-THREE

Within the hour, as the bells were ringing for four o'clock, Louise was standing in Plaats.

'Here,' she said, pressing a coin into the boy's hand, 'and there will be another when you bring me the information I want.'

The child gave a cheeky salute, shoved his cap back on his head, then vanished into the crowds behind the Stadhuis. Louise began to walk slowly around the square, feigning interest in the merchants selling wax-coated rounds of *boerenkaas* from farms in the flat countryside surrounding Amsterdam, or the sweet latticed pie filled with custard known as *vlaai*. Though Louise enquired as to price and quality, as if she was any other middle-aged Dutch housewife looking for a bargain in the market, her basket remained empty.

She'd had to work hard to persuade him but, in the end, Gilles had agreed that she should at least try to negotiate with his mother on his behalf. He would never be rid of her else. But first, Louise had to find out where the woman was lodging. She didn't want to risk her coming back to Warmoesstraat or, worse, hunting Gilles down at the harbour.

Just as Louise was beginning her third circuit of Plaats, the boy reappeared. She watched him stop, jigging from foot to foot until he saw her, then he ran over.

'I found her, mevrouw,' he said, his face pink with success. Louise looked down at him. 'Tell me.'

'A woman like you described – foreign, fat – took a room in a boarding house near the flower market.'

'There are plenty of foreigners in Amsterdam.'

The boy sniggered. 'Like you said, la-di-dah, lots of frills. Everyone knew who I meant, airs and graces, but no class. Not Dutch.'

'Where, precisely?'

'A wooden house at the end of Rokin by the bridge. A tile with a beer glass over the door, you can't miss it.'

She handed him the second coin. 'Not a word to anyone.'

Without showing any signs of haste, Louise crossed Plaats and walked slowly down Rokin. The Amstel was busy, flotillas of barges and tiny boats ferrying goods and people up and down the river. The boy was right, the boarding house was easy to identify. From its position in the street, she doubted if there was a rear entrance. Though the door stood open now, she suspected it would be locked at dusk. This neighbourhood would be less than safe at night.

She crossed the street and went inside.

The hall was empty and opened into a mean-spirited corridor with tallow candles in wooden sconces on the wall. The smell of herring and human waste was overpowering. Yet Louise knew that, on the scale of things, there would be few better affordable lodgings available in the heart of the city. Everything in Amsterdam came at a price and the constant flow of travellers and merchants meant that in the spring, just before the sailing season began again in earnest, boarding houses could get away with charging whatever they liked.

There was no one about, so Louise began to check every room. Knocking on doors, peering through cracks into each dismal chamber. Most were empty, a single cot, a nightstand, a piss pot and a chair.

*What if she's not here?*

The thought of Gilles kept her going. He needed the situation resolved. Louise hoped to be able to come to some kind of agreement with the woman, even though she had initially counselled against it. It was what Gilles wanted – for his mother to go away and leave him alone, nothing more. She paused.

*Is Gilles still 'him'? Should I still think of him as a man?*

Louise pushed the question from her mind. There would be time enough.

On the first floor, a door stood open. Inside a dark chamber, with the shutter half closed, a man was snoring on the floor, propped up against the bed. His hand was still clasped round his tankard, dripping beer onto his breeches.

Up on the second floor Louise finally found the room she was looking for. As she carefully pushed the door wide, the hinges creaked and Madame Roux's head shot up. She was sitting at the table peeling an apple. Louise was entranced by the coil of peel, falling to the floor, the scrape of the knife.

The woman laughed. 'Here so soon? I thought so. You have an answer for me?'

Louise closed the door behind her, placing her basket carefully on the floor.

'I would like to discuss your proposal.'

'There is nothing to discuss. It is a simple yes or no. Does my *son* agree to my terms?'

Louise heard her stress on the word.

'If you think to shock me, you are mistaken. Gilles has told me everything,' she said coldly. 'Why you think you have such a hold over him, I do not know. You were the perpetrator of the deceit, Madame Roux, no one could blame him. He was only a child; he had no choice.'

If Louise had thought to shame the woman, she was wrong. Madame Roux did falter, but only for a moment, then continued cutting the apple into pieces.

'But he is not a child now. And you know, as well as do I, that his true nature is not something he wants known. Deceit is seamed into his soul. He is unnatural, an invert. What would people think if they knew you had taken such an abomination into your house? Or allowed such a creature on board a ship? What would your aunt say? Mevrouw Gerritsen is so very devout, is she not?'

Louise felt sick at the thought the woman might take it into her head to visit Bernarda in the almshouse on Zeedijk, too.

'So did you put my proposal to him, Madame Reydon-Joubert, or not?'

The words stuck in her craw, but Louise forced herself to answer.

'Gilles wants nothing more than for you to leave him alone. Against my advice, he is prepared to accede to your terms, provided you give him a written guarantee that you will never approach him again and that you admit your part – both in the deception and in your brother's murder.' She stepped forward. 'And you are to give me the will.'

The woman's eyes darted to her nightstand.

'So you can destroy it? I don't think so. That's my insurance policy. It's all very simple. My daughter, with the intent to defraud her uncle, masqueraded as a boy.'

Louise struggled to keep her temper. 'If you do not produce the will, I cannot agree to your terms.'

The widow laughed. 'Then we are at a stalemate. But I guarantee you will regret what happens next.'

Louise hesitated only for a moment, then rushed for the nightstand. The woman roared with anger and flew at her, knife in hand. Louise was desperately trying to open the drawer, but felt herself being dragged back by her hair. She lashed out, sending her attacker stumbling back against the bed and falling forward with what sounded like a whoosh of air.

Louise spun round, her hands raised ready to defend herself, but Madame Roux was now kneeling on the ground clutching her hands to her belly. She had fallen on her own knife. Horrified, Louise could see the hilt buried in Madame Roux's stomach, and a haze of red seeping into the woman's skirts. Was this her fault? She froze in disbelief, looking wildly from left to right, as if someone might come and tell her this was all a nightmare. Except now Gilles' mother was slipping sideways, her eyes wide with surprise.

'May God damn you.' She tried to say more, but the words died on her lips. 'You will—'

*So much blood.*

And now Louise was back in another room. Looking down at another knife, a blade in her child's hand. Looking up at the man with a white streak in his hair. And, finally, the picture was complete. She could see herself thrusting the blade into his belly, a glimpse of pale skin between the open folds of his shirt. Remembered the same look of surprise in his eyes, the same dead weight as he dropped to his knees, as if the air had been taken from him, then collapsing onto the floor beside her mother's body. A memory Louise had pushed to the very back of her mind, forgotten for most of her life.

*I have killed before.*

The realisation hit her like a wave crashing on the shore. How vividly she remembered the sound of the knife in Kalverstraat dropping from her hands, as if it was nothing to do with her. How the metal caught the light as it fell, twisting, turning. Reaching down and unclasping her mother's locket from her neck, before running from the chamber. A single red child's handprint on the white-washed wall the only evidence she had been there.

Louise started to shake. A memory held in her muscles, in her bones, in her blood, suppressed for twenty-five years. She was ice cold, breathless with shock. Hours might have passed, minutes, she could not have said. She could hardly breathe. A weight was pressing down on her chest, the violent thudding of her heart as if her ribs might break.

She wasn't sure how long she stood there. Little by little, the roaring in Louise's head started to subside. The dismal room came back into focus. This was Rokin, not Kalverstraat. She was not a child any more. She forced herself to look at the blood pooling on the floor. She knew instantly there was nothing she could do for Madame Roux. She had been defending herself, but the woman lay dead all the same. She was appalled to feel no pity.

Then, her instinct for survival took over.

She couldn't run the risk of being found here. And she had to protect Gilles. Quickly, Louise turned back to the nightstand. The legal parchment was, thankfully, inside. She scanned it, satisfying herself it was Achilles Barenton's will naming his nephew as his heir, then put it in her pocket. Trying to avoid Madame Roux's dead eyes, she scoured the room to see if there was any other evidence that might connect the scene to her, to Gilles, or to the house on Warmoesstraat. She found nothing.

Already, the colour was fading from Madame Roux's cheeks. Louise didn't want to touch her, but she crouched down and felt inside her pockets. Tucked inside a cheap pocket book, she found a bill of passage dated early December, giving Madame Roux permission to travel from France into the Dutch Republic. She must have changed coaches many times to have made the journey overland. Louise had to hope that no one would remember one middle-aged woman among so many.

Taking deep breaths to try and calm herself, Louise scattered a few coins on the floor to give the impression of a robbery, and disarranged the bedding. There was a drab travelling cloak on a hook on the back of the door. Louise took it to cover the specks of blood on the hem of her own skirts. Then, with a final glance around the room, she picked up her basket, and left.

On Rokin, the lamps were being lit, setting flickering light dancing in the waterways and canals. As Louise hurried home to Warmoesstraat, her thoughts kept pace with her quick steps.

She had sought only to defend herself, but an insidious voice in her head was telling her something else. She had killed before. How had she hidden that truth from herself all of these years? She was repelled, sickened. From her grandmother's journals, Louise knew she was the daughter of a murderer, the grand-daughter of a murderer, too.

*Is a murderer born or is she made?*

Louise looked down. She had been careful, but there was a streak of blood on her gloves, too. Quickly, she pulled them from her hands and flung them into the canal as if that act could cleanse her.

*I have killed before.*

The further she went from Rokin, the less certain Louise became that she had not overlooked anything. Her nerves were as taut as wire. Was it guilt, or conscience? Several times, she had to prevent herself from turning back. What if someone had seen her entering or leaving the boarding house? What if the messenger boy told someone he had been paid to find the lodging of a Frenchwoman, or a neighbour had seen them together on Plaats?

*How will I live with this?*

Louise forced herself to stop. Her hands were still trembling. She took a deep breath, then another, to steady her tell-tale heart. All she could hope was that when the body was found, today or tomorrow or the day after, there would be nothing to connect a disreputable French woman robbed of her savings in a boarding house in Amsterdam to one of the city's wealthiest families. She had done everything she could.

But what was she going to tell Gilles? What would she say to Cornelia and Alis, if anything at all?

*I have put myself beyond God's grace.*

As Louise crossed Plaats in the twilight, she knew her grandmother would have known what to do. Minou would have prayed for Louise's immortal soul. But as she stood outside the house, gathering her courage, Louise thought her mother would have understood.

# CHAPTER FORTY-FOUR

The clock was chiming six as she entered the hall. She was still trembling, shaking with cold. Any chance of keeping her own counsel was impossible.

'What is wrong?' Alis asked instantly.

Louise opened her mouth, but no words came.

'Is that Louise?' Cornelia out called from the salon. 'I would talk with her.'

She felt Alis's hands on her shoulders. 'You are as white as a ghost. What has happened?'

Louise shook her head. She tried to untie the stolen cloak, but her fingers wouldn't obey. Alis reached up and, without a word, slipped the clasp, dropped it onto a chair, then she undid Louise's own cloak beneath, too.

'You are bleeding?' she said quietly. 'Are you hurt?'

'It's not my blood.'

She felt Alis stiffen beside her. 'Come into the warm.'

Feeling as if she was in a trance, Louise allowed Alis to steer her into the salon and onto a chair. She felt the two older women exchange a glance over her head, saw Alis gesture to the sideboard. A moment later, Louise felt a glass being pressed into her hand. Brandy, she thought, though she could not drink it.

'Now,' Cornelia said. 'What is it?'

'I . . .' She swallowed hard. 'Is Gilles here?'

Another glance passed between Alis and Cornelia.

'I believe he arrived home a little while ago,' Alis replied.

Louise looked at her. 'Will you fetch him? This concerns him also, this . . . please, will you?'

Cornelia nodded.

Louise remained silent, counting the minutes it might take for Alis to go to the kitchen, send a servant to the top floor, and for Gilles to come down and join them. She knew Cornelia was watching her, but she couldn't meet her eye.

Alis returned. A few more long minutes passed, then Louise heard Gilles' footsteps on the stairs. Now he was standing in the doorway, looking as if he had dressed hurriedly. Even in the depths of her torment, she noticed that one of his cuffs was caught inside the sleeve, and his collar was unfastened.

'Come in, Gilles,' said Cornelia.

Louise found she could not look at him either. 'There has been an accident,' she said simply, and felt the tension in the room tighten another notch. 'I should explain.'

'What kind of accident?' asked Cornelia.

Louise raised her head. 'I killed someone. A woman.'

She saw Alis's hands fly to her mouth, the expression of disbelief on Cornelia's face. And what of Gilles? She was terrified of what she might see in his eyes.

*The daughter of a murderer, the granddaughter of a murderer.*

'It was an accident. I did not mean for it to happen.'

Gilles did not hesitate. Paying no heed to what Alis or Cornelia might think, he crossed the room, knelt down at her feet and took her hands in his.

'Thank you,' he whispered.

An hour had passed.

In the plainest terms, Louise told them what had happened, from the moment she walked into the boarding house to negotiate with Gilles' mother to the moment she threw her gloves into the canal. The only thing she did not tell them was Gilles' secret – that was his to share, or not – nor what she had remembered. A red handprint on a white wall. How could she? Fortunately, Cornelia and Alis were more concerned with protecting her from the consequences of her actions than interrogating the reasons for them.

'You say you left no evidence you had been there?' Cornelia said.

'I cannot be sure, but I was careful.'

Alis ran her fingers through her hair, setting her grey curls standing on end. 'Madame Roux came here. Someone might have seen her.'

Louise nodded. 'And she mentioned Bernarda and Zeedijk, so she may well have called there too.'

'The truth is we cannot know who, if anyone, knew she was in Amsterdam,' Cornelia said, then turned to Gilles. 'Nor her relation to you, young man.'

After his moment of indiscretion, he had said nothing more and had removed himself to a place by the window.

'Gilles?' Louise prompted.

'I think it is simple,' he said eventually. 'A crime was committed on my account. I must take responsibility. You, Madame Reydon-Joubert, have given me everything.' He turned to Cornelia and Alis. 'You welcomed me into your home. You gave me the opportunity to learn and work and . . .'

He faltered, his face betraying his anguish. Louise couldn't bear it.

'Gilles,' she began, but he kept talking.

'My mother's body will be found.' He paused. 'You may think I am unnatural, but I cannot grieve that she is dead. She was—' He swallowed. 'That is of no matter now. She will have gathered her evidence before coming here. Someone will have seen her in Warmoesstraat, someone will remember her.' He turned to Louise. 'When it is announced a body has been found in Rokin, do you not think the boy will remember the lady in Plaats who offered him two cents for information? So, as I say, it is simple. I will go to the authorities and confess to her murder. I cannot let you, any of you, suffer on my account.'

'No!' Louise cried. 'It was an accident. If I tell them that—'

Gilles shook his head. 'It is the only way,' he repeated.

Louise stood up to go to him, but he stepped away and she sank back defeated in her chair.

'It is the only way. A crime has been committed. Someone has to pay.'

'I will not let you do this,' Louise shouted.

Cornelia had been watching the exchange between them. 'Your words do you credit, Gilles. However, there is an alternative.' She held up one finger. 'It is to be understood that I do not condone taking justice into one's own hands – it is only God who dispenses, not those of us who walk this earth for our brief lives – but this woman has clearly been the cause of much wickedness in the world. She came here for the purpose of blackmail and her own behaviour led directly to her death.' She fixed Louise with a stare. 'This is how it happened, yes?'

Louise felt a sliver of hope. 'I give you my word, Cornelia, yes. The paring knife was in her hands. When I tried to take the will from the nightstand, she came for me. I was only trying to defend myself when she fell on the knife—'

'Enough, then.'

Louise leant forward in her chair. 'What are you suggesting?'

'As Gilles said, it is simple. My proposal is that the *Old Moon* must sail tomorrow. Four days early.'

Louise understood immediately. 'So, we will have left Amsterdam before anyone has time to make a connection between Madame Roux and my looking for her. Or her visit to this house.'

'Exactly so.'

Louise turned, and saw the same spark of hope in Gilles' face, too.

'Can the ship be ready, young man?'

'Provided Captain Joost is available, then yes. The crew is ready to sail.'

Cornelia waved her hand. 'Then go, now. Put things in motion.'

'And if anyone asks why the sailing has been brought forward, what should I say, mevrouw Van Raay?'

For the first time, Cornelia smiled. 'Tell them that it is on my orders. That is all.'

*Could it be this simple?*

Louise stood up as if to follow. She desperately wanted to talk to Gilles, to reassure him she had the will.

Cornelia's clear voice held her back. 'Leave him be. And Alis, if you will excuse us?'

Alis looked surprised, but she nodded. 'Of course.'

Cornelia got slowly to her feet and held out her hand to take Louise's arm. 'We will talk on our way.'

'Where are we going?'

'To the Oude Kerk. What you did today, *lieveling*, will leave a stain on your soul. I can help you here on earth, but you must find a way to make your peace with Heaven for what you did.' She caught her breath. 'Come.'

# CHAPTER FORTY-FIVE

*Friday, 19 March*

Louise and Gilles were standing with Cornelia and Alis on the quay, waiting to be taken out on the rowing boat to the *Old Moon*.

Every moment since Louise had confessed to what she'd done had been filled with activity: frantic packing, orders sent and received, the urgent stocking of the ship for its six-week voyage to Las Palmas with provisions had occupied the hours. Louise, alone, had done nothing. Having returned from the Oude Kerk – where she had wept for the child she had been and for the forgotten crime committed so long in the past – she had sat, numb and in shock, in the drawing room, as if in the still eye of a storm with the hurricane blowing around her. She did not regret the death of Madame Roux, nor her part in it, but her conscience would not let her be.

*I murdered my father.*

It would take a lifetime to come to terms with that. A decades-old secret buried, even from herself, for most of her life. Louise had not slept at all, and doubted if anyone else had either.

But this morning, she felt resolved. If there had been any gossip about a foreigner found stabbed in a boarding house on Rokin, it had not so far reached Warmoesstraat. All the same, Louise was nervous and could see the same strain in Alis's and Cornelia's eyes, too. None of them would breathe easy until the *Old Moon* had sailed out of Dutch waters.

Gilles was pale, but seemed calm as he supervised the loading of her wooden travelling chest and her leather bag containing personal items, medicines and clothes onto the *boot*. They had still not been left alone together, but there would be time enough on the voyage.

Louise kissed Alis, then turned to Cornelia. 'I don't know how to repay you.'

'I promised Minou I would look after you,' she replied gruffly, then put her hand on Louise's elbow and steered her out of earshot. 'You remember what I said before.'

Louise did not pretend to misunderstand. She nodded.

'Gilles loves you, you know that. He would do anything for you. Especially now. You cannot marry, of course, but you will be six weeks or so at sea. Do not do anything that you will regret when the ship docks in Las Palmas, nor set the captain against you. Joost is . . .' She tailed off.

'Cornelia, what is it?'

The older woman sighed. 'This last quarter has been difficult, Louise. A guilder is no longer worth what it was. The loss of the *New Star*, all the changes to my licence – it is becoming harder to make ends meet. Joost's father has been generous in buying his son a commission. Indeed, he has increased his investment in the fleet itself. Dear Captain Janssen was loyal to the company above all things. Joost is different, I fear. I have no reason to believe he will not be an excellent captain – the sea is in his blood – but I suspect his first loyalty is to himself. Remember that.'

'Does he know that I own the *Old Moon*?'

'His father has seen the books. I imagine he will have told him.'

Louise frowned. 'But he was still prepared to have me on board.'

'Very much so. Perhaps too much so.' Cornelia paused. 'You

may own the *Old Moon*, but he is the master and commander at sea. Never forget that, once you have set sail, it is his ship.'

'You seem very worried.'

'Ach, everything will be fine. This business yesterday has put my nerves on end. These are just the murmurings of an old woman at the quayside.' She clapped her hands. 'And if a letter comes from Chartres, I will send it out with the next ship. It is due to sail within the week.'

'Thank you.' Louise flushed, then hesitated. 'Why did you say we could not marry? Not that there is any question of it – I feel affection for Gilles, for everything he has suffered – but—'

'*Lieveling*, do you not think I have eyes? When I first saw my Alis, I thought she was her brother, Aimeric, come back to life. Did you know that? She arrived here in Amsterdam dressed as a boy, having fled from a refugee camp in La Rochelle months after the massacre in Paris. Minou thought she was seeing a ghost.'

A shiver went down Louise's spine. 'You knew that Gilles is . . . that he is . . .'

Cornelia gave a gentle smile. 'Not for certain, but I suspected it. And there had to be a powerful reason for his mother continuing to exert so strong a control over him.'

Despite the circumstances of their departure, Louise was relieved that their secret was known with Cornelia appearing to accept it. She glanced over her shoulder at Gilles, then back to Cornelia.

'What should I do?'

Cornelia patted her cheek. 'Be true to your heart, to yourself. Nothing else will matter. Alis has been the great love of my life, but it has not been easy. As I said, be careful. There are many for whom how we live is a sin. And sailors are old-fashioned in many ways, especially where women are concerned.'

The bells of Sint Nicolaas began to ring the half-hour.

'Madame Reydon-Joubert, if you are ready?' Gilles said, holding out his hand.

'We shall miss you,' said Alis, with tears in her eyes. 'It has been our pleasure to have you with us for the winter. Your mother would be proud to see the woman you have become.'

Louise smiled. 'Aunt Bernarda not so much.'

'She means well,' Alis replied loyally, as she always did. 'If a letter does arrive for you, Cornelia will send it out with the next ship.'

'I have told her this,' Cornelia grumbled. 'My love, you must let Louise take her leave.'

Louise allowed Gilles to help her down into the large rowing boat, the *boot*, to take them out to the ship, before taking a seat behind her. Even now, she expected to see a messenger come running with a warrant for her arrest. She could imagine the sound of the stamping feet of the watch ready to march her to the prison at Sint Antoniespoort, where her grandfather and Cornelia's father had once been imprisoned. She could almost hear the charges read out in court. Accused not just of one murder, but two.

*How do you plead?*

She caught her breath, so real was the image. But, at last, the men began to row, steadily at first, then picking up the pace. Gradually, the thudding in her heart subsided. Louise looked back at the outline of Amsterdam, getting smaller with each stroke: the towers and turrets of the old medieval walls, the spire of Sint Nicolaas towering above the forest of masts in the harbour, the jetties and tiny boats shuttling backwards and forwards around them. She would miss all that, too.

Gulls wheeled above their heads as the boat bobbed and cut through the water. Blue skies and a bright March sun glinted behind the clouds, setting sparks of silver across the surface of the sea. Conditions were perfect. Soon, Louise could no longer pick out Cornelia and Alis on the quay, though she could see the outline of the Shreierstoren, the weeping tower, named for all those women who wept as their husbands and sons sailed away.

Prompted by Cornelia's confidences, her thoughts found their way back to the silence from Chartres. So much had happened in the five months since she had received the letter, it had become little more than a splinter under her skin. What Cornelia had told her changed everything. Louise had resigned herself to the loss of her fortune, but if Cornelia's business was failing, then what would that mean for her? For them all? When she had a chance, she would ask Gilles. He saw the books, he might know something more. Then another thought came to her. She was leaving as a fugitive, a criminal. She felt a wave of nostalgia for the home she might never see again.

*Will I ever come back to Amsterdam?*

The catch and the dip of the oars, and the boatswain calling the stroke, calmed her spirits. And now, ahead, the familiar three masts of the *Old Moon*, her sails furled but ready to deploy, looking fine in the spring sunshine. And her mood lifted a little more.

Captain Joost was already on board, standing on the quarter-deck awaiting the arrival of his esteemed passenger. Wearing a black bicorne hat, a short black coat with silver studs over a long red waistcoat and matching breeches, Louise thought he looked every inch the master of the ship. Joost raised his hand to greet her.

She acknowledged the gesture, then glanced at Gilles, so formal and sombre in dark clothes, but his eyes were shining bright.

'The *valet d'épées* can represent someone at the beginning of a journey,' she said. 'New beginnings.'

She spoke very softly, but Gilles heard her, and smiled.

A rope ladder was thrown down, and the cumbersome business of clambering up the side of the ship began. Mindful of Cornelia's words, Louise allowed herself to be hoisted in a chair rather than climb up the ladder herself, then she watched as their luggage was passed from hand to hand until everything was stacked on the deck.

'Madame Reydon-Joubert,' Joost said warmly, advancing to meet her. He ignored Gilles. He clicked his fingers and a cabin boy came running. 'Stow the lady's luggage in her cabin. Be quick about it.' He turned back to Louise. 'Might you honour me with your presence before we sail? A glass of wine perhaps?'

Louise allowed Joost to escort her to the captain's cabin in the stern, very aware of Gilles being taken in the opposite direction.

In Warmoesstraat that night, Cornelia and Alis sat in the salon. A mere six hours after the ship had sailed, a messenger had finally arrived from Chartres.

'Should we open it?' Alis asked.

'It is your choice. This is your family.'

'But it matters to us both.' She shook her head. 'I cannot bear to. You do it.'

Alis passed the letter to Cornelia, who noted the same red Evreux seal, the same heavy white paper as the previous communication. Cornelia took the paper knife from the table, cracked the seal and smoothed the letter out flat. This time there was a name at the top of the paper. She read in silence, then handed the note back to Alis.

'It is from a Phillipe Vidal,' Cornelia said, 'who claims to be the son of the late Lord Evreux and his wife Anne. They were married in Chartres on the second day of January in the year 1594. He has, so he writes, the marriage certificate to prove it.'

Alis frowned. 'A matter of weeks before he saw Marta in the cathedral.'

Cornelia slumped back in her chair. 'So, it's true. If only it had arrived sooner.'

Alis looked across at her companion and, to her distress, saw that tears were rolling down the older woman's face.

'What is it, my love? This is not the end of everything, you told Louise that yourself. It is not clear, even, what this Phillipe might want.'

Cornelia put her hands on the arm of her chair. 'We cannot afford to continue.'

'What do you mean?'

'The changes to the VOC terms, the ending of the truce with Spain, the loss of the *New Star*. I have decided this season would be my last. I have already made adjustments that sit ill with me.'

'You have not negotiated for the transfer of all your shares?' Alis said, appalled.

'No, of course not. What I had told myself was that if we had a successful summer, negotiated well and got a good price for our goods, it would be enough to keep us. But not Louise, too.'

'Does she know?'

Cornelia nodded. 'Not the extent of things, but she is aware I have already sold much of the stock in my fleet to Joost's father. She knows how much this voyage matters.'

For once in their long relationship, Alis took charge. 'Well, then, there is little we can do. There is too much about the matter that we don't know. Phillipe Vidal has given no indication that he intends to challenge Louise's inheritance. It is possible he simply wishes to meet the woman he knows to be related to him by blood. His half-sister.' She paused. 'As you promised, we will send a letter after Louise. Which ship is next due to sail?'

'The *North Star*.'

'Good. Though she won't receive the message until they land in Gran Canaria, we will at least know that we have done our duty by her brother.' Alis took her lover's hand. 'Do not worry, dear Cornelia.'

# PART FOUR

## The Atlantic Ocean &
## Las Islas Afortunadas
### *April–May 1621*

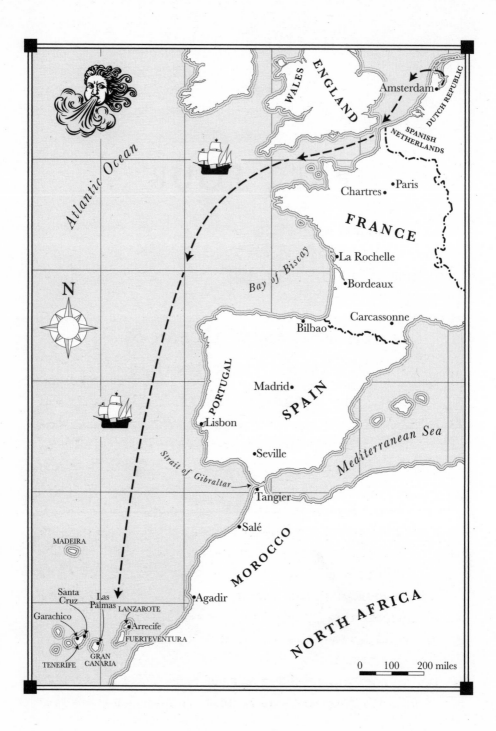

WALES

ENGLAND

Amsterdam

DUTCH REPUBLIC

SPANISH
NETHERLANDS

Atlantic Ocean

Chartres •Paris

FRANCE

N

La Rochelle

Bay of Biscay

Bordeaux

Carcassonne

Bilbao

PORTUGAL

Madrid•

SPAIN

•Lisbon

Mediterranean Sea

•Seville

Strait of Gibraltar

Tangier

•Salé

MOROCCO

MADEIRA

Santa
Cruz

Las
Palmas

LANZAROTE

Garachico

•Agadir

NORTH AFRICA

•Arrecife

FUERTEVENTURA

TENERIFE

GRAN
CANARIA

0    100    200 miles

# CHAPTER FORTY-SIX

## The Atlantic Ocean
*Thursday, 1 April 1621*

They had been at sea for thirteen days.

That the *Old Moon* felt changed, Louise knew was down to the character of the new, young captain. Under his command, it was a different ship. Joost was eager to make a good impression. He had excellent manners and was well-informed and, to her, he was charming. Nothing was too much trouble. To begin with, Louise had found his company congenial. But as the days passed, she began to notice how he was short-tempered and dismissive with his officers and boatswain. To his crew, he was harsh and quick to hand down punishment for the slightest infraction. A lad of no more than fourteen – Pieter – had been flogged on the third day out of harbour simply for dropping a tray of drinks in Joost's cabin. The copper-topped De Groot brothers from Rotterdam were particular targets for his tongue because of the colour of their hair. Even his first lieutenant, Jan Roord, was scared of him. A gentle man from Antwerp, pale with a thin brown beard and moustache, authority sat ill on Roord's shoulders and he winced every time a sailor cussed or used language that offended his devout Catholic sensibilities. The second lieutenant, Joris Bleeker, an experienced seafarer with angry skin, barely spoke.

For his part, Joost took no pains to hide his dislike of Gilles. It was Joost's command and he made it clear that the young

Frenchman was there on sufferance, a man of paper and ink with no real role to play at sea, an encumbrance. Louise started to dread a knock on her cabin door with another request from the captain to join him, but she was in a difficult position. For Cornelia's sake, given the size of his father's investment in the Van Raay line, she could not afford to offend him.

Gilles felt caught between two worlds. When he had sailed from La Rochelle to Amsterdam in November last, he had been numb with grief and shock, seeming younger than his years. The seasoned sailors, at the tail end of a year's voyage, had been inclined to treat him with kindness.

With this new Dutch crew, it was different. Now he was a paid representative of the Van Raay shipping line, a civilian not a mariner. He had plenty of technical knowledge, but no practical experience of the sea. Since Joost made it clear he had no use for him, and they feared invoking the captain's displeasure, the other men avoided him too. In some ways, this was good – his need to conceal his true nature was made a thousand times harder by living at close quarters. He had found a solution in Amsterdam, by visiting the public laundry during his monthly courses. On board ship, he lived every moment in fear of being caught out. That he did not piss like other men, he knew they put down to a fastidious nature – he was French, after all – and Gilles played up to the image. He was a clerk, a paper-pusher, what more could they expect? But it was difficult.

The hierarchy of the ship, enforced fiercely by Captain Joost, also meant there were strict rules as to where he was allowed to walk. He saw Louise from a distance, but could not approach her unless summoned. He slept in a wooden cot in the hold, rather than a hammock, with a table and a covered candle hanging from a hook, but queued up to collect his rations from the galley with the other crew members. The De Groot brothers did not invite him to sit with them on deck when their watch was over, the grizzled Amsterdamer, Jorgen, did not offer to share his tobacco. Their stories, overheard as he sat alone at his desk, were about how they would spend their wages when they returned to shore, not tales of creatures of the deep or exotic lands. They were pragmatic Dutchmen looking for advancement, not dreamers seeking adventure. More concerning, they whispered how they would never want to sail under Joost again.

Despite the ever-present dread of exposure, Gilles was delighted to be back on board. He watched and he listened. In return for a little wine in the galley, he persuaded the cook, Albert, to teach him how to tie mariner's knots. In return for reading a letter from a sweetheart in Haarlem for Lange – the nickname for the tallest member of the crew – he learnt how the rigging was managed: the mainstay and the shrouds, the crosstrees and the ratlines that led up to the crow's nest. He studied the names of the sail edges – foot, head, leech, clew – until he understood how each worked, the admired great white square sails and the elegant triangular lateen sail at the stern. And his aptitude with numbers turned out to be of value to the second lieutenant, Bleeker, at the whip staff, helping to avoid one or two navigational errors, but he never claimed the credit. And tucked beneath his pillow, with his Tarot card, he kept a chart he was drawing on a sheet of paper salvaged from Louise's cabin, and plotted his own version of their course.

Little by little, Gilles earned the crew's trust.

From Amsterdam into the North Sea, through the channel dividing England from France, tacking against the prevailing sou'westerly wind, beyond the tip of Cornwall to Ushant, the westernmost point of France. Two days of rain meant the deck was slippery and it was impossible to get purchase on the rigging and sails, but there was no interference and they made good time despite the head wind.

There was so much Gilles should be thinking about. The will Louise had recovered in Rokin confirmed he was his uncle's sole heir, but he did not want to accept the bequest. He was not the person his uncle had thought he was. Louise had advised him not to act rashly. For now, her steward would continue to keep an eye on the shop and business – that had been arranged before they left La Rochelle last October. In the future, Gilles could not say what he might want. For now, it was enough to be on the *Old Moon* with Louise.

Twelve days after leaving harbour, the wind swung round to the north-west and they picked up speed. They rounded Cape Finisterre with the square masts on the main and fore masts in full sail, billowing and cracking, riding the winds that would carry them south towards the Spanish coast, then on towards North Africa.

This, Gilles decided, was the life he had been set on earth to live.

After nearly two weeks at sea, Louise could no longer deny that Joost's interest in her went beyond the usual duty of care of a captain for an esteemed passenger.

He was some five years younger than she was, unmarried and it was clear he had decided that she would be a good match. For the sake of the harmony of the ship, Louise could not rebuff him and accepted his invitations, but did nothing to encourage his suit. She needed to keep everything on a formal footing.

The only sizeable private quarters on the *Old Moon* were the two primary cabins at the stern: the captain's cabin had been improved over the winter, thanks to Joost's father's investment, as had Louise's own, smaller cabin, which was adjacent. Though she hardly thought Joost would force himself upon her, she took to dragging her trunk across the door when she retired for the night, her dagger beneath her pillow.

And she missed Gilles' company. They had had little time to talk about what had happened on Rokin, though she had managed to tell him she had found his uncle's will. But she felt the depth of his gratitude. Acknowledged his guilt, too, that she had acted for his sake. She wanted to reassure him, but there was never an opportunity.

Before his mother's death, there had been an ease between them. She thought often of that day in November in Sint Luciensteeg – and suspected he did also. But Cornelia's warnings rang in her ears and she knew Joost was watching. The confined quarters of the ship made any private conversation risky. The captain made no effort to hide his antipathy to Gilles, even from her, and she did not want to give him any cause for jealousy.

All the same, on the afternoon of the fourteenth day at sea, Louise decided to ask Joost to invite Gilles to join them for dinner. The seas were calm, the weather mild and they were making time. She had found the perfect, and legitimate, excuse for the three of them to dine together. Her idea was to invite Joost to learn a little more about the cargo they would be carrying back to France and Amsterdam. Though the captain was a man of great confidence in his own abilities, Gilles' knowledge of wine was superior and Joost could not deny that.

Louise knocked on his door. There was no answer, so she

gently pushed opened the door and peered inside, knowing better than to enter the master's cabin without permission.

'Might I have a word? Captain Joost?'

She was aware of the constant song of the ship, the creaking and sighing of timber, as she let her eyes roam around the cabin. A long oak dining table with six chairs sat four-square in the centre of the space, a desk and chair were bolted to the floorboards, and there was a globe, much like the one in Warmoesstraat. Joost's portolan, his own personal mariner's map, lay on the table with a divider. Beautiful and intricate, he had shown her the important ports marked in red and the lesser ports in black, the compass roses with rhum lines forming a pattern across the sea like a spider's web. Beside the vellum map stood a brass astrolabe used for calculating the altitude of the sun. There were also a range of hourglasses, set to run for one hour and one half-hour, used for judging speed and to mark the changing of the watch. Finally, Joost's pride and joy – a compass handed down from his father, who had also served as a captain in the Van Raay fleet. It was a beautiful instrument, the lodestone and magnetic needle housed in an exquisite ivory case.

Joost appeared, to find her hovering in the doorway.

'My dear lady, to what do I owe the honour?'

Louise took pleasure in watching his self-satisfied expression fix, like a man in a portrait, as she explained.

'If it is what you wish,' he said in a brisk voice, 'then, of course, it shall happen.'

Louise smiled. 'It is a matter of business rather than pleasure, captain. Mevrouw Van Raay is keen to extend the range of wines she imports from Gran Canaria. I know she would be pleased to hear of your interest.'

Joost took her hand, and kissed it. 'If you consider this an education I need to have, then I am yours to command.'

'Until this afternoon, then,' Louise said, as he opened the door for her.

As soon as she was back in her own cabin, she took her handkerchief from her pocket and wiped away the stain of his lips.

# CHAPTER FORTY-SEVEN

At four bells, Louise took herself back to the master's cabin. Gilles and the captain were already there, standing in silence, each with a glass in his hand.

Joost was immediately solicitous. 'Dear lady, come in, come in. We have been waiting on your arrival. Barenton was ahead of the hour.'

Louise held out her hand. 'Captain,' she said, then nodded to Gilles.

He bowed. 'Madame Reydon-Joubert.'

She noticed Gilles had a little colour in his cheeks, perhaps from hours spent on the deck as the ship sailed south, and was pleased to see him looking well.

'Please, dear lady, sit.' Joost's hand somehow brushed the back of her neck as he pulled out her chair. 'My cook has prepared you a meal fit for any table in Amsterdam. Later in the voyage, of course, we will be dining off preserved rations.' He turned to Gilles. 'Pass the decanter, will you?'

Louise bridled at his tone, but Gilles simply did as he was asked.

'Would you like me to pour, sir?'

Joost waved his hand. 'Why not, since we have no one to wait upon us. Forgive me, Madame Reydon-Joubert, but this is a small crew and we need all hands on deck.'

'Oh? The sea seems calm.'

He wagged his finger. 'Ah, dear lady, it is an illusion. The

Bay of Biscay can be treacherous this early in the season. The wind has gone round. I fear there might be a squall of bad weather to come, though nothing that should concern you.'

Louise stared at him. 'This is not my first time at sea, captain.'

Hearing the rebuke in her voice, he raised his hand. 'Of course, you are a seasoned traveller. You know, as well as I, the challenges of these waters. Unlike you, Barenton. This is your first time on board the *Old Moon*, I believe.'

'My second, sir,' Gilles replied respectfully.

'Well, let's hope you have your sea legs. The dishes are ready to serve. If you would.'

Without demur, he brought the pewter dishes to the table. Joost kept up a steady stream of conversation directed at Louise, ignoring Gilles to the point of discourtesy. Every time Louise asked him a question, or attempted to have a three-way conversation about the vineyards in Las Palmas, Joost interrupted and told a story of his own. He boasted of his father's wealth, their house in Leiden, his ambitions to own his own fleet and to expand into the Americas. The slave trade offered great opportunities, he thought, for men prepared to seize them. Louise began to regret having suggested the dinner. Except, when she caught Gilles' eye and saw how he looked at her, she was grateful for the snatched time in his company.

'Are you enjoying life on board, Monsieur Barenton?' she said, when Joost had paused to draw breath.

'I am, madame, thank you. I have much to learn but –' he turned and nodded to Captain Joost – 'every member of the company is being most kind.'

'I am glad to hear it.'

Joost poured himself another glass and ignored Gilles. Louise covered hers with her hand as the captain returned to his own stories.

At six bells, after an hour that had felt more like a day, Joost pushed back his chair and stood up.

'If you will forgive me, Madame Reydon-Joubert, I should go up to the quarterdeck. Make sure that everything is as it should be.'

'Your sense of duty does you credit, captain.'

He raised her hand to his lips. It was all Louise could do not to snatch her fingers away. 'If you are not too fatigued, might you join me for a nightcap a little later?'

She found a smile. 'How kind, but I have letters to write. Tomorrow, if your duties permit?'

'Of course. I am yours to command.' He gave a sharp nod. 'Barenton. I am sure you have matters to attend to.'

'Yes, sir.'

'Well, then, I will bid you good evening.'

They all three jostled for space as they left the cabin, and walked out onto the deck. Joost bowed to Louise, then raised his hand and shouted for his first lieutenant. Roord called back, and Joost went to join him.

For a moment, Louise and Gilles stood beneath the canopy of stars. It was almost the first time they had been alone since leaving Amsterdam.

'Are you well?' she asked quickly, before the opportunity was lost.

'I am.' He paused. 'Are you?'

'I am. Captain Joost is most attentive.'

'I have observed it.'

Silence stretched between them. Louise didn't want to say goodnight, but neither did she feel she could risk extending their conversation. From the bow, she could hear the gentle sound of a shanty. Mournful notes, singing of loss and regret.

'Will you come up to the top deck?' Gilles said. 'There is something I would show you.'

'Are you sure?' It was one of the most public places on the ship.

'No one is watching.'

As they moved across the shifting deck, they collided. Louise laughed, as Gilles stood back to let her go ahead. His hand brushed against hers, and a shudder went through her entire body.

*This cannot be. I must remain on my guard.*

Her heart was saying otherwise. Above them, the black sky sparkled with stars.

'What is it?' She shivered again as he put his hands on her shoulders and turned her round.

'There,' he said.

Louise looked towards the horizon and saw, perhaps three or four miles away, a storm. Beautiful and magnificent, a show of lights dancing and flickering as it moved across the distant water.

'Ah,' she breathed with delight. 'But that will not come our way,' she said, reckoning on the direction of the wind.

'No, but the crew say the swell is rising. They think something is building in the west.'

'A storm?'

Gilles nodded. 'They say so.'

Louise turned to face him. 'Are you scared?'

In the darkness, she was sure he was smiling. 'Should I be, madame?'

'Louise,' she whispered. 'Didn't we agree?'

'No, I'm not scared, Louise.'

And then his hand was on her cheek, and he was drawing

her to him. The lightest of kisses. She felt herself lean into his body, like two halves of the same coin.

They stood together for a moment, listening to the lapping of water against the hull, the distant strains of the pipe, the sound of their hearts beating. For the first time since she had watched Madame Roux fall to the floor, for the first time since she had remembered what happened in the chamber in Kalverstraat, Louise felt completely at peace.

Then the harsh voice of Joost came from below, and they sprang apart.

'Forgive me for interrupting,' he said, his voice rigid with anger, 'but we are running into bad weather. You, Madame Reydon-Joubert, retire to your cabin, if you will. Barenton, go to your quarters. Do not make me regret allowing you the run of the ship.'

# CHAPTER FORTY-EIGHT

*Friday, 2 April*

The storm hit at three o'clock in the morning. A single gust of wind, a warning shot across the bow, then the ship began to roll and buck and plummet, being smashed leeward. Within moments, they were trapped by successive walls of water, black and green, as the *Old Moon* began to fight for her life. She was twisting and sliding, crashing into the waves that threatened to sink her.

The boatswain Jansz, the De Groot brothers and Lange struck the sails and battened the hatches. Every rope tied, every lantern secured, starboard and larboard, lights guttering in their wooden cages before being extinguished by another wave booming at starboard. Monstrous waves, crested with white, hovered and loomed over the ship, before thundering down again onto her deck.

Gilles had never heard such a roaring, a screaming of wind and rigging. With every crack of thunder, every fork of lighting, every vertiginous plunge of the ship down into the depths, before being tossed back up like a cork, it seemed impossible that the *Old Moon* would not break in two.

Joost was at the helm, with the second lieutenant, Bleeker, beside him. The crew was frantically scooping up water with wooden pails, trying to clear the deck. Down below, others worked the bilge pump, hammering the metal lever up and down to rid the lower deck of seawater. Water was sheeting down from the quarterdeck and back under the door of the captain's cabin, the sandbags giving little protection. Gilles slipped and fell heavily on his side, before dragging himself up and, hand over hand, making his way up to the quarterdeck.

'What can I do?'

'We're taking in too much water.' Lange thrust a pail at him. 'She'll go down, else.'

Gilles joined the crew, struggling to keep their footing, as they desperately attempted to bail the seawater from the deck. Then he saw the boatswain go flying, being thrown back against the mizzen mast and cracking his head. Against the wind, Gilles managed to drag Jansz along the deck, down into the hold and to his own cot, leaving a trail of blood behind him. Suddenly, Louise was at his side in the hold, offering a cloth to stem the wound on the boatswain's head. Gilles pressed the cloth against the gaping gash, but the blood kept flowing.

'Will you stay with him?' he said urgently. 'They need me on deck.'

Louise put her hand on his arm. 'Take good care.'

He nodded then, lurching like a drunken man, careered his way to the ladder, and hauled himself back up into the eye of the storm.

Jansz was a wiry man, with a crooked nose broken from more than one past misadventure. Louise knew she had to clean the gash before a dangerous contagion crept in. She needed honey to purify the blood and help clot the wound. She set off for the galley, sideways like a crab, hauling herself along the rolling deck to prevent herself from being thrown the length of the hold like a child's doll. It was a slow progress to the galley and back, where the embers of the fire burned unsupervised.

The boatswain groaned as Louise treated and staunched the wound, until the bleeding finally stopped.

She wanted to go back up to be with Gilles, but she forced herself to stay below. Her presence would be a distraction. As for what had happened between them beneath the stars, she tried to put it from her mind. She still marvelled that what he had told her about his nature should have changed nothing. He was Gilles, no more, no less.

*Is this love, she wondered, this calm acceptance?*

There was a deafening crack and she heard men shouting overhead. The ship listed dangerously to starboard. Louise held tight to the edge of Gilles' wooden bunk, her stomach plunging with every roll of the ship, and prayed that he would survive the night. That they would all live to see the dawn.

For several hours, the wind was relentless. Vicious, steady, unyielding. Even below deck, water foamed as high as a man's knee, pouring over the low ship's side and finding every crack or chink in the wood, as if a dyke had burst. Seawater was drowning the floating city. Though she had experienced storms in the Bay of Biscay and the biting winds of the North Sea, Louise had never before feared for her life. She could not believe that the *Old Moon* would withstand the tempest.

Then, soon after six o'clock in the morning, suddenly there was calm. With the light, the wind died as quickly as it had blown up. The ship began to steady, rocking backwards and forwards on the diminishing waves until the swell had gone. Louise raised her head from her arms, listening to the quiet, then glanced at her patient. Jansz was sleeping, with no signs of a fever.

Tentatively, she got to her feet. There was blood on her gown, and her shoes and stockings were soaking, but she was unharmed. Unsteady, her body still pitching with the memory of the storm, Louise made her way to the ladder and climbed up on deck. She looked around in horror at the devastation. The mainsail was ripped and hanging by a thread, the topgallant mast had split, and lay splintered on the deck. Lanterns were smashed and broken on the quarterdeck. The De Groot brothers and Pieter were sweeping the ship of the storm's detritus. Lange and Jorgen were beginning to repair the rigging. Bleeker was back at the helm, an expression of grim determination on his face.

*Where is Gilles?*

Lieutenant Roord stumbled past, his face as white as milk. Louise grabbed his arm. 'Did we lose anyone?'

'Not a soul,' he said, crossing himself. 'Praise be to God.'

Joost was up on the quarterdeck surveying the damage. They had not spoken since the few sharp words before the storm came in. She knew he had seen her and Gilles together, his anger had been testament to that, but decided the best thing was to pretend that he had not.

'Captain, may I congratulate you on bringing the ship through the storm,' she said.

He looked coldly at her. 'Is there something you need, Madame Reydon-Joubert?'

'Where is Gilles Barenton, do you know? I would have him write a report for mevrouw Van Raay.'

'That is not his job,' Joost snapped. 'I will inform Amsterdam what they need to know in due course.'

Louise held up her hand in apology. It would do no good to antagonise him further. 'I was thinking only of the inventory of provisions but, of course. My mistake. I would not wish you to think I was meddling. Might you at least be able to tell me if you intend to find a safe haven and make repairs, or continue on our course to Las Palmas?'

'There is nothing we cannot mend at sea.'

'I am glad to hear it.'

He folded his arms. 'If there is nothing else?'

She met his gaze. 'You have not answered my question, captain.'

A sly look crept over his face. 'Barenton? He is locked in the storeroom aft.'

Louise thought she had misheard. 'I beg your pardon?'

Joost came down the ladder and stood in front of her, his eyes glinting with malice. 'He is a thief, madame.'

'Whatever do you mean?'

'My compass has been stolen. The only person to have been in my cabin, apart from myself and Barenton, is you.' He leant towards her. 'I would not show such discourtesy as to accuse you of theft, madame. No doubt he took advantage of the weather to help himself. It is of sentimental value to me, it belonged to my father. The casing is made of ivory from Africa.'

'That is ridiculous,' she said sharply, then she turned cold. If Joost searched Gilles, then he would discover his secret. She found a more conciliatory tone. 'Surely, the compass has been misplaced in the storm. Might I help you look?'

'I do not need your help, Madame Reydon-Joubert. Barenton will stay locked up until I am ready to deal with him. I am sure there is no need to remind you that you are a guest on board. Now, if you will excuse me, there is a great deal to do. Not least of all disciplining the boatswain, who deserted his post.'

Louise was appalled. 'Captain, no. Jansz was injured, knocked unconscious. I tended to him myself. He could not have stood upright.'

'He was not there when I needed him.'

'Out of courtesy to me, I ask you to reconsider.'

Joost narrowed his eyes. 'Your name might be on the deed of purchase, madame, but I am master of this ship.' He made to walk away, then turned back with a calculating look on his face. 'If you care to join me for dinner tonight, we can discuss Barenton's situation.'

Louise wanted to protest further, but there was nothing she could do. Her ownership of the *Old Moon* meant little when they were at sea. The captain's word was absolute. Tyrant or benign dictator, it depended on the man. She was on the point of withdrawing to her cabin, when she heard a noise from the hatch leading to the lower deck.

There was a scuffle as the boatswain, still dazed, was dragged along the deck by the De Groot brothers. Lieutenant Roord, his profound distaste for the orders he'd been given written plainly on his face, reluctantly pulled Jansz's bloodied shirt from his back, and tied his hands around the mizzen mast with a cord. Louise thought she saw him whisper an apology. Jansz slumped against the mast, unable to hold the weight of his own body.

'Stand up, man,' the captain ordered, as Pieter put the whip, known as the cat, into Joost's hand. Strips of leather with seven knots at the end.

Louise forced herself not to look away as the captain delivered ten blows across the boatswain's naked back, each delivered with a little more ferocity than the last, aware that Joost intended this as a warning to her: this is what Gilles could expect if he was found guilty as charged. She was sickened, both at her failure to stop the brutal punishment and at the absurd situation that left her subservient on her own ship.

Jansz flinched with every blow, but did not cry out. When his hands were untied, he slipped broken to the deck.

*Skin and blood and bone.*

Joost had proved his point. Louise grieved for the boatswain – and vowed she would write to Cornelia to tell her what had happened. She saw the same contempt and hatred for the captain in the eyes of every other crew member, too. Roord had closed his eyes and was murmuring a prayer. But what mattered now was to get Gilles released.

'I will join you this evening, captain,' she said, as he strode past her, his cold eyes sharp with the pleasure of his sadistic exertion. 'I would discuss this.'

He paused, breathing heavily. 'There is nothing to discuss, madame.' Then he smiled. 'But I shall look forward to your company.'

# CHAPTER FORTY-NINE

From the dark and airless storeroom, Gilles could hear the hammering of the nails and sawing of wood above him as the crew worked to repair the storm damage. That, and the whimpering of the boatswain, who had been beaten for the 'sin' of having been injured, and so deserting his post. He now lay half-conscious on the floor beside him.

Gilles removed his own linen collar and used it to try to staunch Jansz's bleeding. Ten claw marks on his back, each raw and weeping, were spotted with fresh blood. He used his handkerchief to stem the wound on Jansz's forehead, which had split open again.

He had only once been moved to violence – when he'd attacked his mother in the alley in La Rochelle – but if the captain had appeared in the storeroom at that moment, Gilles would have killed him. Joost had done everything to inflict maximum damage, landing the whip in the same place each time to deepen the wounds. Not only savage and cruel, but stupid. The boatswain was responsible for the sails, the rigging, the anchor, all work on deck, so Joost had disabled one of his most important crew members. It was foolish, especially in the aftermath of the battering the ship had taken during the night. There was no one else to take his place. Lieutenant Roord was a gentle man promoted far above his physical abilities, and tolerated rather than popular with the men. Though he was discreet about it, the fact he was Catholic sat uncomfortably with the Calvinist crew. The second lieutenant, Bleeker, also kept himself to himself. Jansz, on the other hand, was liked and respected. He was fair.

A rat ran over his foot. Gilles kicked it away. There was barely room to stand upright, but he braced his knees and stretched his arms, wondering what Joost had planned for him. He had not taken the compass – did not even remember seeing it when they had dined – and suspected Joost of lying. He had no fear of a beating – he had learned long ago to separate his mind from his body – but the thought that Louise might be in some way implicated worried him. He didn't even know if she had survived the storm unscathed.

Gilles laced his fingers and felt his muscles tense. Since making his confession to Louise of his double nature in Amsterdam, and their time beneath the stars last evening, his emotions had veered between delight that she had simply accepted him and terror that she would come to think differently. He was an in-betweener, neither one thing, nor the other. And if Joost decided to punish him as he had punished Jansz, then the whole ship would know his secret the moment his shirt was pulled from his back and the strapping that bound his breasts was revealed. He went in fear of discovery – already, he had nearly been caught with his soiled cotton rags. The crew had accepted him, liked him even, but they were superstitious. The presence of a man-woman like him would be seen as a portent, responsible for the storm and any other misfortune that might overtake them: the failing of the stars, the dying of the wind, a weed-choked rudder, freak squalls from the north. All would be put at his door.

At his feet, Jansz was still weeping. Louise had cleaned his head wound, but the damage to his back was extensive. The longer he was down here in the filthy bowels of the ship, the more likely it was his blood would poison.

Gilles sat down beside him. '*Het komt allemaal goed,*' he said in his careful Dutch. 'It will be all right. Try to keep still, and you will be all right.'

Louise listened to the bells, marking each half-hour of the watch, until she thought she would go mad. Eight fore noon, eight after noon, into the first bells of the dog watch. Pacing around her confined cabin, she was restless and unable to settle to anything, just like when she was a child.

Several times, she sat down to pen a note to Gilles, to let him know she was doing everything she could to have him released. Each time, she thought better of it. If the message was intercepted, it would make matters worse. At least by agreeing to dine with Joost, she had stayed the captain's hand for now. She was certain he would do nothing until after they had met.

*Only a few hours more.*

Louise picked up her dagger, tested her finger on its sharp point, then put it down again. She was not yet resolved as to the best course of action. She had a plan, but was not certain she could pull it off. Everything would depend on the crew. Louise hoped Joost's brutal treatment of the boatswain would be a tipping point. Jansz was popular, and known as a fair man, but that did not necessarily mean the men would stand with her against Joost. They had their livelihoods to think of and good employers like Cornelia van Raay were as rare as hen's teeth. Then she remembered Cornelia's confession at the quay that Joost's father now owned a significant stake in the fleet, and desperation took hold.

*Three hours to go.*

She looked at the hourglass, the grains of sand trickling down to mark the time, then turned it over and waited for the evening to come.

# CHAPTER FIFTY

Louise dressed with care. She pinched her cheeks to give them colour, and chose her green gown with slashed sleeves and a low neck. She curled her hair beneath a lace cap and paired it with a matching purse. She wanted Joost to be off his guard. She was very conscious of the powders tucked inside her sleeve, prescribed years ago by an apothecary in Amsterdam for nights when she could not sleep. They were so old, she had no idea if they still had any efficacy, but it was her only hope.

Louise was ahead of time, so she decided to take a turn around the deck to gauge the mood of the ship. Tonight, there were no tankards raised in a toast for their deliverance, no songs on a penny whistle or shanties to help the work along. It seemed to her as if the *Old Moon* itself was holding its breath.

She stood holding the taffrail for a while in the lea of the lateen sail, listening to its gentle sigh. The sea was calm, barely a breath of wind, and the ship was quiet. The moon came out from behind a cloud, sending diamonds of light scattering over the rippling surface of the water.

At the prescribed hour, Louise knocked on the door to the master's cabin. Everything looked the same as it had the previous evening, despite the storm – the long dining table and chairs, the captain's desk, the globe in the centre of the table, the cot in the corner. Except, this time, only two places were set – two pewter cups and plates, a spoon and knife beside each – and the hourglass primed to run for one-half hour had been moved to the chest beside the door. Wax candles had replaced the everyday tallow sticks that smoked and fouled the cabin air. Everything, Louise thought grimly, was in place for a bargain to be struck. And tonight, the youngest member of the crew, Pieter, was waiting on the table. He looked terrified.

'Madame, welcome,' Joost said, pulling out her chair. 'Please.'

The meal began: the last fresh cabbage for a salad, a dish of onions, a filet of seabass baked in salt. As each course was taken, Louise encouraged Joost to refill his glass whilst managing to keep her own virtually untouched. She set out to be charming, listening attentively to Joost's grandiose plans for his own fleet, feigning not to hear his sly asides about the state of Cornelia's finances. All the time, she was waiting for an opportunity to act. She expressed herself delighted with the main course of salted pork followed by Gouda cheese, though she could barely swallow.

'I dare say you thought I was harsh earlier,' Joost slurred. 'Ladies have such tender hearts. But one has to keep a firm hand else all authority is lost.'

Louise kept her smile in place. 'A man who leaves his post puts the entire vessel at risk.'

His eyes glinted. 'Just so, dear lady, just so.' He clicked his fingers. 'Boy!'

Pieter rushed forward.

'More wine for Madame Reydon-Joubert.'

'The jug is empty, captain,' he mumbled.

'Then fetch more, idiot.'

Joost threw the keys at Pieter's chest. The boy fumbled with the lock, growing ever more nervous, then dropped the keys on the floor.

'For the love of God,' the captain thundered, pushing his chair from the table, shoving Pieter out of his way and striding to the cabinet.

Louise took her chance. Quick as a flash, she pulled the paper of laudanum from her sleeve, emptied the powders into Joost's cup, and sat back, her heart thudding.

'If you want something done . . .' Joost said with self-importance, as he dropped back in his chair. 'My lieutenants are just as useless. Roord is sickly and Bleeker's face – those pustules, warts – is enough to turn even the strongest stomach.' He stopped talking as Pieter timidly approached with the jug of newly decanted wine.

'About time,' Joost said, pointing to Louise's cup.

She shook her head. 'The captain should take the first drink,' she said. 'Now, Hendrik, if I may address you so?'

He took it as an invitation, reaching across the table to grasp her hand. 'Dear lady, within these four walls you may do whatever you like,' he leered. 'Whatever you like.'

'I would talk about the secretary, Gilles Barenton.'

Joost scowled and tried to pull his hand away, but Louise held on tightly. 'If you are certain that he is responsible for the theft then, of course, you must take any action you see fit. *If* you are certain.' She looked him in the eye. 'But I would say this. The young man is a distant relation of a dear friend of mevrouw Van Raay and she has chosen to take him under her wing. She would be distressed to know that there was any kind of misunderstanding and . . .' She leant in closer. 'Now, of course I know that your father is a major share-holder, and we are all grateful to him for his generosity. But you would be doing a great service to me personally if you made sure this unfortunate incident did not come to her attention.' Praying that Cornelia might forgive her, she added: 'She is an old woman, Hendrik. This may well be her final season. If so, the entire fleet may need a new commander. A new owner, even.'

Louise could see the indecision in his eyes. A man drunk on his own power and privilege. He swayed in his chair, blinking as if he was struggling to focus.

'I thought you might have a special interest in Barenton,' he mumbled, the words sloppy in his mouth.

Hating herself for playing her role so well, Louise laughed. 'What an idea! I have always been kind to the boy, for the sake of mevrouw Van Raay – and last evening after our dinner, he was homesick for La Rochelle, so I felt obliged to reassure him – but more than that, of course not.'

Louise watched the expression on Joost's face, trying to work out if the laudanum was having an effect. She couldn't tell.

He waved his hand. 'I thought you and he—'

'If the young man has misunderstood my courtesy to him,' she interrupted, 'I regret that. But can I be held responsible? Kindness is so often mistaken for something more.'

'So true.'

Joost was now finding it hard to keep his concentration. His elbow slipped from the table, as he attempted to square what she was saying with what he had witnessed last evening. Arrogance won.

'If I release Barenton,' he slurred, 'he must be confined to his quarters. I cannot have a thief given the run of my ship.'

'No, indeed. How wise.' She smiled. 'Will you send the order now, Hendrik?'

He banged his fist on the table. 'Paper, pen!'

It seemed to take an eternity for Pieter to return to the table. Louise watched as Joost tried to focus his swimming eyes. His hand slipped more than once as he formed the letters. But finally, the order was written.

'Thank you,' she said. 'I am in your debt.'

Joost thrust the paper at the boy's chest. 'See it done.'

Louise waited until Pieter had left the room before raising her glass in a toast. 'Now we are alone, let us raise a toast to your continued success, Hendrik. I have no doubt that you have a distinguished career ahead of you.'

'It would go better with the right wife at my side.'

'There must be many suitable candidates in Leiden, in Amsterdam,' she said playfully, pretending not to understand.

Joost's hand reached across the table. 'Come now.'

Thinking of Gilles, of Cornelia, Louise forced herself not to pull away.

'Does your father not wish an alliance with another of the leading families?'

'Simpering ninnies,' he sneered. 'I would have someone of mature years. Someone who might guide me, and . . .'

Suddenly, Joost launched himself at her. Although Louise had been expecting something, she was still taken by surprise by his agility.

'Captain Joost! You forget yourself.'

'No need to play the innocent with me,' he muttered, grabbing her wrist. 'You have been playing with me all night. Do you take me for a fool?'

'Captain, no,' she protested, as he forced his hand under her skirt. She tried to push him away, but he was too strong. Suddenly, a new memory of her father and her mother flashed into her mind. Petticoats and flesh, not understanding then what she was witnessing. Now, she did. 'Stop,' she shouted, fear and memory giving her voice power. 'Let go of me!'

The door opened.

Pieter took one look, then rushed towards them and dragged the captain away. Joost seemed to stare at him for a moment, then at her, as if he had no idea who she was or where they were, then slid slowly to the floor bringing his goblet and dinner plate down with him. His eyes fluttered, his hand twitched and spasmed, then he was still.

'I'm sorry, ma'am,' the boy was gabbling. 'I thought he was—'

'He was,' Louise said, her voice shaking. 'I am grateful to you, Pieter. You were very courageous.'

Louise looked at Joost, his arms and legs splayed on the ground, a splash of wine on his shirt. The first part of her plan had worked. The question now was would the crew support her next course of action. She took a deep breath.

'You witnessed what happened?'

'Yes, ma'am.'

'In which case, please could you fetch Monsieur Barenton.'

Within minutes, Pieter arrived back bringing Gilles with him.

'Madame Reydon-Joubert, how may I be of service?' Then he saw the captain unconscious on the floor. 'Oh. Is he –?'

'I fear he has taken too much wine,' Louise replied calmly. 'And that caused him to behave in a manner not appropriate to his station nor my position. In front of this young man, too.'

Gilles spun round. 'You saw him?'

'Yes, sir.'

'How much wine did he have?'

'I wouldn't like to say, sir.'

'But more than was good for him?'

'Yes, monsieur. And when I came into the cabin he was—'

Louise interrupted. 'That will do, Pieter. Will you find Lieutenant Roord and ask him to join us.'

The moment the boy had gone, Gilles took her hand, then saw the red mark on her wrist. 'My love, what happened? Did he hurt you?'

'I am fine.' She put her hand to his cheek. 'What about you?'

'Did he make an attempt on you? If he did, I will break his neck.'

'I gave him laudanum,' she said quietly. 'The rest, he did to himself.' She could see him looking at her, not knowing what to say, or what to ask. 'I couldn't think of how else to persuade him to release you,' she added, seeing the question in his eyes. 'A sleeping draught from my own cabinet.'

'Louise, you cannot keep putting yourself at risk for me, I cannot bear it.'

'I love you,' she said simply. 'And it is for the good of the ship, too. But if we are to take the crew with us, I need your help.'

Gilles shook his head. 'I don't understand.'

'I need you to speak to the men, Gilles. Tell them what has happened, and what I intend to do.'

He looked at her. 'And what is that?'

'This is my ship,' Louise replied. 'And I intend to take it back.'

Just before midnight, Louise stepped up onto the quarterdeck. There was a full moon and the crew had been summoned to hear her address.

Every man already knew Joost was locked in her cabin. He had not yet woken up, but Gilles had spread the word of how the captain had made an attempt on Madame Reydon-Joubert's virtue and so been confined to quarters. Pieter had confirmed the story.

'*Mijne heren*,' she said, her voice clear in the crisp night air. 'Gentleman. The lewd behaviour, and now indisposition, of Hendrik Joost casts ignominy over this ship. If anything, it might remind us of the evils of drink. But, together, we will fare forward, we have no choice. Each of you has pledged allegiance to the Van Raay company and I know all of you will fulfil your obligations.' She looked slowly around the deck, holding the eyes of each man in the glinting moonlight until she arrived at Jansz, sitting in a chair beside Gilles. Her voice sharpened. 'Many of you have been ill-used, many of you would have wished for the chance to serve a more honest master.'

The crew exchanged glances, not yet sure what was happening. The natural succession, while Joost was relieved of his command, should pass to First Lieutenant Roord. But he was standing behind Madame Reydon-Joubert with his hands folded in front of him, the second lieutenant beside him.

'It is why,' Louise continued, 'with the authority vested in me through my ownership of the *Old Moon* and my close relationship with mevrouw Van Raay, I am taking it upon myself to assume command of the ship.'

Someone gasped, and was quickly hushed.

'I understand that, for many of you, this will be unthinkable. A woman in charge, such a thing does not happen. And I understand. But gentlemen, I give you this pledge. I will be as fair as any man, and will reward handsomely all who serve me. Though I have not spent much of my life at sea, it is in my blood as much as it is in yours. I understand the tides and the winds as well as do you. Moreover, I know how to bargain for a good price and believe in the Dutch way that any bounty fairly and honourably come by belongs, by right, to the entire crew.' She nodded to the officer by her side. 'Since Lieutenant Roord is on his first commission, he has generously agreed to give his support to me. So, I ask you now, will you serve under a woman?'

For a moment, no one spoke.

'I say "aye",' shouted Jansz, and he began to clap.

'Aye.' Albert, the cook, stepped forward. His broad shoulders, moon face and huge beard wobbled as he spoke. 'I say aye.'

One by one, the others followed suit, until the deck was filled with sounds of clapping hands and stamping feet.

'Lieutenant,' Louise shouted above the noise, 'if you might provide our crew with a drink? God speed, and I thank you all for your trust.'

As Roord gave the order for a tureen of bumboo to be brought on deck, Gilles came quietly to stand beside her.

'Mistress and commander,' he whispered.

Louise looked at his beloved face. He appeared overwhelmed with pride. She had no idea what would happen when Joost returned to his senses but, for now, the first hurdle had been overcome.

'Together we will do great things, Gilles,' she said. 'Things to make the heavens sing.'

Later that night, at the changing of the watch, someone slipped into the cabin where Hendrik Joost was confined. A single thrust into the captain's side pierced his lung – a point so fine, so narrow that the wound almost closed as the blade was withdrawn. Joost gave a gasp, like a sigh, and appeared to carry on sleeping. A little blood seeped into the cot. Eventually, his breathing slowed, his heart stuttered and stopped beating.

The murderer watched until they were sure Joost was dead, then stole away into the night as silently as they had come.

# CHAPTER FIFTY-ONE

*Saturday, 3 April*

At seven bells fore noon, the body of Hendrik Joost was committed to the deep.

Louise had arranged a simple service to be held in the presence of the entire crew, with Lieutenant Roord acting as pastor. Though he was a Catholic, his years in Amsterdam had made him conversant with the rites expected by the Calvinist mariners. Louise thought Roord had missed his vocation. Inadequate and nervous as a sailor, he read well in a voice both clear and honest. He belonged in the pulpit not at the helm of a ship.

As he closed the prayer book, she nodded her thanks. She might have led the committal herself, but though the pragmatic seafarers had accepted a woman as the temporary captain of the *Old Moon*, to ask them to listen to a woman preach a sermon would have been too much.

They had sewn Joost's body in a Dutch flag, weighted with shot, so he could be buried at sea. The *Old Moon* would not make land in Las Palmas for some weeks more, and they could not keep a dead body on board. Louise would write a full report for Cornelia, and a letter of condolence to Joost's father, though she was under no illusion that he would let the matter rest. One way or another, there would be consequences. Lieutenant Roord had certified that death appeared to be due to a sudden and fatal loss of breath. Joost had suffocated. What she would not mention was that it was brought about by a stab wound that had pierced his lung.

'Such a tragedy in one so young.'

Plain Calvinist words were spoken at his committal, she would put that in the letter, too. How his men had loved him and been honoured to serve under him.

A tapestry of lies.

Louise had no idea who had crept into the cabin late last evening – every man had a knife or a cutlass and everyone on board, without exception, had reason to hate Joost. But it was a far step from hatred to murder.

*And what right do I have to judge?*

Louise glanced at Gilles, who was standing beside Jansz. Was it possible he was responsible? Hadn't he threatened to break Joost's neck? But when she caught his eye, he met her gaze with a clear and untroubled look, and she was reassured. She was beyond redemption, but she did not want Gilles to damn his soul for her sake.

As for the memories Joost's assault on her had stirred, she put them to one side. She did not have the strength to deal with what she had witnessed when she was a little girl. Not now, not yet.

'In the name of the Father, the Son and the Holy Ghost,' said Roord, making the sign of the cross. 'Amen.'

Louise gave a nod. Jorgen and Lange stepped forward and tipped the plank. The body slid slowly into the sea with barely a splash, and was pulled down beneath the waves by the heavy weight. The crew remained with their heads bowed, until the boatswain rang the bell to signify the service was over. A moment of silence followed on deck, then a shuffling of feet.

'Gentlemen, a moment of your time,' Louise said, stepping up to the quarterdeck. She looked around the men in their tatty slops, Albert, the cook, in his apron, Lieutenant Roord in his long coat, Jansz, Lange towering above everyone else, the red hair of the De Groot brothers, Jorgen's grizzled beard, Pieter's scrawny arms and legs. 'Be under no illusion, this will not be the end of things. Hendrik Joost was the son of a wealthy man, an influential man. Someone amongst you knows what happened. I tell you this. I do not intend to investigate. But I will be in my cabin until the next bell should anyone have something they might wish to confide. For the sake of their conscience. After that, I shall consider the matter closed pending our arrival into Las Palmas. In return, I ask you all – for the good of the ship and the companionship we share – not to allow this incident to be the subject of gossip either on board, or on shore.' She paused. 'It would be a kindness for his father to believe his son to have been a fair and beloved commander, even if many of you might feel he does not deserve such consideration.'

Louise gave a final look around, to ensure that her message had struck home, then turned to Roord. 'Thank you for your address, lieutenant. I am in your debt. If I might finish with words from the psalms: "They that go down to the sea in ships, that do business in great waters; these see the works of the Lord, and his wonders in the deep. For He commandeth, and raiseth the stormy wind, which lifteth up the waves thereof."' Louise allowed time for the solemn words to sink in. 'Remember, despite the misfortune of Captain Joost's untimely death, we are fortunate, gentlemen, to be sailing on such a worthy ship. Now, back to work.'

'Aye, aye, captain,' said Jansz.

One by one, the men dispersed, and Louise finally allowed herself to breathe.

# CHAPTER FIFTY-TWO

*Saturday, 10 April*

Seven days had passed since Joost's body had been committed to the deep. They were benefitting from a north-westerly, helping them to pick up speed as they sailed south, not far from the coast of Portugal and Spain onwards to the Strait of Gibraltar. There, God willing, Louise hoped they would be lucky enough to pick up an easterly wind, the Levante, to push them towards the coast of North Africa. All being well, they should make landfall in Islas Afortunadas in three weeks' time.

From listening to Joost, Louise knew the difficulty of maintaining a course. Their speed was measured by the ship's log, so she joined Joris Bleeker on the upper deck to learn more. Joost, for all his faults, had been an expert navigator. Louise watched as the log – a thin rope with knots tied at intervals, with a flat, triangular piece of wood attached from each of the corners with short lines and a lead weight on one edge – was thrown over the taffrail, the thirty-second sand glass timing the rope running out from the reel, then braked to assess their speed.

'Three knots, ma'am,' Bleeker said.

Beside the log bucket stood the lead and the line used to determine depth, another skill essential when sailing closer to the coastline.

So long as the sun and horizon were visible, Louise knew they could calculate latitude. By night, if the sky was clear, they could plot their course by the North Star. All of this taken together, alongside Bleeker's estimate of any sideways drift according to wind speed and direction, enabled them to work out the position of the ship by dead reckoning. The more Louise watched, the more her admiration for her lugubrious second lieutenant grew, a man who had stepped into the breach when they most needed him.

They had provisions enough. The small crew worked well together and there was no flux on board, no sickness or gripe. It was now a harmonious ship. Apart from another storm, the biggest threat, so far as Louise could see, were corsairs as they sailed closer to the Barbary Coast. But the *Old Moon* was nimble and seaworthy. She thought they would be able to outrun any pirate ship.

In the past week, Louise had taken to wearing a plain skirt and a shirt and tying her long brown hair back from her face with a red scarf. Her dagger was in her cabin, her mother's locket she now wore concealed around her neck, and her face was tanned by the sun and wind. She had inherited Joost's vellum map and his cutlass – not wishing to be the only person on board without a fighting weapon of her own – though she knew she would have to return them to his father. Each was valuable and, in the case of the 'stolen' compass and the portolan, of sentimental value. The ivory-encased compass had been found beneath Joost's pillow, confirming Louise's suspicion that the captain had hidden the object himself in an attempt to discredit Gilles.

Louise lifted the spyglass and looked out to sea. Nothing. No clouds on the horizon, no sign of any other ships, no corsair flag fluttering in the April sunshine.

On the deck below, she saw Gilles patting Pieter on the shoulder. She knew the boy was homesick. Thanks to Joost's harsh treatment, his initial excitement of being at sea for the first time had faded quickly. Louise smiled. Gilles was always kind, his childhood having given him a sixth sense for the suffering of others, and she loved how the men had come to respect him. He wrote his own log each day, making a record for Cornelia of everything that happened on board. But he turned himself to practical tasks, too, and helped Lieutenant Roord, who was frequently confined to his cabin with some malady of the stomach. It seemed her second-in-command spent more time on his knees in prayer than fulfilling his duties at the helm.

Louise knew the new informality on board could not last. Once they docked in Las Palmas, the usual protocols would come back into play. But for now, this was the life she had dreamt about as a child. This was the freedom she had hungered for, and she knew Gilles felt it, too. For all the mistakes of Louise's life – those of her own making and those forced upon her – for all the fears of what the future might hold, here, on the deck of the *Old Moon*, she was the person she was born to be.

*Mistress and commander.*

She no longer tried to pretend that everything wasn't better with Gilles at her side. She accepted, now, that she loved him. There were few secrets on board a ship, eleven people living at such close quarters, and the fact that Gilles' true self remained undiscovered was testament to his intelligence and discretion. People saw what they wanted to see – he had learnt that in La Rochelle all those years ago. He had now lived as a boy for as long as he had been a girl.

Louise was careful they did not overstep the mark. As a breed, sailors were inclined to live and let live, but were superstitious and had firm opinions about everything from God to the price of beer. They had accepted a female commander, grateful to be freed from Joost's vindictive command, but she felt her Calvinist crew would baulk at a love affair between her and a man some fifteen years her junior. She smiled.

*As if that would be the true objection if they knew.*

Still, they sometimes managed to be alone with one another, if only to check the books or to discuss the wines they might purchase in Gran Canaria. Otherwise, an occasional touch of a hand had to suffice, leaving Louise always wanting more. Was not this also what her grandmother had counselled, to have someone at her side?

Once they made land that, too, would change. She would have to hand back command of her ship to another captain and return to a constrained female life. It would be her responsibility to report Joost's death. She had managed to put thoughts of Gilles' mother from her mind, but the closer they got to shore, the more Louise started to dread what news might be chasing her from Amsterdam. Or from Chartres. Or both.

*I do not want this adventure to be over.*

A few days later, as the dog watch was coming to an end, there was a knock on her cabin door.

Louise had asked Roord to come and see her when he came off duty. They had picked up the trade winds off the coast of Portugal and were making fair progress in the afternoons, before a slower pace at night. A good north-to-north-westerly had sent the *Old Moon* flying across the water, but they needed the wind to shift to the east to see them beyond the Strait of Gibraltar. The particular geography of the region funnelled the wind between the mountains of Spain and those of North Africa, making the straits difficult to navigate in a westerly. The danger would be running into a stretch of calm weather along the

Moroccan coast, so Louise wanted to discuss Roord's forecasts with him.

'Come in, lieutenant,' she called.

Gilles grinned and raised the charts he was carrying in his arms. 'He is indisposed. I am his emissary.'

She smiled with delight. 'What ails him this time?'

'A bad piece of salted pork, so he thinks. He is praying for deliverance. May I come in, or am I not welcome?'

Louise laughed. 'Of course you are.'

He lightly placed his hand on her waist, then spread the charts on the table.

'Roord seems to be concerned about the wind dropping as we pass the North African coast. He is praying that it will not.'

'He is right. The danger is us being becalmed and losing several days, perhaps as much as a week.' Gently, she slid her hand along the table until it was resting lightly against his.

'Would that matter so very much?' he asked.

Louise forced herself to concentrate. 'We have provisions enough to allow a few days' slippage, and we still have fresh water. No, the bigger concern is that we might be a target for Barbary corsairs operating out of the port of Salé, if we are becalmed. For the most part they are Moriscos, expelled from Spain. But their numbers are swelled by Christians who have turned Turk. Their most valuable cargo is people, seized from villages and coastal towns in Spain and France, even from as far as England.' She shook her head. 'It is their trading example, I regret to say, that the VOC hopes to emulate. The slave markets in Salé and in Valetta, Moslem and Christian alike, are notorious and profitable.'

'Jansz mentioned there is a Dutchman among their number.'

Remembering one of the stories Captain Janssen had told her on the night of his banquet in La Rochelle, Louise nodded.

'Jan Janszoon was originally a privateer from Haarlem. Some twenty years ago, he was issued with letters of marque allowing him to harass Spanish ships, but he overstepped the boundaries of his agreement and was penalised for it. Subsequently, he found his way to the Barbary Coast, where he launched attacks on ships of pretty much every foreign state. He flew the Dutch flag when he attacked a Spanish vessel, and the crescent moon and star of the Turks when he attacked any other – English, Portuguese, French, Italian.'

'Why did he convert?'

'The tale is that he was kidnapped by Moslem forces in Lanzarote, and converted to their faith. After that, he sailed with another Dutchman who had also converted – Ivan Dirkie de Veenboer, who went by the name of Sulayman Rais. When de Vennboer was killed, two or maybe three years ago, Janszoon moved his operations to Salé.'

Gilles glanced back down at the chart. 'But if we find ourselves becalmed, how would they be able to attack us if they were subject to the same weather?'

Louise entwined her fingers with his. He caught his breath.

'The conditions near the shore are not the same as out here in the ocean,' she said.

'And, because of the manpower on the oars, they are not reliant on the wind, as we are.'

'Precisely. Cornelia lost a ship last season in this stretch of water – and another ten years previously, the *White Dove*, the ship on which Janssen was taken captive. Her insurance premiums consequently are high, hence the need for investment from Joost's father. All this is why I wanted to discuss the forecast with the lieutenant.'

'I see.'

Louise continued to examine the chart for a little longer, then stepped away from the table, letting go of Gilles' hand with regret. 'Roord's prediction is that we will be lucky, and sail through to arrive in Las Palmas on time. But it is hard to have faith in a man who is mostly prostrate in his cot rather than at the helm. Bleeker's navigational skills are good, but the situation is not ideal.'

Gilles grinned. 'Roord is not made for a life at sea. But I would say, with a compass and spyglass, his monitoring of the clouds and the winds is excellent. Or so it seems to me. I am sure he can explain his calculations, however agitated his stomach.'

Louise looked through her long, narrow window. It was pitch-black, no stars over the sea tonight.

'I suppose it can wait until the morning,' she said lightly.

The candle guttered in its cage and she shivered, suddenly overcome.

*This is the moment.*

The ship was holding steady, the sea was calm, the wind gentle in the north. Beyond her closed door, Louise could hear the usual evening sounds of the late watch: the De Groot brothers rolling dice; Pieter singing in his reedy voice; Lange's bellowing laugh.

'Will you take a cup of wine with me?' she asked, and her heart lifted as delight lit his face.

'I would be honoured. And I have something for you.'

'You do?'

Gilles reached into his doublet and pulled out a sheet of paper. 'This time we have spent—' He stopped, began again. 'I know you regret how things will change when we arrive in Las Palmas. As do I. And I know how little you wish to relinquish command of the ship – of your ship – and that is a source of sorrow for you, too. So, I wanted to give you something to remember these weeks at sea.'

He handed the paper to her. Her heart sped up, not knowing what to expect. Louise looked down to see an exquisite painting of the *Old Moon*: the red, white and blue of the VOC flag, Cornelia's colours of green and gold, her own mark of an emerald drop on a silver background. Surrounding the ship were waves and sea monsters, copied from memory from the globe in Warmoesstraat. And in the four corners, the Tarot cards: the page of swords, Justice, the ten of cups and the lovers, *l'Amoureux*, bearing, or so she imagined, a marked resemblance to her and to Gilles.

'It is exquisite,' she said softly. 'I had no idea you could draw.'

'I cannot, not really.' He paused. 'I made the labels for my uncle's casks and designed his crest, nothing more.'

Louise was silent, then touched the image of *l'Amoureux*: 'You remember that day?'

Gilles laughed. 'I think of it all of the time – the eighth day of November in the year of Our Lord 1620.'

She smiled. 'I thought I had done the wrong thing by taking you to the cartomancer. That I had presumed too much.'

He shook his head. 'The opposite. I have never forgotten how you wanted to give me a gift, something that would matter to me. No one, not even my uncle, had ever done that before.'

She stepped a little closer. 'I am glad.'

'And since then – and before that in La Rochelle – you have given me everything.' He gently touched her hair. 'So, I wanted to give you something in return. It's not much.'

'It's beautiful.' Louise looked down again at the painting. 'You have given me more than you know, Gilles, but this is perfect.'

She placed her hand flat upon his cheek, then using the motion of the ship, tipped forward on her toes and kissed him on the lips.

'Will you stay with me tonight?' she asked. The hour glass was running down. For one night, the real world could be forgotten. It was time out of time. 'Stay here with me.'

He met her gaze. 'Do you order it, mistress captain?'

'I do.'

Gilles smiled. 'Then I am yours to command.'

# CHAPTER FIFTY-THREE

*Sunday, 11 April*

The following day was Easter Day. Louise arranged a service on deck, with lieutenant Roord once again officiating.

Though she could hear the words, her head was full of the memories of last night, the softness and gentleness, each seeing herself reflected in the other. The passion, too. Louise had never thought to experience such feelings.

They could have lain in one another's arms all night, but wisdom prevailed. At five bells, when the sky was still as dark as ink, Gilles crept from her cabin and returned to his own bunk, leaving her to wonder at how something so complicated could be so simple, too. She could not ever have talked frankly about such matters to Cornelia or her great-aunt, Alis, but she would have liked to ask how they had managed. Hiding in plain sight, she supposed. It was true that society had an abhorrence of men lying together – though it was far from uncommon, especially at sea – but it saw female companionship as a given, without suspecting physical love.

'Alleluia, He is risen. He is risen indeed, Alleluia,' preached Roord, and the crew muttered their amens.

'Amen,' Louise said automatically, thinking of Gilles.

She forced her attention back to the matter in hand, looking around at her crew with something approaching affection: Roord, pale and insubstantial, but his face lit with divine inspiration; the navigator, Joris Bleeker, with his raw skin;

Dirk Jansz, wiry and snub-nosed, his face a map of the life he'd lived; Albert, the cook, in his leather apron, his extravagant beard and his forearms and hands scarred with burns where flames had licked him; the cabin boy, Pieter, looking more his old self; general mariners the De Groot brothers, Lange and Jorgen in their slops, tall and short. Louise felt grateful for their trust and wondered what they were expecting to happen when the *Old Moon* docked in Las Palmas. It had been assumed that her command of the ship was temporary. But what if they, like she and Gilles, did not want the voyage to end?

*Might it be possible?*

'In the name of the Father, the Son and the Holy Spirit, amen.'

'Amen,' Louise proclaimed. So be it.

Another week, and Louise felt spring tipping into summer. Here, off the coast of Africa in mid-April, the hotter months felt closer at hand. The air was more oppressive and the days longer. Red sands blew from the east. The winds filled their sails, billowing white clouds against an endless blue sky, sending the *Old Moon* skimming over the water.

The ocean beneath the ship was alive. Shifting colours of green and blue; leaping silver-backed swordfish and dolphins racing alongside; sea dogs, and translucent jellyfish hovering below the surface of the water; creatures with ancient spines and gaping mouths, nothing like the sea pigs and sirens on Cornelia's globe, but wondrous all the same.

Roord had recovered from his latest bout of indigestion and, as Gilles had said, proved to have a good grasp of the weather and wind. He reported to Louise each day, explaining in his dry voice the course he thought they should follow.

'In my estimation, captain, we are on track to arrive in Las Palmas de Gran Canaria on the twenty-sixth day of April.'

Louise's hand stole to her mother's locket at her neck, not sure if she was perturbed by the coincidence, or if it meant nothing at all. Being in the company of sailors and their superstitions had made her see signs and portents where none had existed before.

'Why is the date significant?' Gilles asked later, as they stole a few minutes together at midnight. It was a cloudy night with no moon. Louise could not tell where the sea ended and the sky began.

'It is the anniversary of my mother's death.' She had not told him what else she had now remembered in the wake of Joost's attack. It was still too raw, too difficult, to share.

'Which, in turn,' he said, 'was two days after you first set foot upon this ship—'

'– and nearly drowned.'

They both smiled at how easily they finished one another's sentences. Their growing intimacy had, of course, not gone unnoticed. But because Louise took care never to favour Gilles, and he was popular with the crew, there had been no rumblings of complaint. At least, she believed that to be true.

'In which case,' Gilles was saying, 'we must make sure that this April the twenty-fourth – and the two days after that – are remembered for wonderful things. For you commanding your ship safe home to harbour.'

'Replace the bad memories with new.'

'Yes. You are not that same person, Louise,' Gilles said, placing his hand beside hers on the rail. 'Touch wood, things are different now.'

She stroked his cheek, moved by the loyalty in his voice. 'Ah, you are superstitious as any mariner, too.'

'I am now.'

'There is no need to be. I am here. We are together.'

Suddenly, in the darkness behind them, came the sound of running footsteps.

'Captain?'

They quickly moved apart at the sound of Pieter's anxious voice.

'Captain, will you come?'

Louise looked down to the deck below. 'What is it?'

The cabin boy gulped, his face white with fear. 'Lieutenant Roord thinks there is another ship to starboard.'

# CHAPTER FIFTY-FOUR

'Tell me what you heard, lieutenant,' Louise said. She and Gilles were both now standing with Roord on the quarterdeck, looking out over the sea's inky-black expanse.

'I took the middle watch,' he began. 'The ship was quiet. There was barely a breeze.'

Louise waved her hand, nerves making her impatient. 'Go on.'

'I thought I heard a faint washing and splashing of another craft moving to our starboard side. Some way off, but there all the same. Then, though I could not swear to it, a kind of a creaking, then a series of dull thumps.'

'You are sure it was not the sounds of our own men?'

'No, it was further away. Astern of us.'

'What do you think it can be?' Gilles asked.

'I cannot be certain, but it sounded like a ship opening her hatches and running out her guns.'

Louise walked to the highest point and looked out to starboard. She could see nothing through the night-time mist, nothing but blackness. She stood for a while, feeling the gentle pitch of the ship.

'Our speed has dropped.'

'Yes, ma'am. As I feared, the wind has decreased in this patch of cloudy weather. But it should pick up as we get closer to the Islas Afortunadas.'

Louise looked back over her shoulder. 'And we hope to out-run them, if it comes to that?'

'Yes, that is our best hope.' The lieutenant paused, his eyes scrutinising the darkness. 'I might be mistaken.'

'You're not.' They had been a month at sea. Louise knew what the emptiness of the ocean felt like and she, too, could sense they were no longer alone. Somebody was out there. Like a giant creature in the mist, stalking its prey. 'Where, precisely, are we?'

'We passed Agadir some four hours ago.'

'And the nearest landfall would be Lanzarote?'

'Yes, ma'am.'

She thought for a moment. 'What do you suggest?'

'There is nothing we can do until morning,' Roord replied, 'when we will know for certain if there is another vessel. Then, we can assess if she is a danger or just another merchant ship like us, intending no harm.'

'But you heard them arm their guns?' Gilles said.

'I *think* I did, but there is no way of knowing if that was for the purpose of attack or defence.'

Louise clutched the taffrail tightly, the memories of Cornelia's loss of the *New Star* and her crew last season at the forefront of her mind. None of the men had ever come back. Drowned, or lost to the slave markets of Salé, Tunis, Agadir and Valetta.

'We should make our guns ready, too,' she said. 'Prepare for the worst, but hope for the best. It is possible their captain is having the same discussion about us as we are having about them.'

'And then?' Gilles asked.

'We wait,' she replied grimly. 'As the lieutenant says, we can do nothing until it gets light.'

Watching the sky turn from black to white, Louise thought the night would never end. There was almost no wind and they were barely moving. The *Old Moon* rolled gently from side to side on the almost still ocean, becalmed.

Louise paced up and down at the stern, waiting and watching. Gilles brought her a cup of cloudy beer and a ship's biscuit to stay her, but she couldn't eat. Counting the minutes down. Until, there it was. Unmistakable even in the early morning mizzle, the outline of another ship. A furled lateen sail and a ladder of long oars in the water.

'Lieutenant,' she said quietly, passing the glass. 'I fear it is a corsair galley.'

Roord raised the spyglass to his eye, then exhaled. 'Yes.'

'Can you see her colours?'

He adjusted the setting. 'No, ma'am.'

Louise narrowed her eyes and tried to fix the vessel in her sights. Some oared galleys, powered by enchained oarsmen, might have as many as twenty-five pairs of oars, requiring five men to operate each one. Galleys were typical corsair ships, long and low and sleek, with a projecting beak at the bow, but it was odd to see one out in the open water of the Atlantic alone – they were better suited to the relatively calm conditions in the Mediterranean and Corsairs usually hunted in packs.

'How many oars?'

'I would wager no more than six,' Roord estimated.

She nodded. 'I agree.'

'Which would make how many crew?' Gilles said, appearing at her elbow.

'It is impossible to know, but many more than us.'

'Where are their cannon?'

'Mounted in the bow,' Roord answered.

Gilles frowned. 'Which means to aim the cannon, they have to aim the ship head on rather than come alongside.'

Louise nodded again, as always impressed with how immediately Gilles understood. 'Precisely. But it is rare for corsairs to do more than fire a warning shot across the bow. Their trade is in people and cargo, so they want to capture a ship intact. Lieutenant, what do you think is our best course of action?'

'We are wholly at the mercy of the wind, captain.'

'Whereas they have manpower in their oars.'

'Yes, ma'am.'

'And if they mean us harm? Attempt to board us?'

'We should seek to negotiate.'

'With pirates?' Gilles exclaimed. 'Is that possible?'

Louise turned to him. 'Each of the ports negotiates its own trading treaties. If this galley has, say, come from Tunis, with whom there is a trade agreement with the Dutch Republic, they are not permitted to attack Dutch ships or steal our cargo. Dutch citizens should, in theory, be protected. Although, of course, they do not always abide by such terms.'

'And if there is no agreement?'

'Then we are fair game,' she said, turning her gaze back towards the galley. 'It depends on the flag they are flying.' She paused. 'Lieutenant, does it not seem to you that the oars are dragging in the water? The sail is furled. The galley looks as if it is drifting.'

Roord handed back the spyglass. 'It looks like that.'

'What does that mean?' asked Gilles.

Louise shook her head. 'I don't know. Either that they do not intend to pursue us, in which case why are they here? Or there has been some catastrophe on board. An outbreak of contagion, perhaps.'

'Or mutiny,' said Roord.

# CHAPTER FIFTY-FIVE

The *Old Moon* was silent, the crew standing along the starboard rail. All had heard terrifying stories of the Barbary corsairs and their ruthless capture of merchant ships. Louise knew that each and every man would be thinking of home, that he might never see his family again. She saw Gilles put his hand on Pieter's shoulder to give him courage.

*This is the greatest challenge of my command.*

Yet the galley still didn't seem to be getting any closer. Louise knew how the thickening light on the horizon, and the motion of the sea beneath them, distorted judgement. It was hard to gauge the distance between the two vessels.

*What are they waiting for?*

At five bells, their luck changed. A gust from the north-east filled their sails and they began to pick up speed. The same was true for the galley, which was windward of them. Louise told Roord to change direction and come round behind the other ship. A hunter and its prey, Louise thought, trying to steady her hammering heart.

At six bells, the galley was close enough for them to be able to distinguish its colours.

'They are flying three crescent moons on a green ground,' she said.

Roord nodded. 'So, most likely a slaver ship out of Salé.'

'And they are gaining on us,' she added, lowering her voice. 'Are the cannon primed?'

'Both to port and starboard, yes.'

'Then there is nothing more we can do now but wait.'

Louise had never before felt trapped on the *Old Moon* – at least, not since Joost had died – but now the short hairs on the back of her neck were standing on end. Knowing that there was an enemy in the water behind them, perhaps even gaining on them, filled her with a terrifying paralysis. It was like watching a storm build on the horizon, and knowing there was nothing they could do to escape it.

She had Joost's cutlass tied around her waist and she checked to see every mariner was armed, able to defend himself. On their faces, she saw a mixture of emotions – fear, determination, courage. Lieutenant Roord had given Gilles a dirk, one of a pair inherited from his father. Most of the others had short knives tucked into their tunics, better suited for hand-to-hand combat at sea. Pieter, she noticed, had a long slender blade on his belt, as thin as a needle at its tip.

She gave a low whistle. 'So, it was Pieter,' she muttered to herself, making the connection to Joost's death: a blade like a stiletto, capable of making a wound almost too small to see. Not a born murderer, just a boy who fought back. But none of that mattered now. None of them might live to see the sun rise tomorrow.

Louise wrapped her scarf around her head, covering her hair, then climbed to the quarterdeck. She stood with her legs braced and her hand on the brass grip of the cutlass, ready to defend the *Old Moon* and all who sailed in her. If they were to go down fighting, she would be at their side.

*But if Gilles should die . . .*

Louise pushed the thought away. They would survive, or not, but whatever was to happen, they would face it together.

The galley was getting closer. But as the vessel came within hailing distance, Louise saw her first instincts had been right.

There was no sign of activity. The benches appeared to be manned, though no one seemed to be rowing. Some of the wooden blades hovered on the surface of the water, others seemed to bob in the waves, but there was no sound of oars pulling together, and no overseer shouting the stroke or cracking the whip.

*What horror is this?*

Louise leant over the rail to see more clearly. Now she could make out that although there were men chained to each bench, naked to the waist, most were slumped forwards, as if inebriated. Others seemed to have fallen sideways. No one was moving, except with the rocking of the gentle waves.

She caught her breath.

'Gilles,' she shouted. 'Roord!' In an instant, they were both at her side. 'Do you see? They are dead, everyone is dead.'

'Unless the corsairs are hiding below, ma'am.'

Louise frowned. 'Waiting for us to board, before ambushing us?'

'It is a tactic they have used in the past to good effect.'

She thought for a moment. 'No. The galley is drifting,' she said, then realised what that meant. 'It's drifting,' she repeated urgently. 'Which means if it continues on its current course, it will collide with us. Roord, trim our sails to allow the galley to come alongside.'

The vessel bobbed closer, and closer again, until it was almost beside them in the sway. Louise swallowed hard, as the full horror became evident. Shackled to their benches, open staring eyes, mouths slack, arms loose. On the raised beak, the overseer with a white turban and long moustache was curled on his side as if sleeping, his whip still in his hand. Another lay between the benches, with two more in the shadow of the lateen sail.

'In the name of God, what happened here?' Roord whispered.

Louise exhaled. 'It's the ghost ship,' she said.

# CHAPTER FIFTY-SIX

Roord began to pray.

Louise felt an overwhelming sense of pity, of shock. It was a floating charnel house. She had no explanation for how an entire company could have been killed at the same time, nor how the galley came to be drifting this far out in the ocean, but Louise had heard of such a thing once before. That night of Captain Janssen's banquet – the night she had met Gilles for the first time – he had told her of a ship, crewed by the dead. Every man, slave and corsair alike, suffocated. Killed by noxious air that sucked the breath from a man's chest, leaving no mark, no signs of violence. She had dismissed it as the inebriated ramblings of an old sailor home from the sea, another of his tall tales.

*And yet . . .*

Janssen had been captured by Barbary corsairs. He had certainly sailed this same route from Amsterdam to Gran Canaria on many an occasion, and on this very ship, the *Old Moon*. There was no knowing what manner of stories he might have heard. Louise wished, now, she had paid closer attention.

How long had the galley been drifting? Where had it come from? The colours announced it was from Salé, but given so many ships flew false flags, that might well not be true.

As thoughts tumbled through her mind, Louise was also conscious of a deep sense of relief. They were not out of danger, far from it – whatever had afflicted the vessel and its crew might affect them, too – but there would be no battle today.

'Lieutenant, tell the men to stand down.'

Roord crossed himself, and went to deliver the order.

One by one, Louise watched her small band of sailors sheath their weapons. Though grateful they did not have to fight, she could see they were as scared by an enemy they could not see as they might have been by the scimitars of the corsairs. Pieter was muttering to Lange, and the boatswain Jansz unexpectedly fell to his knees, with his hands pressed together in prayer.

'Could it be some kind of contagion?' Gilles said. 'A sudden plague, as you suspected.'

Louise shook her head. 'There's no evidence of sickness, or flux; do you see? No stench of blood, or human effluvia, which there would be if it was the plague. From here, we would smell it. They all look as if they simply stopped breathing at the same time. The crew, as well as their prisoners.'

Gilles nodded. 'And no evidence of attack, either.'

'So far as I can see, none.'

Then, unmistakably, they heard the sound of a human voice from somewhere within the ghost ship. Louise leant forward, both hands gripped on the gunwale.

'Did you hear that?' She narrowed her eyes and scanned the galley, looking for signs of movement somewhere.

'There!' Gilles cried, pointing to the beak at the bow.

Louise saw an emaciated figure get to his feet. A man with pale skin, with brown hair, bare to the waist. Northern European, not Moroccan. He stood unsteadily, tilting with the gentle lapping roll of the galley, staring at the *Old Moon* as if he couldn't believe the ship was real.

'Ahoy,' Louise called.

The figure swayed, but didn't respond.

'Is anyone else alive?' she shouted in Dutch. Nothing. She tried again in French. '*Est-ce qu'il y a quelqu'un d'autre de vivant?*'

This time, a reaction. A slow, stunned shaking of the head.

'Can we risk bringing him on board, lieutenant?'

Roord frowned. 'If it is a contagion, then he could be infected too.'

'Dying, but not yet dead,' she murmured.

'We must put ourselves first, ma'am.'

'How long have you been alone?' she called out across the water, speaking slowly and clearly. It was evident the man was in shock, possibly suffering from lack of water. Captain Janssen had told her of how men deprived of water began to hallucinate, seeing creatures that were not there, tearing at their own skin. How they were crazed enough to drink seawater, which swelled their bellies and killed them. 'If you cannot speak, give me a sign.'

The man held up six fingers.

'Hours or days?' Gilles muttered at her side.

'*Six jours?*' she shouted. '*Tu es seul depuis six jours?*'

The same slow, steady nod.

Louise turned to Roord. 'If he is telling the truth – and he knows how much time has elapsed – surely then the contagion has passed him by.'

'We cannot be sure. A true quarantine is forty days.'

'You think we should leave him to his death?'

Roord flushed. 'It is a matter of the good of us all.'

Louise turned to Gilles. 'What do you think?'

He hesitated. 'The lieutenant is correct in that we must protect our ship and crew. But the fact seems to be that this one man has been spared.' He glanced at Roord. 'God has saved him.'

'Unless the corsairs are hiding below.'

'But we can see several of their number, Roord, and they also are dead.'

'It is too great a risk.'

Louise considered for a moment more, then made her decision. 'You are right, it is a risk. But, in all good conscience, we cannot leave him. And we need to know what happened. What befell this galley might also affect us. He is the only witness to it.' She looked between them. 'Are we agreed?'

'Agreed,' Gilles said.

Roord held out for a moment longer, though in truth he knew she did not need his agreement, then nodded.

'Do you think he will be able to climb up, if we throw the ladder down?' Gilles asked. 'Or should someone go across to fetch him?'

Louise looked at the distance. The highest point of the galley was at least six feet below their gunwale. 'No, I won't risk any one of our men setting foot on the galley. But, if he can hold on to the struts, then we can pull him up. It's not far.'

With Gilles shouting instructions as the only other speaker of French, the survivor managed to understand what was required of him. He stumbled, but then got up again and staggered to the edge of the beak.

Jansz threw across a grappling line and, with the help of Lange and the De Groot brothers, dragged the galley closer. The boatswain then lowered the ladder and the man twisted the rope around his arms and held on to the wooden struts.

'Heave,' Jansz shouted, and they began to haul the ladder back up the side of the hull. 'Steady does it.'

The survivor's head appeared, then his pale arms, then the sailors put their hands under his armpits and heaved their new passenger onto the deck.

Gilles immediately crouched down beside him. 'You are safe, now,' he said. '*Tu es entre amis.* With friends.'

Louise felt a wave of fury when she saw the shackles around his ankles, his skin bleeding and cracked, then noticed a mark in the shape of a crescent moon on his shoulder. Was he a Morisco?

*Is that what had saved him from the oars?*

Louise saw that the entire crew was watching, understandably suspicious of the man they'd just rescued. 'Take him to the small cabin, we will treat him there. He is one of us. We need to know what happened to prevent it afflicting us, too. Do you understand?'

There was a pause, then Pieter spoke. 'Aye, aye, captain,' he said, his high voice ringing out clearly.

There was a moment of delay, then Jansz stepped up and, in one motion, picked the man up from the deck and carried him to the cabin.

'Begging your pardon, captain,' Lange said, 'but if there is cargo, shouldn't we salvage it?'

Louise considered for a moment. 'No, I would not have any one of us set foot on the ghost ship. Not until we know what happened there.'

# CHAPTER FIFTY-SEVEN

As eight bells were rung for the end of the fore noon watch, Louise and Lieutenant Roord entered the cabin where the survivor was resting. Gilles, as the unofficial ship's doctor – the ship's crew being too small to warrant a dedicated sawbones – was waiting.

'Captain,' he said, standing up. 'Lieutenant.'

'How is he?' Louise asked.

'Hard to say. In a state of shock. Given he has been the only one alive on the galley for almost a week, his condition is reasonable. I think he will be able to talk. He has no injuries, there is nothing wrong with him beyond a lack of food and drink, and the horror of what he witnessed.'

'His shackles?'

'Jansz managed to remove them. His skin is broken, but there is no sign of infection.'

'Thank you.'

Leaving Roord by the door – he was still fearful of contagion – Louise crossed the cabin and sat on the chair Gilles had placed by the bed. The Frenchman still looked stunned, pale and under-nourished, but she could see he was returning to himself. Fresh clothes, a tankard of watered rum and ship's biscuit – the first food he had eaten for nearly a week – had helped. He looked more like a man, less like a ghost. He struggled to get up.

'Please, stay as you are,' she said in French. 'You need to conserve your strength.'

'*Merci*,' he whispered. 'Thank you.'

'Can you answer a few questions?'

'Yes, ma'am.'

Louise nodded. 'Good. Then will you tell me your name?'

'Marco Rossi, as it pleases you.'

'And how old are you?'

'I have seen eighteen summers, ma'am.'

As if it was not a matter of consequence, she calmly said: 'Can you tell us what happened? Take as long as you need.'

For a moment, Rossi said nothing. 'I come from Vieste,' he began, almost too quietly to be heard.

Louise raised her eyebrows. Vieste was within the Hapsburg-controlled states of the Italian peninsula. 'You are Italian? But you also speak French?'

Another pause, as if every word he spoke caused him pain. 'My mother was French, my father Italian. He served in the guard of Marie de' Medici.'

'I see. And when did you return to Vieste?'

'Four years ago, when the Queen Regent was banished from Paris.'

'And then?' Louise prompted gently.

He swallowed hard. 'They came in the evening, came into the church and took us all – men, women, children – at the point of the sword. Put us on a ship for Salé.' He closed his eyes. 'In retaliation, they said, for the slave markets of Valetta. All the thousands of Moslem souls taken by the Knights Hospitallers.'

Louise nodded. Cornelia had once told her that Malta was considered the heart of the Christian slave trade in the Mediterranean. Not only Ottomans, but captives from southern and central Africa – and places unknown even to the globe in Warmoesstraat – were traded and sold in the markets there.

*Like for like, an eye for an eye.*

'We sailed south around the coast of Sicily to Salé,' Rossi continued. 'I was taken to the market, stripped naked, my father and mother, too.' He took a deep breath. 'I never saw them again. I know not whether they live.'

Gilles rested his hand on the man's shoulder.

'And from there?' Louise asked.

'I was bought by a slaver and put to work on the oars. In the market, I spoke to a man taken from a Spanish ship. He told me that, if I was offered the chance to turn Turk, I should take it. He claimed they treated those captives better.'

'Hence the mark on your shoulder?' Gilles said.

Rossi nodded. 'It's from a branding iron in the market. I will never forget the smell, nor the agony, but it bought me a privileged position on the bench and better rations, though they were meagre enough. And I was permitted to walk freely on the deck, rather than always being shackled to the bench. Others were condemned to sit day and night in their own filth. We were Italians, mostly, but Dutch and English, too. Some French.'

Gilles held the cup to his lips, and Rossi took a sip of rum.

'We sailed from Malta along the coast of North Africa, putting in at Tunis, before attempting the Strait of Gibraltar. Though I couldn't understand much of what was going on – the corsairs spoke a mixture of Berber and Dutch—'

'Those villains were Dutch?' Roord interrupted from the doorway. Louise had all but forgotten he was there, and had not realised he understood French.

'The captain was Dutch by origin, though he had taken a new name and wore the turbaned cap, and buttoned and tasselled tunic of the Salé rovers.'

She smiled. 'You are observant.'

Rossi gave a faint smile. 'I was apprenticed to a tailor in

Vieste, before we were taken. It was this that saved my life. I listened carefully and from what fragments of conversation I could understand, I learnt that we were heading to Lanzarote, one of the Islas Afortunadas, to raid coastal villages there.'

'Slaving raids.'

'Yes. To start with, the wind was with us but, in truth, it made little difference to the mood on board. The overseers shouting and constantly beating any man who mistimed his stroke. Every day, someone died of exhaustion or lack of hope. But then the sea turned against us. A storm blew up. It became impossible to know which direction we were travelling in.'

Louise knew the westernmost tip of the Alboran Sea, coming into the Strait of Gibraltar itself, was notorious. The graveyard of many ships. It was said the voices of the drowned could be heard when the wind was in the west.

'That was where the *New Star* went down,' she said to Gilles, then added for Roord's benefit: 'One of Cornelia van Raay's ships.'

'I had never known such hell,' Rossi continued, shutting his eyes as he re-lived the horror. 'I prayed for God to take me. Waves breaking over the topwale, men choking in their own vomit as the galley pitched. Even the corsairs themselves, accustomed to the vagaries of the weather, prayed to their God for deliverance. Then, just as quickly as it had blown up, the wind dropped and the skies cleared. That was when the captain summoned me to his cabin – he had a favourite tunic he wanted repaired and the lining had caught and been torn during the storm.' Rossi swallowed. 'It was the saving of me. I was taken up to the top deck at the stern and left there to work.'

Louise was starting to understand. 'The highest point of the ship.'

Rossi nodded. 'I was left alone. There was no need to guard

me, for where would I have gone? I started to sew and, for a while, I forgot where I was. Then the wind tended east.'

'Bringing with it a sea fog.'

He nodded again. 'It descended upon us out of nowhere. One moment we were on the open sea, the next the oars and benches had disappeared under the yellow fog that smelt of sulphur and salt.'

'You were above it?'

'The bad air covered the ship. I was looking down on it, like a heavy blanket of dirty wool. Even under the captain's door. I couldn't see anything, but I could hear the men were choking. Our captors too, suffocating.' Rossi covered his face with his hands. 'Such terrible sounds.'

'The *Ghost Ship*,' Louise said, glancing at Gilles. 'It's a tale Captain Janssen told me. I never gave it any credence before.'

Rossi took another sip of rum. 'I was too terrified to move. I prayed that, so long as I stayed above the cloud and didn't breathe the foul air, I might be safe. I don't know how much time passed, but I must have slept. When I next came to, the fog had gone.' He shook his head. 'I have never seen such a sight, and hope never to again. Everyone else was dead, the breath sucked from them were they fell. Captives, our captors, not a soul spared.'

Louise placed her hand on his arm. 'What did you do then?'

'I did nothing,' Rossi replied. 'I was too scared to move from my platform, in case the pestilence came back. I knew that there was no hope, anyway. There was no one to steer the ship; we were drifting. Even if I'd had courage enough to venture down in search of provisions, they might have been tainted with the foul air. Besides, what right did I have to be saved?' He gave a long sigh, as if he had come to the end of his strength. 'When I saw this ship, I thought it was a mirage. Then I heard your voice – a woman's voice speaking to me in French. I thought it was my mother come to take me home.'

Tears welled in his eyes, then he started to sob.

'You are safe now, Marco Rossi,' Louise said gently. 'This is my ship. She's called the *Old Moon* and we are sailing from Amsterdam to Las Palmas de Gran Canaria. Once we make land, we can work out how to get you home to Vieste. Tomorrow, or the next day – whenever you are sufficiently recovered – you can make yourself useful. Your skill with a needle saved you. I am sure we can find plenty of work for you to do.'

'Anything, *capitana*.'

Louise was touched by his natural acceptance of her position. She stood up.

'Remain here for now. Later, Monsieur Barenton will show you where you can sleep.' She dropped her voice. 'Gilles, will you stay with him in case he remembers anything else? Anything he says, can you write it down?'

Gilles gave her a quick smile. 'Of course, *capitana*.'

# CHAPTER FIFTY-EIGHT

*Tuesday, 20 April*

After the strains of the long day, Louise retired to her cabin. Though the origin or cause of bad air was uncertain, it was thought to be the result of some pestilential fermentation in the deep of the ocean. There were several documented cases, all in the same stretch of water. When she reached Las Palmas, she would investigate further.

She sat down on her cot, intending only to rest for a while but, when she next woke, it was dark. Her candle had all but burnt out. She had slept without dreaming, as she mostly did at sea.

But now, as too often in the middle of a wakeful night, unwelcome thoughts flooded her mind. The sight of the ghost ship, its dead crew tethered like animals to their benches, had filled her with pity, but also with fury. If the galley had taken on water or been scuttled, the captives would have been unable to save themselves, dragged down by their chains into the deep ocean. Louise had a profound revulsion to the trafficking of men and women. It did not matter who was the victim, who the captor – Christian, Ottoman, men who served only Mammon – she believed it was wrong. Cornelia felt the same, though Louise knew that sticking to her principles was costing her dearly. Cornelia was accused by fellow voc ship owners of being naïve, of putting sentiment before business in an ever-expanding world.

*I do not believe that we are lone voices.*

Now that Louise had seen the reality of it at first hand, and heard Rossi's account, her opposition was strengthened. And although Janssen had told his story until it was threadbare with retelling, those who, like him, were taken captive, escaped and made it home, were rare birds indeed. She vowed, if she ever made it back to La Rochelle, that she would seek him out and ask him to tell his tale again. This time, she would listen.

*There must be something we can do.*

For a moment, she entertained the possibility that the Stadhuis in Amsterdam might be persuaded to reject any goods transported by slave labour, then dismissed it. The VOC was driven by profit, and sought any advantage over their competitors.

Louise got to her feet and stretched, relieved to feel the forward motion of the ship beneath her feet again. The wind must have picked up. She took a fresh candle from the drawer of her nightstand, held the wick against the guttering flame of her nearly spent candle and lit it. She knew she should go on deck and check that all was well, but she had the glimmering of an idea . . . She sat back down on her cot to think. A ghost ship, a vessel that no one knew if it was real or not.

There was a tap at the door.

'*Kom binnen*,' she replied, assuming Roord had come to report. But again, it was Gilles.

He peered into the candlelit cabin. 'May I come in, *capitana*?'

Louise laughed. 'The *capitana* would be delighted if you did!'

She heard the click of the door being closed, his feet crossing the boards, then he was standing in front of her. Gently, Gilles leant down and kissed the top of her head. She put her arms around his waist and buried her face in his soft belly for a moment. Warm, safe, familiar.

'How is our guest?' she asked, patting the bedding.

Gilles sat down beside her. 'He is doing well. The men are still wary of contagion, of course – no one more so than Lieutenant Roord – but Rossi makes no trouble and he has already set to repairing the luff of the lateen sail.' He grinned. 'Much thicker material than he is used to, of course, but it will be the most elegant stitching ever seen on a ship's canvas.'

'That's good.' Louise sighed, feeling herself relax a little in Gilles' presence. 'Would you like a drink?'

'Let me fetch you something,' Gilles said, going to the side-board, pouring them both a measure of wine, then returning to the bed.

'What time is it?'

'Three bells have just been rung for the middle watch.'

'So late.' On dry land, that would be a half past one in the morning. She had an unexpected pang of nostalgia for the *grosse horloge* and the sound of bells that filled the streets of the Huguenot capital.

'Do you miss La Rochelle?'

For a moment, Gilles didn't answer. 'It's hard to say. Though so many memories – of the town, of my mother, of the night my uncle died – are painful, it was the only home I had ever known. So, the places I used to play, the harbour front, the towers and the lighthouse, those things I do miss.' He paused, then corrected himself. 'No, I don't miss them. Rather, I think of them as I might remember old friends from another life.'

Louise nodded. That she understood.

'What about you, Louise? Do you miss your house in the rue des Gentilshommes? Such a fine building. I had admired it often, even before I knew that its owner was the most beautiful thing about it.'

'Flatterer!'

Gilles put his hand over his heart. 'My lady, I speak no more than the truth. But, in faith, do you see yourself returning? After this?'

Louise sighed. 'I was always restless, Gilles, even as a child. I couldn't stay still. Amsterdam, La Rochelle, Paris, Carcassonne, I never felt I belonged anywhere. When I think of my beautiful house, standing empty with only the servants for company, it means little to me. I would be glad to know my uncle and his family were making use of it – I wrote to him when we left for Amsterdam and gave my steward orders to welcome Jean-Jacques if he came – but if I lost it tomorrow, and I might, I would not mind.'

'You would mind losing this ship, though.'

'Yes, and my independence with it. And with things as they are for Cornelia at present . . .' She broke off. 'Of course, you know.'

'Things are changing in Amsterdam. It is hard for the smaller fleets to adapt to the voc's new demands.'

They sat in silence for a moment, his head on her shoulder, moving in tandem with the comforting sway of the ship.

'I noticed Pieter's weapon. A stiletto,' she said quietly. 'Did you know it was him?'

Gilles sat up. 'I guessed as much.'

'Did you task him about it?'

'No. I think he did it as a service to you. As you did for me in Amsterdam.'

'What happened with your mother was an accident . . .' she said, as she always did, then she stopped. She knew that the secret she continued to carry made them unequal. If he did not know the full truth about who she was, then how could he truly love her?

*I must have faith.*

'But it was not the first time I had taken a life.' There. She had said it. Her words seemed to fall like stones into a pond, sending ripples across the surface of the water. 'I have only just remembered.'

In the semi-darkness, she felt Gilles take her hand, giving her the courage to continue.

'You don't have to tell me.'

She exhaled. 'The day after I fell from the *Old Moon*, my mother returned to Amsterdam, as you know. She was in a state of high excitement. I thought it was because of my accident – my grandfather told her of how he had fished me out of the IJ only just in time – but now I wonder. Whatever the cause, Marta didn't let me out of her sight the whole day long. But just before dawn the following day, the twenty-sixth of April, she slipped out of the bed beside me and put on her clothes – her favourite dress and best slippers.' Louise stopped to gather her thoughts. 'To this day, I still don't know why I didn't call out, or ask her where she was going. Perhaps I just knew better than to draw attention to myself.'

'Children always know,' he said quietly.

'I waited until she had left the room, then I put on my new clogs and my bonnet and cape, and followed.'

'To Kalverstraat?'

'Yes.' Louise took a sip of wine. She had buried this secret so deep inside her – from herself, as well as anyone else – for most of her life, she hardly knew how to bring the words into the light. Her hand went to her mother's locket.

'You needn't go on, not if it is too painful.'

'I want to,' she said, gripping his hand more tightly. 'I was frightened to be out on my own so early in the morning but I thought that, so long as I kept my mother in my sights, I would be all right. I followed her over the canals, across Plaats and into Kalverstraat. I didn't understand what she was doing, except

that it was secret, so I stayed a few steps back. Halfway along
the street, she stopped outside a shop front – it sold fabric and
cloth then, too – and then went inside. I waited, expecting her
at any moment to come back out again. But she didn't.'

'How long did you wait?'

'I don't know.'

'So, you went in to find her.'

Louise nodded. 'When no one was looking, I slipped inside
and up the stairs. The door to the chamber on the first floor
was ajar. I put my eye to the gap and—' She caught her breath.
'I saw him first. A man with a white streak in his black hair,
his doublet unbuttoned and his shirt untucked.'

'Your father.'

'I didn't know that then. He looked dazed, as if he couldn't
comprehend what was happening. Then I heard something hit
the floorboards, metal. I looked down. There was a knife beside
my mother, who was lying on the floor in the blue dress I had
watched her put on that morning. Her skirts and petticoats
were pulled up around her waist.' Louise swallowed. 'I think
he had made use of her – that, too, I only just remembered
when Joost tried . . .' She waved her hand, as if to push away
the memory. 'Nothing of what I was seeing made sense. It was
like a tableau set for a painter to copy, yet I knew my mother
was dead.'

'And then?'

'I pushed open the door wider and went into the room. I
don't think he saw me at first. Then, he seemed to come to.
Whether he knew who I was, or not, I don't know. "I loved
her," he said, looking directly at me. I remember it word for
word now. "I could not live without her, but she would not
have me."'

Louise closed her eyes. 'That angered me. It sounded as if

he was blaming her.' She swallowed hard. 'Then somehow the knife was in my two hands. The hilt was slippery with blood, my mother's blood. Without thinking, as if my hand was not my own, I thrust it into his belly – I was tall for my age, and strong. His eyes widened with shock. He collapsed onto his knees, then fell forward across my mother's body, driving the blade deeper in. It was seeing your mother—'

'– that helped the memory return.'

Louise nodded. 'I was horrified. I don't know what I had intended, perhaps to scare him, or hurt him. Oddly, I think I was more worried that I would be told off for going out on my own than for what I had done. All I could think about was getting home before I was discovered missing. I took the locket from my mother's neck and fled, almost losing my footing at the top of the stairs, then ran out into the street.'

Gilles exhaled. 'Did anyone know you had been there?'

'No one knows but me.'

'And now me,' he said, echoing his words to her in Amsterdam.

'So, you see, Gilles, my soul was already damned before I went to Rokin to confront your mother.'

'No, I won't accept that,' he cried. 'Killing to defend someone we love, how can that be wrong? The entire human race would be damned and thrown into perdition if we failed to protect those we care for.'

For a while, they sat in silence, her confession seeming to shimmer in the air. Louise was conscious of a great weight having lifted from her shoulders. In Carcassonne, all those years ago, she had nearly admitted to her grandmother that she had been in Kalverstraat, but had not wanted to burden her. After Madame Roux's murder, she had almost confessed her earlier crime to Cornelia, as they knelt in the Oude Kerk, but again she had not wanted to burden the elderly woman. Now it was as if something evil inside her had been exorcised, something she had not even known was there. Gilles had not pulled away, he was not judging her.

'Do you think he did love her?' he asked quietly. 'Or she him?'

Louise paused. It was a question she had been asking herself for more than twenty-five years.

'That cannot be what love is,' she said eventually.

The flame guttered and Louise realised they had been talking for some time. As if reading her mind, Gilles fetched another candle from the drawer, lit it from the dying wick, then knelt before her and held her hands between his.

'Would you like to know what I think?'

Exhausted, now, Louise could only nod.

'I think you have spent your life trying to make amends for the great loss you suffered. And now, you have remembered something more. Something so huge, terrible, that it could overwhelm you. But you were a child, Louise – as I was a child when I became who I am now. You have to forgive yourself.'

'I was too late to save her, Gilles,' she said. 'How can I forgive myself for that?'

'It was never in your power to save her, don't you see? But you saved Pieter and Dirk Jansz, you saved Marco Rossi.' He lifted her hand to his lips. 'You saved me.'

Louise felt a spark of hope, a spark of possibility.

'And we could save more,' she said. 'Listen.'

# CHAPTER FIFTY-NINE

*Monday, 26 April*

Over the next six days, Louise and Gilles spent time with Marco Rossi, gathering every detail they could about the corsairs who had taken him from his village – the ways in which they transported their captives, the nature of the markets in Valetta and Salé. Put together with everything she already knew, what became clear was that although the corsairs, the Ottomans and the slavers from France, the Dutch Republic, Spain and Portugal had different justifications for their activities – faith, profit, revenge – their tactics were similar. They all depended on fast raids, superior manpower, making an example of one or two of the men as a warning to the others. Christian or Turk, they were brutal, efficient and cruel.

To be a 'privileged prisoner' – as Rossi had been – was to have certain freedoms. He had heard it said that some captives, when the corsair galleys were laid up in ports such as Alexandria or Tunis over the winter, were even permitted to run taverns in the town, or take a wife, before the hunting season began again. The shackles on their ankles marked them out from free men, but they adapted. Most had no such chance. Louise was horrified to learn that many were held captive for twelve, thirteen or fourteen years. They lived, and died, enslaved. How could she hope to make any difference?

But then, Louise would pull herself up. Saving one Marco Rossi was better than saving no one. Everyone was someone's son, someone's husband. And always her grandmother's words were at the back of her mind, half-remembered, well-worn advice, shared on Minou's last morning on the earth: 'Do not dwell on what is not possible, but rather what you might do in the world.'

Hadn't she already done that? Hadn't she chosen to stand alone, when a woman's lot was to marry and bear children? She had already lived a life so much larger than her ten-year-old self had thought possible, the child who nearly drowned from disappointment. And now, following in the footsteps of her grandparents, of her great-aunt, Alis, and her lifelong companion, Cornelia, she had found love with one who, like her, lived outside of the bounds of normal society. On a ship, for all its challenges, it was still possible. Louise was aware that, every day she sailed further south, the ties binding her to La Rochelle or to Amsterdam were loosening. Soon, they would barely hold her at all.

With her plan taking shape, she realised something more – that the threat of losing her fortune had made her timid. In the sharp brightness of the southern air and the shifting ocean, Louise understood that rather than seek to protect her wealth, she should use it. So, if eventually there was nothing of her fortune left, the claimant from Chartres might pursue her to the four corners of the earth but it would be futile. Louise smiled. That thought, too, was liberating.

Louise perused Roord's charts. Weather permitting, they were due to make landfall in a few days' time and dock in Las Palmas, as arranged. Once there, rather than spend time talking to the wine producers of the island, she intended to set about transforming the *Old Moon*. She would release those of the crew who might prefer to sail with a more conventional captain and crew, and engage a broader range of seamen – perhaps a rope maker and a caulker, as well as those who had skills acquired on warships. Their current crew of eleven was not enough for what she had in mind. She needed to arm the ship – they had only two cannon and two swivel guns – and they would need more.

She was determined to become not a pirate herself, but the scourge of pirates – a 'she-captain', the huntress and hellion of the high seas. The *capitana* of the *Ghost Ship*.

Waking just before dawn on the early morning of Tuesday, 27 April, Louise realised the anniversary of her mother's death the previous day had passed without her thinking about it once. Sharing the burden of the secret she carried had eased her conscience. Louise had released herself from the burden of guilt. She had done what she could. She had no right to take a life, but justice had been done. In the case of Madame Roux, too. Just desserts.

Had it always been that? A matter of forgiveness?

She turned to her love, lost in sleep, and ran her fingers down his arm. Then, she sat bolt upright. Gilles was still beside her. Last night, weary after their long discussions about her plan to turn pirate hunter, they had forgotten their usual night-time precautions.

'Gilles,' she whispered, shaking him awake. 'It's almost light.'

He blinked, then realised where he was and leapt out of bed. He kissed her, quickly gathered his clothes and scuttled back to his own cabin. Still half-asleep, he failed to take his usual steps to keep himself covered.

Neither realised, until much later – and when the damage had already been done – that Lieutenant Roord had seen him leave and so discovered Gilles was not what he claimed to be. Roord was bewildered, then horrified. Did not the holy book say that marriage was between one man and one woman? Did not the holy book condemn abomination and immorality? Was what he had witnessed evidence of a sin against God's laws? In truth, he wasn't certain what he had witnessed, only that it troubled him deeply.

As the first rays of the sun touched the pennant on the main mast, Roord took his hidden rosary from his pocket, sank to his knees and prayed for guidance.

# CHAPTER SIXTY

*Friday, 7 May*

'Land-ho!' shouted Jansz.

Louise raised her spyglass to her eye.

*She had done it.*

After fifty days at sea, and having navigated the treacherous waters of the archipelago of Las Islas Afortunadas past the island of Lanzarote, the *Old Moon* began her final approach into the port of Las Palmas on the north-east coast of Gran Canaria.

Louise stood at the bow as the coastline came closer, delighted by her first sight of the famous palm trees that gave the city its name. Everywhere she looked, green fronds swaying against a blue sky and the austere grey rock of the ravine in which the city had been built held the bay tight. Golden sands, so very different to the stone and wood jetties of La Rochelle and Amsterdam, stretched as far as she could see. Louise had seen paintings of Las Palmas, but it was more beautiful than she had ever imagined.

The history of the city she knew from the detailed information kept in the Van Raay offices and her conversations with Cornelia. Las Palmas was the de facto capital of the archipelago, not only the administrative centre but also its religious centre and where the Inquisition had their headquarters. The elegant, pale buildings with their latticed balconies had been constructed by the Spanish invaders nearly one hundred and fifty years previously and the cathedral of Santa Ana, a mixture of Gothic and Moorish architecture, dominated the main square.

Gran Canaria was a vital staging post not only for Spanish ships, but also for Dutch expeditions to the Cape and the East Indies. Its position further from the coast of North Africa gave it a little more protection from the slaver raids that plagued Tenerife, though Las Palmas had also suffered. The most devastating attack had taken place in June 1599 at the hands of the Dutch privateer, Van der Does, and had never been forgotten.

For so long as the truce between the Dutch Republic and Spain was in force, Louise knew merchant ships such as the *Old Moon* would be welcome here – trade was trade – but the Dutch were not popular and there was a great deal of uncertainty as to what would happen once the VOC licence with Spain lapsed. This did not overly concern her. She had much to accomplish in the days ahead if she was to set quickly back to sea. Piracy was rife during the summer months before winter storms set in, which allowed her at least three months to put her plans into action. She glanced up to the heavens and thought her grandparents would be proud. She smiled. Her mother, too.

A crowd had gathered on the dock to watch them come in, much as they might in La Rochelle or Amsterdam. Except here, everything was brighter and more vivid.

The crew had already trimmed the sails, as Lieutenant Roord steered the *Old Moon* safely towards the dock, with the navigator, Bleeker, at his side.

Louise watched with joy as children with dark curly hair ran up and down, shouting and waving at the ship. A widow – dressed head to toe in black with a long lace veil held in place by a comb at the top of her head – crossed herself as the *Old Moon* entered the harbour. And all along the quay, young women with their jet-black hair drawn into buns at the nape of their necks beneath straw hats stood beside men with brown blankets tossed over their shoulders, and waved. At that moment, on the hill above the town, a cloud of tiny blue birds flew out of a forest of palm trees, like blossom shaken from a bough in spring. It was all Louise could do not to clap her hands with pleasure.

Louise remained at the bow as the heaving line was thrown ashore. Black-eyed men jostled to pull in the thick berthing hawsers, one at the bow, one at the stern, and wound them around the bollards on the quay. On board, her crew began to stow the cannon and shut the gun ports.

Despite her eagerness to explore this new world, she was suddenly reluctant to leave the ship that had been their home for the past seven weeks. Not only would she lose her intimacy with Gilles – they had agreed that they had to revert to their former formal relationship – but there would be a great deal to do once on shore. Not to mention the faint hope that the crew would stay true to their word and not take the story of Hendrik Joost's demise into the taverns and boarding houses of Las Palmas.

*But they will talk. Men always do.*

Louise pushed it all from her mind.

Gilles was waiting with her travelling chest and personal leather bag, as she joined Lieutenant Roord at the starboard taffrail.

'It is a wonderful sight, is it not?'

'Yes, ma'am.'

'Is it as you imagined?'

Roord did not answer. Louise turned to look at him. He was pale and sweating, his eyes fixed on some point straight ahead. 'Lieutenant? Does something ail you?'

He did not meet her eye. 'No, ma'am.'

Perplexed, Louise left him to his reflections.

'There you are, *capitana*,' said Jansz cheerfully, as he put the plank in position. '*Bienvenida a Las Palmas.*'

At half past four in the afternoon of the seventh day of May in the year 1621, Louise Reydon-Joubert walked slowly down the gang plank, still feeling the roll and sway of the ocean in her legs, and stepped onto Spanish soil for the first time.

# CHAPTER SIXTY-ONE

LAS PALMAS
*Saturday, 8 May*

The day after their arrival, Louise was summoned to the Casas Consistoriales, the town hall, to explain what had happened to Hendrik Joost.

It soon became clear that the men who ruled Las Palmas were not accustomed to having to deal with a woman. The chief prosecutor, Felipe Arauz – an anaemic man originally from Bilbao – made no effort to hide his disdain. Two members of the Inquisition were in attendance, though no explanation was given for their presence and they were not introduced. The fact that Louise was the owner of the *Old Moon* meant nothing and although Joost was Dutch, and Calvinist, his father, Andries Joost, had many trading contacts in Gran Canaria. He was evidently an important and influential man. After a morning of barely courteous questioning, Louise even found herself remembering her meeting with *Prévôt* Arnaud in La Rochelle with fond nostalgia.

Prosecutor Arauz was different. It was with a great deal of difficulty that Louise finally convinced him to accept that the captain's death had been a sudden, and wholly unexpected, tragedy. The ship's first lieutenant had certified the death, she reminded him, and there was no evidence that Roord had falsified evidence. Her second lieutenant, Joris Bleeker, had ratified it. She showed Arauz the letter to Andries Joost she had written

332

whilst still on board. It was witnessed, then sealed by the authorities, and Arauz recommended that it should be sent back to Holland with the next Dutch ship bound for Amsterdam – he clearly did not trust Louise with it. The entire process left her frustrated and angry.

'Is everything settled?' Gilles asked, as she stepped out into the sunshine two hours later.

'It was disgraceful,' she said, her colour high. 'My word counted for nothing. They made me feel like a criminal. And there were two inquisitors there, like vultures, watching proceedings.'

The Spanish Inquisition was notorious for its brutal methods to eradicate heresy and the forced conversion of Jewish and Moslem peoples within Spain and Spanish overseas territories.

'Whatever for? Their role is to hunt down heretics, is it not?'

'And to stamp out immorality, anything contrary to Catholic statute. I had no power, Gilles, no voice at all.'

In the next few days, Louise had no reason to change her mind that this was a society where women were invisible. They were not present in the courts or the town hall, they were not there at the corn market where the price of goods was set. The fact that she was a spinster of middle years, with no children, marked her out as unnatural in this Spanish city where the grip of the Catholic Church was absolute. Men laid down the law, women obeyed it. In Amsterdam, even in La Rochelle, she had been unusual, but respected. Here, in beautiful Las Palmas, Louise was nothing.

It was a far cry from life at sea.

Despite her frustrations, Louise loved her lodgings over-looking the Santa Ana cathedral and the city itself. Each morning, she woke to the sight of flocks of wild canaries, the colour of the Canarian sun, swooping in and out of the plaza Santa Ana. From her window, she could see the Casas Consistoriales, the Bishop's Palace and the Casa de Colón, the house where the Genoese explorer Columbus had stayed more than a hundred years before. Latticed wooden balconies and red wallflowers sparkling like rubies against the white-washed walls. Calm internal courtyards providing shade from the heat of the sun. Everywhere, palm trees swayed in the warm wind.

But the beauty concealed an uglier history. It was from Las Palmas that the first Spanish invaders had conducted their conquest of the neighbouring islands of Tenerife and La Palma, slaughtering the original inhabitants of the island, the Guanches. The fighting had been bitter and fierce. In recent years, the town itself had been the subject of several merciless attacks – by the English and the Dutch, by Barbary corsairs – its treasures looted and the sanctity of the cathedral defiled. It seemed to Louise that Las Palmas was a town in a permanent state of fear and siege, even though there was no discernible threat.

Her bad dreams returned at night. Vivid images, the look on her father's face as he fell, her mother's long hair, the colour fading from Madame Roux's lips. Hollows started to appear beneath her eyes and her skin began to lose its bloom.

The plaza Santa Ana was also the headquarters of the Inquisition. Although evidence of Moorish influence was wide-spread, Las Palmas was a fiercely Catholic city and the diocesan heart of the Islas Afortunadas. Etiquette and status and repu-tation were everything. Inquisitors from mainland Spain had enormous power, conducting tribunals behind the white-washed walls, condemning heretics and infidels, those who engaged in adulterous behaviour or immorality. The intimidating tendrils of the Inquisition spread into every corner of life. Louise had been told in whispers that mass public proclamations of faith – *auto da fé* – were common. So, too, were the burnings that sometimes followed.

She and Gilles never saw one another except in company and she missed him. But Louise knew they had to be especially careful. She had seen women chastised in the street for immodest dress, or for the crime of being out after dark without a male escort. However much she missed his presence at her side, she couldn't allow anything to prevent them from being able to sail.

As she waited in her chamber full of shadows, listening to the tolling of the bells of the cathedral, Louise sensed danger ahead.

A stone's throw away from the plaza Santa Ana, Gilles walked along the sand and wondered when he would have the opportunity to present Louise with her birthday gift. He had enlisted Marco Rossi's help, and thought she would be delighted.

His heart ached for her. He kept hoping she would summon him, on some pretext or another, but the days passed and still no messenger came. He understood, but deeply regretted the caution that kept them apart. The *North Star* was due to arrive in Las Palmas any day now – she had sent a maid to tell him that – possibly bringing letters from Amsterdam. If so, he would want to be with her.

Tomorrow, perhaps?

All along the water's edge, far from the bustle of the harbour, Gilles saw rows of smoking racks. Fishing boats rested on the shore, while men mended their nets. Women with weather-worn faces feeding the fires with dried seaweed, flooding the beach with the pungent smell of burning salt and ash. Silver-backed fish were being cooked head to tail on wooden racks: it was reminiscent of the harbour front in La Rochelle, yet could not have been more different.

Gilles was finding it hard to sleep without the constant motion of the ship, though he was entranced by this colourful new world. A childhood spent trying not to be noticed served him well, so he managed to move through the squares and streets without attracting much attention. Even his black garments helped him to melt into the background, in a city where Catholic priests and inquisitors and widows of the sea could be found on every street corner. He soon learnt that Las Palmas was like any port town. Everyone knew everyone else's business – who was due into harbour, whose business was on the rocks, who was filling the back pockets of the wine producers or the customs officer. There were few secrets that could not be bought or sold. The Inquisition, in particular, had very deep pockets.

Preparations for transforming the *Old Moon* were almost completed. Dirk Jansz was going to remain with the ship, together with the cabin boy, Pieter, and Albert, the cook, Lange and the De Groot brothers, too, Second Lieutenant Bleeker and Rossi. Jorgen was not, and Louise wanted to extend the crew, leaving them three places to fill. It was proving hard. The fact was that most men did not want to serve under a woman. As for Lieutenant Roord, Gilles did not know what afflicted the man and he had not confirmed his plans. His manner had been strange even before the *Old Moon* had docked.

# CHAPTER SIXTY-TWO

*Friday, 14 May*

A week after their arrival, the *North Star* sailed in to Las Palmas, bringing news from Amsterdam.

Louise had adopted the local habit of drinking a little Canarian rum in the morning, served with raisins and hot water. Here in Las Palmas, she felt always on her guard. At any moment, a messenger might arrive with another summons to the Casas Consistoriales. With a whole city to explore, she nevertheless felt confined in a way she had never felt on the *Old Moon*.

She knew she was being charged over the odds for the weapons and timber she was purchasing. All the same, the *Old Moon* was now equipped and almost ready to sail. The two additional swivel guns had been installed, the hull cleaned and the running repairs completed. Iron davits had been secured at the stern and Jansz had negotiated the purchase of a larger *boot*, a single-masted small boat, that could be lifted in and out of the water and used to carry goods and people from the *Old Moon* to the shore where the water was not deep enough.

Louise was greatly indebted to both Gilles and to Jansz. Without Jansz, she would not have been able to negotiate what she needed. He was a regular visitor to Las Palmas and had many contacts and a working knowledge of Spanish. Together with the other remaining members of the crew, they were lodging in a boarding house down at the port.

The bells of the cathedral rang out the three-quarter hour. Willem de Klerk, captain of the *North Star*, would be here presently. She had a favour to ask of him. And perhaps he would have letters for her? She prayed he would, but also hoped he would not.

While she waited, Louise's thoughts returned to her missing lieutenant. She had expected to rely on Roord's help in Las Palmas – he spoke passable Spanish – but he had been notable by his absence. In fact, his manner had changed even before they had docked. He had become oddly formal, distant even. Louise didn't know what to make of it. For all his faults – his over-zealous faith and his weak stomach – she had come to like the gentle and quiet lieutenant, and had hoped he might consider remaining with the *Old Moon*. Now, she wondered if he had resented her taking command of the ship after all. It was frustrating. If Roord turned down her invitation – and for that to happen, she needed to find him – then she would have to secure another second-in-command quickly. Bleeker was eager to help, but spoke no Spanish and his pustulant skin meant people shied away from him. He could not replace Roord.

The maid came into the chamber. 'Captain De Klerk is here, *señora*.'

'*Gracias*. Show him in.'

A tall, red-haired man walked into the room. For a moment, Louise was taken aback. The captain was as a twin to her uncle Jean-Jacques, at least as she remembered him. She received letters from time to time – his son had died in his infancy, a great loss – and enjoyed hearing about his daughter, Florence, now fifteen years old, who sounded spirited and intelligent.

She stood up. 'Captain De Klerk, you are most welcome.'

He gave a small bow. 'It is kind of you to receive me, Madame Reydon-Joubert.'

'Not at all. Please, take a seat.' She gestured to a woven-backed chair of dark wood, the companion to her own. Between them stood a low brass table with wine, two glasses and a plate of salted almonds. 'Will you take something to drink, or to eat?'

'Perhaps some wine?'

Once the drinks were poured and the maid had withdrawn, Louise got straight to business, asking about De Klerk's voyage from Amsterdam to Las Palmas, explaining how she had been obliged to take command of the *Old Moon* after Captain Joost's untimely death. She went into more detail than was necessary, conscious that she was prolonging the moment when she would have to ask if he had letters for her. De Klerk was amusing, and it was a pleasure to talk to him, though he confirmed that the voc changes being put into place were continuing to affect Cornelia's business adversely.

'Although it may be disloyal for me to say so,' De Klerk concluded, 'I fear many of my crew will join other ships after this season. The rewards in the Americas and the East Indies are so much greater.'

'The risks, too,' she added.

De Klerk spread his hands. 'That is true. How long do you intend to stay here? Are you going south to the vineyards in Monte?'

Monte was a fertile valley of volcanic soil, and consequently the most popular region for wine production.

Louise shook her head. 'I had originally thought to take a pony and trap to the Agaete Valley, or even into the highlands of San Bartolome de Tirajana. They tell me the high altitude means the grapes are exposed to huge temperature differences over a long period of time, which produces a very different taste.'

'But no more?'

Louise hesitated. She knew Cornelia valued De Klerk. He

seemed straightforward and honest, and he had made many journeys to the Islas Afortunadas during his long career at sea. But she had learnt to be cautious.

'With the loss of Joost, my plans have changed.'

'Ah. You need to secure the services of a local captain, which will be far from easy.'

'A first lieutenant, in fact,' she clarified, and saw surprise flash across his face. 'I intend to keep command of the ship myself.'

'Well, I wish you the best of luck,' he replied politely. 'It was one thing for you to step in when Joost unexpectedly died and your lieutenant – did you say he was called Roord – fell ill?'

'Yes.'

'But it is quite another to command in your own right. Forgive me for speaking plainly, Madame Reydon-Joubert.'

Louise smiled. 'I value your candour, captain. Do you speak Spanish?'

'Passing well, yes.'

'In which case, I have a favour to ask you. Might you be prepared to help secure me a second-in-command? For this season only. As I said, I hoped to retain Lieutenant Roord's services, but I realise now that he is perhaps more orthodox in his views than I thought. However, most of the crew who sailed from Amsterdam are remaining with me, including our boat-swain, Dirk Jansz.'

'I know Jansz. He is a fine mariner.'

'He is. In addition, we have taken on a gunner, a caulker, and a third seaman. Jansz has done his best, but of course he cannot help secure a ranking officer. Lieutenant Bleeker intends to remain with the ship. He has excellent navigational skills, but lacks authority.'

'This sounds more than a simple refit for trade?' De Klerk probed.

'As I said, my plans have changed,' Louise replied in a level voice. 'Gilles Barenton has the list of our requirements.' Louise felt a moment of pleasure at saying his name out loud. 'Mevrouw Van Raay values him highly.'

'I have heard so. Barenton worked in the Van Raay office in Lestrange, I believe?'

'Yes. He came with me from La Rochelle, as a secretary. His knowledge of wine is second to none.'

De Klerk was silent for a moment, then he nodded. 'It won't be easy to find a lieutenant at such short notice, but I am happy to help. We have only to load our cargo and return presently to Amsterdam. If the *Old Moon* could be ready in time, we could sail in convoy?'

Louise prevaricated. It was a generous offer, but it was not what she wanted. 'That is generous of you, captain, but I would not have you alter your plans on my account.'

De Klerk paused, then nodded. 'If you change your mind, let me know.'

Louise raised her glass. 'To new beginnings.'

'To the *Old Moon*, and all those who sail in her.' They drank the toast, then De Klerk put his cup on the table. 'Now, lest I forget, I have letters for you from Amsterdam.'

Though she had braced herself, Louise felt her stomach clench.

'Thank you,' she said, as calmly as she could manage. 'That is kind of you. If you leave them with me, I will read them later at my leisure.'

'Mevrouw Van Raay asked particularly that I should bring back any response with me when I returned – in point of fact, she was most insistent. Though, admittedly, if you are sailing in the next couple of days, the *Old Moon* will be back in Amsterdam before we are.'

Louise smiled. 'In which case, I will be able to thank you in person. In turn, there is a letter for the father of Captain Joost to be taken. The authorities would like you to deliver it, rather than entrust the obligation to me. They feel it would be better.'

De Klerk raised his eyebrows. 'Do they indeed? Well, of course, I will be happy to oblige with that, too.' He got to his feet. 'It has been a pleasure. I have been somewhat starved of congenial conversation these past weeks. I shall make enquiries and see if anyone suitable might be available. Shall I meet with you – Barenton, too, if you wish it – later this afternoon? Shall we say four o'clock at the harbour?'

'Thank you,' Louise said, studiously ignoring the sealed letter lying on the brass table. 'Until this afternoon, captain.'

# CHAPTER SIXTY-THREE

Lieutenant Roord walked quickly through the square and into the cathedral. He had wrestled with his conscience ever since that night on deck, and knew the only way to find peace was to make his confession. It was Friday. The priest was certain to be there.

He dipped his finger in the holy water in the baptismal font and made the sign of the cross. He stood still a moment, allowing his eyes to adjust to the contrast of the brightness outside and the sombre grey within. Ahead of him was the high altar. The familiar smell of dust and incense and prayer soothed his troubled spirit.

Roord was not here as a traveller come to admire this temple to God, but as a penitent. His eyes searched the shadowed space until he found the confessional booth, in the side nave. With the same short, hurried steps, he went towards it. There were two heavy red felt curtains either side of the priest's seat. One was drawn – Roord could see the skirts and boots of a woman beneath the curtain. The other was unoccupied.

Roord slid onto the wooden kneeler, drew the curtain and waited his turn. He heard the rings rattle on the other pole, and the sound of the woman sobbing as she left the booth. Then, he heard the priest turn towards him and murmur a few words of welcome. Roord sank to his knees with relief, crossed himself again, then pressed his head against the metal grille.

'Bless me, Father, for I have sinned. It has been sixty-two days since my last confession. I have been at sea.'

'The Lord understands.'

He took a deep breath. 'These are my sins.'

Over the next minutes, Jan Roord unburdened himself, confessing all that he had done, all he had witnessed on the journey from Amsterdam to Las Palmas. The sin of the two people who were not married lying together. How he had seen, upon the table in the cabin, Madame Reydon-Joubert's jewelled paper knife, and his concerns over the death of Hendrik Joost. He hesitated, then finally shared his confusion about Gilles Barenton. Looking back, he had doubted the evidence of his own eyes and feared it might reflect badly on him to have allowed such impure thoughts to enter his mind. Besides, he liked the young man, and wished him no ill. But secure in the knowledge that his words were private, and wanting to rid his soul of sinful thoughts and deeds, he tentatively described what he thought he had seen. From time to time, he faltered, unable to remember the correct word in Spanish, but he was certain the priest understood. He knew that God was listening. He expressed his hope that Madame Reydon-Joubert would find her way to penitence, too. He had come to admire her, though she lived in a manner inappropriate to her sex. All she needed was to be shown the error of her ways.

With each word, spoken in the sure and certain confidence of the secrecy of the confessional, Roord felt his soul lighten. He felt God's grace upon him.

When Jan Roord stepped out into the sunshine of the square a few minutes later, he felt like a new man. He had made a true and good confession, and been forgiven – for partaking in a Protestant service, for not bearing witness when he should have spoken out, for turning a blind eye to abomination and lewdness.

But it was over. His sins were wiped clean.

He would go to Madame Reydon-Joubert and tender his resignation – no need to give the reason for it. She was a good woman, but sinful. He could not serve under such a person. His plan was to approach the captain of the *North Star* and see if he might have passage with him back to Amsterdam.

As he walked across the square, Roord started to plan a new life. He wondered if he might take holy orders. To minister to sinners, to save souls, that would be to do God's righteous work on this earth.

Ignoring the pews of veiled women waiting to make their Friday confession, the priest left the booth. Waving his hand in apology, he walked quickly across the central nave, pausing only briefly to cross himself before the altar, then on through the vestry and out. A rotund bustling black figure, he looked like a shabby crow.

In the orange orchard separating the cathedral from the Bishop's Palace, he stopped. What he had just been told had shaken him to the core. The penitent's Spanish was muddled, so it was hard to be certain, but he had talked of abomination and immorality, even of treason. Murder, possibly. If he had understood the man's confession correctly, the she-captain and her lover were part of a plot to terrorise the waters of the Islas Afortunadas. And they were heretics, followers of the renegade Church – Huguenots – who had resisted lawful Spanish rule in Holland for more than fifty years and brought about the death of thousands of devout Catholics.

The priest respected the Seal of the Confessional – it was the bedrock on which his ministry was founded – but this situation was exceptional. What of his responsibility to God? What of his duty of care to all the Christian souls who would surely suffer, be corrupted and defiled, if he did not speak out? What he had heard – treason, murder and intrigue – was too important to be bound by his duty to a foreigner.

He glanced up, looking for guidance. God would forgive him.

The priest took a step forward, out of the shadow of the orange trees and into the light. It felt like a sign. Now he knew how to do it. If he confessed what he had heard to another, then he was not – strictly speaking – breaking the bounds of the confessional. The chief inquisitor would be grateful for the information and his Eminence would decide what should happen next. The matter would be out of his hands.

He changed direction and walked instead to the Inquisitional Tribunal. At no point did the priest allow himself to acknowledge that, by taking this step, he might also benefit himself. He felt his lack of advancement within the hierarchy of the cathedral keenly – too many of the senior clerics were incomers from mainland Spain, rather than islanders like him. This act of service – to uphold God's laws and protect the security of Gran Canaria from treachery – would surely bring him the notice he deserved.

# CHAPTER SIXTY-FOUR

'Take this to Gilles Barenton,' Louise ordered, passing a note to the maid. The girl looked blank. 'Quickly. *Ve rápido.*'

It was unwise to summon Gilles here, she knew that, yet she had to talk to him.

*Else I will go mad.*

The news from Amsterdam was worse than she had expected. Cornelia's letter was dated the twentieth day of March, only the day after the *Old Moon* had sailed. What might have happened in the past two months since the ink had dried and the letter had been sealed, Louise had no way of knowing.

*There might by now be a warrant for my arrest.*

She placed her jewelled knife on the table, and started to pace up and down, her skirt dusting the tiles of the chamber. It was hot, airless, and she felt cumbersome and weighted down.

*Not for much longer.*

Any day now, with the right tides and a willing crew, the *Old Moon* would sail away from Las Palmas. She would be the commander of her ship, once more. She would be free, once more. And Gilles would be at her side.

Dirk Jansz was pleased with himself. With the promise of wages better than they would get on most merchant ships – and a guarantee that they would be paid on time – he had managed to secure another three mariners to join the crew. True, there would be a babel of tongues spoken on board, but they were men who needed employment and weren't too fussy. He had asked around, and almost no one wanted to serve under a woman. Some of the things they'd said would make even the most hardened sailor blush.

He'd tried to tell them. It wasn't what they imagined. The *capitana* – as they'd all taken to calling her, thanks to the Italian, Rossi – was the best man he'd served under. Honest, firm, bold. Not like a woman at all.

Jansz smacked his own hand, knowing Barenton would chastise him for making such a comment. Gilles was a funny one. He was knowledgeable, he never complained, was kind to everyone. Hadn't he saved him when that bastard Joost had flogged the living daylights out of him? But Jansz couldn't say he knew him. All those weeks at sea, but he still couldn't work out what the Frenchman was thinking. Not really one of the boys. Didn't like getting his hands dirty.

Jansz stumbled, and threw his hand against the wall to steady himself. The rum in the tavern by the port was strong, not watered-down piss. A good job, he thought to himself as he staggered on, that they were not due to sail for a while yet. His head would ache in the morning.

He tripped over his own feet and nearly fell. Perhaps he'd had one too many? But then hadn't he earned it? Hadn't he done well? Hadn't he delivered a crew to Madame Reydon-Joubert, who was the most beautiful woman he had ever seen? He stopped, swaying happily on his feet. Honesty compelled him to admit that she was not to his fancy. Too tall, too broad, not enough flesh on her. Now, the girl he'd lain with last night. What was her name? Rosana? Rosita? Sparkling eyes, full lips, something for a man to get hold of. 'But she's a good captain,' he muttered as he tottered on, as if arguing a point in a court of law. 'A great captain, any man would be proud to serve under her.' He laughed at his choice of words. He reckoned Barenton carried a torch for her.

Now the ground was coming up to meet him. Jansz tried to tell himself it was no worse than a ship in a storm, but the earth was shifting, tipping, everything jumping about in front of his eyes. Just in time, he wrapped himself around a palm tree. He looked up at the fronds through dancing eyes. Had they always been so green? Had they always been so tall? Gently, Jansz slid down to the ground until he was sitting with his legs outstretched, still propped up against the trunk. Perfectly comfortable.

Then, on the far side of the square, he caught sight of Lieutenant Roord. He tried to wave his hand, but his arm wouldn't obey him. Roord was a feeble streak of a man, always sick and rattling on his prayer beads, but Jansz felt well-disposed to everyone today.

'Lieutenant!' he called, the word echoing loudly in his head. 'Ahoy . . .'

Then Jansz saw two men approach Roord. He narrowed his eyes, trying to focus. Not black robes, but red. The Inquisition. He didn't know what that meant, but he knew the lieutenant was a papist. They seemed to be talking, but then Roord took a step back. And now two soldiers appeared, one of whom took hold of his arm and the other stepped behind. Roord began to struggle.

'Lieutenant,' Jansz called uncertainly, his voice tapering away. He tried to stand up, minded he should help. But his legs didn't work, his arms didn't work. 'I say . . .'

Slumped hopelessly against the tree, he watched as Roord was escorted towards a building in the far corner of the square and into a garden beyond.

'I should tell someone.'

Jansz managed to get to his feet. Gradually, he started to stumble across the square in the direction of their lodgings. Perhaps Barenton would be there? He was an odd one, no mistake, but the Frenchman would know what to do.

# CHAPTER SIXTY-FIVE

'So, you see,' said Louise, astonished at how calm she sounded, 'it is bad news on both counts.'

Louise was pacing the room, while Gilles was sitting in the chair previously occupied by Captain De Klerk. Bright beams of sunlight fell through the slatted shutters, leaving strips of light on the tiles.

The two letters from Amsterdam lay open on the table.

Gilles was frowning. 'Who do you think told the authorities my mother had been looking for us?'

'I warrant it was my aunt. Cornelia says the city guard came to Warmoesstraat the day after we sailed. A woman had been found knifed in a boarding house in Rokin, a proclamation had been posted asking for information, and a lady in Zeedijk had come forward suggesting that our household might know something. Bernarda is always very determined to do the right thing. I have no doubt she told them more of our business than was needed.'

'She would betray her own family?'

Louise gave a wry smile. 'Bernarda would not think of it in those terms. Rather, that it was her *duty* to provide any information she possessed.' She thought for a moment. 'The fact is they have no evidence linking me to your mother's death, Cornelia is clear about that. All that can be proved is that your mother came to Warmoesstraat to see someone. The day after that, she was found dead.' Louise gestured at the letter. 'But this was written two months ago. It is possible the boy from

Plaats also came forward later, if there was a reward being offered for information. If he did, that would link me personally with Rokin.' She paused. 'And though I was careful, I cannot be certain no one else saw me.'

'This is my fault.'

'No,' she said, taking his hand. 'None of this is your fault.'

For a moment, she allowed herself the pleasure of feeling his skin against hers. 'So that was the first piece of unwelcome news. The second should feel of as much significance, but oddly does not.'

'The letter from Chartres.'

Louise sighed. 'I think from the very beginning I knew the claim was true. This man, Phillipe Vidal, asserts that my father married his mother in Chartres on the second of January in the year 1594. I would have been nearly eight years old.' She smiled wistfully. 'Do you know, I always wanted a brother. He has, so he writes, a marriage certificate to prove it.' Louise knew she was talking as much to order her own thoughts as for Gilles' benefit. 'There is no way of knowing the circumstances of their marriage. It might have been a long-term arrangement between his family and hers, or a love match. Her name is Anne of Evreux – and Evreux was the name of my father's former family estate. Perhaps he was seeking to regain possession of it?' She shook her head. 'But why sell the land in the first place?'

Gilles picked up the letter. 'He doesn't say what he wants, beyond wishing to make your acquaintance.'

'No, nor what his circumstances are.' She paused. 'He cannot be much older than you, Gilles. Even if his mother was with child when they married, the very earliest he could have been born is in the year of the marriage itself.'

'Making him twenty-seven at the oldest.'

'I have written to him, and will give the letter to Captain

De Klerk, to deliver to Cornelia. She will make sure it finds Phillipe.'

'Are you certain that is the right thing to do?'

'I am.' Louise went to Gilles, put her hands on his shoulder and dropped a kiss on the top of his head. 'So many questions with no answers, but at least it has given me the chance to see you. So, already I am grateful to my half-brother for that.' She kissed him again. 'How I have missed your company.'

He turned around in his chair and Louise brushed her lips with his, then walked to the window and peered through the slats. She felt curiously peaceful. After the first shock of reading Cornelia's news and the enclosed letter from Chartres, she'd realised it was the not-knowing that had been so hard to bear. Now, at least, she knew where she stood.

'What time are you meeting De Klerk?' Gilles asked.

'At four o'clock,' she answered. 'Most of our existing crew are already on board. The three new recruits will report at three o'clock. A full inspection was carried out this morning. Everything is in order, the repairs complete. If De Klerk has found me a new first lieutenant, then we can sail straight away.' She was about to turn from the window when something in the corner of the square caught her attention. 'Gilles, can you come here? Is that Jansz? Over there, by the cathedral?'

Gilles parted the wooden blind with his fingers, then sighed. 'By the looks of things, I think he spent the night with some drinking companions.'

Louise shook her head. 'Can you go and see if he needs help? I would have him in a fit state to sail.'

'And still no word from Roord?'

She shook her head. 'He seems to have vanished off the face of the earth. It's a pity.'

Gilles put his arms around her waist and held her tight. 'It is better to have men who are committed to the ship than someone like Roord, especially with the plan you hope to put into action. For all his virtues, he was often unable to fulfil his duties.'

'How wise you are for one so young!'

'I live to serve you, *capitana*.' He grinned. 'Right, I will go and offer my assistance to our inebriated boatswain.' He paused in the doorway. 'Oh, and I forgot to say, I have a gift for your birthday yesterday. I will give it to you once we are back on board.'

'I will look forward to it, my love. *À bientôt*.'

Roord could see the inquisitor's lips moving, and he could see words being spoken, but he did not understand why he was being questioned. Why was this happening? He was a Dutch citizen, honest and law-abiding. He had done nothing wrong.

It seemed no time had passed since the soldiers accosted him in the square and dragged him into this cellar below the Inquisitional headquarters. The Seal of Confessional surely meant that the priest could not, under any circumstances, betray his confession. Yet, another part of Roord's brain realised he must have done, for the inquisitor had asked question after question about Madame Reydon-Joubert, about her lewd behaviour, about the unnatural relationship between her and her secretary. They had asked about piracy and the arming of the ship, and about Hendrik Joost's death. Murder, he had called it. All of Roord's speculations and imaginings had been twisted inside out and turned into something reeking of treason and treachery.

'There has been some misunderstanding,' he protested again in his faltering Spanish.

The inquisitor lost patience, and flicked his hand. 'Stretch him.'

Now Roord felt himself being pulled from the chair and

dragged to the rack. He was forced down onto the wooden board, then ropes were tied around his feet and his hands, and pulled up above his head.

How could this be happening? He was a good Catholic. He said his prayers and did his best to abide by God's commandments. He had been wiped free of sin. Then the first of the levers was turned. Roord bit his tongue to avoid crying out.

'Tell us precisely what you told the priest in the cathedral of Santa Ana?' the inquisitor hissed. 'You have done nothing wrong. She has. They are traitors. It is their sin that concerns us, not your conscience. It is in my power to show clemency if you provide me with the information I require. Tell us what you saw.'

Roord thought of Madame Reydon-Joubert's kindness to him, Barenton's too. Then the lever was turned a second time and he felt the sinews in his shoulders start to stretch.

'Stop,' he cried.

The inquisitor raised his hand. The torturer released the pressure from the rack.

Roord began to talk.


'Monsieur!' Jansz said, with swaggering bonhomie. 'I was on my way to find you . . . have something to tell you.'

'Do you indeed.' Gilles put his arm around the boatswain's shoulder and steered him towards a bench. 'You need to sleep this off, Jansz. You are no use in this state. What will our new crew think?'

'No, no.' Jansz started to shake his head. 'Must get back to the ship. Taking the next watch. On duty at three bells.'

'Up you get,' Gilles said, hoisting him to his feet.

'All engaged and ready to go,' he slurred. 'Three of 'em. A motley band, it's got to be said – Moriscos, foreigners, but good mariners, I give you my word.' He tapped his nose. 'Young Pieter's staying with us . . .'

'I know.'

'And that Italian, Rossi. Not much of a sailor, but willing to work.'

'He will learn.'

Jansz was shaking his head. 'But not Lieutenant Roord, oh no. They took him. He can't come.'

'He is going to join another ship,' Gilles admitted. 'But we will have a new first lieutenant this afternoon, God willing.'

For a moment, Jansz seemed to come to his senses. His eyes cleared and he frowned. 'No. They took him,' he said, flinging his arm wide and striking Gilles in the chest. 'Roord. Over there. Papists took him.'

'You're drunk, Jansz.'

'I may have had one or two, but I know what I saw.'

Gilles sighed. It was going to be a long walk back to their lodgings, and he needed to be at the harbour at four to meet Louise and De Klerk.

'Come on.'

'I'm telling you,' the boatswain insisted, lurching to his feet. 'Two men in red.' He tapped the side of his nose. 'Inquisitors. Poor old Roord didn't want to go, but the soldiers made him.'

'Where did they take him?' Gilles said, humouring him. 'To the Bishop's Palace? Perhaps he is invited for dinner.'

He stopped. 'Not the cathedral, beside it. There.'

Gilles turned and, for the first time, a trickle of alarm pricked his spine when he realised Jansz was pointing in the direction of the Inquisitional headquarters.

'Jansz,' he said, steering him to a wall and sitting him down on it. Gilles crouched in front of him. 'Dirk, look at me. Tell me exactly what you saw.'

# CHAPTER SIXTY-SIX

The shadows were lengthening.

At the harbour, Louise was taking her leave of De Klerk, having shown the new lieutenant he had found for her around the *Old Moon*. She had liked what she'd seen of the mop-haired Englishman, Tom Smith, and had immediately offered terms for him to join as first lieutenant for the remainder of the season.

A mariner originally from Cornwall, Smith had been taken captive by Barbary corsairs five years ago. He had managed to escape, with the help of the wife of the Ottoman gaoler when the ship was laid up in Valetta for the winter. He was experienced, had the navigational skill and authority Bleeker lacked, knew the waters around the Islas Afortunadas well, and had knowledge of the North African corsairs from his years in captivity. Best of all, for Louise's purposes, he had a burning hatred of piracy and slaver ships.

'There is nothing left for me there,' he had explained when Louise asked why he had not wanted to return to Cornwall. 'My whole village was taken. Many died on the journey to Salé, or on the oars from exhaustion.'

'Well, you are very welcome, Lieutenant Smith. All of the crew, bar our boatswain, are already on board.'

Smith nodded. 'I will go and make their acquaintance, and get my bearings.'

Still wondering why Gilles had not joined them as promised, Louise turned back to De Klerk. 'Smith is an excellent choice. I am greatly in your debt, captain.'

'And you have a full crew now?'

'Yes. Other than Roord, we only lost one. He has been replaced by a local mariner, Sanchez, and we also engaged a Morisco by the name of Ali Al-Bayt – from Gran Canaria – and a French gunner, Pierre Rémy. With Bleeker and Rossi, our cook and cabin boy, and now Lieutenant Smith, as well as Gilles Barenton, that takes us to thirteen. Fourteen, including me.' Louise took the letter she had written to Cornelia and Alis from her pocket. 'If you might do me this final service, captain, and give this to mevrouw Van Raay.'

'Of course, though you might well be home before me.'

Louise smiled, keeping up the pretence. 'Indeed, I might.'

He returned her smile. 'God speed, Madame Reydon-Joubert. I hope our paths will cross again.'

'As do I,' Louise said, and she meant it.

At last, she saw Gilles coming towards her on the paved quay-side, and her heart leapt. She was relieved to see Jansz was with him, followed by a boy with a cart. She shielded her eyes. Though a little unsteady on his feet, the boatswain was walking fast and had his sea bag slung over his shoulder. Gilles was carrying something in his arms. As the little gang got closer, she saw it was her wooden travelling chest, and that her leather bag and Gilles' own effects were piled on the cart. She frowned.

'Captain,' Jansz said when they drew level, attempting to draw himself up straight. 'I may have had a little to drink.'

'So I see,' she said curtly. 'It won't do, Jansz. Go on board and sober up.'

'Aye, *capitana*.'

She turned to Gilles. 'Is everything all right? Why have you brought my belongings?'

He didn't answer, but signalled to the boy. 'Take the bags on board. Jansz, show him where to stow them.'

Perplexed, Louise watched as Jansz scrambled on board with surprising agility, followed by the boy and luggage. 'Has something happened?'

'The new recruits were due to report at three, that's right?'

She knew there would be a good reason for his odd manner, so she answered. 'Rémy, Ali Al-Bayt and Sanchez are on board.'

'And the lieutenant secured by De Klerk is satisfactory? When will he arrive?'

Louise could hear the strain in Gilles' voice and he kept looking over his shoulder, as if he was afraid of being overheard.

'Tom Smith is already acquainting himself with the ship. He seems excellent.'

'Good.' Gilles dropped his voice. 'We should sail tonight.'

Louise took a step backwards. 'That's impossible! We cannot. There are only two hours of daylight left.'

'We must,' Gilles said in an urgent whisper. 'They have taken Roord.'

Louise felt her chest tighten. 'What do you mean? Who has taken him? Taken him where?'

'Jansz saw him arrested by two soldiers. He's been taken to the Inquisitional headquarters.'

Louise shuddered, remembering the terrible stories her grandfather told her of the Inquisitional prisons in Toulouse and Carcassonne. How few who were taken were ever released. How those who were set free emerged as shadows of their former selves, broken men.

'What could he possibly have done?'

'I cannot imagine. Roord is a devout Catholic, he is pious. But the fact remains Jansz witnessed his arrest.'

'Jansz is inebriated.'

'Yes, but he was coherent about what he saw.'

Louise had a sinking feeling in the pit of her stomach. 'What do you think?'

Gilles took a deep breath. 'Roord has been troubled for days. His mood changed before we even came on shore, we both noticed it.'

'Yes.'

'It is Friday today. Roord might well have gone to confession.'

She frowned. 'And confessed to what?'

Gilles let his hands drop. 'It's impossible to know, but if he shared what was troubling him with the priest—'

'The confessional is sacrosanct.'

'It is supposed to be, but there is no way of knowing for certain if that secrecy is always respected. Priests are men, too. They could be tempted to break their vows.'

Louise nodded. Wasn't her own paternal grandfather an example of that? Her grandmother's journals had described how, though a cardinal in the Catholic Church, he had murdered any who got in his way.

'Do you think Roord voiced suspicions about Joost's death?'

'He may have done,' he replied. 'He examined the body. He might have seen the puncture mark.'

'He signed the death certificate.'

'What else could he do?' Gilles hesitated, gathering his thoughts. 'But there could be something else. The night we fell asleep together, remember? Roord had taken the watch.'

Louise turned cold. 'You think he saw you leaving my cabin?'

'I think he may have done. His behaviour towards you, towards me, changed after that.'

'Because we are not married?'

'Yes, and – Louise, it was early in the morning. I didn't take my usual precautions.'

Louise flushed. 'You think he might have seen you for who you are?'

'I don't know, he may have done. Either way, he would think any relations between us sinful outside the sanctity of wedlock. The Inquisition in Las Palmas has punished as many women for adultery and immorality as it has men for heresy.'

Louise glanced behind her at the *Old Moon* rocking lightly in the water, then up at the beautiful palm trees on the hillside, and suddenly the world felt a dark and treacherous place. The situation with Roord might have nothing to do with them, or it could have everything to do with them, but they could not risk waiting to find out. Her treatment at the Casas Consistoriales was testament to how little power she would have should they decide to pursue her.

'Should I try to get Roord released?' she began, but realised there was no point. 'In fact, I will see if De Klerk can help.'

Quickly, she scribbled a note to the captain, asking him to look into the matter, then sent it back to the town with the boy and his now empty cart.

'Louise,' Gilles insisted, 'you must give the order. We should leave, while we still can.'

She took one last look around the quay, remembering how she had felt in Amsterdam, dreading an imminent arrest, and made her decision. There was nothing keeping them in Las Palmas, and every reason to leave quickly, provided they could navigate the harbour and make it to clear water before night fell.

'Come, I will introduce you to Lieutenant Smith.'

Gilles breathed a sigh of relief. 'I am sure this is the right thing to do.'

Louise looked up at the rigging, at the flags snapping at the top of the masts, and the jolly boat hanging proud at the stern below her colours. 'The wind is with us. Let's prepare to sail.'

The next hour seemed to pass painfully slowly. Louise scoured the quay, desperately hoping not to see soldiers appear at the far end of the dock or, worse, the red robes of the inquisitors.

Pinpricks of light – candles and lamps in windows and on balconies – started to appear around the harbour. The quayside and the sands now were empty now, the palm trees silhouetted against the dusk sky. The sound of the cathedral bells striking six floated from the town across the water.

Finally, they were ready.

From the quarterdeck, Louise gave the order to cast off and the *Old Moon* began to move through the water.

Soon, they cleared the harbour wall. Her heart steadied a little. Louise turned to talk to her new first lieutenant.

'The open sea is a beautiful sight.'

'It is indeed,' Smith agreed, then added, 'Might I know where we are going, and why we left in such haste?'

'I apologise for not consulting you, lieutenant. It was a decision born of circumstances – not of my own making. As for our destination, we are heading for Garachico.'

Louise had elected to make her operational base on the island of Tenerife, rather than Lanzarote – which had suffered terribly at the hands of the Barbary slave trade – hoping their activities would be less observed there. She needed a safe haven from which to conduct her sorties.

'I see,' Smith said, though clearly he did not.

Louise waited, wondering if he would press her. Jansz and Gilles between them had apprised the former crew members of her intention to sail the waters of the Canary Islands until

October rather than return to Amsterdam by way of La Rochelle as usual. Smith, however, was not yet aware of their plans. Louise knew it was a risk – he might object – but she was paying wages considerably over the odds and also hoped his own personal history would make him sympathetic to her cause.

'We will talk further when we are clear of Las Palmas,' she said. 'I would value your opinion, lieutenant, and your advice.'

Louise knew this moment would be a mark of the partnership between them, and his acceptance of her authority. So, though she saw the questions in his eyes, she was pleased when he simply nodded.

'Aye, captain,' he said, then shouted down to the men. 'There are hidden rocks to the portside, so be on your guard. After that, set a north-east course to Tenerife.'

Louise climbed up to the top deck, feeling her muscles start to relax the further they got from Gran Canaria. Their new *boot*, suspended on davits above the water, rocked gently on its ropes. From time to time, she caught sight of Gilles, and allowed herself to wonder what birthday gift he had found for her. She looked with affection at Pieter and Jansz, good men both. At Marco Rossi, and the way Rémy, Sanchez and Al-Bayt were already fitting in to the existing pattern of life aboard the *Old Moon*. She thought, with regret, of Jan Roord and hoped that De Klerk would be able to secure his release. Holding her locket between her fingers, she said a prayer for her mother, and remembered the debt she owed to Cornelia and Alis.

Gradually, the lights of Las Palmas disappeared completely. Louise felt her heart return to its usual rhythm. Tomorrow, she would change into the clothes she wore on board, and the claustrophobia of the past week and more would be gone.

*Captain and commander once again.*

# PART FIVE

## THE HIGH SEAS
*May–August 1621*

# CHAPTER SIXTY-SEVEN

For everyone on board, the first hours of their voyage were spent adapting themselves to the new rhythm of the *Old Moon*. A calm night was followed by a gentle dawn, with dolphins playing alongside the ship. The log line was thrown over the taffrail to gauge their speed, and the compass reassured Louise they were holding their course steady. Conditions were perfect.

Lieutenant Smith was an immediate success with the crew, even the old guard. The Englishman was straightforward, with natural authority matched with the confidence not to belittle others. Marco Rossi had a sense of fellow feeling – they had both been captured by corsairs and lived to tell the tell – and Ali Al-Bayt, Sanchez and the gunner Pierre Rémy quickly found their feet with the De Groot brothers, Pieter and Lange, Jansz and Albert.

Louise was grateful to them all, and to Gilles and Captain De Klerk, for helping to assemble so harmonious a band of brothers. It was a relief to return to a world bounded by the ringing of the ship's bell and regimented activity on board. When finally she did retire to her cabin – she'd stayed on the quarterdeck until late into the night, not wanting to leave until she was certain they were safely away from Las Palmas – she had found Gilles' birthday surprise waiting folded on her pillow: a pair of men's breeches and a skirt combined into one, stitched by Rossi – he had sewn his initials into the waistband. Such a thoughtful gift, appropriate for a woman to wear without causing offence, yet comfortable enough to give her some measure of freedom moving about the ship.

She wished she could thank Gilles in person. But aware of how close they had come to being caught – and still not certain what, if anything, Lieutenant Roord might have said – she knew they had to take care. Gilles did not come to her cabin that night. For the time being, they would have to survive on looks and smiles. It was so little, but it was better than nothing.

Holding his gift close, imagining it smelt of him, Louise snuffed out her candle, and slept without dreaming.

At the end of the next day, she invited Lieutenant Smith and Gilles to join her for dinner in her cabin. Albert had surpassed himself: newly caught wreckfish, cooked in oil, and the local delicacy of *gofio* served with honey. Once they were properly at sea again, fresh food would be scarce. The cook was enjoying this rare opportunity to show his culinary skills.

It was the first time Gilles had set foot inside her cabin since arriving in Las Palmas. Louise saw he was looking around as if to check that everything was still the same. She saw his eyes pause on the painting he had done for her, now pinned above the dresser, and they caught one another's eye and smiled.

Though she had not been able to forewarn him that she intended to share her plans with Lieutenant Smith this evening, Louise knew Gilles would support her decision. In truth, there was little choice. Smith was a sharp man and had immediately realised that this engagement was not to be a simple return journey to Amsterdam as he might have expected. But Louise had been watching him, and admired the way he carried himself. She felt the time was right to take him into their confidence.

'Gilles, might you?' she said, gesturing to their glasses.

'It would be my pleasure.'

While he chose and decanted the wine, Louise drew her chair to the table. 'Lieutenant, I told you I would appreciate your advice. I will also need your support.' She was encouraged to see that although Smith looked interested, he did not appear ill at ease or wary. 'How are you finding our ship, lieutenant?'

'She is a pleasure to sail,' he replied warmly. 'I am not accustomed to such a flat-bottomed craft – I imagine she might struggle to hold steady on rough seas – but she is trim, and efficient.'

'She has done great service.' Louise paused. 'I imagine, though, you are wondering why she has been equipped so particularly?'

A broad smile crossed the Englishman's face. 'I assumed you would inform me when you thought it fit to do so.' He cleared his throat. 'Though two cannon and four swivel guns is more than I would expect to see on a merchant ship.'

Gilles carefully poured them each a cup of wine, and sat down.

'Lieutenant, I fear I employed you under somewhat dishonest circumstances. I have a plan I would like to put into action. I have no idea if it will work, or if it is foolish of me to think that one ship might make any difference, but I would like to try.'

Smith leant forward. 'I am listening, ma'am.'

Seven bells had rung before Louise had finished speaking.

'So, what do you think, lieutenant?' she asked finally, somewhat nervously.

Smith sat back in his chair. 'I hardly know what to think, *capitana*. It is . . . ambitious beyond anything I have heard.'

'But possible?'

He hesitated. 'Possible, yes. Easy, no.'

Louise smiled, relieved. He had not dismissed her idea out of hand.

'No, it won't be easy. Gilles and I discussed our strategy, after our conversations with Rossi. The idea that a single merchant ship – even with such additional firepower as we now possess – might take on a Spanish galleon or a corsair galley powered by enslaved men, *c'est de l'utopie.*' She smiled. 'As you might put it, lieutenant, pie in the sky. And even if we did launch a successful attack, how would we disarm the captors without harming their hostages?'

Gilles nodded. 'Also, if we fired on the slavers and the galley went down, that would be many souls lost, shackled to their oars. We wouldn't be able to get to them in time.'

'But what if we could intercept them, and disrupt their passage?' she said, her eyes flashing. 'What if we could scare them? I think there is a way that we can make it impossible for them to ply their trade in these waters.'

'With just one ship?' Smith asked. 'How?'

'This is where I need your advice, lieutenant. Your knowledge of firearms, Rémy's too.'

'It is why we need to make a port of call into Garachico, where we might acquire the materials we will need,' Gilles added.

'The question is, lieutenant,' Louise asked again, 'are you with us?'

A smile broke across his broad face. 'I would be glad to teach those villains a lesson. They owe me five years of my life.'

Louise nodded. 'So as to help stop such things happening to anyone else.'

'That's right. This is why we are sailing to Garachico rather than Santa Cruz and the reason for our o'er hasty departure?'

Louise and Gilles exchanged a look.

'It is true that I would like our presence on Tenerife to be discreet,' she replied carefully, 'but there was also a reason to think that the authorities in Gran Canaria might have felt it incumbent upon them to prevent us leaving. There was an incident with my previous captain . . .'

Smith laughed. 'I heard something of that. A lady commander and a Dutchman who drank himself to death and was buried at sea, the taverns were full of it.'

Louise did not laugh. 'What else did they say?'

Smith blushed. 'What you'd expect. Nothing worth repeating.'

She could imagine. 'There is no reason to believe they would send a ship after us,' she said steadily, 'but there is no need to court trouble. Garachico is on the furthest side of Tenerife from Gran Canaria, facing west to the Americas rather than east to the Barbary Coast. I do not think they will look for us there.'

'Aye, *capitana*,' Smith said. He stood up, bowed to Louise, then held out his hand to Gilles. 'May I ask who else is aware of your plans?'

Gilles answered. 'Jansz, though not the specifics. Rossi, too. No one else. Well, Roord was aware of something, but he is no longer with us.'

'If I might make so bold, I would recommend we keep it that way for now. A tot of rum in their bellies, and the crew will take the gossip on shore.'

'I am in complete agreement with you, lieutenant. Thank you for your time, and your support.'

The same broad grin. 'Aye, *capitana*. There is much to do.'

# CHAPTER SIXTY-EIGHT

*Monday, 17 May*

On the morning of their third day out of Las Palmas, Louise caught her first sight of El Teide, the black mountain standing at the heart of Tenerife. Ali Al-Bayt and Sanchez had regaled them with stories of how the ancient people of the Islas Afortunadas, the Guanches, believed that a devil lived inside. When he was angry, he sent rock and fire up into the sky.

Louise raised her spyglass and saw black rock above sweeping green slopes. It reminded her of her first sight of the Pyrenees from the battlements of the medieval Cité of Carcassonne. As with the ocean, there was a timelessness in the mountains that made the affairs of men seem insignificant.

She tightened her headscarf, adjusted her cutlass at her waist, then saw Gilles was watching her from below. Louise smiled, holding his gaze for just a moment. He smiled back, his eyes alight with pride and affection.

Then Lieutenant Smith gave the order and the *Old Moon* began her preparations for the approach into Garachico. The crew trimmed the sails on the main and fore masts, and turned the ship portside to bring her safely in. Marvelling at how different Tenerife was to Gran Canaria, Louise took up position on the bow, watching the elegant villas, palaces and haciendas of the town come into view. On the hills above, sat richly endowed convents and monasteries.

Prosperous and secure, Garachico was the most important

port on the island – perhaps of all the Islas Afortunadas – so Louise was confident that they would soon be able to find what was necessary to put her plan into action.

Over the next two days, Gilles, Smith and Jansz, accompanied by Sanchez and Al-Bayt, ventured out into Garachico to acquire everything they would need – two barrels of lime saltpetre and charcoal, additional pails filled with sand, and two pairs of matchlock pistols. Although he was a Morisco – and so mistrusted by some of the Spanish merchants – Ali Al-Bayt understood how the minds of the islanders worked. He proved invaluable. After talking to men in the market, he led their little band down tiny streets, into a small and nondescript building where an armoury of weapons was on offer to those with deep pockets.

'Looted from wrecked ships, do you think?' Gilles muttered to Smith, as the merchant stood back to let them inspect the wares.

'Best not to ask.'

The lieutenant tested the weight of the weapons and checked the mechanisms. He had never served as a soldier, but had been brought up on a farm in Cornwall, so was a fair shot. 'Rabbits, not men,' he said, lifting his arm and pretending to take aim, 'but the principle's the same.'

Back on board, it became clear that Pierre Rémy had the best eye. With the lightest of the muskets, he could hit a piece of driftwood floating some fifty yards away in the water. He was assigned one of the pistols, with one apiece for Smith and Gilles, and a spare in case the mechanism of any of the others jammed. Second Lieutenant Bleeker and Jansz were trained to operate the swivel guns to support Rémy and Lange.

Louise was aware of the danger firearms posed on board ship. Fire was an ever-present threat, so mariners and corsairs alike favoured cutlasses and daggers over pistols. But Louise intended to turn the corsairs' own tactics against them, and she knew that the moment of 'surrender or die' was often brought about by threatening, even shooting, the captain. Muskets were not always accurate, even in the right hands, but with Smith and Rémy on board, she reckoned they had a good chance.

Pirates mostly targeted lone merchant ships full of cargo, which had limited room for heavy weapons. This time of the year was prime piracy season, when corsairs would scout the less-travelled sea lanes, avoiding the likelihood of running into a Spanish or English warship. They would follow and watch their quarry, judging its speed and manpower, before deciding on a strategy for attack.

Louise intended to do the same.

'And then?' Gilles had asked.

'Then,' she replied, 'we give them a fright they will never forget.'

Flying false colours was commonplace, to lull the quarry into an unwarranted sense of security, as was sending a couple of warning shots across the bows to make sure of surrender without damaging the ship.

Again, Louise intended to do the same.

The difference was that the *Old Moon* alone could not hope to take on a corsair galley and defeat it. Instead, she proposed to intercept them as they were coming out of Salé or Tunis and stop them from carrying out their raids, rather than catching them on their way back and attempting to free any captives they might have on board.

*Prevention not cure.*

\* \* \*

On the morning of the third day on shore, Rossi returned to the ship triumphant, having secured a measure of loom-state linen, the last item they needed. From that, he would cut face masks for the entire crew. Louise wanted to ensure no harm would come to anyone on board.

By the evening of the fourth day, everything was ready. Louise again invited Gilles and Lieutenant Smith to her cabin to take stock.

'Is there anything we have forgotten?'

Gilles smoothed his inventory on the table, striking off the items as Smith catalogued what they had bought.

'Everything present and correct,' he confirmed.

'And you think the cauldron will work?' Louise asked.

Smith nodded. 'We will need to experiment with the proportions, the mixture of saltpetre to the other ingredients. A great deal will depend on the wind direction, and how quickly the saltpetre ignites. But, in principle, it should work precisely as the charge for the cannon does, just on a larger scale. We'll add the powder and spirits of wine from a priming horn – we'll mix the dye with the saltpetre in the cauldron – then set the charge and "boom".' He mimed the explosion with his hands.

'But that will be very dangerous for whoever sets the charge, surely?' Gilles said.

'It will require a long trigger line and some kind of shield, yes.'

'Would a wooden barrier be effective?' Louise asked.

'Provided it was doused with water to protect it from the sparks, it might.'

Louise put her fingers to her temples. She had the beginnings of a headache. From time to time, she thought she heard a rumble of dry thunder over El Teide. 'Ali Al-Bayt's devil is waking up,' she murmured, and felt Gilles look at her in surprise. 'Are we due for a storm?'

'Dry thunder is common at this time of year in Tenerife,' Smith said. 'It usually comes to nothing.' Then came the familiar sound of the ship's bell ringing the changing of the watch – though they were in harbour, they were maintaining the discipline. 'If you will excuse me, ma'am. Barenton, I will see you in a few hours.'

Louise smiled. 'Thank you, lieutenant.'

'*Capitana.*'

'Monsieur Barenton, if you might stay a moment longer? I would like to go through the books with you.'

'Of course, ma'am.'

They waited until the cabin door had clicked shut. Then, without a word being spoken, they moved together. On the eve of this new adventure, they wanted to be – had to be – with one another. Gilles pulled her heavy wooden chest across the door, Louise covered the candle, then they lay together in one another's arms as thunder cracked over the black mountain and the sky lit up with lightning.

This time, they did not fall asleep afterwards – they would not make that mistake again – though they whispered of love and destiny, until the sky was nearly light.

# CHAPTER SIXTY-NINE

*Saturday, 22 May*

On the third Saturday in May, as the sun was rising over the rocky terrain behind the town, the *Old Moon* sailed out of the harbour of Garachico on the high tide under a boundless blue sky. An armed merchant ship some hundred feet long, two swivel guns at the bow, another two at the stern, she was a sight to behold. The two square sails on the main and fore masts trimmed, the wind astern, the lateen sail helping to steer their passage. Spirits on board were high.

Louise stood on the fo'c'sle, hands on the rail, as they struck out into the Atlantic Ocean. As the ship sailed east, towards the coast of North Africa, every part of the vessel seemed to sing – the creaking and lilting, the rise and fall of the hull in the water bouncing against the swell.

Dawn to dusk to dawn, the bells marking the hours, Smith and Bleeker taking turns at the helm. Though the wind was against them, they made fair progress, measuring speed, maintaining their course by the stars and the sun.

On the fourth day out of port, they ran into huge breakers approaching in La Bocayna, the strait of water that separated the island of Lanzarote from its southern neighbour, Fuerteventura. Gigantic rolling waves, steep and unforgiving, set the vessel bobbing like a cork. A wall of water broke over the bow, sending white sheets of sea spray across the deck. But the *Old Moon* came through with no damage and though Lange was hit by a piece of wood, and the older De Groot brother slipped on the ladder coming up from the hold, there were no significant injuries among the fourteen-strong company.

Louise had decided the waters around Lanzarote would be a good place to start their campaign of disruption, since it was often a target for Barbary raids. So many captives had been taken that most of the villages along the eastern coast of the island were deserted, ghost towns. Everyone had fled inland. It was where Rossi's slaver ship had been heading when the storm and the blanket of choking bad air knocked them off course.

They dropped anchor in the lea of the tiny island of La Graciosa.

Louise supervised the preparations for their first attack, inspecting the cannon and making sure they were primed, checking that the swivel guns were in good working order. Beside each stood pails filled with sand to dampen any rogue sparks. Each man was ordered to wear his linen face mask should the wind blow the saltpetre cloud back in their direction. The flat metal dish, twice the length of a man's forearm, had been set at the highest point of the fo'c'sle; the torch was ready to light it and the noxious agents prepared to make it spark. Behind it, a large square of sail – soaked in a solution of lime to make it fire-resistant – had been constructed to help funnel the 'bad air' in the direction of the pirate ship on the prevailing breeze. Three long lines, to work like a fan, were attached to pegs on the deck and, behind the sail, a defensive square of timber had been constructed, with a small hole for the trigger line, to protect the operator from sparks and the heat.

Only once everything was ready did Louise's nerves get the better of her. There was no guarantee this would work. Was this foolish, dangerous, putting her crew in danger for no valid reason? She would find it hard to explain, to anyone apart from Gilles, why she felt the need to right such a wrong. She hardly understood herself.

But then Louise caught the expression on Smith's face – and looked at Marco Rossi, making last-minute adjustments to the sail he had helped rig behind the sparking dish. Though he had recovered his health, she knew he would bear the scars of his ordeal for the rest of his life. Sanchez and Al-Bayt had lost several people to slavers – a family member, a friend, a neighbour. She drew a deep breath. They were right to try. If everyone looked away, then how would the world ever change for the better?

'Everything is ready,' Gilles said.

Louise looked out to sea. 'So, we wait.'

Eight bells had just rung for the end of the dog watch on the following day, when Pieter spotted something out of the corner of his eye in the fading light. A movement out at sea, some distance northwards. He took a moment to be sure, then called down to Jansz. The boatswain confirmed the sighting, then came to inform the captain.

'About half a mile, give or take,' he offered.

Louise raised her spyglass to her eye and adjusted the setting. Her heart started to beat heavily. They had company. She nodded to Lieutenant Smith, who gave the call.

'Ship a'port,' he called, repeating it in Dutch, French and Spanish. This was to be their first engagement and Louise wanted no misunderstandings. Since this was a crew of many languages, she had ordered all critical orders to be given four times over.

'Raise the anchor,' she commanded, 'and man the sails.'

'We will need to come round behind them,' Smith said, 'otherwise the wind will blow the cloud back upon us rather than towards them.'

Louise nodded, and gave the order to change course.

'Can you see their colours?'

'No, but they are sailing away from the coast not back to port, so I wager we are seeing the beginning of a raiding trip.'

Beside her, Louise heard Gilles draw breath.

'Are you scared?' she whispered.

'A little.' He paused. 'Are you?'

She gave a light laugh. 'Apprehensive, yes. Doubting my judgement, yes. At the same time, not scared. I feel as certain of this as I do of you.'

Beside her, she saw him smile. Then his voice grew grave. 'If we can see them, can they see us?'

'We have to assume so.'

Louise adjusted the spyglass again. She couldn't see their colours, but it was a single-masted vessel with a slender hull and low freeboard – a typical corsair galley. Maybe no more than five sets of oars. No way of knowing if it was powered by corsairs or slaves from another raid, but it was not too big for them to take on. And luck was with them – the vessel appeared to be alone, not part of a flotilla.

Beneath her feet, Louise felt the *Old Moon* change direction, leaning against the heavy rudder. She heard the clap and rustle of the sails being trimmed, tacking through the wind and picking up speed. Anticipation tightened in her chest. As Smith said, they needed to sail north and then turn and approach the corsair galley from behind, to take advantage of the wind.

*A hunter tracking its prey.*

As in a strange dance, the two ships, though still some distance apart, were almost circling one another in the water. Louise felt as if she was locked in a battle of wills with her invisible opposite number.

When the light started to fade over the Atlantic Ocean, Louise ordered every candle to be extinguished on deck, so their position could be less easily seen. Moments later, the corsair galley did the same.

'They know we are here,' she muttered. 'Good.'

As night fell, a few clouds rolled in, cloaking the moon. From time to time, the silver light broke through, glistening on the surface of the sea. The ships were changing position, moving away from one another, coming closer. Louise could imagine the pirate galley's confusion. A merchant ship with Dutch colours should be heading away from them, taking flight. It was not a warship primed to attack.

Then the play of wind and the current brought them closer. In the shifting shimmering light, Louise was straining to hear – the gentle lap of the waves against their hull, the sway around their gunnels. She smiled with satisfaction. The corsairs had lifted their oars from the water. Good. They were not yet ready to attack. They, too, were waiting. She whispered to Gilles, who relayed the order to Lieutenant Smith, that the ship's bell was to be muffled. Then, without warning, the wind dropped. A stalemate, both vessels becalmed. Neither ship was moving, but the advantage now was with the galley with its oar power.

Louise thought the night would never end. Waiting, watching, listening. Everyone was in position on deck and ready to put their plan into action. She had no idea what the crew truly thought of what they were about to do – Gilles said they had taken the orders in their stride – but no one was showing signs of dissent.

Finally, the first crack of light appeared in the east, profiling the corsair galley on the horizon. The wind started to pick up.

'It's time,' Louise said.

Slowly, the *Old Moon* began to advance. They covered some distance before the corsairs noticed, and a shout went up on the galley. Smith had brought the ship round behind the vessel, so they had the advantage of the north-easterly filling their sails. They were now skimming across the surface of the water.

Louise watched their prey change direction but, even with the advantage of their oars, they were no match for the wind. The *Old Moon* was gaining on them. Everything was going to plan.

'Masks on,' she ordered. 'Is Rémy in position?'

'Yes, ma'am,' replied Smith.

Acting as Rémy's powder monkey, Pieter was holding the gunpowder ready in a flannel cartridge. Another mariner loaded the cartridge into the gun, pushing in the cloth wad and securing it home with a wooden rammer.

'*Fais attention*,' Rémy muttered. 'Take care.'

He pierced the flannel with a small length of wire, then placed it down the touch-hole in the breech of the gun.

'Home!' he shouted, once he had made contact.

Next, a round shot was loaded into the barrel, followed by another wad to keep it in place. From her position on the quarterdeck, Louise heard the rumble of wheels and knew they were hauling the first of the cannon up to the port so that the front of the gun carriage was hard up against the ship's bulwark. Rémy primed the touch-hole with a mixture of fine powder and spirits of wine from the priming horn, made sure everything was safe, then raised his left hand to signal the gun was ready. In his right hand, he held the linstock.

Louise turned to see the barrel was now protruding out of the gun port and was being manoeuvred into position to send a warning shot across the bows of the galley.

'And are we also ready above, lieutenant?'

He looked up to the upper deck where Ali Al-Bayt was crouched behind the wooden barricade, Sanchez behind him holding a flaming torch ready to light the trigger line. The De Groot brothers were holding the ropes for the limed-sail, ready to fan the cloud towards the galley.

'We are,' Smith confirmed.

Louise took a deep breath, and shouted the command. 'Fire!'

Rémy applied the linstock to the touch-hole, which ignited the priming powder, in turn setting off the main charge. The shot was propelled out of the barrel, the gun itself hurling violently backwards in recoil until it was stopped by the breech rope.

A roar exploded from the bowels of the *Old Moon* as the ball flew through the air and the cannon juddered to a halt. The shot missed the galley by a matter of feet, as was intended, setting a wash by its bow that caused the craft to plunge down, then rear up in the turbulent water. On the deck of the pirate ship, Louise could see the corsairs lined up – ready to defend their ship or attack the aggressor, she couldn't tell which. She estimated there were perhaps a dozen men. An equal match.

The two vessels were now just fifty yards apart.

She held her nerve, waiting until she saw Rémy appear on deck with his musket, poised to take aim.

'Are you ready?'

'Ready, ma'am.'

Louise dropped her arm. The Frenchman took aim, and fired. At the beak of the galley, Louise saw their captain in his turbaned cap and long-buttoned jacket go down. She dropped her arm again and gave the command to Ali Al-Bayt waiting in position.

'Fire!'

Al-Bayt took the flaming torch from his colleague's hand and held it to the first of the trigger lines buried in the lime saltpetre in the metal dish, which also contained a substance mixed with charcoal and a measure of turmeric. Instantly, there was a flash, then an explosion, and a noxious yellow cloud of bad air was sent upwards. The De Groot brothers pulled on the ropes and the sail began to billow. Turning his face away, Al-Bayt repeated the process twice more, until a foul blanket of yellow cloud was hovering over the sea. Caught by the wind, it was blown towards the galley, as Louise had prayed it would be, settling over the lower part of their ship. Above the cloud, on a platform like the one that had kept Marco Rossi safe, Louise saw two corsairs reaching for the captain's body to drag it away.

'Rémy!' she shouted.

The Frenchman fired again, taking down another of the corsairs. Smith aimed and took down the other. Chaos erupted on the slaver ship as the yellow cloud covered the deck. Panicked orders to withdraw, followed by the sound of oars dipping without pattern in the water.

'Shall I fire again, *capitana*?' asked Rémy, his eyes bright.

Louise hesitated, then shook her head. The galley was rowing away, battling against the prevailing wind. There was no need to waste any more of their ammunition.

Their trick had scared the corsairs, and confounded them, but Louise knew that if the pirates had mounted a proper defence, the bad air would not have held them at bay for long. The cloud was already dissipating. Next time, she thought, they would need to adjust the balance of ingredients, or find some other way of making the noxious air last for longer. But, for a first attempt, she was pleased. The wind had been with them, they had threatened the galley without destroying it. She had no doubt they had delivered a warning to be taken back to Salé.

'*Capitana?*' Rémy repeated.

Louise removed her mask and lowered her hand. 'No. It's over.'

Rémy let his arm drop. One by one, all around the ship, the crew started to remove their masks and lower their weapons. Pieter came up on deck, then surprised everyone by letting out a whoop of delight.

Louise laughed. Soon, the entire ship was shouting, slapping one another on the back, celebrating the success of their first engagement. She gave them a few moments, then she sheathed her cutlass and sighed with relief.

Louise remained on the quarterdeck a while longer, weighing up the success of the mission. On balance, the stratagem had worked. They had suffered no injuries, and no damage. Next time, there were things they should do differently. But, today, she was proud of the *Old Moon* and her crew, the old hands and the new.

Gilles came to join her.

'*Capitana*,' he said. 'Your men salute you.'

Louise smiled. 'Let us raise our cups to the *Ghost Ship* and all who sail in her.'

# CHAPTER SEVENTY

## Las Palmas de Gran Canaria
### *Saturday, 12 June*

Felipe Arauz was a disappointed man. He had come to Gran Canaria from the mainland some years ago, an idealistic and hopeful young lawyer from Bilbao. He had married into an important local family, and risen up through the ranks to reach the role of chief prosecutor to Gran Canaria. But he had never got used to the heat. His wife nagged him, his children despised him and his house in the hills, where his mistress currently resided, was costing him a fortune. The Inquisition was always breathing down his neck, interfering and exceeding the bounds of their jurisdiction.

Now this.

He dabbed his nose with his handkerchief. 'What does it mean?' he asked again.

The clerk stood in front of him. 'I know no more than I have reported, Señor Arauz. That we are receiving reports of ships being overcome by clouds of noxious air.'

'When you say "we", who do you mean exactly?' Arauz snapped.

'The harbourmaster has recorded comments from crews of several ships who have docked, who have heard it spoken of.' He hesitated. 'Some say there is a ship seen in the vicinity when these incidents have occurred.'

'What kind of ship? A pirate vessel?'

'No one seems to know, señor.'

Arauz threw his hands in the air. 'I fail to see what I am supposed to do about it. This is clearly a maritime matter, not a civil one. The harbourmaster is paid enough. And,' he added, warming to his theme, 'didn't you say this was happening in the waters around Lanzarote?'

'Yes, señor, but there—'

'Well, then. I've told you before. I have no time to waste on problems that are nothing to do with us. Let Lanzarote sort out its own concerns.' He flapped his hands. 'That will do.'

Arauz sat back in his chair. For a moment, he considered what the clerk had told him, then put it from his mind. Lanzarote was a law unto itself. No reason that this problem – if indeed it wasn't just an old wife's tale – would spread to their waters.

He opened the drawer of his desk and pulled out a small flask of rum. His wife didn't approve of him drinking so common a swill, but then she did not approve of anything he did. As the liquid slipped down his throat, working its usual magic, his ill-temper started to ease. His thoughts went to his mistress and what he might take her, to encourage her to receive him favourably this evening. A lace mantilla, white for the summer?

Arauz put his feet up on his desk, and smiled. Yes, that would do nicely. As for this ridiculous rumour, it would blow over. Even if there was some truth to it, it was nothing to do with them. Gran Canaria had problems enough of its own. Satisfied he had dispensed with the matter, he poured himself another tot. A little more wouldn't hurt.

But in the taverns and boarding houses of Las Palmas, the Saturday-night crowd was in full throat. Talking of a warship that came out of nowhere, attacked corsair galleys from Salé, and vanished just as quickly.

And further away, in the Barbary ports and in the villages along the coast of Lanzarote, stories were being carried on the breeze. Whispered at first, then getting louder, gaining credence. Rumours of a ghost ship coming out of nowhere – trailing with it a cloud of bad air, that stole the breath from a man's chest, making his eyes burn and his skin blister – and vanished just as quickly. Tales of cannon shot and musket, of men taken down by a less-than-human hand. The stench of sulphur and the judgement of Hell itself, some said.

More than this, it was rumoured that the ghost ship was commanded by a she-captain, a hellion, a monstrous yet beautiful creature, some ten feet tall, her hair wrapped in a long red scarf, who would turn a man to stone if he looked upon her. A being neither wholly of the land, nor of the sea. Mothers started to threaten their children that, if they were disobedient, the ghost ship would come and take them away. Men in the taverns, emboldened by drink, would boast of how they would be able to defeat this siren of the high seas.

On board the *Old Moon*, Louise was unaware of how quickly their notoriety was building. The sun was growing hotter, the winds fiercer, giving speed to merchant ships and corsair galleys alike.

As June progressed, the *Old Moon* patrolled the waters around Lanzarote and the tiny island of Lobos in la Bocayna Strait. They carried out six more attacks on suspected slaver ships – five successful, one aborted because of a change in the direction of the wind. With Gilles' and Lieutenant Smith's help, Louise had adapted her stratagem: the timings, the speed at which they could attack and withdraw, the way to make the cloud denser and to last for longer. They discovered their masks were more effective when damp; Al-Bayt experimented with the proportion of saltpetre to charcoal, and added a measure of laudanum from Louise's own supply, to further disorientate their opponents; Rémy trained Lange to prime the cannon, so they could prepare more than one for each attack; and, in his turn, Lange showed Sanchez and Pieter how to manage the gunpowder, rammers and cloth. On days when the sea was as flat as a looking glass, Jansz and Smith improved their skills with the musket, so they were not solely reliant on Rémy leaving the lower deck to take the first shot. For it was evident, from each sortie, that the speedy removal of the master of the slave galley was critical to the success of their mission. If they ever came across a loaded ship, shooting the commanding officer would offer a slim chance that the enslaved men might be able to overpower the remainder of the corsair crew and free themselves.

As time passed, the crew became skilled in their tasks. Little by little, the *Old Moon* became a fighting ship, its trading past forgotten. An independent band of confederates, owing allegiance only to one another and to their captain. No longer citizens of France, or Holland, or England, or Italy, or Las Islas Afortunadas, but elite members of an independent republic under the command of the *capitana*.

They were making a difference. Louise hoped that their resistance would give others the courage to fight back.

## THE ATLANTIC OCEAN

In mid-June, they were forced to detour into Arrecife on the east coast of Lanzarote for provisions.

Louise intended to send the *boot* in and out, under the cover of moonlight, rather than take the *Old Moon* itself into harbour, but, even so, their presence did not go unnoticed. As they replenished their supplies of fresh food and water, some dozen islanders came to wish them well on the quayside in the moonlight. Women threw flowers and men shouted thanks for what they were doing.

The crew was delighted, and talked late into the night. Rossi imagined how his village might have been spared had the ghost ship patrolled the waters around Vieste, Smith and Ali Al-Bayt, too. Louise was touched, but concerned. They were not operating with any authority and she wanted to remain incognito. But there were no repercussions.

Their attacks on slaver ships grew bolder and they went hunting further afield.

Gilles still lived with the fear his true nature would be discovered but, with Louise's help, he kept his secret. And, as the boundaries of nationality and social standing blurred, the knowledge of an affection between the *capitana* and Gilles Barenton became openly accepted.

At night, the gentle Frenchman now slept in the captain's cabin and the crew knew to find him there. It was a form of *matelotage*, a kind of partnership existing at sea that all mariners understood, in place of a marriage or a formal agreement.

All the same, Louise wanted to make things official. The more the crew's confidence rose, the more successful their sorties, the more she worried that their good fortune would not last.

So, on Thursday, the twenty-fourth day of June – with Tom Smith officiating, and in the presence of the entire crew – Louise Reydon-Joubert and Gilles Barenton pledged their worldly goods to one another and vowed to fight alongside one another as true friends.

'In the power *not* invested in me –' the lieutenant began and everyone cheered – 'not invested in me by either God or man, I declare this partnership entered into willingly by one woman, and one man, both of sound mind, to be binding for so long as you both shall live.' He grinned. 'So help me God!'

As they exchanged rings – a twist of red cotton for her, a twist of blue cotton for Gilles – Louise remembered, from Minou's journals, how her grandparents had first pledged themselves to one another with a ring made from straw, and was glad she was doing something similar. As if it were an echo calling back through the generations.

The festivities lasted late into the night, until, finally, Louise and Gilles withdrew to their cabin, to the accompaniment of ribald comments and good wishes – Albert even threw a handful of his precious grain over them to wish them prosperity and fertility.

Later, when the ship was quiet and the celebrations over, they lay in one another's arms in the quiet of the early morning.

'Will you regret the lack of children?' Louise asked.

Gilles sighed. 'I would not wish a childhood such as I had on any living creature.'

She propped herself up on her elbow. 'I am serious. Don't most people want to leave something of themselves when they die?'

'Do you?'

Louise considered. 'I suppose I have always wanted to do something myself, be known for that rather than for having my life reflected in another.' She sighed. 'But then I think of my niece Florence, and how I wish I knew her better, then I am not so sure.'

'This is our family,' Gilles said quietly, kissing her bare shoulder. 'Here on this ship. We don't need anyone else.'

\* \* \*

By the very tail-end of June, Louise knew that they had to return to Garachico to restock their ammunition. There was nowhere on Lanzarote that could provide them with what they required, and they needed more fresh water and beer, too. She delayed for as long as she could and was uneasy at the thought of setting foot on dry land again. Come the autumn, there would be no choice. They would have to over-winter some-where, and Garachico seemed as safe a place as any.

Again, rather than take the *Old Moon* herself back into the harbour, Louise decided to send a small landing party on the *boot* to pick up what they needed: Jansz and Gilles, Lange and Sanchez to row, with Rossi and Al-Bayt. The expedition should take no more than six hours, depending on the tides, and they could be back on the open sea within the day.

The visit was successful. Although their reception was more muted than in Lanzarote, it seemed that their exploits were well-known in Garachico too. Gilles said tales of the ghost ship terrorising the corsairs away from Las Islas Afortunadas were commonplace. He heard them spoken in the markets and the taverns, the stories wilder and more fantastic with each retelling: a vessel crewed by the undead; a ship some thousand feet long that floated above the water; a galleon commanded by a red-horned she-devil; a miasma of bad air that swallowed any craft that came within its orbit; old European superstitions mixed with the ancient mythology of the islands.

While the crew congratulated one another – they were folk heroes, the stuff of legend – Louise felt the same tightness in her chest, listening as Gilles and Jansz reported all they had heard.

*It was working.*

The consequence was that fewer ships were coming across their path, and Louise started to discuss the possibility of moving further east to the African coastline with Gilles and Lieutenant Smith. What if they left the waters around Lanzarote and sailed towards the territories controlled by Ottoman-ruled Agadir?

'Although I am not sure,' she mused. 'We have a strategy that works. We are keeping the waters of Las Islas Afortunadas safe. Is there any need to put ourselves further in harm's way?'

'If there is more we might do,' Smith urged, 'then, yes.'

Gilles nodded. 'Or head towards Malta. The Christian slave markets are just as bad. Rossi was taken in retribution for Valetta, wasn't that what he told us?'

Louise gathered up her charts. 'We will sleep on it,' she said, aware of an undertow of anxiety she could not shake.

*As if our good fortune cannot last.*

# CHAPTER SEVENTY-ONE

## THE HAGUE
### *Thursday, 1 July*

In The Hague, Andries Joost was preparing to board a ship for Gran Canaria. Most of his expanding fleet was registered in the port city on the west coast of the Dutch Republic – though, since acquiring a majority stake in the Van Raay shipping line, he had also extended his operations into Amsterdam. His home in Leiden was midway between the two.

A man of middle years, with a deeply lined face, curled brown hair and a trimmed moustache, he was wearing a high black hat and a long blue waistcoat with silver studs. Everything about him spoke of wealth and power. A man used to getting his own way.

The letter informing him of his son's death had been delivered three days previously by the captain of the *North Star*. Written by Louise Reydon-Joubert, it informed him that his only son had been taken ill and, tragically, had died at sea on the night of the second of April. His death had been registered with the authorities in Las Palmas. She sent her heartfelt condolences for his loss.

Andries Joost did not accept this version of events. He knew Reydon-Joubert was the registered owner of the *Old Moon* and, although mevrouw Van Raay had professed shock that he could even suggest such a thing, Joost believed the harridan had murdered his son in order to seize command of the ship.

Poisoned, or stabbed in his sleep, he knew not. Only that his son had been healthy, in the prime of his life. He suffered from no ailments or weaknesses that could have caused his heart simply to stop. The woman was a thief, too. His son's prized possessions – his portolan and the ivory-cased compass that had been Andries' father's before him – had not been returned to him by the captain of the *North Star*. De Klerk had claimed to know nothing about them.

The truce between the Dutch Republic and Spain had ended three months previously and, already, the battle lines between the trading routes were being drawn. Next season, Joost intended to begin sailing to the East Indies – the trade in people was profitable – and had already given Van Raay notice that he would be moving all of his operations to The Hague, away from Amsterdam. She had entreated him not to do so – begged, even – but he been unyielding.

He would kill two birds with one stone. First, he would bring Reydon-Joubert to justice, then he would call Van Raay to account for allowing such a situation in the first place. It was common knowledge that Van Raay's company was in financial trouble. Joost intended to accelerate that collapse, which would leave him free to acquire both the *North Star* and, if justice was served, the *Old Moon*, which he would have seized. He had been at great pains to avoid taking sides in the conflict between Catholics and Calvinists. Finance and trade were his religion and he would negotiate with anyone for the right price. But with the loss of his son, his ambition had been dealt a heavy blow.

Even before learning about his son's death, Joost had decided to offer a substantial inducement to the authorities in Las Palmas and make Gran Canaria his base, rather than Malta. They were men of business. They knew that their harbour was less advantageously placed, so there was a deal to be done. Initial discussions had already begun. Now, there would be an additional condition. His fleet would come to Las Palmas, but only if they brought his son's murderer to justice.

He would see Louise Reydon-Joubert hanged. And all those who had been on the voyage with her and failed to protect his son, every single one of them.

# CHAPTER SEVENTY-TWO

*Wednesday, 11 August*

The *Old Moon* had served them well, but after three months at sea, there were signs of wear and tear. There were also signs of fatigue amongst the crew.

Louise knew that was when sloppiness slipped in and accidents might happen. An exhausted man with his mind not entirely on his job might fall from the yardarm; a gunner thinking of a quart of ale in a harbourside tavern might forget to pack the wad securely; a man dreaming of a girl might leave a candle burning and cause a fire down below.

And the punishing temperatures were unlike anything Louise had ever known. During the day, the crew covered their heads with damp cloths to keep the sun from burning their necks as they went about their chores. Louise still wore her red headscarf and breeches, but her forearms and face were tanned brown by the sun. Gilles, whilst needing to keep his collar high to his chin, wore a looser fitting shirt. Bleeker suffered terribly, his skin angry and raw in the heat. The mariners took off their slops and worked with bare backs.

The fierce winds blowing from the Sahara Desert, the *calimas*, had the heat of a furnace and covered the deck in gritty white sand that stung the eyes. The flags atop the masts of the *Old Moon* and at the stern snapped and tugged, as if trying to break free. The rigging slapped with a permanent hum, the sails stretched and billowed, making the ship sometimes hard to control. Rossi was kept busy with repairs. Ali Al-Bayt, the caulker, struggled to keep the hull watertight.

Louise had a permanent ringing in her ears from the wind. It was too hot to sleep and, everywhere she looked, she could see tempers were starting to fray. Jansz had a permanent scowl on his face and snapped at everyone. Whenever he was not on duty, Pieter sat slumped in the shadiest corner of the deck looking miserably into space, Rossi worked tirelessly before complaining that it was impossible to hold a needle in such heat, Rémy spent hours cleaning the muskets, complaining at the lack of opportunity to use them. Lange and the De Groot brothers talked of home. For three weeks, they had not had sight of another ship.

Only Gilles and Lieutenant Smith seemed unaffected.

It was mid-afternoon, and Louise and Gilles had withdrawn to their cabin – one bell had just been rung for the start of the dog watch. The wooden floorboards and furniture seemed to have swollen in the heat and motes of dust danced in the over-heated afternoon air. It was suffocating, as hot as a furnace, but it was only here that Gilles could risk loosening the top buttons of his shirt to let his skin breathe for a while.

'We should go ashore for a few days,' Louise said, fanning herself with a piece of parchment. We need provisions, our water is running low again, and I would replenish our stores of saltpetre and powder before September.'

'You would like to make a final few sorties this season?'

'I know you and Lieutenant Smith think we should be bolder. I don't disagree, but I would rather remain in the waters we know for August and September—'

'Even though there are no corsairs in sight?'

'They might be biding their time, too.'

'True,' Gilles agreed.

'So, my plan is a final patrol in the waters of Lanzarote and Fuerteventura – they might well have moved their operations south to avoid us – then winter in Garachico and take our time to decide what to do next season.' Louise wiped her hot face with the edge of her scarf. 'It is by no means certain that everyone will want to stay with the ship.'

'Do you still have sufficient funds to pay for all this?'

'For now. There is gold in the strongbox in my cabin. I have more available on shore.' She pulled a face. 'That is, unless my mysterious half-brother has, in my absence, somehow managed to steal my fortune.'

'What are you proposing?'

'I think we should return to Garachico for a brief sojourn. It will do everyone good. Ali says that the most important festival on Tenerife, the Feast of the Virgin of Candelaria, takes place over the night of the fourteenth to the fifteenth of August. Though he says the largest gathering is in Santa Cruz, there will be plenty of people in Garachico, too, over the two days and a night.'

'Meaning that we could be there and meld into the crowd, be less obvious.'

'Precisely so.' Louise's expression darkened. 'I know you think I am over-cautious, but I fear our activities coming to the attention of the authorities.'

'I do not believe the authorities give credence to the rumours of a ghost ship,' Gilles said, walking around behind her and massaging her shoulders. 'Even if they did, there is no reason to associate the *Old Moon* with such stories. Though unorthodox, the only female captain—'

'– that we know of.'

'Very well, the only female captain that we know of. Despite our hurried departure from Gran Canaria, you are a respected woman of business from Amsterdam, the owner of a merchant ship that has traded with Gran Canaria for many years.'

'Perhaps.'

'You are,' he smiled. 'In any case, we are doing the authorities' work for them. We are keeping their seas free of pirates. The people love us.' He dropped a kiss on the top of her head. 'Having said that, your plan is an excellent one. The crew needs a diversion, a rest, something to entertain them. The heat is setting them against one another.'

Suddenly overwhelmed with love for him, she cupped his face with her hands.

'You, Gilles Barenton,' she said, 'have been the great blessing of my life.'

# CHAPTER SEVENTY-THREE

### GARACHICO
*Saturday, 14 August*

Three days later, Louise dressed herself in the clothes from her former life – a wide skirt and bodice, a light cloak, a white lace cap – and went on shore. Lieutenant Bleeker had offered to stay on board with a skeleton crew, claiming he had no appetite for religious indulgence.

Although she felt constrained and uncomfortable in her old clothes, Louise had forgotten what it was like to have no responsibilities, or to lose herself in a crowd come to celebrate. She felt light-hearted and determined to enjoy herself.

There were people everywhere, children running backwards and forwards as the procession snaked through the narrow streets of Garachico to the main square. The Virgin Mary – a Black Madonna – was carried on a painted wooden platform by four men, a replica of the statue at the heart of the legend. At the head of the procession was an officiating priest in black soutane with buttons down the front, flanked by acolytes carrying a gold cross and a thurible. Though Louise had a Huguenot's horror of the gaudy pomp of Catholic parades, it had the atmosphere of a carnival. Drummers, fire-eaters, street vendors selling roasted almonds, all competed for their attention, and Louise let her cares slip away for an hour or two. She was a woman in her middle years, but she felt like a girl again.

The bells started to ring for ten o'clock as the procession approached the steps of the church. Louise glanced at Gilles, and saw the same joy and delight in his face.

'Come on,' she said, taking his hand, 'let us get closer to the front.'


## LAS PALMAS

Andries Joost waited until the bells of Santa Ana had finished striking ten, then shook his head.

'I do not think you are quite understanding the situation, Arauz,' he said, in careful Spanish.

He was in the Casas Consistoriales, the town hall in the plaza Santa Ana, in the office of Felipe Arauz, the chief prosecutor.

Arauz frowned. 'Señor Joost, forgive me. If you might explain, again, what you would like me to do.'

In the same, cold voice, Joost repeated everything he had said, stressing the significant amounts of money involved, money that would be lost to Gran Canaria – indeed, to Arauz personally – if his wishes were not carried out.

'I do not blame you,' Joost said magnanimously, 'but the situation is clear. My son was murdered and I expect you to administer justice.'

The prosecutor wiped his face with his handkerchief. 'But, Señor Joost, we do not know where Madame Reydon-Joubert went. She left Las Palmas in mid-May, I presumed to return to Amsterdam.'

Joost's eyes narrowed. 'Have you not heard of the ghost ship?' he asked.

'No such thing exists,' Arauz blustered, remembering the ludicrous tales his clerk had told him back in June. 'The people are fools; like children, they will believe any fairy tale.'

Joost tapped his manicured nails on the table. 'I am not in disagreement with you in general terms, but this is different. The *Old Moon* is the vessel that the Reydon-Joubert woman put into the hands of my son before—' Joost broke off, as if it was too painful to speak.

'Señor, do not distress yourself.'

'Do you have a son, prosecutor?'

His face hardened. 'I have not been so blessed.'

Joost waved his hand. 'Would that I had never had a son rather than suffer the torment of him being taken from me.'

Arauz rang the bell. 'A glass of wine for Señor Joost,' he said quickly.

'If you will join me.'

The prosecutor hesitated, then nodded. 'If you wish it, of course.'

A more convivial atmosphere established, Joost continued with his story – all the reasons why he believed the *Old Moon* and the phantom ship haunting the waters of Las Islas Afortunadas were one and the same; the rumours he had heard; the coincidence of Louise Reydon-Joubert vanishing at the same time as stories of the ghost ship started to surface; the fact that the captain was said to be a woman; and hadn't Reydon-Joubert usurped his son's place on the *Old Moon*?

'You are an intelligent man, prosecutor.' Joost leant forward in his chair. 'It would be greatly to your benefit to try to find the harridan. If you help bring her to justice, I will ensure that you have the funds you need to keep your estate in the Agaete Valley a secret.'

His hand shaking, Arauz put down his glass. He didn't understand how this Dutchman could know about his private house in the hills above Agaete, nor about the mistress he kept there. But he did know that if his wife's family got to hear of his indiscretion – or, worse still, the Inquisitional court – he would be ruined.

## GARACHICO

Dirk Jansz was sitting at a table outside a tavern in the port. Not for him the noise of the jamboree. An honest quart of ale, a comfortable stool and a full pipe; he was a man of simple needs.

He looked down into his tankard and saw it was empty. He tipped it upside down, unwilling to believe the evidence of his own eyes, then scrambled in his pocket for a coin.

No coin. He would have sworn on his mother's life he'd had another.

Jansz peered around, hoping to see Pieter or Rossi or Lange. Ali had vanished into the crowd the moment they'd stepped off the boat, and he realised he hadn't even noticed if Rémy had come ashore or not.

He stood up, finding himself a little unsteady on his feet. Perhaps he'd spent all his coins already. He didn't remember doing so, but his pockets were empty. And he had two hours before he was due back at the ship. Jansz surveyed the crowd, all hard-working men like him looking for a little peace and quiet from the toils of the day. Men like him who had no interest in wandering around in a procession worshipping a bit of painted wood.

His eyes fixed on a table with three men. They didn't look foreign. He pulled himself up. He supposed that he was the foreigner here – this wasn't Amsterdam, after all – but they were short like him, their pale skin scorched red by the sun like his. What say they were Dutch? Or, at the worst, English? He liked Smith, he liked his stories. He was a gentleman, no doubt about it. Perhaps Smith would stand him a drink? He looked around, but couldn't see him anywhere.

'Shame,' he muttered. He would have enjoyed sharing a pipe with him. 'A good man, the lieutenant.'

Taking it one step at a time, he made his way over to the table. Three men stared up at him, but he thought they looked friendly.

'Gentlemen,' he said. 'Do I have a story for you! If you stand me a drink, I'll tell you. Make your eyes stand out on stalks.'

A man with a thick black beard and hair combed back behind his ears turned to look at him. 'Is that so?'

Jansz put his hands on the table to keep himself steady. 'Have you heard about the ghost ship?'

'No such thing.'

Jansz tapped his nose. 'Says you.'

There was a pause, then the man clicked his fingers. 'A quart of ale for our friend.'

The boatswain sank happily onto the stool. 'Don't mind if I do.'

## LAS PALMAS

It took Prosecutor Arauz little more than an hour to discover that the rumours Joost had recounted were widespread. He spoke to the men in the secretariat, to the guards on duty outside the gate. He even interrogated the elderly servant, who was too terrified to make any sense, but finally admitted that she had heard stories of such a vessel.

'It's the Devil's work,' she said, crossing herself.

At eleven o'clock that night, he sent a messenger down to the harbour. Within half an hour, the man returned. The stories were the same: from Tenerife to Lanzarote, they were talking of a ship that brought bad air that choked a man to death, a ship that hunted corsair slaver galleys, of how the waters were safer than they had ever been. Not a single captive had been taken from the villages of Lanzarote or Fuerteventura this entire season.

Though he had not approved of her – women who spoke too much and lacked in feminine virtues were a plague on society – Arauz did not believe Louise Reydon-Joubert had anything to do with the so-called 'ghost ship', even if such a vessel existed. But then it came back to him that the inquisitors had talked to her former lieutenant, a Dutchman by the name of . . . he couldn't immediately remember, only that the interrogator had been over-zealous. The man was alive, but only barely so. Roord, that was his name. Yes, Roord had made allegations about treason and the woman's lack of decency, hinted at some kind of conspiracy between the Reydon-Joubert woman and her secretary? Had there also been something about the sudden death of Joost's son?

Half past eleven and the heat was still intolerable. Arauz put his head in his hands, trying to remember precisely what he had been told. Nothing else came back to him. At midnight, he gave up and went to tell the guard to organise a scouting party. The messenger had reported that the chatter at the port was that a Dutch merchant ship had docked twice in the past few months in Garachico to take on provisions, though no one knew where it was going or where it had come from. He scratched his chin. Could it be the *Old Moon*? He supposed Garachico was as good a place as any.

In the end, it didn't matter what was true. If Joost wanted the woman arrested and brought to justice – whether a crime had been committed or not – he had better do his level best to find her. He was not entirely certain of his authority to try a Dutch citizen of French heritage on Spanish soil, especially given the crime was committed in international waters. But Joost was insistent and Arauz was more concerned with placating him than worrying about courts a thousand miles away, if they ever got to hear of it.

He poured himself another glass of wine. The French had a phrase for it. They always did. He swilled the liquid in his glass, wracking his brain until it came back to him.

'*Sauve qui peut,*' he muttered.

Yes, that was it. Every man for himself.


GARACHICO


When Louise and Gilles returned to the *Old Moon* at two o'clock in the morning, all was quiet. Lieutenant Smith reported that Bleeker was at the helm and everyone, bar Jansz, had returned from shore leave. The ship was ready to sail on the first high tide.

Louise, her eyes bright from the magic of the evening – and the local wine – struggled to take Smith's report. She managed to nod her head and thank him, before retiring to her cabin.

'This has been one of the finest nights of my life,' she said hazily. 'Will you come to bed?'

'I think I had better and go and look for Jansz,' Gilles said, steering her to their cot and removing her shoes.

Louise flung out her hand. 'Send someone else.'

'Better if I go. You know what he's like when he's three sheets to the wind. I won't be long.' He paused to give her one last kiss. 'I love you.'

'I know,' she said, and fell instantly asleep.

# CHAPTER SEVENTY-FOUR

*Monday, 16 August*

Because Jansz had been so late returning to the ship, they missed the first tide and were forced to wait for the next. It was a mistake that was to cost them dearly.

They were now two days out of Garachico sailing into a headwind, at the changing of the fore noon watch, when Louise spied a three-masted caravel to starboard, the red cross of Burgundy flying atop the main mast. The Spanish tended to use caravels, which were shallower and lighter, to travel between the islands, but she couldn't remember seeing one out in this stretch of water at this midway point between Tenerife, Gran Canaria and Lanzarote.

'Lieutenant Smith,' she said, summoning him to the quarter-deck. 'Can you think of a reason this ship would be here? They are flying Spanish colours.'

'Bound for Tenerife?'

Louise glanced at the compass. 'Except they appear to be heading due north.' She paused, remembering, with a flash of concern, the official caravels belonging to the authorities moored at the harbour in Las Palmas. She raised her spyglass. 'Is it possible they are seeking to engage with us?'

Smith frowned. 'Possibly. In Garachico, I heard it said there had been some recent clashes between Spanish and Dutch warships. But caravels are usually patrol ships.'

'They are armed, though.'

'Yes, ma'am.'

It was another ferociously hot day and there was a heat haze over the surface of the water, so it was hard to gauge the true distance between them.

'Bring her round to port forty degrees, lieutenant,' she said, giving the order to change direction to see if the caravel would alter course.

It did.

Louise looked around and saw several of the crew had noticed they had company. Bleeker was at the helm, but Rémy, Rossi, Al-Bayt and Sanchez were standing on the starboard rail.

'What do you advise?'

Smith shielded his eyes. 'We are in Spanish waters. The truce between Holland and Spain has ended. We could outrun them, but for how long?'

'You think they might attack us?' Gilles asked, joining them.

'I have no idea,' Smith replied. 'There is no reason to believe they mean us harm.'

'Nor any reason to think they do not,' Louise murmured. 'Lieutenant, what do you advise?'

'That we keep our powder dry and hold our course.'

Louise agreed. Not having expected to run into any corsair galleys in this stretch of the ocean, they were unprepared for an attack – the smoking dish was cold, the screen was not in place, there was no way they could put their usual plans into action quickly enough to enable them to get away. Besides, it would be seen as an aggressive act. As Smith said, they were in Spanish waters and this was a Spanish ship.

The *Old Moon* was windward of the caravel. A gust of hot air caught their sails. Despite the heat, Louise felt a trickle of cold sweat run down her spine. Her hand stole to Joost's cutlass at her waist.

She called down to Rémy. 'Are the cannon primed?'

'They can be, *capitana*.'

'Do it.' It was as well to be ready, just in case.

Rémy nodded, and waved for Pieter to follow him.

'Arm the guns,' she ordered.

Jansz – just released from the storeroom after his tardy arrival back on board – and Al-Bayt took up position at the swivel guns on the fo'c'sle. Gilles rushed to Louise's cabin, returning immediately with weapons for Smith, for Lange, for Louise, keeping the last for himself.

Louise tightened her headscarf, then stood with her legs braced, watching in silence as the caravel came closer and closer. There was no doubt now that the other ship intended to intercept them.

'So far as I can see, four cannon on the upper deck,' Smith said quietly, 'and six on the main deck. Swivel guns on the fo'c'sle and aft.'

Louise frowned. They were very considerably outgunned.

Finally, the two ships were in hailing distance and Louise recognised the livery of the state fleet of Gran Canaria. Her eyes swept the deck, and identified the captain, with at least two other officers, and perhaps fifteen crew.

The captain raised a speaking trumpet to his mouth: 'We are the *San Pedro* from Las Palmas. Lay down your arms.' He repeated the instruction in halting Dutch to be sure his message had been understood. '*Leg je wapens neer.*'

Louise stared across the expanse of water at her opposite number, and cupped her hands to respond: 'We are the *Old Moon* from Amsterdam, a merchant ship, sailing from Garachico to Lanzarote.'

'We have instructions to escort you back to port.'

Louise glanced at Gilles, then back to the captain on the opposite ship. 'On whose orders?'

'The harbour authority.'

'For what purpose?'

There was a pause, then the captain shouted: 'If you will come with us, señora.'

Louise would never know what might have happened had she acceded to the request there and then. But suddenly, from behind her, she heard the sound of a gunshot as Lange discharged his musket.

'Hold your fire!' she shouted. The caravel gave a warning shot across their bow. The *Old Moon* plunged down into the turbulent water, then reared back up.

'Drop your weapons,' the Spanish captain shouted. 'This is your last warning.'

'Lange, hold your fire,' she yelled, but it was too late. The Dutchman had already fired another shot.

Gilles launched himself sideways, throwing Louise flat to the deck as a bullet slammed into the bulkhead, precisely where she had been standing.

Then the *San Pedro* let off a broadside, every gun on their starboard blazing.

'We're hit,' Smith shouted, as shot hit their hull below the fo'c'sle.

'Fire!' Louise ordered, dropping her arm. Rémy applied the linstock to the touch-hole, igniting the priming powder and setting off the main charge.

'A hit!' Smith cried, firing his musket.

Louise saw one of the Spanish mariners go down.

'*Capitana!*' Rossi cried, pointing up to their main mast where an ember had caught the rigging. The younger of the De Groot brothers was already shinning up to the spar, but was brought down by a musket shot from the enemy ship. Louise watched in horror as the young man was thrown backwards, and fell down to the deck.

Pieter turned his head away, and vomited.

'No time for that, boy,' Rémy said, moving to the next cannon and letting loose a second ball.

Jansz and Al-Bayt were doing excellent work, targeting the marksmen on the caravel, but Louise knew they were outgunned, and outnumbered. The Spanish launched a second broadside. Behind her, she heard a cry as Sanchez was hit by splinter from the ball. A second shout from Rossi, as the aft mast was struck.

'Smith, how many men are down?'

'Four.'

'How many dead?'

'One.'

Louise had to make a decision. If they kept fighting, their causalities would no doubt rise. They had no hope of overpowering the caravel – they were outnumbered and outgunned. She didn't want to lose anyone else. She didn't want to lose her ship.

# CHAPTER SEVENTY-FIVE

'Strike our colours,' she commanded, as another assault was launched from the caravel. The older De Groot brother, already in shock, was struck by a bullet in the arm, and fell to his knees.

'We surrender,' she cried across the water, though the words stuck in her craw. 'We submit.'

Slowly, Smith and Gilles lowered their muskets. All around her, Louise heard the sound of weapons being laid on the deck. Jansz and Al-Bayt stepped back on the fo'c'sle and raised their hands. Pieter and Rémy, too.

*Should we have tried to outrun them? Should we have taken our chances?*

Louise looked at her beloved ship, now floating silently on the water. All guns silenced, all voices quiet. The *Old Moon* had seen more than its fair share of action. Now, its hull was splintered, her sails tattered and burnt.

'I am sorry,' she murmured.

The guns of the enemy ship were also quiet. As the smoke began to clear, she could make out the shape of the Spanish captain with his dark trimmed beard, red breeches and hat.

'I am sending across six of my men to join you,' he shouted. 'Do not resist or try to prevent them from boarding.'

'I have surrendered, captain,' Louise replied. 'I will abide by that.'

As their helmsman began to bring the caravel alongside the *Old Moon*, Louise quickly turned to Gilles.

'I do not know what this is about, or why they attacked us, but I think we should hide any evidence of our activities.'

'We have done nothing wrong,' Lieutenant Smith said. 'We were not in restricted waters. We are flying our colours, we responded when they hailed.'

'But we fired first,' she said, 'though it was unintended.' She was glad to see someone had covered De Groot's body with a sheet. She dropped her voice. 'When they board, they will find the saltpetre, the gunshot, our masks. It would be easy to make a case that we were a threat to their fleet. Let's not make it easy for them.' She glanced at Gilles.

He nodded. 'Leave it to me.' He beckoned Pieter to join him, and they crept below deck.

Louise stayed where she could clearly be seen, trusting Gilles to hide anything that could be incriminating. She wasn't sure what would be worse: that the Canarian authorities had discovered that the *Old Moon* and the *Ghost Ship* were one and the same, or that the attack had something to do with Lieutenant Roord? Her stomach lurched. Surely not, after all this time?

She heard a heavy splash, and realised that Gilles had thrown the smoking dish overboard. The saltpetre and lime too, she suspected. She caught her breath, only now acknowledging how incredibly lucky they had been that the hold hadn't taken a direct hit. The *Old Moon* would have gone up in a flash. The embers in the sails had burnt themselves out.

Then she saw a red *capotain* hat as one of the Spanish commanders climbed over the rail, holding a coil of rope.

'That will not be necessary,' she said, holding up her hands to show she was unarmed.

The man shook his head. 'Orders.'

Livid, Louise held out her arms, but he tied the rope around her waist instead. Out of the corner of her eye, she saw Gilles appear on the main deck, then dart back again out of sight.

Now more Spanish sailors were coming over the rail and taking up position beside her crew. She raised her voice so Gilles could hear her, speaking in French in the hope that their enemies would not understand.

'When we dock, get everyone away, if you can. It's me they want.'

From below, she heard Gilles speaking quietly to her. 'I'm not leaving you.'

'You must. If this is something to do with Roord, then you are in danger too. You cannot let yourself be taken.'

'Louise, no.'

'Quiet!' the Spanish commander ordered.

'*Perdóname*,' Louise replied. 'I was praying.'

The man looked at her suspiciously, then pulled her towards the rail. Louise suddenly realised they were going to take her onto the caravel rather than allow her to remain with her crew on board the *Old Moon*.

'I am the captain,' she protested. 'I must stay with my ship.'

The Spaniard's voice was rigid with disdain. 'You are a woman.' He gestured to Smith. 'He will sail the ship.'

Tied to the mainsail of the caravel, like a common criminal, Louise felt as if everything was happening in slow motion.

The two ships sailed slowly in convoy back towards Las Palmas. Despite the hole in her hull, the *Old Moon* was seaworthy – there was no danger of her sinking. Two of their five sails were damaged, but they were not lagging too far behind the caravel, which had trimmed its sails.

Though the sun was sinking lower in the sky, the heat was still fierce. Her limbs were heavy and she could feel the skin on her face burning. Had she made a mistake? Should they have tried to flee? The questions went round and round in her head, but she had no answer. All she knew was that she was a prisoner now, and the *Old Moon*, and her crew, captured. She had known their good fortune was too good to last. They should have stayed in Garachico.

Louise shook her head. There was no sense thinking like that. What was done, was done. And until they arrived in Las Palmas, and she discovered why the authorities had run the ship down, she did not know what she might have to face.

She closed her eyes, and thought of Gilles, praying that he would put his own safety above hers. That he would do everything he could to keep her crew safe.

This time, there were no crowds cheering as the two ships came into harbour, no children waving or women crossing themselves to give thanks for their safe delivery.

Louise could see Prosecutor Arauz waiting for her on the quayside. He was accompanied by two soldiers. The captain of the *San Pedro* untied the rope and dragged Louise to the rail. Seconds later, she felt hands on her arms, and she was half lifted, half dropped, over the side of the ship to the quay.

Arauz stepped forward and threw a cloak at her. 'Cover yourself,' he spat. 'You are indecent.'

Louise looked down, realising that she was still in her breeches. If they wished to charge her with public immorality, she was making it easy for them.

Arauz stepped back, as if he could not bear to stand close to her. 'Louise Reydon-Joubert,' he said, 'I am arresting you for the murder of Hendrik Joost.'

Louise stared at him in disbelief. 'That is ridiculous. I told you what happened. You accepted my statement.'

'And,' Arauz continued, 'for the theft of valuable property – to wit, one vellum portolan, one ivory-cased compass and one globe of great personal value – belonging to this same Hendrik Joost.'

Her stomach twisted. She should have handed over the items to Captain De Klerk, and had meant to do so. In the rush to leave, she had forgotten.

'That is an oversight, something that can easily be put right.'

But her arms were being dragged behind her back, and her hands shackled together.

'If you want to behave like a man,' Arauz hissed in her ear, 'then you shall be treated like one.'

Behind her, Louise heard a roar as Pieter threw himself from the *Old Moon* and barrelled into one of the soldiers, who batted the boy away with the staff of his pike. Pieter staggered back, a trickle of blood running down his cheek.

'Help him,' she mouthed to Gilles.

She could see the anguish in Gilles' eyes, but to her relief, he didn't try to intervene. She saw him reach for Pieter and help him to his feet. She was aware, too, of the concerned faces of her crew watching from the deck of the *Old Moon*, not knowing what to do.

As she was marched along the quayside back towards the town, Louise tried to work out what had happened. Though they had taken some persuading, the court had accepted her report into Joost's death back in May. What had changed? She prayed that Gilles remained at liberty. For if they arrested him, they would discover his true nature soon enough and she didn't dare imagine what would happen then.

'Stay safe, my love,' she murmured. 'Be safe.'

# PART SIX

*Six Weeks Later*
Las Palmas de Gran Canaria
*October 1621*

# CHAPTER SEVENTY-SIX

'Will the court rise?'

Louise watched the judges in their judiciary gowns haul themselves to their feet. They had been looking forward to this day since her arrest on the quayside six weeks ago.

She looked straight ahead, uncomfortable in the clothes they had forced her to wear. Women's clothes of the island, designed to strip her of her authority. She raised her chin and fixed the chief prosecutor, Filipe Arauz, in her sights. She would not let them decide who she was. She was the she-captain, the hellion of the high seas, as the common people had taken to calling her. There were eight of them sitting in judgement, and only one of her in the dock, but Louise would not bow down before them.

'Will the prisoner state her name.'

She almost smiled. This was the moment they intended her to submit. They were expecting modesty and contrition. She would not give them that satisfaction.

'I am *la Capitana*,' she replied, her voice ringing out loud and clear. 'Mistress and commander of the *Ghost Ship*.'

A murmur went around the courtroom.

Arauz tapped his stick on the bench. 'Your given name,' he barked. 'Do not force me to hold you in contempt.'

Louise held his gaze. 'If you do not consider that name

appropriate, *estimado señor*, I beg you to choose one that suits better the purposes of the court.'

A ripple of consternation. Such insolence, such lack of feminine obedience, the honourable men of Las Palmas did not know what to make of it.

'I command you to give, before this court, your legal name.'

She paused a moment. 'I am Louise Reydon-Joubert, former resident of La Rochelle, a daughter of Amsterdam, the child of Marta Reydon-Joubert and Louis Vidal.' She smiled. 'And, as I have already stated, the lawful owner and captain of the *Old Moon*.'

This time, Louise heard a low murmur of appreciation from the congregation. Arauz again rapped the stick on the bench, his colour rising.

'Silence, I say. I will have silence!'

The courtroom was slow to obey. As the noise abated, Louise looked around the chamber. In other circumstances, it was a room she might admire: cedar wood panelling to the dado rail with white walls above, blue and white tiles below, the shutters half open. It was an unusually dull day for October, a grey sky filled with clouds. She caught a flash of colour as an aria of wild canaries, the colour of the sun, flew across the windows and, despite everything, she felt a stirring of joy at such a beautiful sight.

*A good omen?*

As the clerk began to read a long statement establishing the authority and competence of the court, bestowed by the King of Spain for his overseas colonies, Louise let her thoughts wander. She could only understand one word in ten anyway. She glanced to her right, where the red robes of the inquisitors filled the benches, hands folded in front of them, wearing their piety like armour. A rotund priest, like a shabby crow, looked pleased with himself. In front of her sat the men who would pronounce judgement – the governor of Las Palmas, Arauz and his scribes. To her left, a mixture of invited *burguesía* – the great and the good of Las Palmas – and a man whom she struggled to place. A deeply lined face, curled brown hair and a trimmed moustache, he was wearing a high black hat and a long blue waistcoat with silver studs. She stared a moment longer, but could not remember where – if – she had seen him before.

*Who is there to speak for me?*

Her love was nowhere to be seen – they had agreed it would be too dangerous for him to attend – but her heart ached at the absence of him. Her hand stole to her locket, to give herself strength. Louise still had faith that Gilles would find a way to save her from the gallows. Images of their lives flashed through her mind: the traumatised boy cradling his dying uncle in his bloodied arms in the alleyway behind her house in La Rochelle; the almost-mute boy stepping on board the *Old Moon* to sail with her to Amsterdam; that first kiss in the chamber in Kalverstraat and his hands turning over the Tarot cards in the cartomancer's studio in Sint Luciensteeg. She thought of their life together at sea, lying in one another's arms; the boy-woman who was the love of her life.

Louise gave a half smile, though her nerves were singing. Today's date was of significance, too. As they had brought her up from the cell which had been her home for nigh on six weeks, she realised it was exactly a year to the day that she and Gilles had first met.

If she believed in portents, this surely was a good one?

Then Louise thought of the image on Gilles' treasured Tarot card – Justice with her sword and scales – and knew there would be no justice for her here. Whatever she said, these men would condemn her. This was a show trial. They did not intend to find her innocent.

The clerk concluded his recitation and Arauz cleared his throat to state the capital charge against the laws of Spain and her territories. She felt the atmosphere in the chamber sharpen.

'Louise Reydon-Joubert, you are charged with murder. It is the court's contention that you did wilfully, and with malice aforethought, take the life of Hendrik Joost. How do you plead?'

*Now the game begins.*

Louise took a deep breath. 'Not guilty,' she said.

# CHAPTER SEVENTY-SEVEN

Gilles slipped through the network of backstreets behind the Casas de Consistoriales, in search of the one person who might be able to help them.

The past six weeks had been torture, though initially luck had been on their side. Arauz's men had been so intent on arresting Louise, that they had been slow to board the *Old Moon* to apprehend any other crew members who had been with them when Hendrik Joost had lost his life. That had been time enough for Gilles to do what Louise had asked him.

The crew of the *Ghost Ship* were folk heroes, feared by the authorities but beloved of ordinary Canarian people, who were grateful to them for keeping their waters free of pirates. Ali Al-Bayt had family all over the island, so had smuggled Pieter, Albert, Bleeker, De Groot, Lange and Jansz to his second cousin's house in the hills. They had exchanged their slops and mariner's kit for plain shirts and breeches, and Ali's family had kept them hidden. Their skin brown from the sun, they were quickly absorbed into the life of the village.

By the time Arauz thought to give the direct order to board the *Old Moon* some hours after the ship had docked, the soldiers found only Tom Smith in possession, with Rossi, Rémy and Sanchez, who knew nothing.

'Gilles Barenton?' Smith had said, shaking his head. 'He remained in Garachico.' He refused to be shaken. And Smith had remained loyal since, staying with the *Old Moon*, working on the repairs to her hull and the mast, making her seaworthy.

Gilles himself was lodging with another of Al-Bayt's cousins in Las Palmas. He had managed to get a message to Louise that the crew was safe and that Smith was in possession of the ship. By day, he listened to gossip and tried to discover what evidence, if any, Arauz held against Louise. It was all, of course, circumstantial, hearsay. Only three of them knew what had happened to Joost, and Gilles had persuaded Pieter not to speak. As for Lieutenant Roord, it was common knowledge in the town that the severity of the inquisitor's questioning had left him unable to stand, to feed himself, to talk. He was still alive, but barely so.

Gilles had also kept safe Louise's journal, her wooden travelling chest and leather case, her jewelled dagger. The last of her laudanum had been jettisoned overboard with everything else that exposed their previous lives as pirate hunters. There was no evidence of the *Ghost Ship* left to find.

They had been apart for six weeks, six weeks of Gilles trying – and failing – to find a way to get Louise pardoned. He knew he could not live without her. 'Let me say that it was I who killed him,' he had whispered at the quayside, but she had refused. He would have given his life for hers.

Lying awake at night, listening to the loving squabbles of Al-Bayt's large family in the kitchen below, Gilles held her beloved face in his mind. What he could not bear was that Louise would be telling herself how it was only right she was finally being called to account. How she would accept her fate.

Pick a card, any card.

Gilles did not accept it, he would not, though it was becoming harder to keep faith. It was common knowledge that the father of Hendrik Joost was in residence in Las Palmas awaiting the trial. By every account, he was a favoured guest of Prosecutor

Arauz. Everyone, even the Al-Bayt family, knew how unlikely it would be for the verdict to go in Louise's favour.

All the same, Gilles did not give up. Each morning, he left the house with Al-Bayt's aunt's good wishes. He approached everyone of influence in the town, trying to convince them to take on Louise's case. Trying to persuade them to offer a ransom to have her released. No one was prepared to go against the inquisitors or the town council. Each evening he returned despondent and was welcomed back with a smile. '*Shukran*,' he learnt to say. 'Thank you for your kindness.'

Day after day, week after week.

Then, at the beginning of October, Gilles heard a rumour that there was a new visitor to Las Palmas. Not from the Dutch Republic or Spain, but from France. A spark of hope. No one seemed to know who he was, or why he had come to the island, but the stranger was not the usual kind of traveller. He was neither a sailor nor a merchant, but rather a gentleman. Perhaps he would have less fear of the Casas Consistoriales?

For twenty-four hours Gilles had been scouring the town, gathering morsels of information until he found out where the Frenchman was lodging and who he was. It hardly seemed possible, but he finally managed to confirm that the rumours were true.

Louise's trial had already started – a day he had hoped would never come. He was almost out of time. But now, for the first time in six weeks, Gilles felt there was a chance.

He stopped in front of the Casa de Colón, the house famous for being the lodgings of Christopher Columbus. Louise did not know he was here – Gilles prayed she would not be angry with him – but he had to try. Why else would the man have come all the way from France if not to find her?

In the end, he had no choice. If he did nothing, Louise would be hanged. This was their last chance – their only chance. His hand went to the Tarot card in his pocket.

Then Gilles took a deep breath, knocked on the door and waited to be admitted.

# CHAPTER SEVENTY-EIGHT

The chief prosecutor rested his hand on the mountain of paper set before him on the bench.

Louise marvelled at the pile of documents – all, no doubt, signed and countersigned, and stamped with the Inquisitional seal – and realised Arauz was going to persuade the court of her guilt by cloaking his lack of hard evidence in official language and process. He could hardly produce his star witness. From gossip inside the prison, Louise knew the trial had been delayed these six weeks in the hope that Roord would recover enough to give evidence. He had defied them by finally, two days ago, dying of his injuries. Louise had said a prayer for him, though he had been the cause of her undoing, knowing that the gentle man from Antwerp would never have had the strength to withstand the brutal questioning of the Spanish inquisitors.

'Acting on information received from Jan Roord on the four-teenth day of May, in the year of Our Lord 1621,' Arauz intoned, 'it is the court's contention that the prisoner did, on the second day of April of that same year, bring about the death of Hendrik Joost by means of stabbing with a knife. It was common knowledge that the prisoner was in possession of a narrow blade with a jewelled handle, a single emerald on the hilt.'

Louise was amazed at how easily the facts could be made to fit.

*But a lie is still a lie.*

Arauz continued, his voice pompous. 'The crime took place

in the second cabin astern the *Old Moon* where Hendrik Joost, a man from a leading and honourable Leiden family, was engaged as captain. It was his first command. It is the court's contention that, using wiles such as only a woman might employ, the prisoner encouraged the victim to take an excess of drink and fed to him a sleeping draught, rendering him helpless. It is the court's contention that she bound her victim and, under cover of night, later went to the cabin where he had been taken and punctured his lung with a blade, causing his death from suffocation.'

Louise listened, almost fascinated by the narrative that held enough detail to be closer to the truth than Arauz realised. She was surprised. She had not thought Roord so observant.

'The prisoner then, by use of threat and deceitful female stratagems, forced Lieutenant Jan Roord, a Catholic of good name and reputation, to falsify the record in order that the remains of Hendrik Joost might be committed to the deep with unseemly haste, thereby ensuring that no further examination of the victim's body might take place.'

As Arauz talked, Louise kept her expression steady. She was determined not to react, not to lose her temper, nor show any weakness. Whatever the provocations, the falsehoods spoken against her, she believed the murder of Joost was a pretext – the truth was they hated the fact that a woman had made their seas safer. That she had done more to disable and thwart attacks by corsairs during the past five months than they had done in the past five years. It was an affront to their power and authority. That they were not charging her with piracy meant nothing more than they were aware of the public mood, which was firmly on her side.

*They will make an example of me, evidence or no.*

'Moreover,' Arauz droned on, 'it is the court's contention

that she did, in addition, appropriate valuable personal possessions belonging to the victim – namely, a cutlass of tempered
steel with a brass hold, an ivory-covered compass of antique
value, an heirloom of the Joost family, a vellum portolan, which
is to say a mariner's map, and a globe also of sentimental value
to the Joost family. All of these objects were found on board
the *Old Moon* in the prisoner's ownership.'

At that moment, Louise realised who the man with the deeply
lined face might be. Older, his expression hardened by time,
but the family resemblance was clear – Andries Joost. She
remembered Cornelia had pointed him out to her once. That
he was here in person to see his son's murderer condemned
made one thing clearer. She caught her breath: if Joost was
driving the case to be made against her, then there was even
less hope of a reprieve. Her courage faltered. He was clearly a
man used to getting his own way.

Louise jumped at the sound of the prosecutor's hammer
striking the bench. She raised her eyes and realised Arauz had
stopped talking. He was staring at her, clearly waiting for her
to respond. Everyone was staring at her.

'Madame Reydon-Joubert,' he said sharply, 'you are bound
to answer the question put to you. Having now heard the
evidence put before the court, I ask you again. How do you
plead?'

She exhaled. This was her one chance to speak, and she would
not squander it. That it would make no difference to the verdict,
she put aside. Whatever was to happen, she wanted this moment
in the court in Las Palmas remembered as one where a woman
took the stand and spoke with dignity.

'*Estimado señor*, gentlemen of the court, I am innocent of
the murder charge set against me. My other crimes, though they
are not before the court, I do not deny. I confess I have taken

a life – more than one – but each and every one of them deserved to die. My actions were measured, they were just. They have, as all those who are not blinded by the fact of my sex, saved many souls from the evils of the slave galleys. My courage, as those who sailed with me will testify, as your own citizens will testify, has made the seas of Las Islas Afortunadas safer. I deserve your thanks, not your opprobrium. So, yes, I have killed, but only ever in self-defence or to protect those I love. Never for gain. Never without due cause.' She paused to allow her words to sink in. 'Gentlemen, as I stand before you and God, I am innocent of the murder of Hendrik Joost, a man whose loss to my ship was a tragedy. As for those personal objects belonging to Captain Joost, there was no intention to keep them for myself or to claim them as my own. They merely remained on board ship until such time as they could be safely returned to their rightful owner.' Louise turned slowly. 'If I may extend my condolences to his father.'

Andries Joost got to his feet, his face red with fury. 'How dare you speak his name. You are an unnatural woman, usurping a man's role, wearing a man's clothing, you are nothing but a whore.'

'Señor Joost,' Arauz said hastily, 'please remember you are in a court of law.'

Louise fixed Joost with a look. 'You do me a gross discourtesy, *mijn heer*.'

'Harridan!' he roared and leapt out of his seat. He would have stormed the dock and laid hands on her, had not two of the court officials placed themselves in his path.

'Señor Joost, do not make me remove you from the courtroom.'

There was a moment's hiatus, then Joost shrugged off the officials' hands and returned to his seat.

'You have the sympathy of this court,' Arauz said. 'We appreciate how great is the burden of a father's grief.'

Louise waited. There was no evidence against her, just the word of one man who had naïvely trusted in the sanctity of the confessional. There were no other witnesses, no proof. She knew Gilles had been as good as his word and ensured that every one of her crew, who had been on board the *Old Moon* on the night in question, were safe in the hills with Ali Al-Bayt's family. She no longer feared they would be forced to give evidence. It was her they wanted. Her greatest relief had been that there had been no charge of immorality, or any suggestion that Gilles was not who he claimed to be.

*Pray God that he is safe.*

His absence was a permanent ache in her heart. But even knowing he was in Las Palmas, gave her courage. He would be doing his best to find a way to save her.

Arauz pulled himself up straight. Louise's heart hammered.

'Gentlemen,' the prosecutor intoned, his voice now sombre, 'this was a wicked crime. Hendrik Joost, a young man of great promise and reputation, was in the prime of his life. He was brought down by a scheming and imprudent woman seeking to usurp command of the ship. That her name is the name on the bill of sale of the *Old Moon* should not distract you from this evil felony. It has long been known that, in the Dutch Republic, there are practices that would never be countenanced here. Does not it say in Ephesians that wives should submit themselves unto their husbands? A woman without a husband is as a child and we see here where such laxity of morals leads. The fact is that some are born to evil – the prisoner, Louise Reydon-Joubert, is one such. She has admitted as much. She is an unnatural woman, indecent and sinful, a self-confessed murderer. That she denies this one charge, again should not distract you. Her word is worth nothing.'

Below the rim of the box, Louise clenched her fists.

'Therefore, by the power invested in me and in accordance with the laws laid down by the supreme court of Spain I accordingly pronounce that the prisoner, Louise Reydon-Joubert, shall at dawn tomorrow be taken to a place of execution and hanged by her neck until she is dead. May God have mercy upon her soul.'

Louise gasped. Hearing the verdict spoken out loud, and so quickly after the charges, stole her breath from her. She was not ready to die, not for a crime she did not commit. Finally, her self-control broke and she leapt to her feet.

'No!'

'Return the prisoner to her cell,' Arauz ordered.

'I am innocent,' she shouted, but already she was being pulled away.

# CHAPTER SEVENTY-NINE

*Friday, 8 October*

A maid walked through the Casas Consistoriales opening the shutters and letting the first rays of daylight into the long corridor outside the chief prosecutor's office.

Gilles sat up with a jolt, appalled to realise he must have fallen asleep on the wooden bench. He looked down at the Justice card in his hand, remembering the words of the cartomancer in Amsterdam: how Card VIII was a powerful card, how it might indicate he would be called upon to right some wrong. He had carried it with him these past weeks like a good luck charm. Had it worked?

Some twelve hours had passed since Gilles entered the Casa Colón resolved to do anything in his power to save Louise from the gallows. In point of fact, the man he had found there needed little persuading. Instantly, he had agreed to go to the town hall to speak to the chief prosecutor. Gilles had tried to say he could not accompany him, fearing he would be arrested if they discovered who he was, but the man had been adamant.

'You would be under my protection,' he had said, with the authority his status and influence gave him. Though he was French, not Spanish, he was an esteemed Catholic in a Catholic world, and known to be in favour with Rome. 'All will be well.' He had glanced at Gilles' clothing, and raised an eyebrow. 'Besides, they will take you for a local man.'

Gilles slipped the card into his pocket and got to his feet, wondering why it was taking so long. The debate had lasted all night and yet still the door to the prosecutor's offices remained closed. He raised his eyes to the narrow windows with mounting desperation, hearing the sound of hammering as the gallows were erected in the execution yard.

The man had come out of the chamber at two o'clock in the morning to tell him how negotiations were progressing. The issue was not, as Gilles had at first assumed, the unwillingness of the Catholic inquisitors to negotiate – they were attracted by the sum of money on offer in return for the sentence being overturned – but rather the prosecutor himself, speaking on behalf of Andries Joost. It seemed that neither Joost's father, nor his counsel, were prepared to countenance the sentence being rescinded.

But with a determination and single-mindedness that reminded Gilles of Louise herself, the man had evidently continued to press his point. He had suggested that, perhaps, Arauz did not actually have the authority to try a citizen of France and Holland. At four in the morning, the man had sent out a further message. They were expecting Andries Joost. Gilles kept his head down when Joost arrived at the Casas Consistoriales, accompanied by two soldiers.

Inside the room, the level of ransom was rising – an endowment to the monastery of Santo Domingo, a contribution to the Inquisitional coffers until finally, in this corner of the Catholic world where cultures collide, the *diyya* was agreed: blood money to be paid to Andries Joost for the loss of his son.

It was now nearly seven o'clock. In a matter of minutes, the sun would rise and the drum would begin to beat. Gilles couldn't bear it. Trapped here, doing nothing, knowing Louise was so close at hand. What would she be thinking? Had she given up hope?

Suddenly, the door to the prosecutor's office was thrown open. Gilles could see Arauz and the Frenchman shaking hands. Then he saw him turn to Andries Joost, who hesitated before also accepting his two hands to seal the bargain.

The Frenchman strode out.

'*Allez vite*,' he said to Gilles. 'The prosecutor will draw up the full papers of release. Go!'

Gilles hurtled down the long corridor, throwing open the door to the outside world, running as if the Devil himself was at his heels.

# CHAPTER EIGHTY

Alone in her cell, Louise thought of all the sleepless nights she had endured in her life: in her childhood in Amsterdam, in La Rochelle in her days of bourgeois respectability; on board the *Old Moon* with Gilles talking the hours of darkness away. Not one of them had seemed either so long, nor so short, as this.

*Today I am sentenced to swing.*

Outside her window, the sky had grown white, giving shape back to the world and the scaffold. A single gibbet mounted on a wooden platform, steps up the side. One solitary prisoner to be hanged today.

Louise shivered, and turned back to the cell that had been her home for nigh on six weeks: the rough bunk affixed to the floor, a blanket lousy with fleas, her trencher and tankard, a night pot. Familiar now, safe now. She ran her fingers over the bricks close to the floor where she had scratched her initials, so that future prisoners would know that, in the year 1621, a woman was here confined: LRJ, captain and commander, innocent of the crime for which she was condemned.

Louise could hear the bells of Santa Ana marking the start of another day. At the port, the fishermen would be mending their nets, their fingers red and swollen. Their wives would be gutting the morning's catch and their children curing seaweed with smoke on the sand. In the harbour, the wind would be whispering in the shrouds and snapping at the rigging of the tall ships as they prepared to journey south to the Cape of

Good Hope where two oceans met. The journey she had, one day, hoped to make.

She leant back against the wall, thinking of how much she missed the lilt and sway of the waves beneath her feet, the buck and the tilt. The solitude of the night-watch and the black sky scattered silver with stars. The endless, treacherous, beautiful shifting water.

*It was nearly time.*

In the Casas Consistoriales, scribes would be preparing their paper and ink. The priest would be sharpening his prayers and preparing to hear her confession, expecting repentance and a desire for absolution. Louise did not intend to give him that satisfaction.

During her weeks of captivity, she'd had time to write. She smiled as she realised how, at the end, she had followed in her grandmother's footsteps and written everything down. Minou had believed that those she loved would be waiting for her when she died. Louise wished she had such certainty. She thought of Cornelia and Alis in Amsterdam, and how her death would grieve them. She thought of Jean-Jacques and his copper-haired daughter, Florence, and wished she had known her better. Perhaps Jean-Jacques would one day learn the truth and tell Florence stories about her wayward cousin, the pirate commander? Perhaps she would grow up to travel the seas, too.

Louise had thought herself composed, but her hand was unsteady as she wrote her final words. She had paid the guard well to smuggle away her papers, and could only pray that he would be honest.

She stood up and began to pace around the tiny cell. Six steps across, eight steps from window to door. Back and forth, wearing the stone away, if such a thing were possible. Though the sands had all but run out, she still believed Gilles would find a way to save her. After all they had been to one another, all they had seen and done together, she could not accept that she would never see his beloved face again.

Six steps across, eight steps from door to window.

Starved of company, she had been left alone with her own thoughts. Day after day, week after week. Yet there was still one question that she had been unable to answer.

*Is a murderer born, or is she made?*

Was there such a thing as bad blood? Some are born to evil, that's what the prosecutor said. And how could she – the daughter of a murderer, the granddaughter of a murderer – refute that? During her imprisonment, Louise had scrutinised every moment of her life and wondered. Were the seeds of her downfall sown in her childhood among the wooden masts of the *fluyts* and flat-bottomed barges of Amsterdam? In the boarding house in Kalverstraat when she picked up the knife? In La Rochelle when she saw Gilles for the first time?

*Or the instant I realised I was in love, and so had everything to lose?*

The sky was now the palest of blues. It was quiet in the gaol, as it always was on a day of execution. Louise could almost hear the silence. Outside the prison walls, it was different. She could hear the growing roar and clamour of the populace gathering at the gate. Louise could picture them, armed with their needlework and their lace, flasks full of Canarian wine and parasols held aloft. It had been one of the hottest autumns on record.

Suddenly, a memory of the day on the Place de Grève in Paris. The day before her twenty-fifth birthday, two days before the assassination of the old king. The good king, *le Vert-Galant*. Remembering the ugliness of that crowd and the lost child, remembering the rattle of the cart bringing the prisoners from the Bastille and the four bodies twisting and turning in the air. The boy with the blue lips dying alone. The twelfth day of May, 1610.

*I was another person then.*

Now, faintly in the distance, Louise heard the clink of keys and the tramp of boots, and knew they were coming to fetch her. She wrapped her arms around her body to stop herself from shaking.

She had rejected the hood. She wanted the *burguesía* and the common people alike – all those who had come on this dull morning in October to witness the execution of the notorious she-captain of the seas – to see how a woman could face death as bravely as any man. She had petitioned to be allowed to die in her captain's clothes, but they decreed that since she had come into this world as a woman, she was condemned to leave it as one.

Louise stopped, took several deep breaths to steady the racing of her heart. Last evening, she had overheard the guards say they were expecting it to be the largest crowd ever for a hanging. They had seen corsairs swing many times before at this turning point of the Atlantic Ocean and the Barbary Coast where piracy was a fact of life, but it was only right that she should be such a draw. She was, indeed, notorious, feared over sea and land. She was the one they did not believe could exist.

The commander of the *Ghost Ship*.

Now the key was turning in the lock, and her cell door was being pushed open. The gaoler was holding out his hand. Without a word being spoken, Louise passed him her writings and a purse of coins. He glanced over his shoulder, tucked them beneath his tunic, then nodded.

'For this last service, my thanks,' she said.

He bowed his head. '*Capitana*.'

Touched by his courtesy, Louise smiled. Then emotion caught in her throat, and she turned away.

*She had not truly believed this hour would come.*

Louise Reydon-Joubert, mistress and commander, took a final look around her cell. Then, with her head held high, she stepped out into the chill corridor that led from the dungeon beneath the prison to the execution yard, and began her final walk to the scaffold.

# CHAPTER EIGHTY-ONE

Even though the sky was dull, it was still too bright after the gloom of her cell, and Louise raised her hand to shield her eyes. Then, she checked herself. She would show no sign of weakness, no sign of distress.

Ahead, she could see the scaffold, the rope and the noose swaying gently in the early morning air. She shivered, but did not break step. There were guards stationed all around, as if they feared she would even now escape. Louise could feel every eye upon her as she walked slowly forward, a single drumbeat keeping pace with the thudding of her heart.

*After everything, can this be how my story ends?*

As the gaolers had predicted, the yard was full. A mounted bank of seats had been erected for the *burguesía* come to witness the execution of the she-captain in comfort. A sea of hats and feathers, rich doublets and wide ruffs, ostentatious Spanish fashions. In the crowd, she could make out the local people bright in their striped skirts, brown blanket coverings and straw hats.

Louise could see mouths moving, lips that whistled and hissed as she walked through the crowd, but she heard nothing. Everything was as if it was happening underwater, muffled and distant. She had thought she would feel fear, or regret, or grief to be leaving a life she had come to love. But now it seemed every emotion had been spent in the weeks of confinement. All that was left were her memories of Gilles and their life she had held so dear: the night sky out at sea, the gentle movement of the *Old Moon* beneath her feet, the dolphins that played alongside the ship. This, today, was a spectacle happening to someone else. Someone who looked like her – though grown thin and pale in her cell from lack of sunlight – but who was not truly her. A ghost.

Louise searched the crowd and far up into the stand, hoping for one last glimpse of her beloved's face and not finding him. Then, finally, despair hit her, like a vast wave, stealing her breath. She stumbled and her hand flew to her chest, caught by an incontrovertible truth.

*I do not want to die alone.*

Louise stopped, regained her composure. She felt the movement of the crowd, craning forward to see what was happening, jostling for position. She took a deep breath, her moment of crisis over, then lifted her chin and walked up the wooden steps to where the executioner stood waiting. In his hand, a black scrap of material and, strangely, the sight of it gave her courage. They had not believed her when she told them she did not want the hood.

The man held it out and she shook her head.

'*No, gracias,*' she said, in a voice that was clear and strong.

With what looked like regret in his eyes, the executioner dropped the hood to the platform, then took the noose and placed it gently over her head. So very gently.

'I have measured well,' he whispered. 'The drop is sufficient.'

Louise nodded. 'For that kindness, I thank you.'

The rope felt heavy, rough, around her neck. Her hair was loose. They had intended that as another mark of her shame, but she was grateful for it. Louise looked around the crowd, silent now. Holding its breath. She bowed to the rich women and men of the town in their front-row seats, and she bowed to the crowd. They had come for a spectacle, and she would give them a lesson in how to die.

She had asked to be allowed to speak, a request the prosecutor had denied. Now the moment had come, Louise realised they could hardly stop her.

'*Señoras y Señores*,' she began.

'Stop!'

Her words caught in her throat as a shout went up at the back of the crowd. A murmuring of discontent, of confusion, as everyone turned in the direction of the noise. Louise stepped forward, and felt the executioner grab her arm, as if he feared she would try to flee.

'In God's name, stop!'

Louise caught her breath. She had so long imagined hearing his voice that, at first, she doubted the evidence of her own ears. Was she dreaming? Then he shouted again and relief flooded through her.

'Gilles,' she whispered, almost afraid to speak his name for fear he would vanish.

But now she could see him pushing through the crowd, forcing them to let him through. He took the steps to the gallows two by two, and then he was standing before her.

'By order of the prosecutor,' he panted, in careful Spanish, 'the execution is not to go ahead.'

The executioner looked around wildly, uncertain as to what he should do. His hand went to the lever. Gilles launched himself at the man, sending them both tumbling off the platform onto the ground.

The guards rushed forward, whether to protect the hangman or seize Gilles, Louise wasn't certain. The crowd roared, not sure if they were to be deprived of their entertainment or if this was merely the beginning.

Then another cry rose from the back of the crowd.

'*Parad!* Stop!'

Louise recognised the voice of Chief Prosecutor Arauz, the man who had traduced her for hour upon hour before condemning her to death. She did not understand.

As if they were all figures in a painting, everyone became still. No one moved, no one spoke. The crowd was silent as the prosecutor himself strode towards the platform holding a piece of paper in his hand. At his side was a tall man dressed in a short blue cape, embroidered breeches and doublet, sporting a blue hat with a feather.

The prosecutor handed the paper to a representative of the court. 'Publish this,' he said, then turned on his heel and left as abruptly as he had come. He clearly feared the wrath of the crowd.

The clerk looked down in disbelief, then climbed nervously onto the scaffold. 'By order of the prosecutor of Las Islas Afortunadas on this eighth day of October in the year of Our Lord 1621, the sentence is commuted from death to permanent exile. The prisoner has seven days to leave Gran Canaria, the Islas Afortunadas and the surrounding seas.'

Then all was chaos.

Robbed of their entertainment, the crowd surged forward. Many cheered. Even the bourgeoisie stood up in their comfortable seats, waving their fans. Louise felt the noose being removed from her neck – by Gilles, she thought – and herself being guided down from the platform, then rushed towards the gate back into the underground prison. Behind her, the guards dropped the bars, leaving the mob on the other side.

For a moment, no one spoke. Louise reached out and took Gilles' hand, felt the familiar touch of his fingers, and everything else faded away.

'You came for me. I knew you would.'

'How could you doubt it?'

Gilles was clearly desperate to take her in his arms, but he maintained his self-control. 'There is someone you must meet,' he said in French. 'Madame Reydon-Joubert, might I introduce you to the gentleman who paid the ransom and secured your freedom.'

Still in a daze, Louise turned towards the stranger. '*Merci,* monsieur. You have my heartfelt thanks.'

He bowed. 'Louise, if I might address you thus, it is a pleasure to make your acquaintance. Barenton here has been most assid-uous on your behalf. You have him to thank as much as you might me.'

She nodded. 'For this, as so much else.'

Then the Frenchman removed his hat. Louise caught her breath. A man of twenty-seven or twenty-eight years of age, with black hair with a white streak, stood in front of her. She didn't know how he came to be here in Las Palmas, or how he had known to find her here, but there was no doubt.

Louise looked into the face of her half-brother, and smiled. 'Monsieur Vidal – Phillipe – it is a pleasure to meet you.'

# CHAPTER EIGHTY-TWO

Three hours had passed since her reprieve.

Louise and Phillipe Vidal were sitting in the elegant interior courtyard of the Casa de Colón. After the privations of her cell, it felt like a different world.

The past four months already seemed like a dream to her. At every second of her ordeal in the court, Louise had expected the charge of being the commander of the *Ghost Ship* to be added to the list of her crimes. But Gilles had been right on that night in Garachico: the common people were grateful to them for keeping their villages and coastline safe. She, and her crew aboard the *Old Moon*, had done what the authorities had failed to do. The chief prosecutor and the men like him would prefer to pretend that the ghost ship had never existed, than face their own shortcomings.

Louise had finally stopped shaking. The piece of paper with her pardon, and the terms of her exile, was on the table beside her. She kept glancing at it to confirm it was real.

A sudden memory of the first of Minou's notebooks came back to her – a journal inherited from Minou's own mother, the first châtelaine of Puivert: spidery browned ink and the antique language reaching down the generations, the letters and sketched maps and testaments held within its leather covers. The first line forever etched into Louise's memory.

*This is the day of my death.*

How she wished she had brought all the journals with her, but she had thought they would be safer left in Alis's and

Cornelia's safekeeping. She would never have a daughter of her own, but perhaps Jean-Jacques' daughter Florence might inherit them and so learn she was descended from a family of women who believed they could change the world.

Louise shook her head, bringing herself back to Las Palmas on this extraordinary day. Phillipe had brought his own household staff with him from Chartres, servants who silently appeared bringing trays of wine, sweet biscuits, a platter of cheese and cured meats.

Phillipe raised his glass. 'To your good health.'

The silence stretched between them. Louise sipped her wine. Made from Malvasia grapes, grown in the arid volcanic soil in the highlands of the island, Gilles had chosen well. She wished he was with them, to help ease the slight awkwardness between her and her half-brother, but there was so much to do. Having seen her comfortably settled with Phillipe, he had taken his leave to ride to the mountains. The terms of her release and exile meant they needed to reassemble their crew immediately and make ready to sail the *Old Moon* from Las Palmas within the week.

In the time it had taken for them to walk here to the Casa de Colón, Gilles had told her everything that had happened while she had been in gaol. How, in the confusion of her arrest, the prosecutor's men had failed to secure the ship; how Ali Al-Bayt had hidden the old crew in his family's village in the centre of the island, so they could not be called as witnesses or persuaded to talk; how Smith, Rémy, Sanchez and Marco Rossi had remained on the *Old Moon* to keep the ship safe.

'They are all good men,' he had said. 'They would have followed you to the ends of the earth.'

'Perhaps, now, they will get that chance,' she had replied.

Louise glanced up to see Phillipe was looking at her, an

expression of enquiry in his dark eyes. She blushed. 'Forgive me, I am not very good company.'

'Not at all.'

They were formal with one another, walking on eggshells. The debt on her side felt so immense that no words could be adequate. There was so much she should say to this half-brother of hers, yet they were strangers. For his part, he seemed content to let her lead the conversation into gentle waters, and she was grateful for that. What linked them most closely – their father – was a topic neither was yet ready to raise.

Louise had already told him a little of her childhood in Amsterdam and her life in La Rochelle, but after six weeks of imprisonment, with only snatched conversations with the gaolers and the guards, she had lost her talent to amuse.

'You said that La Rochelle has been blockaded by royal troops since June?'

Phillipe nodded. 'The conflict between Catholic and Huguenot forces is escalating.'

'The King is reneging on his father's promises,' Louise said with some of her old spirit, then stopped herself. While the Reydon-Joubert side of the family was with the Huguenot camp, she was aware that Phillipe and the Vidal-Evreux contingent were close allies of the Catholic throne. 'I feared as much,' she resumed carefully. 'When I was still in Amsterdam, all the signs were so.'

'Your house in La Rochelle has stood empty for a year?' he asked, changing the subject. He was clearly also keen for there to be no dissent between them.

'To my knowledge, my steward and housekeeper are still there. And it is possible my dear uncle, Jean-Jacques, and his family have taken possession.' She added, 'He left Paris to serve with Henri de Rohan some time ago. I wrote to him that he should make use of the house, should he wish.'

'I hope he and his family are safe.'

Louise smiled. 'As do I. It is some years since I have seen them, though I am particularly fond of his daughter, Florence.'

'Does she take after you?'

She smiled. 'Perhaps.' She took another sip of wine. 'And you? I hope you will not think me too bold to ask if you have a wife and family?'

Louise knew Philippe's parents had married in January 1594, and he had been born nine months later. Also, as she had suspected, that it was a match made for advantage, not love – Anne of Evreux was the daughter of the man to whom his father, their father, had sold his estate and title.

'My mother was a gentlewoman,' Phillipe said, 'but disappointed. She was aware she was second best.'

'What do you mean?'

He drummed his fingers on the arm of his chair. 'I was only a child. I barely knew my father – he died before I was two years old – and I was aware this was a great sadness for her. But as I grew older, and heard the servants tattling, I realised she suffered from more than grief. She was, how can I put it, tormented by jealousy. It ruled her life. My father—' He stopped, corrected himself. '*Our* father never stopped loving your mother. But Marta had left him, vanished. He tried to find her, but in vain. In the end, he gave in and married my mother. Only weeks after the wedding, at the coronation of the late king in Chartres cathedral, he saw Marta again.'

Louise shivered. 'I remember. I was there – we all were: my grandparents, my mother, my aunts and uncle.'

If he had noted her reaction, he said nothing. 'Again, I was too young to understand what was happening, only that my father was rarely at home. My mother cried all the time. I tried to comfort her, but there was nothing I could say or do—' Phillipe broke off. 'Did you ever meet him, Louise?'

She felt her stomach clench. Though she liked what she had seen of Phillipe so far, she was cautious. She owed him her life, but how could she tell him the truth? Neither did she feel she could tell him an outright lie.

'No,' she replied. 'I never knew him.'

Phillipe sat back in the chair. 'Ah, I hoped you might have. My memories are so few. He was a great man.' For a moment he was silent. Louise watched the shadows play across his face as the palm trees shifted in the wind within the secluded court-yard. Then he waved his hand, as if pushing away this painful part of the conversation. 'A pity. But to answer your question, no. I have no wife, no children.' He paused. 'And you also chose not to marry.'

'I did not – do not – wish to be a wife. To have my life constrained.'

'But there is an affection between you and Barenton,' he said, more a statement than a question. 'His concern for you goes beyond that of a servant for his mistress.'

Louise was about to deny it, then she stopped. There could be no harm in admitting to that now and, surely, she owed Phillipe that truth at least? In just a few days, she would sail into exile and most likely would never see him again. She could not work out whether she would regret that, or not.

She smiled. 'There is. Gilles has been by my side this past year. We have an understanding, such as is common on board a ship. As much as I owe you my life, Phillipe – and I do and am more grateful than I can say – Gilles has saved me twice over: once at sea; a second time, by finding you and bringing you to me.'

Again, silence fell between them. There was so much more beneath the surface that was not being said. Louise had barely had time to think since her miraculous reprieve. As a result, she had failed to ask the one question from which everything else led.

*What does Phillipe Vidal want of me?*

# CHAPTER EIGHTY-THREE

Louise put down her glass on the table.

'It is my turn to be blunt.'

He waved his hand. 'You can ask me anything, Sister.'

'Why did you write to me, Phillipe? You knew of my existence long ago – at least, your mother did. Why wait so long?'

'Ah, yes. That is a reasonable question. The simple answer
is that I did not.'

'I don't understand,' she said, then suddenly, she realised. Of
course. Although the first letter had borne the Evreux crest and
the seal, it had been unsigned. 'Your mother sent the first letter.'

He nodded. 'I only knew what she had done when your
response arrived from Amsterdam in March. I taxed her with
it and was angry – not with you, with her. I accused her of
meddling. We parted on bad terms, and that I regret. But she
should not have interfered.'

'Surely she was only protecting your interests?'

'I had no need of her protection,' Phillipe said curtly. 'Answer
me this, Sister. When the letter came, did you not wonder why
it had taken so long for the claim to be made?'

'I did, yes.' Rather than relate all that she had imagined and
feared – she did not want to offend him – Louise waited for
him to continue.

'I love my mother,' Phillipe continued, 'but she is easily
swayed. While I was away from Chartres, she had come under
the influence of a new parish priest. He was young and ambitious. She confessed to him how she still found it hard to forgive

the fact that her husband's son – his legitimate heir – had not received his rightful inheritance, which instead had gone to a child born out of wedlock.'

Louise frowned. 'Are you saying it was this priest who encouraged her to write? After all those years? What business was it of his?'

'Quite,' Phillipe said, his voice hardening. 'Whether the scoundrel was hoping for some significant contribution to his parish coffers, or to line his own pocket, I know not. When I became aware of his influence over my mother, I made the strongest possible complaint to the Bishop of Chartres. The priest is no longer in the diocese. As you might imagine, it is another reason why my mother and I are estranged from one another.'

'You will find a way to repair that.'

'It's possible.' Phillipe took a sip of his wine. 'So, this was the situation I found myself in. I wasn't sure what to do. I had no need of money – I am a wealthy man through my mother's family. And though my father sold the estate, in order to provide for you – or, rather, to provide for the child of the woman he loved – he retained control of the remainder of his own father's fortune: property in Paris, treasure and works of art.' He fixed her with a direct look. 'But then I received your letter and I started to wonder what kind of person you might be. I wrote back by return, then became impatient, sitting and waiting for a reply. So, against my mother's wishes, I might say – though she had forfeited any right to an opinion – I travelled to Amsterdam and met with Cornelia van Raay and your great-aunt.'

Louise's face lit up. 'You met them? How are they?'

'I found them both impressive.'

'Oh, they are.' She stopped, still feeling wary of her half-brother. He seemed open and friendly, but there was iron beneath the surface. 'They are two of the people I love most in the world. I very much miss their company.'

'They were, understandably, protective of you. But once I convinced them how I wished you no harm – and explained that, from records at the harbour, I knew you had sailed to Las Palmas on the *Old Moon* – they confirmed it.'

'And you came, Phillipe? Just like that?' Louise frowned. 'I am glad of it, but why?'

He waved his hand. 'Why does one do anything? I have no family other than my mother, no other sisters or brothers. The spectre of your mother – of Marta – was a ghost in my life and now here was a letter from her daughter offering to meet. And I thought I would like to have a half-sister—' He broke off. 'You have her eyes, you know? One blue and one brown. My mother always talked of that, the eyes of the rival who had so bewitched her husband.'

Louise smiled. 'She was a great beauty,' she said, remembering her mother on those summer nights in the orchard in Zeedijk. 'She was rarely in Amsterdam – my grandmother brought me up – and Dutch society did not suit her. But whenever she was there, Marta was dazzling. Like a rare bird that lights up the world around it.'

'She must have greatly loved him,' he said. 'Our father, Louis. She named you for him, after all.'

The comment so casually made pierced Louise like an arrow, the coincidence of her name and his. What did that mean? She was so lost in her thoughts, that she realised Phillipe had asked another question.

'I am sorry?'

He smiled. 'I asked where Marta was now. Your great-aunt did not say.'

Louise's stomach lurched. In the whole of their conversation, it had never occurred to her that he would not know what had happened in Kalverstraat.

'Phillipe . . .' she began.

Seeing the look on her face, he leant forward. 'What is it?'

'I assumed you knew.'

'Tell me.'

She took a sip of wine. 'What did your mother tell you about your – our – father's death?'

'That he died at the siege of Calais in April of 1596, fighting with the Spanish forces against Henri of Navarre. Why?'

Louise's hand stole to the locket around her neck. 'This will come as a shock, Phillipe. I understand why your mother might have told you our father died a hero's death – Louis may well have told her he was going to Calais – but it is not true.'

'Go on,' he said, his expression resolute, and she saw another flash of the steel that had made Phillipe such a force to be reckoned with in the face of Joost's determination to see her hanged.

'Marta and Louis were found together in a boarding house in Kalverstraat in the heart of Amsterdam on the twenty-sixth of April that year.'

He began to drum his fingers on the arm of his chair once more. 'Found together? What do you mean?'

'Phillipe, they were murdered,' she said, hating that she was destroying his memory of his father. 'The knife was found in the room.'

He ran his fingers through his long black hair with its white streak, his expression impossible to read. In that instant, Louise saw the strong family resemblance between him and their father – the man she had killed – and she shivered.

'That cannot be,' he said, his voice rising. 'That cannot be.'

Louise wanted to find some words of comfort, but did not think he would welcome that. 'No one knew how long Louis had been in Amsterdam, or why they were together, only . . .' She tailed off, unable to continue the deceit.

'By whom? Was the killer caught?'

'No one knew,' she said, falling back on her grandfather's explanation.

For a moment, Phillipe said nothing. 'So Marta is dead,' he repeated. 'Twenty-five years dead.'

'Yes.'

He sighed. 'Do you think my mother knew?'

Louise shrugged. 'I cannot say, Phillipe. How would I know?'

'And you were only a child when this happened.'

'I was ten,' she answered, wishing he would not be so kind.

Another long silence followed, as if he was processing the information. His fingers kept drumming on the arm of his chair, his eyes fixed on some point in the middle distance.

'We both lost a father,' he said eventually, 'but I had my mother.' He shook his head. 'I wish I had met Marta, I wish I had had the chance to know my father. But at least . . . it makes it even more important that we have found one another. I believe our father would have been glad of that, don't you think? He clearly never stopped loving her.'

To her dismay, Louise felt tears well in her eyes.

Phillipe was instantly at her side. 'Everything is going to be all right,' he said, putting his hand on her shoulder. 'We have each other. I am going to look after you and keep you safe. Everything will be all right.'

# CHAPTER EIGHTY-FOUR

Las Palmas
*Tuesday, 12 October*

On a bright and mild morning four days later, the *Old Moon* was ready to sail. Since dawn, they had been waiting for the tide and the wind, and conditions were now as good as they could be this late in the season: a light north-easterly, good visibility. It was a year to the day that Louise and Gilles had first stood side by side as the ship left the harbour of La Rochelle bound for Amsterdam in the north. Today, they would be sailing due south. Louise was sad to be bidding farewell to the waters of Las Islas Afortunadas and the people of the islands, but the terms of her exile gave her no choice.

Over the past four days, whenever they had a moment alone, she and Gilles had debated where they should go.

'I cannot return to the dark and the cold of Amsterdam,' she'd said. 'Grey, damp skies, the fear of arrest hanging over me.'

Her heart ached at the thought of never seeing Cornelia or Alis again, but her weeks in prison had taught her that she could not risk that again. If she returned to Holland, she was certain Andries Joost would continue to persecute her, *diyya* or not, and her presence would make life harder for Cornelia. Louise had no doubt of that. In addition, word of how she and Gilles lived as if married would eventually spread: it was one thing at sea, it would be quite another in Calvinist Amsterdam.

And although Louise was learning to make peace with her past and her actions, she could not do that in Amsterdam. The memories were too raw.

Her only other home, La Rochelle, was under siege, and Gilles had no desire to return there in any case. He wanted nothing more than to be with her and Louise felt the same. From her conversations with Phillipe, it seemed evident that the King – and his increasingly powerful chief adviser, Cardinal Richelieu – were intending to continue the persecution of the Huguenots until they had driven every last one of them from France. In southern Africa, at the point where the Atlantic and the Pacific oceans met, a small refugee Huguenot community was already forming, French and Dutch exiles seeking a safer life. She and Gilles would be part of that.

Louise thought back to the Tarot reading in Sint Luciensteeg. When Gilles had turned the ten of cups, how the cartomancer had explained that ten was the number of completion, marking the end of one cycle of life and the beginning of the next. She smiled. Together, they had done that, and would do so again.

*A new adventure, new beginnings.*

Exploration was in her blood. The court had seized Henrick Joost's portolan, but Phillipe had presented her with an exquisite mariner's map to replace it as a farewell gift at their dinner last night. It had been a pleasant and convivial evening. Louise hoped that, between them, she and Phillipe could bring to an end the feud that had so bitterly divided the Reydon-Joubert and Vidal families for two generations. She had not shared what she knew of it from her grandmother's journals, but she suspected Phillipe was aware of the rift between her grandfather and his.

All the same, though her half-brother was charming and engaging, Louise was relieved to be leaving. Phillipe wanted to be with her all of the time, endlessly talking about the past and their families, what they might do together, how he would look after her. He suffocated her. And the burden of deceit, the truth that she had to conceal from him, lay heavily on her conscience. His loving attention left her little time for anything else.

'He thinks he has bought the right,' Gilles had said calmly, when the dinner was over and they were walking back to the ship.

'Do you not enjoy his company?'

'I am grateful to him,' he replied carefully. 'The question is, is he his father's son or his mother's?'

'What do you mean?'

Gilles had put his arm around her waist. 'Only a few hours more, then we can put all this behind us.'

Louise looked around her ship with pride. Gleaming, polished, repaired. The Dutch flag still snapped atop the main mast, and Louise's own private colours at the bow, a single emerald green drop on a silver background. But at the stern, the VOC colours had been replaced by a new flag. Designed by Gilles, and stitched by Rossi, it displayed a three-masted sailing ship with a woman in a red headscarf standing on the deck. One last reminder of an adventure now over.

Once they were out into the open sea, she would change her women's clothes for her captain's breeches – in his weeks in the hills, Rossi had sewed her another pair. Her mother's locket was still around her neck, but her scarf, though still in her possession, was folded at the bottom of her travel chest. It belonged to a different time. Her jewelled knife, confiscated by the court as evidence, had never been returned.

They were almost ready. Around her on the quayside, the sound of last-minute preparations: Pieter, grown stronger and more confident during his time in the hills; Tom Smith as her first lieutenant with Second Lieutenant Bleeker at the helm; Jansz, with his crooked nose, commanding his two new Canarian recruits with a mixture of exasperation and paternal affection; Sanchez with his thick black moustache; Pierre Rémy, on the main deck checking he had everything he would need to defend the ship at sea; Albert in his galley, his arm fully healed; Marco Rossi, inspecting the mainsail to check for loose stitches and tears; Lange towering over everyone; the russet-haired De Groot, still grieving for his brother; and finally, Ali Al-Bayt, still on the quayside, running his hand over the hull. The crew of the *Ghost Ship* reunited. All being well, and with the benefit of the north-east wind, they would reach the Cap Verde islands in time to lay up in safety for the winter. Then next spring, as soon as the weather improved, they would continue down the Portuguese Gold Coast to the Cap de Bonne Espérance, the Cape of Good Hope.

Louise smiled. This would be a different voyage. She was still mistress and commander of the *Old Moon*, but no longer the scourge of the corsair slaver galleys. This was a merchant ship once more, carrying passengers and cargo – a consignment of Malvasian wine from the volcanic highlands of the island, though bound for South Africa rather than Amsterdam.

She looked along the harbour wall. She had expected Phillipe to come to see her off, though privately she was grateful he had not. Her thoughts were focused on the voyage ahead. She was looking forward, to her future, rather than dwelling on her past.

'Louise,' Gilles said quietly. 'Look.'

She shielded her eyes and saw Phillipe, with his tall blue *capotain* hat, long blue coat and black buckled shoes, striding along the quay towards the ship. Behind him, his manservant and two attendants were carrying several bags between them.

'What is he doing?'

Gilles shook his head. 'I have no idea.'

Now Phillipe was standing on the dock smiling up at her. 'I have had a change of heart. May I come on board?'

A wave of disquiet swept through her. 'Why, of course,' Louise replied, 'though we will be sailing at any moment.' She signalled to Pieter, who helped Phillipe over the rail. 'What a wonderful surprise. I am glad. I had feared you might not come to wave us off. Yet here you are.'

'I feared I might be too late.'

'Just in time. Thank you, again, for our wonderful dinner last evening, and for everything. I will forever be in your debt.' Louise laughed, aware she was talking too fast.

Except now, his manservant was lifting the cases on to the deck. She shot a look at Gilles, whose face was an impassive mask.

'Phillipe, I—'

He put his finger on her lips. 'Sister, if I may. We are just getting to know one another. I have so much enjoyed your companionship over these past few days—'

'And I yours.'

'With the consequence that I was sitting in my chamber and suddenly thought, why not sail with you? You have admitted you might never return to France and I have all the leisure and time in the world. There is so much I would like to know, to talk to you about.' He paused. 'And there are letters I think you would like to see.'

She stared at him. 'Letters from whom?'

He smiled. 'From your mother to our father. I had forgotten I had them with me, otherwise I would have shown you before.' His eyes lit up. 'Sister, they are – how shall I put it – letters of such love and passion as to rival those of Héloïse for her Abélard.'

Louise was blind-sided. 'Phillipe, I hardly know what to say. I would, of course, love to read them, but –' she gestured behind her – 'these are not the standards you are used to. We are a small ship, with a small crew. There is very little accommodation.'

Phillipe laughed indulgently. 'Sister, I have served in the field. I have lived in quarters considerably less salubrious than this.' He held up his hands in a gesture of mock surrender. 'But only if you can find a berth for me, that is. And a couple of my people. They know the sea.'

Louise felt trapped. She liked her half-brother, but did not want him on her ship. He would monopolise her attention and there would be no escape. But he was so excited, so honest in his affections, how could she deny him? She owed him her life. And if he had letters written by Marta, then she would want to see them. The oddness of Phillipe not having mentioned them until now, she pushed to one side.

'Of course, it would be my honour,' she said, not meeting Gilles' eye. 'We intend to over-winter in Cap Verde. You could perhaps sail with us as far as that, then return to France when we continue on to Cape Town. I cannot imagine you would want to be away from Chartres – from your mother – for too long.'

Phillipe held her gaze. 'Oh, my estates will manage well enough without me for a month or two.'

Louise forced a smile. 'In which case, Gilles, might the small cabin astern be prepared?' She turned back to Phillipe. 'Your men can sleep with the crew on the main deck.'

Gilles nodded. 'Of course. Monsieur, if you would like to follow me.'

She could hear the concern in his voice, and wanted to explain. But Phillipe had already taken her arm.

'Now, where should I stand?'

Louise gently slipped out of his grasp, and pointed behind her.

'Come with me to the quarterdeck, Phillipe. I will introduce you to my first lieutenant.'

Once she was in position, Lieutenant Smith rang the bell. Bleeker was at the helm. Every man was ready to sail once more. Her emotions in turmoil, Louise looked around at the crew waiting on her command.

'Is our course set, lieutenant?'

Smith nodded. 'Yes, ma'am.'

Louise was waiting for Gilles, expecting him to come up to the quarterdeck as usual, but he elected to remain down on the main deck. She could see the anxiety in his face and gave a smile of apology, hoping he would accept how it had been impossible to refuse to allow Phillipe to join them. She would explain later that it was only for the first part of the journey. Gilles would surely understand.

For now, she put everything from her mind. Louise felt the same fluttering beneath her ribs as always when she was about to set sail, especially on a voyage of discovery such as this. This was no longer the *Ghost Ship*, but they were embarking on another exciting new adventure. The *Old Moon* was sailing into barely charted waters, in search of new lands. She and Gilles were bound for the Cape of Good Hope and the promise of a forever life together.

*Once upon a time . . .*

Full of hope, she lifted her face to the sun. Then Louise Reydon-Joubert, mistress and commander, raised her arm and gave the order.

'Slip the ropes, unfurl the sails.'

# EPILOGUE

CAPE TOWN

CAP DE BONNE ESPÉRANCE

*August 1688*

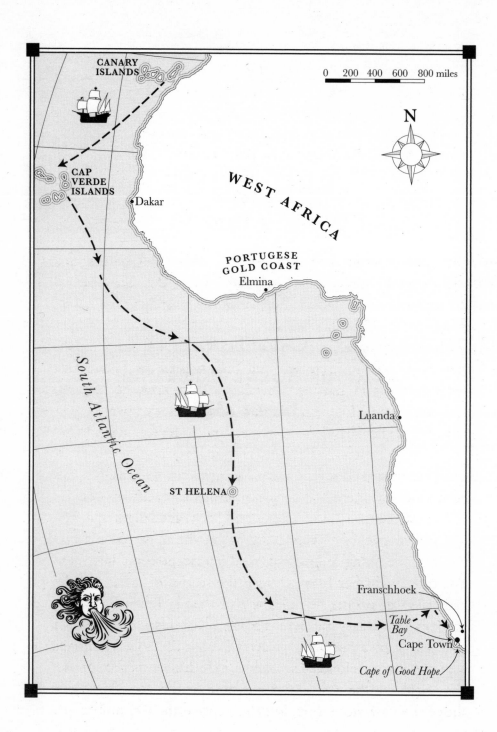

*Sixty-Seven Years Later*

On a cool afternoon in early August, after a voyage that had taken one hundred and forty days from the Chamber of Rotterdam in the Dutch Republic, the mighty *Berg China* dropped anchor in Table Bay.

The *spiegelretourschip*, one of the largest and finest of the voc fleet, was on its fourth and final trip to the Dutch East India colonies in Batavia. Boasting a large crew, it was also carrying several Huguenot families, refugees fleeing persecution, as well as eight girls from a Rotterdam orphanage intended as brides for the men of the voc stationed in Cape Town. There had been several deaths on the journey, but the weather had been kind and there had been no outbreak of flux on board.

Two women – a grandmother and her granddaughter, a spirited girl of twenty – were standing on the upper deck above the stern watching the rugged, wild landscape come into view. The girl caught her breath. From the stories of mariners who had sailed this route before, she had already learnt the names of the extraordinary mountains rising out of this wild and empty land: the Lion's Head, the Devil's Peak and Table Mountain, where the white clouds draped like a cloth over its flat surface. She could see the red, white and blue of the voc flag flying above the new stone fort, built to replace the old timber and earth fortifications established by Jan van Riebeeck on the shore of Table Bay thirty years earlier. The settlement was a replenishment station for voc employees headed for Batavia. She could see huddles of low buildings to her right, where local men in the pay of the voc lived and, beneath the Devil's Peak, a flourishing garden where she'd been told fruit and vegetables were grown. It was unlike anything she had seen before in La Rochelle or Amsterdam. Huge skies, a landscape of red earth and green, mizzle hanging in the air covering the tops of the mountains. In August, in the Cape, it was winter. She had never seen them, but the girl imagined the mountains of the Pyrenees might look something like this.

'It is magnificent,' she said, taking her grandmother's hand. 'Breathtaking.'

'It is,' the old woman agreed, then added: 'You must try to speak Dutch now.'

Though Florence was in her early eighties, there was a strong family resemblance between the two women: both tall and pale skinned, with copper hair and mismatched eyes, one blue and one brown. They were women of courage and determination, forced to flee their house in La Rochelle with what little they could carry on their backs. Forbidden from leaving France, their right to worship taken away, so many of their number had returned to the Catholic Church for fear of reprisals or imprisonment.

Not them.

They were the last surviving representatives of one of the most distinguished Huguenot families of France, and would not disavow their faith. Leaving their home in the rue des Gentilshommes, travelling by night to avoid the King's dragonnades and soldiers hunting Huguenots for sport, it had taken ten months for them to reach safety in Amsterdam. Travelling up the west coast of France, then across to Chartres and Reims, into the Spanish Netherlands. Footsore and weary but defiant still, they had finally arrived in the old family house on Zeedijk, where they were given shelter and loaned enough guilders to buy them both passage to the Cape of Good Hope. It was in Amsterdam that the girl had read the journals of Minou Joubert, who had died nearly eighty years ago, and the prison diaries of Minou's granddaughter, Louise. It was then she had taken the old family name, to link herself to the generations of women who had gone before her.

The first of the rowing boats were getting ready to go to shore. Once they were on dry land, everyone would be processed and registered, then assigned a plot of land to settle. Oliphants Hoek, Drakenstein, these were names of settlements inland the girl had heard spoken. Slowly but surely, the community was transforming itself from a replenishment station to a settlement in its own right and they needed people: winemakers, hurdle-makers, farmers, dressmakers, wives. She could not imagine what it would be like to live in an environment such as this, a place that belonged on the pages of a fantastic story, but she felt excited by the adventure to come.

Most of her fellow passengers were here in search of a better life, a new life, free from fear. They were refugees like them, they had no expectation of riches or a warm welcome. But they had hope. Hope that here, on the far side of the world, they would be free of persecution, that they could live and worship in peace.

The girl was here for another reason. For her whole life, she had grown up with stories about her first cousin twice removed, Louise Reydon-Joubert. She herself had been born in Louise's house in the rue des Gentilshommes in La Rochelle, where she and her grandmother had lived until they had been driven from

France – her mother had died giving birth to her – and there were whispers about a family feud going back generations. She had quizzed her grandmother, Florence, who remembered Louise from when she was a child and from her own father's stories. From other records, held in the old Van Raay shipping offices in Amsterdam, the girl discovered Louise had been the owner of the *Old Moon* and that she had sailed her to the Islas Afortunadas in March of the year 1621. She heard legends, each more fantastic than the last, about how Louise had turned she-captain, a pirate commander in the Atlantic Ocean. Stories of murder and a trial in the Casas Consistoriales, of piracy and revenge on the High Seas, tales too wild surely to be true. Then in October of that same year, the *Old Moon* had left Gran Canaria bound for the Cap de Bonne Espérance. Louise's companion, Gilles Barenton – some said husband – was believed to have been on board, as was her half-brother, a man who went by the name of Phillipe Vidal.

The *Old Moon* had arrived in Cape Town on the seventh day of May in the year 1622, and nothing had been heard of Louise Reydon-Joubert again. She had simply vanished. There was no record of her death, no record of where she might have gone. The *Old Moon* itself had been sailed back to Amsterdam by her first lieutenant, Tom Smith, on her instruction, but the Englishman maintained to his dying day that he had no idea where his captain had been headed nor why she had abandoned the ship she loved so dearly. It was he who had brought her prison diaries back to Amsterdam and handed them into the keeping of Louise's elderly great-aunt, Alis. Among them, a battered Tarot card. Justice.

Sixty-seven years later, the girl was here to walk in Louise's footsteps. She knew it would be difficult, perhaps impossible, but she was going to do her best to find out what had happened to her. She was determined to finish the story and give Louise a proper memorial. A woman like that should not simply disappear from history. The generations to come should know her name: Louise Reydon-Joubert, captain and commander.

Now the ship's officer was calling out the names of the first passengers to be taken ashore. The two women stood in line, then stepped forward together, acknowledging their names.

'Suzanne Joubert?'

'*Hier ben ik*,' she replied, remembering her grandmother's advice to speak in Dutch.

With her leather bag strapped to her chest, Suzanne climbed down into the boat and settled herself on the wooden bench beside her grandmother. She took a deep breath, feeling her nerves singing with excitement. Apprehension, too. The sea was choppy, but she was accustomed to the roll of the waves and the swell and knew she would be all right.

As the oarsmen started to row, Suzanne smiled.

'I'm coming,' she murmured to the air, as the gulls screeched above their head. 'I'm coming to find you.'

# Acknowledgements

There are so many people who have given support during the writing of *The Ghost Ship*.

As always, my dear friend and publisher at Mantle, Maria Rejt, and the London Pan Mac team including Alice Gray, Sara Lloyd, Lara Borlenghi, Jeremy Trevathan, Kate Tolley, Rebecca Needes, Claire Evans, Lucy Hale, Jamie Forrest, Kate Green, Charlotte Williams, Stuart Dwyer, Jonathan Atkins, Cormac Kinsella, Christian Lewis, Marian Reid and the fantastic Pan Mac reps; a huge thank you, too, to everyone at Pan Macmillan Australia, New Zealand, South Africa and India.

My old friend and agent Mark Lucas, and everyone at The Soho Agency and ILA, especially Niamh Grady, Alice Saunders, Nicki Kennedy and Jenny Robson. Thanks also to George Lucas and Inkwell Management. I'm lucky to have so many exceptional foreign publishers and translators, in particular Maaike le Noble, Frederika van Traa, Davy van der Elsken and Koen Lempers at Meulenhoff-Boekerij; and my editor Catherine Richards at Minotaur Books, and the whole St Martin's team including Hector DeJean, Andrew Martin, Kelley Ragland, Paul Hochman, Michelle Cashman, David Rotstein and Nettie Finn; Marie Misandeau and the wonderful team at Sonatine.

For all things to do with ships and the sea, I am deeply indebted to Rear Admiral John Lippiett for his encouragement, endless patience and expert advice. Any errors are mine alone. My thanks to Tessa Murdoch FSA and the Huguenot Museum in Rochester, Kent, and the Huguenot Memorial Museum in

Franschhoek, South Africa. In Carcassonne, as always, thank you to Alain Pignon, Pierre Sanchez and Chantal Bilautou, and to the Pujol family at the Hôtel de la Cité.

My thanks, too, to all my friends and family for their support, in particular Jon Evans, Clare Parsons, Tony Langham, Syl Saller, Saira Keevil, Anthony Horowitz, Jill Green, Linda and Roger Heald, Sylvia Horton, Robert Dye, Lucinda Montefiore.

All love to the legendary Granny Rosie, to my brothers-in-law Mark Huxley and Benjamin Graham (who helps keep the home fires burning), to my fabulous sisters Caroline Matthews and Beth Huxley, and all my lovely nieces and nephews, especially Lottie, Bryony, Rick and wonderful Thea and Ellen.

Finally, as always, I could do none of this without my beloved husband Greg Mosse – my first love and first reader – and our brilliant Martha Mosse and magnificent Felix Mosse, as well as wonderful Ollie Halladay and joyous Finn. I am so grateful for you all.

# About the Author

Kate Mosse is an award-winning novelist, playwright, essayist and non-fiction writer. The author of ten novels and short-story collections, her books have been translated into thirty-eight languages and published in more than forty countries. Fiction includes the multimillion-selling Languedoc Trilogy, the Joubert Family Chronicles (the number one bestseller *The Burning Chambers*, *The City of Tears* and *The Ghost Ship*), and number one bestselling Gothic fiction. Her highly acclaimed non-fiction includes *An Extra Pair of Hands* and *Warrior Queens & Quiet Revolutionaries: How Women (Also) Built the World*. The Founder Director of the Women's Prize for Fiction, she is the founder of the global #WomanInHistory campaign and has her own monthly YouTube book show, *Mosse on a Monday*. A Fellow of the Royal Society of Literature, Kate is a Visiting Professor of Contemporary Fiction and Creative Writing at the University of Chichester and President of the Festival of Chichester.